"A breathtakingly beautiful book. Cook[...] that, in 1914, was poised on the brink of extinction, as ponderous as the huge dinosaurs but just as magnificent. The exquisite intimacy of the writing and of the haunting love story drew me into this elegant world so entirely that I couldn't imagine ever leaving it. The vivid characters and understated heartbreak of their conflicts, above- and below-stairs, are depicted with sensitivity and insight. Superbly researched; a real treat."   —Kate Furnivall, author of *Shadows on the Nile*

"I found myself addicted to *Rutherford Park*, much as I was to *Downton Abbey*. I reveled in delicious detail about life in a great country estate, all the while waiting to learn—would Octavia's family survive or would they be torn apart by the forces converging on them: personal failings, society's excesses, and Europe's Great War?"
          —Margaret Wurtele, author of *The Golden Hour*

"Beautiful, melancholy, and richly detailed, *Rutherford Park* elegantly depicts the lives within an English country house on the cusp of a new age. Elizabeth Cooke evokes classic authors like Vita Sackville-West and Frances Hodgson Burnett."
          —Natasha Solomons, author of *The Gallery of Vanished Husbands*

"Reminiscent of Catherine Cookson, a heart-aching story of an old world order and class divides set against Edwardian England."
          —Judith Kinghorn, author of *The Memory of Lost Senses*

continued . . .

"With its vivid descriptions and memorable characters, *Rutherford Park* drew me in from the first page. Richly textured with historical details, the novel captures perfectly the pre–World War I mood and atmosphere of the grand Yorkshire house and the lives of those who inhabit it. The final page left me thoroughly satisfied, yet wishing for more. Thank you, Elizabeth Cooke, for a wonderful story and the promise of another."   —Kelly Jones, author of *The Woman Who Heard Color*

"Comparisons with *Downton Abbey* on the eve of World War I are inevitable, but *Rutherford Park* gives a more comprehensive and realistic look at the farms and mill villages that sustained the great houses, and shows us the inevitable cracks in their foundations. Compelling."

—Margaret Maron, author of the Judge Deborah Knott series

Titles by Elizabeth Cooke

RUTHERFORD PARK

THE WILD DARK FLOWERS

The Wild Dark Flowers

Elizabeth Cooke

BERKLEY BOOKS, NEW YORK

THE BERKLEY PUBLISHING GROUP
Published by the Penguin Group
Penguin Group (USA) LLC
375 Hudson Street, New York, New York 10014

USA • Canada • UK • Ireland • Australia • New Zealand • India • South Africa • China

penguin.com

A Penguin Random House Company

This book is an original publication of The Berkley Publishing Group.

THE WILD DARK FLOWERS

Berkley trade paperback ISBN: 978-0-425-26259-7

An application to register this book for cataloging has been submitted to the Library of Congress.

PUBLISHING HISTORY
Berkley trade paperback edition / July 2014

PRINTED IN THE UNITED STATES OF AMERICA

10 9 8 7 6 5 4 3 2 1

Cover photo by Edward Steichen © Conde Nast 1924.
Cover design by Diana Kolsky.
Interior text design by Laura K. Corless.

For my mother's eldest brother,
William David Nash of the 11th Battalion Border Regiment.
Killed in action 1st July 1916, aged 20.

The Wild Dark Flowers

Chapter 1

As he stepped down from the upper paths of the woodland, and paused to look over the valley on that still and beautiful May morning in 1915, William Cavendish remembered his father.

William Cavendish senior, the 7th Earl Rutherford, had been a quiet and scholarly man, full of integrity; and William wished now that his kindly father were here, for he needed his advice. He looked down through the trees at five-hundred-year-old Rutherford Park, vast and sprawling, terracotta-colored in the morning light, with its Tudor barley-sugar twist chimneys and mullioned windows; his gaze ran along the line of century-old beeches on the drive that led down to the village.

Rutherford looked, as always, beautiful; alluringly romantic at the head of the Yorkshire valley it ruled. William sat down now among the dancing shadows of the wood, and gazed down at his heritage.

Somewhere down there—his eyes sought out the exact window

on the upper floor of the southwest wing—his wife Octavia was sleeping. It was barely five o'clock, although the sun had risen nearly an hour before on this sublime day.

It was here—he looked around himself—or somewhere very near here, that his father had brought him one similar morning long ago. William had been fourteen years old, and suffering at Eton from some ongoing petty slight that had left him unpopular for a whole term. His father had listened, and said very little; they had walked back and forth along the terraces, the lawns, and the sweeping arc of the river. And then, the kindly hand upon his shoulder, and the face turned to his.

"You must bend like the willow, or break like the oak," he had said. And seeing his son's puzzlement, "It is some proverb or other from the East, William. Heed it in such situations. Whatever you may hear, there is no lasting strength in being obdurate."

William's hands rested now on his knees in two clenched fists. God knew, he had tried to follow the advice all his life, but he had failed miserably. It had finally taken the events of last year, among them his own wife's love for another man, to unwind the stiffness in his character.

After the American had gone (and in his own mind he never gave John Gould a name, merely thought of him as *the American*), William had found to his dismay that he had become as loose, as unfocused, as an unraveling knot. He had found himself helplessly watching Octavia; and the symptoms of her distress, as much as she tried to conceal them, were obvious to him.

He had discovered that his heart was a tender and nervous object, wrapped in a shroud of silence. Even now, he found it hard to explain himself to his own wife; and he had an ominous feeling that Rutherford, for all its glamour, might not keep them together.

He got up and stared over his estate. He could see movement down in the grounds: the gardeners were already about. There was a scribbled line of white blowing on the washing lines behind the farrier's cottage. In the huge glass-walled orangerie, someone was opening the roof lights, and they gleamed in the sun; down by the curve of the river he could see the horses dashing in the grass, fluid lines of vitality.

His father had delighted in Rutherford, both for its own sake and for its ability to rule calmly and with dignity; he had not an ounce of the cruel blood with which his eighteenth-century ancestors had carved the Caribbean into their own shape and laid down the sugar plantations that had brought riches to the family. Nevertheless, William felt the weight, the responsibility of Rutherford deep in his heart rather than its extraordinary beauty. And now he must keep it functioning in the midst of a war that had taken his son away to France.

At the thought of Harry—not yet twenty-one, and serving with the Royal Flying Corps—William felt nauseated with anxiety. Harry was coming home this very evening on a few days' leave; they had received the telegram last night. Octavia had been all a joyful flutter at the news; but, in the later post, William had also received a letter from Harry's commanding officer. A letter that had disturbed him enough to make him wake early this morning and walk the estate, turning its contents over and over in his mind. He had not shown the letter to Octavia yet: he really doubted that he should.

William waited a few more minutes, watching the sun steadily rising, and the sky turning a perfect shade of blue. All this beauty, all this complicated hierarchy of land, farms, moors, river, woods, and gardens: all this might fail if Harry never returned when this damned war was finished. Harry was their sole heir.

"He shall come back," he had told Octavia once, last Christmas, as she had held Harry's latest scrawled letter from the battlefields of France in her hand. "Never fear that, darling."

Never fear that.

It was the utmost irony.

For losing Harry was the thing that William Cavendish feared most in all the world.

*W*illiam had been quite wrong in thinking that Octavia was asleep.

She was lying in the four-poster bed, staring upwards at the yellow satin curtains, and the embroidery that made it seem that a whole flock of bluebirds were flying across the material over her head. The bluebird was the ancient insignia of the Beckforths—William's great-great-grandfather's before he had been given an aristocratic title. Blue was everywhere in the house. All the upholstery in the drawing and sitting rooms was blue and white; on the gateposts, entwined bluebirds, carved in granite, were depicted perched on a sugar cane; in the Tudor hall, bluebirds were in the plasterwork; on the great mahogany staircase, bluebirds outstretched their wings below the huge Singer Sargent portrait of herself.

She sighed, and looked away. The birds, the house, the stifling ennui of ordinary life sometimes threatened to suffocate her. She sat up in bed, threw back the covers, and walked to the window. The Liberty clock on her bedside table showed half past five in the morning.

Harry was coming home today. She would see him tonight; she would be able to hold his hand. Seven months had passed since his last leave: a leave on which she saw that her twenty-year-old boy had been transformed into a man, his face etched with the residue of dark experiences. There had been shadows there, but he had shrugged them off, kissing her and smiling. "You mustn't worry about me," he had told her. "I'm having a jolly time of it."

A jolly time. The retreat from Mons—that frantic scramble that had cost so many English and French lives; she knew he'd been involved in it. But he wouldn't discuss it. He had turned away instead and talked about his little daughter: Cecilia, nicknamed Sessy, born to a housemaid the Christmas before last, a scandalous affair. But Harry's image, and Harry's own. And her granddaughter, who now lived at Rutherford on Octavia's insistence.

She leaned on the windowsill, breathing in the faint scent of the flowers below on the terrace. She would go up and see Sessy later in the nursery, she decided. And perhaps they might take a turn about the gardens. The little child reminded her of Harry at that age: determined, feisty, clutching a rose in her little fist and refusing to cry when a thorn smeared blood along her thumb. So like him; but Harry had been born in an age where war was a distant tremor in the Empire, the stuff of Indian frontiers and Boer conflict. Not here. Not just twelve miles across the English Channel. Not a war that took away sons and obliterated them by the thousands.

Octavia shivered. She took up the wrap that lay across the armchair, and sat down, staring without seeing anything in the room.

It was with surprise that she heard the knock on her door a half hour later.

Frowning, she knew that it was still too early for her maid, Amelie, to be up. "Yes?" she called.

The door opened. William stood on the threshold, dressed in outdoor clothes. "May I come in?" he asked.

"Of course."

She watched him cross the room.

William was almost twenty years older than she; they had been married when Octavia was just nineteen. She had known nothing of men then, and very little of society; she had been kept close by a feared father. But she came with an enormous fortune, and she knew now—had learned over the years—that it was the fortune that had attracted William Cavendish to her. She had been wildly in love with him on their wedding day; he had come to love her only as the years progressed. But it was not love such as she had experienced last year with John Gould. It never would be. It never could; not now.

William took up her hand, and kissed it. He sat down opposite her. "I'm surprised that you are awake. But glad of it." He handed her the morning newspaper that he had been carrying. "Just delivered. I caught the hallboy as he took it across the yard."

She gazed down at it, then up at him. A spasm of panic had touched her. "Not Harry."

"Would we find out in such a way, if it were?" he answered, raising an eyebrow. "No, not Harry. But the Kents. Their son Rupert."

"Oh no," she breathed. The Kents were their oldest friends in the area. They had two boys, both professional soldiers, in France. The last time that she had seen Elizabeth Kent she had, like every other mother, voiced her terror at the war. She had shown Octavia letters from Rupert that talked of the trenches being vilely flooded and the men standing for hours in freezing water; he had talked of how much he had admired the Canadian regiments and their courage under fire.

Octavia still recalled a letter from Rupert that Elizabeth had shown her. It had brought the war vividly into focus. "*To see a good chap taken out is the most disheartening thing,*" he had written. "*We lost a sergeant the day before last. I shall never forget it. He was an old hand, a cheerful fellow. He was instructing a gun team and they were caught by a stray shell. I ran back—the wider scene I shan't describe—but there lay our sergeant on his back. He looked untouched, almost relaxed; there was not a mark on him, but he was quite dead. That is the effect of the close concussion of a shell. He had smiled at me only seconds before, and he lay with the brightness of life still in his face. . . ."*

Rupert Kent had been a fine letter writer.

And now the letters would be all that Elizabeth and Hamilton Kent would ever have of him.

The casualty list noted that Captain Rupert Kent had been killed at a place called Langemarck on the twenty-second of April.

"I must go and see Elizabeth," Octavia murmured. "She will be devastated." She tore her eyes away from the list of casualties in the newspaper, and thoughtfully folded the page. "And what of Alexander?" she asked. Alexander was the Kents' other son.

"I suppose he continues out there," William said.

She covered her eyes with her hand, and all the while she was thinking, *please bring Harry back. Now, this minute.* She felt—she knew it was absurd—but she could not wait a single moment longer; she would not believe that he was safe until she laid eyes on him.

She felt William's touch on her arm. She opened her eyes.

"We made it a policy not to worry," he reminded her.

She couldn't reply. She saw him glance at the bed. He was stroking her hand.

"Would you . . . would you mind awfully if I called Amelie?" she said. "I'm rather desperate for tea."

She saw him take the rebuff; his face almost comically folded in disappointment. "Of course," he murmured, and got to his feet.

When the door closed behind him, she breathed out.

She was cruel and selfish, undoubtedly. She was not what a wife should be, and William was too much a gentleman to press her. But her heart was cold inside her since John Gould had left. She had stayed here for the sake of her children—not only Harry, but also for Louisa and Charlotte, his younger sisters. And of course, little Sessy. She respected William; she sometimes pitied him, and she had submitted to him as regularly as she felt appropriate. But to love him, to *love* him? That was beyond her power.

*B*elowstairs, Rutherford was awake and working hard by six thirty that morning.

The two housemaids, Mary Richards and Jenny Best, had been up for half an hour, swiftly laying fires where needed, opening the curtains and windows, letting in the lovely morning. They moved around the rooms like two contrasting pictures, negatives of each other: Mary moving quickly, short and dark, a bustling image of efficiency; Jenny tall and thin, fair-haired, soft voiced, following self-effacingly in her wake. Stairways and corridors had already been swept, and tea trays laid and delivered to the housekeeper, the chief housemaid, and the butler. Albert, the hallboy, had taken back the master's already-polished shoes, and, later, had spent a bedraggled half hour loading the wood and coal baskets in the storerooms across the yard. Under the sharp eye of the cook, Mrs. Carlisle, the range had been lit, and bread was already baking. And by seven o'clock, the staff congregated in the servants' kitchen, where breakfast was laid out on the huge scrubbed-top table.

They grouped together, but it would not have been this way once. In times past, the footmen and housemaids would have occupied another room. But the war had thinned out the numbers of staff at

Rutherford. Counting the "outsiders"—those that worked in the gardens and stables—only three years ago Rutherford had twenty-four staff. Now there were only eleven, with the occasional help of day staff from the village.

Two stable boys and two undergardeners had gone—they were in training now for France. The kitchen maid, Grace, and one of the chambermaids, the lumbering and complaining Cynthia, had gone to work in the yards at the mills; they had been lured back by the better pay and the pleas of their mothers, whose husbands and sons were on their way to Kitchener's New Army like so many others. The footmen Nash and Harrison had enlisted, too: the tall and blithe Harrison vanishing almost as soon as war was declared, without notice; and Nash—solemn and quiet, unshakably loyal, was still in training in England at this moment.

Mr. Bradfield struggled with only one footman and the dull-witted hallboy, Alfred; Mrs. Carlisle stoically worked long hours, trying to train the scullery maid, Enid, to help her, and regularly pleading with the housekeeper to find her another live-in pair of hands. It was a blessing that, since the war had started, the Cavendishes rarely held large dinners.

Upstairs, only Mary and Jenny were left to help the head housemaid, Miss Dodd, and even then it was generally believed that even Elizabeth Dodd had an idea to return to Sheffield, to be nearer to her sweetheart's family. Amelie, her ladyship's maid; Cooper, his lordship's valet; and the nursemaid never left the upstairs—they may be servants, but they did not mix with those they considered lesser mortals. They were a race apart.

And so it was a sparse group that gathered at the kitchen table at seven o'clock, and, as was customary, they remained standing until the arrival of Mrs. Jocelyn and Mr. Bradfield.

Mary Richards stood impatiently at Jenny's side. Eventually, they heard Mrs. Jocelyn's skittering step on the stone flagstones of the corridor, and then the padded and more measured stride of Bradfield. Mrs. Jocelyn came into the kitchen clutching her Bible; she had been at her private morning prayers. Her eye glittered with malevolent concentration. Mary thought how, over the last year, the woman had become thin, as if in the grip of some permanent low-grade fever; the starched collar was loose around her neck, and, if you looked hard, you could see her bony hands shaking.

Mary glanced from Mrs. Jocelyn to Mr. Bradfield. By contrast, he was the same as always—tall and calm, his sandy hair brushed neatly. In moments when he was caught off guard, Mary would notice a rather sweet and engaging expression on his face, a sort of dreaming and philosophical look.

Bradfield now held out the chair for Mrs. Jocelyn. They all sat down. The food was served, and they began to eat in silence. Breakfast was not a lengthy meal: tea and toast only, while the elaborate kedgerees and egg dishes for upstairs bubbled behind them on the stove. When the last of the cups had been filled a second time, Bradfield took out his newspaper, and he passed whatever letters had been received to their recipients.

One such came to Mary this morning.

She looked keenly at the postmark: *Carlisle.*

"What have you there?" Mrs. Jocelyn demanded.

"If you please, m'm, it's from David."

"David?"

"Mr. Nash, m'm."

Mrs. Jocelyn turned her head away. "It's a wonder he has time to write." She disapproved deeply of a footman mixing with a maid: it was a dangerous quicksand, in her opinion—if not downright immoral. Mrs. Jocelyn was very fond indeed of pronouncements on morals. Next, she stared accusingly at Jenny. "And you?"

Jenny had blushed bright red. She had opened a letter whose bold handwriting on the envelope betrayed the sender: Harrison. She held it out, and then let it drop to the table as if ashamed of it.

Mrs. Jocelyn almost pounced on her. "A man that left the service of this house without a word."

"He is in a London regiment," Jenny ventured.

"And why would he go there?" Mrs. Jocelyn said.

"I don't know," Jenny admitted. And she dropped her voice. "He doesn't write very much."

Mrs. Jocelyn at last left them, making her way up to see Lady Cavendish to discuss the day's menus. Mary could almost see the struggle in the older woman's face not to criticize David Nash and Harrison more severely: they had enlisted after all, and deserved some respect. But Mary thought that the housekeeper probably had decided that fighting for one's country was less important than polishing the his lordship's silver; for nothing at all was more important to Mrs. Jocelyn than William Cavendish's comfort.

Only when she had finally gone, and they heard the green baize door slam above them, did Mary pull a grimace. "Old cow."

Fortunately, the remark went unnoticed among the clatter of plates. Jenny leaned towards her. "Any news? What does he say?"

"He's got a few days' leave."

"Is he coming here?"

Mary stuffed the letter in her pocket. "Maybe. And Donald?"

Jenny showed her the hasty scrawl of Harrison, one side of a single page. It was not a love letter; in fact, it was full of talk of some London concert party that had come to his training camp. She looked up at Jenny, wondering what the other girl made of it. Harrison had certainly been no favorite of her own—he was too sure of himself, too apart from the next of them—but she didn't want to spoil what pleasure Jenny might get from receiving his notes. After all, she was a sweet girl, quite naïve. Mary felt protective of her.

Jenny was frowning. "He says they'll go to France soon. Why does he go, when others that signed up are training still?"

"Some of the London ones are being drafted into the Regulars," Mary told her. "I heard Mr. Bradfield say so."

Jenny folded the letter and put it away. "I don't understand half of what he tells me," she murmured. "I don't know what I am to him at all."

And, to her dismay, Mary saw tears in Jenny's eyes. She wanted to say, *don't let any man hurt you*; but the other girl stood up quickly, taking her plate to be washed, and hurrying out when it was done.

Forty miles away, high in the Westmorland hills, David Nash was walking along the spine of Helvellyn. He had climbed the western side of the great mountain that morning, and he stopped now on the summit, breathing the clean, sharp air deep into his lungs.

With the whole of Cumberland and the Borrowdale and Thirlmere valleys at his back, he gazed out towards the line of Ullswater. The lake was where he was headed that evening; he calculated that it would take him about three more hours to reach it. Far below him, Red Tarn was an almost-perfect dark blue circle at the foot of a smooth, thousand-foot drop.

He was, despite the beauty of the view, thinking of Mary Richards and Rutherford. He would be able to spend a day or so there, he hoped. He had always been too shy to tell Mary what he felt for her—he was better at putting things into words on paper—and Mary was always so seemingly sure of herself. He dreaded revealing himself and seeing her look at him with those narrow, assessing eyes.

The last time that he had been up here—it must be four years ago now, when he had first been promoted to footman at Rutherford—he had not been able to see his hand in front of his face on Helvellyn's summit. Clouds had suddenly descended, and he had found himself stumbling along, disoriented, close to the edge; and looking down suddenly, he had seen the fog below him curling in a funnel, much like looking down into a drain as the water swirled away.

He had stepped back from the edge with all the hairs rising on the back of his neck; he had been that close to falling. But now, on this late-spring morning, there was not a cloud to be seen; he could even make out the distant rise of the Pennines towards Yorkshire and Rutherford. There was barely a sound either; he might have been the only man on earth.

He sat down on the smooth, close-cropped turf and stared back towards Brown Cove Crags, the way he had come. It had been a scramble up the narrow gulley with the gravelly scree slopes vertiginously rolling away beneath him. Down in the valley was the long, shadowy mass of Thirlmere, the reservoir that had been created to provide water for Manchester. There had been such an outcry when that lake was proposed; he remembered his parents saying what an outrage it would be. Now the little valley was obscured, its fields gone. He wondered what other changes would come, and lay back on the grass, and stared at the sky.

His brother worked some miles to the east of Ullswater, in a little village called Orton; he was groom at the Hall there. In September last year, David had taken the three days' holiday owed to him and gone to find Arthur. He had found his brother in the stables of the Hall, mucking out, whistling loudly, with a beautiful grey hunter of the owner tied up in the yard. When he had seen David, Arthur leaned on the shovel and smiled at him. "Are you going?" David had asked. He did not bother to say where. They both knew. It was less than a month since war had been declared. "If you'll come with me," had been the reply.

No more was said. Arthur had gone inside the house and returned half an hour later, and they had walked together to the village center and caught a lift on the back of a cart going down to Keswick. It had been late in the afternoon when they had got to the recruiting hall, but there was still a long line of men waiting. It was all back-slapping and smiles; it was all talk of chasing the Hun out of Belgium. He had gone in first, because he was the eldest; then he had watched Arthur sign his form, and smiled to himself when his younger brother had hesitated and, where it asked for his occupation, he wrote "footman" just as David had done. Arthur was no more a footman that he was the man in the moon, but David had winked at him conspiratorially as they went out, new members of the regiment.

They had gone into the pub afterwards. David grinned at him, "Well, we've done it now," he said.

"Right enough," he agreed. They were all puffed up with pride, flushed and happy. They swatted each other's shoulders, and joined in with the singing. Someone had started "Rule, Britannia!" and "The Flower of the Valley." They had come out of the pub laughing.

It had been no laughing matter, however, when Nash got back to Rutherford and went to see his mother in the village. She had three sons and four daughters; her husband, his father, had died some years before, and three of the daughters were in service. There was another family a few villages along, the children of his father's first wife. They were all grown up—he and Arthur and his sisters were much younger. Fifteen children in all when the two families were added together; but the man responsible—his loving, quiet Dad—was long gone, buried in the churchyard when David had been only five. His mother was left to bring up her own six children alone, and she was a bitter, thunderous storm of a woman, free with her pinches and twists and slaps.

Still, to his complete surprise, she had said nothing when he showed her the enlistment papers, and told her that Arthur had done the same. She just held on to the doorframe, and her eyes filled with tears. It bothered him no end, shocked him; he tried to hold her hand, but she turned away and carried on with the clothes washing at the stone sink. "We'll be back before you know it," he'd told her, trying to be cheerful. "I'll bring you back something pretty from France."

She glanced at him. "Did you have to take Arthur with you?" she asked.

"He wanted to go more than me," he told her.

She had shaken her head as if she didn't believe him. His youngest sister, Gertie, came to the door of the outhouse, and stood there sucking her thumb and scuffing her shoe on the flagstone floor. She was not quite right, poor addle-headed Gertie; and she was the only one that mother would have with her now. "I've got to go, I've got to be part of it," he said. "There's a poster up in the village. It says you're either a man or a mouse. I can't be called a coward, Mother."

"I've seen it," she murmured. She stopped scrubbing and stared at the wall. "Why can't you wait till they call you?"

"They might not call," he said. "It might not come to that. It might be over quickly, and then I'd forever be thinking that I should have gone." He patted Gertie's head, and she looked at him like an adoring dog. "Besides, Lord Cavendish says it's our duty to go."

His mother snorted derisively. "What does he know?" she muttered. "He didn't fight in the last lot. I can't see him fighting in this one."

"He's something in the War Office, though," David said.

"Is he," she retorted sarcastically. "How very fine for him."

"And their son has already gone. The Flying Corps has gone with the BEF."

She didn't reply.

He and Arthur had first been taken to a place called Ormskirk, south of the Lakes, on the way to Liverpool. They had spent all winter training. Then they went digging trenches in the flat open ground of Carlisle Racecourse, and then back again to their tented camp. Endless square bashing, endless marches, endless yelling and stamping and cleaning. They were used to following orders, though; they had both been in service since they were boys. It wasn't so different to get up cold and damp and warm yourself by running, heaving, and carrying.

They were told that France was like this flat countryside, and muddy, too. That was all right, they told each other. A bit of mud never hurt anyone. It was a poor soldier who couldn't stand mud and rain. And what they liked most of all—for they stayed together, trained together—was that they were part of something bigger, and they were all one. One big marching army. One body, with one idea and one purpose.

When they had joined up, everyone had said that the war would be over by Christmas, and the long months of winter training had disheartened them. It seemed as if his own prophecy might come true—that it would all be finished before their regiment got itself organized.

But then, by this spring, the stories of their great derring-do had begun to ring hollow, and he heard it unmistakably in his own voice. The edge had gone off the great adventure; they were glad lads no longer, their jauntiness had been replaced by a more determined grim humor. They had counted the numbers of the dead in the newspapers and started to guess the odds. The word "Ypres," for instance, had taken on a bitter, awful ring since last October. All hell had broken loose there again last month, apparently. And he had no doubt that it was there—or thereabouts—where the regiment would end up. But there was no turning back. If anything, it was even more important to go.

He watched the glorious blue sky now and considered himself, just an inconsequential body of a man lying on the back of a three-thousand-foot-high mountain, of no greater worth than the grass. Not in himself. Not in everyday matters. He was ordinary from the outside; he knew it. But perhaps war would make him better than he had ever been before; of more use, of more purpose. Perhaps it would steel him a bit, make him bigger in some way that he couldn't get a grasp on, couldn't define.

He knew that he was not much to look at; he was not handsome, he would be passed over in a line. The battalion had already had some photographs taken in training, and, when he had come to look at them when they were pinned up at the barracks, he couldn't place himself for a long time. When he did, it was to see with some chagrin that he had nothing striking about him; nothing made him stand out from the crowd. He was tall, right enough, but his shoulders were sloping—he supposed from so many years of service, trying to polish up a kind of obsequious look. He was thin, too—pale handed, thin wristed—he was hardly the soldierly ideal.

Mary had been surprised when he came back and said that he had signed up; she had raised an eyebrow. "I had you down for a quiet man," she told him. His hackles rose at the subtle insinuation. Seeing his frown, she smiled. "I can't see you as a soldier, that's all I meant," she whispered when they saw each other again, passing in the corridor from the kitchen. "With your poetry and all." He had considered her. "A poet can carry a gun," he told her. "I'll come back in uniform, see how you like me then." She smiled back at him. "I like you enough as it is," she replied. Astonished, he had watched her back as she hurried away.

He propped himself up on one elbow now and looked down towards Ullswater. Just below him began Striding Edge, the long narrow ledge that led away from Helvellyn and down towards the distant lake and Glenridding. He'd walked it before; it was not as bad as it looked from here. He would be down in the village by sunset. It was not as hard as the way he had already come, from Dale Head—a grinding, exhausting, exhilarating walk. Tomorrow he would climb to Bampton Common and finish at Shap, where he would rest his back against the Guggleby Stone, a relic of a thousand years or more, of stone circles and avenues that no one understood.

He'd done it so that he could carry the walk and the mountains with him, keep the images of it all in his head—as a kind of invisible keepsake.

This time last year, he had never realized that there would be a war at all—never even dreamed of such a thing. He had been doing what he always did at Rutherford; waiting table, laying out clothes, polishing silver. He thought of the steamy servants' kitchen, where Mary even now would be laboriously laying the trays for afternoon tea, and tried to put himself alongside her, and dreamed of putting his hand, thin as it was, frail as it seemed, over her ruddy, hardworking fingers. He imagined stopping her in her work, looking into that earnest, honest face of hers, seeing those brown eyes gazing back at him with their usual touch of understated humor and kindness. He imagined something he had never done: lifting those same fingers to his mouth, and gently kissing them.

She might laugh at him if he did that; he wondered if she would. Laugh, and turn away, or make a joke of him. Or perhaps, now, she wouldn't laugh at all. Perhaps she would turn her down-to-earth look on him, and tilt her face. He would look down on her thick brown hair held demurely at the nape of her neck. He would watch that mobile mouth turn upwards in a smile. Perhaps she would even lay her hand on his shoulder.

He smiled, despite himself; they would make such an odd couple. It was only that she always talked to him, only that. He liked her voice. He had asked her to write to him, so that he could have that voice wherever it was that he was going. "I shall do that," she said. "A promise?" he asked. "I don't say one thing and mean another," she retorted sharply.

He pushed back his hair, and the cool breeze of the hills blew over him. Out of his pocket, he took a sheet of paper and a pencil. He had rhymes in his head that were not quite rhymes; he savored the words as if they had a taste, arranged them in his mind, trying to get the feeling of the mountain curled under him like a great dog, trying to get its power, its pulse. He shut his eyes and felt the enormity of the miles ahead of him.

Opening his eyes, he smoothed the paper on his knee, and began to write.

Louisa Cavendish had been sitting in her father's library all morning, and had not stirred even to take lunch. Her father was out seeing the estate manager; her mother was shopping in

Richmond with Louisa's sister Charlotte. But she liked her solitariness much more these days: in fact, she enjoyed it.

She sat back now, catching sight of herself in her father's little mahogany wall mirror: a slight, fair, rather pretty girl. She wondered vaguely if she looked different since last year. She was nearly twenty; she sometimes felt more like fifty because of her wretched treatment by Charles de Montfort. She put her head on one side, assessing herself. Perhaps her experiences—her being so dramatically jilted— had actually given her a more interesting air? A darkness, a suggestion of character?

She shook her head and smiled sadly. "You are certainly a ridiculous, silly fool," she told her reflected face.

Since she had come back from France in August last year, the library was the place where she felt most comfortable. She had never been a great reader when she was younger; it had all seemed such a waste of time, and she had skipped her schoolwork whenever she could. Unlike her sister, Charlotte, she would happily fling down a book rather than read it, and the learning of French above all had been torture. It was an irony in itself, she had considered since. French was the language of distrust, of despair, to her now. It was the language spoken by liars like Charles de Montfort.

She would sometimes think of him, when off her guard, in a rather rosy light, as if he inhabited a grotesque fairy story that became more unreal with each telling. He had been handsome—she doubted that she had ever seen a more handsome man—and he had been such fun, so lighthearted. It still mystified her how much she had misjudged him; it made her doubt herself. That, above all, greater even than the whispered scandal and disgrace of having been jilted so theatrically, was the thing that had unnerved her so much. It made her question every opinion she had ever had, and it made her question her own advantages. Because all her popularity and lightheartededness and frivolity, all her good humor, all her prettiness, had brought her to her knees.

For a long time after her father and Harry had rescued her and brought her back to Rutherford after the debacle of her elopement, she had mistrusted herself even to speak, let alone take pleasure in the world. She remembered her mother sitting on her bed last autumn, stroking her face, chafing her hands, saying, "Darling, please talk to me. It's quite all right to talk to me, I shan't criticize you." But her mother's kindness had made it all the worse. Louisa simply lay there with tears streaming down her face. "Don't blame yourself," her father said, the first time that she managed to come down to dinner. "It wasn't your fault." But of course, it was her fault. She knew that. She had failed quite spectacularly to have a grain of sense in her head.

Now, however, pleasure was coming back. And to her complete surprise, she felt it most in the library, carefully looking through the books, running her hand over histories and maps and the records of other lives. Here, and in the archives, where Father kept all his own father's diaries, she felt that her family were wrapped around her, gently protecting her, gently encouraging her to look outwards, past herself.

Her father would come in sometimes and stand next to her. He would say very little. But he would occasionally put his hand on her shoulder, and lean to kiss her cheek. "Read the translation of Homer," he would suggest, or, "Look at the botanical drawings, they are rather fine," or some such thing. She knew he was offering her what he himself most enjoyed. He wanted to share it with her. She would look up at him, and he would blush, and pat her shoulder rather embarrassedly. "There's a good girl," he would say, as if she were five years old. "There's a good girl."

She got up now at last, and stretched. She looked out onto the terrace; then opened the large doors through to the hall, crossed over it, and went into her father's study. There on the desk was the morning newspaper, still folded at the page about Rupert Kent. She laid her hand on it reflectively.

She hadn't much memory of Rupert—he was nine years older than she. He *had been* nine years older, she corrected herself, frowning deeply. Her mind immediately conjured up Harry as he had been last October, putting an arm around her shoulders and whispering, "Buck up, dear girl, won't you? For my sake, if nothing else. I don't want to think of you here moping about." She had smiled at him; one couldn't help smiling at Harry's irrepressibility. "I shall try," she promised him. "There's a love," he responded, pretending to give her chin a glancing blow.

She shook her head at the memory. Slowly, she walked out of the room and through to the orangerie.

It was a building that ran down the length of the south side of the house. Palms reached up to the roof, and there was a warm, heavy scent. She stood for a few moments, gazing out at the grounds, and then seemed to make a decision. Taking up her hat, which was lying discarded on a cane chair, she went out through the double doors and down the long herringbone path, skirting the kitchen garden within its high walls, until she finally emerged in the bright afternoon sunshine at the stable block.

Jack Armitage was just crossing the yard. As soon as he saw her, he stopped dead.

"Good afternoon, Jack."

"Afternoon, miss."

She smiled at him. "Are you busy?" He paused, after a brief glance over his shoulder. "Of course you are," she said for him. "Two of the boys have gone, haven't they?" She knew that the stable hands had enlisted long ago.

"That they have."

"Where are they training?"

"They've gone already, gone to France."

"So soon?"

"Some do," he said. "And the Blessington Pals are going this week, too."

"Are they?" It was the group that had signed up together from the mills that her mother had owned, twelve miles away on the other side of the moorland hills.

"And Harrison, and Nash."

"Yes, of course," she replied.

He stood watching her. She liked it that he had little to say; she found it comforting. The people who distressed her now were the ones that never stopped talking. Jack was a good man; she liked his implacability. He was tall and dark and had been a constant presence when she was growing up. There were only six or seven years between them: he and Harry had almost been childhood chums, as far it was possible between the son of the family and the head groom and his boy. "Jack," she asked now, "have you seen Cecelia—little Sessy—lately?"

He colored a little. The subject of Harry's daughter was still a tender one. Since the little girl had come to live at Rutherford, the staff shied away from the subject; there was a conspiracy of silence, it seemed to Louisa. She tried to be careful; she didn't recall Emily Maitland exactly—she only had a memory of the pale, frail girl who had been one of the parlor maids. She had known nothing at all about Sessy being Harry's daughter by Emily until after she came back from France. She had even sat the child on her lap at the late-summer dance for the staff, sat with her and held her little fingers in her own, and gazed down at her—all without knowing that they were in any way related. It was her mother who told her just before Christmas. "The child who comes here," was the way she had introduced the subject. "Will have a nursemaid. I've employed one. She'll come to live here."

"The village child—Sessy?" Louisa knew that Octavia had a soft spot for the girl, and that she was regularly at the house. But, in the dense fog of her own recovery from her shock and illness after Paris, Louisa had not realized the significance of it all.

Octavia had sat beside her in the morning room as she told her the news; it was a bitterly cold morning in late November, and a fire was roaring in the grate as they took their morning tea. Louisa had a magazine open in her lap that she was not truly reading; the fashion pictures had no interest anymore. And so the importance of what her mother was saying only filtered through slowly. "She is Harry's daughter, darling. Surely you understood that."

Louisa had stared in surprise. "No, I didn't," she admitted. "How awfully stupid of me." And Harry suddenly came back to her as he had been in October, gazing out of the window at the little dogcart that went down to the village. "So that's why he went down there so much," she murmured. "I thought it was some girl. Or rather, you know, someone he was fond of down there in the village." She looked up at her mother. "But of course, it *was* someone he was fond of."

"Yes," Octavia said. "And now she'll come and live here. Your father has agreed to it."

Louisa took some time to think about it. "And the mother. . . ."

Octavia sat sitting with her shoulders squared as if she dreaded an argument. "Emily Maitland."

"Well," Louisa replied, after a moment or two of astonishment and horror. "We have both been rather a trial to you, Harry and I, it seems. You've borne it awfully well."

Octavia's face had broken very briefly into a smile, but she said nothing else. Thinking about it alone in her room afterwards, Louisa had considered how what might have been an absolute scandal even a year ago had now been utterly overshadowed by the war. Life was fleeting, it was temporary: that was a lesson drummed into them all in the past few months. She could see how the little girl was something else: some beacon of hope, of vitality, in a war-dreary world. Yet, even considering this, it was still remarkable that Octavia—and her father, good heavens!—was prepared to face down the whisperings that would inevitably accrue. And what would Cecelia be to her? A niece. A Cavendish. Another girl growing up in Rutherford, and taking, presumably, Harry's name as her own.

She had sat for a very long time staring out of her own bedroom window, in the comfort of her beautiful room, thinking about Emily Maitland, who had died as her daughter was born, and whom she herself she had never really known and now would never know.

Sessy had duly come into Rutherford, though still hidden away by the sheer distance of the nursery from the main house. As often as she could without being a nuisance to the sturdy woman who looked after Sessy, Louisa would creep in to play with the little girl.

"You needn't be embarrassed," Louisa said to Jack now. "She's up in the nursery, you know."

"I know."

She took a step closer to him. "She's a dear little thing," she said.

"That I wouldn't be party to, as I don't see much of her."

"Very strong, and rather willful, I'm afraid." He made no comment. "I've been wondering . . . do you think it's too soon to find her a little pony to ride?"

He looked surprised. "She's only a bairn."

"She's seventeen months old, and walking."

"Aye. Maybe."

"Well, do you think it's time to sit her on a pony? I'm sure she would love it. I had Grey Goose when I was ever so little."

He smiled. "That were a grand little one."

"Yes," Louisa agreed. "I still miss her, you know."

They gazed at each other in silence; after a moment, Jack dropped his eyes and seemed to take a great interest in the sandy gravel under his feet.

"I'll ask Father."

"Aye," he agreed.

"And will you help me find the right sort of animal?" He raised his eyes. "I can't very well do it without you," she told him. She smiled when he shrugged by way of reply. "That's settled, then," she murmured. She turned to go, stopped, and looked back at him. "Do you remember when we danced in the orchard?" she asked.

"I do."

She smiled hesitantly. "Carefree days," she murmured. And, almost to herself, added, "I was such a little beast most of my life, I'm sure. So pleased with myself generally. So thoughtless." She looked at him. "Did you ever dance again to that song?"

"I don't dance much," he told her. "There's not the opportunity."

"It's very frivolous, I suppose, to talk about dancing just now."

"I suppose," he agreed.

She turned to go, then stopped and looked back at him. "You're not going to enlist, are you?"

"Your father has said he can't spare me."

"But you'll not listen to all this talk of going anyway?"

"I can't say," he replied quietly. "I must go in time, I think." She frowned; he nodded at her and made a kind of shrugging gesture. "I'm away down to the farm then, if there's nothing else."

"No, no, of course," she told him.

And she watched him go, until he was out of sight beyond the gates of the yard.

As the motor taxi trundled along the narrow lanes from York station that evening, exhaustion crept up on Harry Cavendish.

It was strange, because he had managed to keep awake all the way from London, relishing the green peacefulness of the world beyond the train window. Other passengers had engaged him in conversation too, eager to hear his version of the war.

Perhaps it was the strain of keeping a positive slant on his stories—it was not done to suggest even a fragment of the nightmare in Flanders, it was perceived a duty to be insouciant, even offhand—but it was only when he stepped onto the platform at York that an overwhelming need to sleep gripped him.

It was not long before his head tipped back and his eyes closed as the taxi went along. He felt himself to be lolling gently on a warm tide, and the patchwork landscape that moments before had been his home country now became monochrome reconnaissance photographs of France all laid out in an endless line, one after the other. Scribbled lines in the mud that were once farms and fields and cottages.

His hands were relaxed in his lap, despite the thick bandage on the left; but in his dream he was hefting the camera in a mahogany case, weighing ten pounds, over the side of the Avro to try and take pictures. He was dimly aware that his observer was dead, a bloody red mess behind him; somehow he had got hold of the camera case, and he felt the plane tilt as he partially released his grip on the controls to take the photograph.

And then, absurdly, he was dreaming of sketching the lines below them. Trying to figure out which trench belonged to which side was something of a challenge—for it looked like someone had gone mad with an ink pen that dripped blotches between the hairsbreadth wriggling lines. But he knew all too poignantly that deep in the lines were thousands of living men, and deep in the blotches were shell holes, full of the dead.

And all the time they shot at him from far below while he tried to keep a steady grip. "You bloody sods!" he muttered.

The driver looked back at his passenger, saw he was asleep, and smiled to himself.

Those photographs that Harry had helped to take mapped out Neuve Chapelle in March this year. Horrible Neuve Chapelle. Dreaming still, slumped in the depths of remembering, the strange otherworldliness of the images suddenly became more real. He was above Saint-Omer last year, and it was a clear, fine day. Harry looked over the side of the aircraft, his BE2, and he saw the Maubeuge road crowded with retreating troops.

He had been so jaunty on those first few days last year, before everything went to hell. The BEF and the corps were chasing, chasing; they were pushing the Germans back. Or at least that was what was supposed. They were all innocents then. All optimists. All so supremely confident in the last few weeks of the summer of 1914.

He tried to struggle out of the depths of sleep now; he didn't want to see this picture: it was an awful, impotent memory. Because the BEF and the French didn't chase the Germans away; my God, no.

In just a few short hours, in silent mime below him, thousands streamed back the way they had come, the wounded being carried by men who threw away their rifles, artillery guns stuck in the center of the road, horses backing up, and in among them all civilians towing carts and cattle, and children running, screaming, in and out of the summer wheat that would never now be harvested.

The retreat to Saint-Omer. The Battle of Mons, August 23. He and the other pilots had only landed in France ten days before. He had only got his commission in the Flying Corps a few days before that, and his Royal Aero Club certificate a week previously. He had thought that, despite all he had said about hating the air, his father had some hand in making things go so straight and true for him. But Harry hadn't had time to see his father to thank him, or to go home to Rutherford. In what seemed like the blink of an eye, they were qualified, commissioned, and gone. Anyone who could fly a plane was in one.

Harry had gone out and looked at the planes the night before they left England, and the light of day was very slow to fade—it was one of those balmy, lovely evenings of summer. And he stood alone and thought, *I am twenty years old. I am twenty years and two months old. And tomorrow I am going to war.*

The next day, he had crossed the Channel in a Farman, a ridiculous sloughy machine that wouldn't go more than fifty or so miles an hour. He longed for the Blériot that a chap at Hendon had shown him; it went twenty miles faster. The Farman lumped over the Channel, and he had headed for Cap Gris Nez, the quickest route.

It had taken him nearly an hour with a rough sea underneath him and a distrustful passenger, a driver who had been seconded into the role of mechanic and who prayed loudly all the way. Harry had never felt so desperately frightened or so exhilarated; not even his very first flight could compare to that crossing to France. He sat rigid and hunched, eyes on the controls, the plane, the sea, the horizon: it all became a jigsaw of navy blue and white. He kept thinking of the absurd luggage that he had with him, most particularly the tire inner tubes that had been bought from bicycle shops in Dover, and which he was meant to inflate by mouth if he ditched in the sea.

By the time that they crossed land, his teeth had been chattering and his face felt frozen, wind whipped; his lips were sticking to his teeth, his throat was closing up. Seeing the first piece of shoreline, he felt triumphant, as if he had won the war all by himself.

They had got to the aerodrome at Amiens and he had seen, to his astonishment, fifty planes all lined up as if they were at a show, and crowds cheering them. To his embarrassment, his passenger, the surly mechanic, had waved. When he had got the Farman down, he had grabbed the man as they had walked away from the machine. "Don't do that showboating business ever again," he'd told him, "Or I shall box your bloody ears."

Oh, the dark, dark water of the Channel and the drizzling rain of Amiens, and the feeling of being an avenging angel ready to fly out over northern France and watch the BEF hound the Germans back over the Belgian frontier; oh the delight of it. He would have rather been in his aircraft, whatever they gave him, than be on the ground. The minute that he was in the air he was more alive than he had ever been in his life; even the controls in his hands felt surreal, brightly lit, more than three-dimensional. He would walk to his plane as if he were going on a morning stroll, jingling the change in his pockets. He liked to think he could make any plane dance; it was freedom itself.

He was knocked back, of course, by older men. "The callow care-lessness of youth," he had heard one say of an eighteen-year-old boy, newly qualified like himself, who had managed to crash his machine on the South Downs before ever reaching the Channel. "Brief candlelight."

Harry had asked the man what he meant. "Sir, 'brief candlelight' . . . ?" He was wondering if it was some sort of jargon for a technical term. The man had downed the whisky in his glass; they were standing at a makeshift mess in the aerodrome. "There's husbandry in heaven; its candles are all out. Or some such thing," the man had replied. And he had eyed Harry, smiling. "You don't know the play?"

"No sir." The officer had laughed.

"Just as well, perhaps. Supposed to be bad luck."

Harry had come to the conclusion that the officer had been one over the odds, drunk. But the phrase remained. The snuffing out of candles; and they were all candles. Particularly the young ones. Brief candles flickering in the dark. He understood that, finally.

It was true that the young ones died. But then, they all did, whatever age they were. He'd known so many go the reckless maddening way of the boy who had smashed into the Sussex soil, including poor Allentyne getting shot in a place that guaranteed no little Allentynes would ever emerge—"right through one fuselage to mine own," the man had joked as he was taken from the wreckage. Wreckage of a reconnaissance flight only four days after they got to France.

The motor taxi suddenly slowed, and made a sharp right-hand turn.

Harry woke up, shuddering briefly: Allentyne's face had been so absolutely clear that he was convinced for a moment that the poor devil was right here next to him. Harry shot upright, and the driver noticed the movement.

"Just coming up to the house, sir," he said.

And so it was. There, in the sweet evening air, Rutherford. To Harry's absolute chagrin, he felt like crying; he ran his right hand rapidly over his face.

As he watched the view of the house steps ahead of him on the drive, he saw the great door suddenly swing open, and his youngest sister Charlotte stepped out. She clapped her hand, and ran back the way she had come, and suddenly his parents were there: his mother looking radiantly happy, his father smiling, one hand in his pocket and the other on his hip. *My God*, Harry thought. *The old man looks tired.*

The taxi came to a halt; Harry pushed open the door. Charlotte had run down the steps; he saw Bradfield at the door, smiling.

Charlotte threw herself into her brother's arms. "Harry!"

He started laughing. "Hello, scrap," he said.

She pushed herself away from him. "Scrap?"

"I do beg your pardon," he replied. He kissed her extended hand. "Quite the grown-up lady, I see."

His mother waited as he climbed the steps. She held out her arms to hug him. "Darling," she murmured. "Darling boy." He could feel her trembling. She stepped back from him, and, frowning, touched the scar on his cheek. "What's this?" she asked, horrified.

"Little present from Fritz. Flew a bit low one day."

"A *bullet*?"

"There are one or two about, you know."

"Oh, Harry." She looked at his hand. "And this??"

He shrugged. "Well now, that's why they gave me a couple of days. Went to see the doc in London, though. He gave me the all clear." And he wagged his fingers above the bandage. "Can't blame Fritz for it, though," he said. "Some fellow put a chair on it. Blow me if it didn't numb the hand right up. Couldn't grip anything for a while."

"A chair? But how could he do that?"

Harry smiled at her. "I'm afraid I was lying on the floor. *De trop vino.* Embarrassing."

Out of the corner of his eye, Harry saw his father frown.

Then behind them, in the shadows of the doorway, a voice called out. "You're awfully late," Louisa admonished him. "Someone's been kept up past her bedtime."

Harry had been quite all right until that moment; disengaging himself from Octavia, he was in the act of shaking his father's hand. And then, in a flurry of movement, Louisa was at his side, and Sessy was thrust into his arms, and a small starfish hand reached up and grabbed hold of the collar of his uniform jacket, and he looked down into a serious little face, very fair, framed by almost starched-looking curls. And saw Emily Maitland's eyes gazing back at him.

And suddenly it was all one: the children running screaming along roads from Mons; the tilting terrors of reconnaissance; the snuffing out of human candles in churned seas of mud, or up on thermal currents pricked by brown pockets of antiaircraft fire.

He buried his face in Sessy's small round shoulder, and felt those same inquisitive little hands touching the crown of his head like a blessing.

Chapter 2

Twice a month, Edwin Bradfield walked from Rutherford into the village. He was always alone; he did not mix with the staff beneath him, nor the family above him. Others might have considered this fact both a blessing and a burden; but he was not a man to dwell on his personal requirements. In fact, after so many years of serving the Cavendish family as their butler, he did not know what personal requirements he might have. The pursuit of happiness was, in any case, an empty thing, he had found. It rarely brought satisfaction.

He walked steadily, as he did so much else: calmly, at a measured pace. For a young man—and he had indeed once been a young man on this walk—it might have taken an hour or so to cover the four miles. Now, in his sixtieth year, it took him considerably longer than that.

He stood on the bridge and watched the water go by, and then took himself to the bench seat built into the churchyard wall. The little village—much like the great house hidden now beyond the trees and slight hill—was a picture of perfect peace. Mellow stone cottages were grouped around the green, and the Norman church was framed by a large and picturesque lych-gate; the churchyard itself was surrounded by horse chestnut trees. Bradfield looked out along the lines of graves to the modest new stone in the grass on the west-side corner: *Emily Maitland,* read the inscription. *1895–1913.* He frowned, and folded his hands in his lap.

Emily Maitland. He could see her now, a frail little thing swamped by her uniform: thin and pretty. She had been hardworking, he would give her that. But she had made two errors: she had listened to Harry Cavendish, and she believed what he told her. Young men tell lies to young women; he might have advised her of that, had he himself been more watchful. Mrs. Jocelyn, the housekeeper, lectured the maids about proper behavior and quoted the Bible at them mercilessly; but it was of no practical use once the girls were alone with a man. Especially a young man like Harry Cavendish.

Bradfield had been a young man himself, just thirty, when he came to Rutherford. The year was 1884, and he had replaced old Watbridge, who had worked for Lord William's parents for fifty years. Times were very different then; Rutherford had been a man's house. Lord William's parents were soon to go and leave their son alone in the place. A year or two later, Mrs. Jocelyn was hired as housekeeper, and between them they ran Rutherford—Bradfield in charge of the men, the cellars, the service, the practicalities; Mrs. Jocelyn in charge of the kitchens, the furnishings, the maids.

He had known early on that there would never be any chance of a friendship with Mrs. Jocelyn; she killed any instinct at close harmony. Edwin had realized within hours of meeting her that they would each live in their assigned kingdoms in their rooms below-stairs; each in a small, hot furnished room along at either end of a stone corridor. The housekeeper was a frightening woman.

But it was only lately, in the past year, that Mrs. Jocelyn had actually begun to worry him. She kept to her room more, and the maids said that they often found her fervently praying. She had taken against Lady Octavia in a serious way after the young American, Gould, had visited last year. She talked obliquely, at odd times, about loyalty and disgrace, and gave dark warnings about the war being the visitation of God on mankind. She had frightened some of the younger girls, he knew. But he was at a loss as to know what to do about it.

Bradfield had always thought that Lord William would never marry. In the old days he had been a silent and self-conscious man. Busy with his Parliamentary life in London, his lordship would come back at Christmas, Easter, and in July. By rote, Bradfield and Mrs. Jocelyn went to London to run the house there, and occasionally they traveled together if a large occasion were planned in the capital. But that was hardly ever the case, for his lordship had rarely enter-tained.

Bradfield had partly admired his lordship's simplicity; part of him felt that it was a shame. He had looked at William and seen himself: obsessive, upright, lonely. All the master's affection was lavished on dogs; mastiffs sat by his lordship's side in the breakfast room, they traveled with him, they slept in the bedrooms. Mrs. Jocelyn, surpris-ingly, tolerated the mess. "It is his lordship's wish." She idolized the man.

Rutherford had become Bradfield's world from the moment he had stepped through the door. In that first year of his service, he had read news of outside events in the newspapers—the siege of Khartoum, the presentation of a great statue depicting Liberty to the USA, the publication of a book called *Huckleberry Finn*, which would much later become young master Harry's favorite—but these had all very quickly become distant echoes. He had heard Lord William discuss Gladstone with the men who came to shoot, and of course the Queen's name was uttered with holy respect. But they had not been matters of importance to Edwin Bradfield.

Nevertheless, times changed. And the greatest change had come with Lord William's marriage. Rutherford had been torn apart, physically, after Octavia came. In went the enormous staircase to link the two wings of the house; in went the broad upstairs gallery; up went the glasshouses and the two extra cottages for the "outsiders," the gardeners and undergardeners; up went a suite of extra bedrooms, and two upstairs bathrooms where none had been before. The kitchens were extended, and a new range added, and a proper laundry. Octavia Cavendish's wishes had flowed through the house like fresh, cleansing water. Instead of a man's house reeking of dog and dust and mildew came a glamorous, gilded home. Rutherford had emerged like a butterfly from a chrysalis.

"I see you are enjoying the day," a voice said. Jolted from his reverie, Bradfield looked up into the face of Stephen Whittaker, the village vicar. He had not heard him walking towards him along the path. The man smiled. "May I join you?"

"Please do."

Whittaker sat down. "Fine weather."

"It is indeed." Bradfield was not the best at conversation; he was used to keeping silence. Opinions were rarely required of butlers.

"What news at Rutherford?" Whittaker asked. "Your employers are well?"

"Yes, quite well."

"The staff have been seriously depleted, I hear."

"Yes," Bradfield agreed. "I have been speaking to Mr. Gray, the land steward, about it today. There is no one from the tenant farms whom we can bring up to the house; no one suitable. We have only Edward Hardy now as second footman. I need at least two others." He paused. "Although I doubt that I shall find them."

"They are all enlisting," Whittaker observed. "It is the same everywhere. My mother tells me that in London women have been taken on to drive the omnibuses, and to take tickets and so on. And they are making munitions in the factories, I believe."

"Good heavens," Bradfield murmured.

The two men sat in silence. After a moment, Bradfield noticed the agitation in Whittaker; he was sitting forward, his face pale. Bradfield saw how thin he was; the sunlight only made him look paler. His neck looked scrawny in the clerical collar.

"I have been making a decision," Whittaker suddenly announced.

"Yes?"

"A decision . . ." Whittaker's voice faded away momentarily.

"I ought to be in France. There is a need there for me."

"There is a need here."

Whittaker smiled briefly. "Oh, to utter platitudes. That is all. And two burials, but no marriages or christenings or confirmations—that does not constitute a busy life."

Bradfield was shocked. He gazed at the man, at the blue eyes that always looked on the verge of weeping. He knew that Whittaker was not entirely well; he had suffered tuberculosis as a child. He kept very much to himself, isolated here with his books and his prim daily walks that never muddied his polished shoes.

"But surely you can't abandon your parish here?"

"I don't see it as abandoning my parish, Mr. Bradfield. I see it as following my parish. There are chaplains in France, you know, doing essential work. Men like those who have left Rutherford will need me far more in France than they ever did here."

"I don't doubt it. But . . ." Bradfield's unease was as much for the feeling that England, in all its little villages and towns, was being pulled to pieces, its very fabric threatened, as it was for Whittaker himself. What would communities do without working men, or priests? What did cities do without transport drivers? What did homes do without women in them?

"I have asked for a commission."

"Will you get it?"

Whittaker put his head on one side, shrugging. "You mean my health."

"I do. Is it wise?"

The vicar paused. He looked across the road to the fields beyond. Four horses were grazing in the narrow pasture between the river and the hedgerow. "These are going, too," Whittaker said.

"You mean the horses?"

"Yes, the horses. Don't you recognize them? They pulled the dray carts for the brewery."

Bradfield followed Whittaker's gaze. He could not honestly say that he was familiar with dray horses.

Whittaker turned in his seat to face him. "Do you know that they are shipping thousands of horses from America to France?" he asked. "And from India and China. From China! It is unimaginable, is it not? The poor beasts. Do you know what happens to them, out there?"

Bradfield shook his head.

"I have a distant cousin who writes to me," he said. "He is with the signalers. The horses are used for everything. They take them down to the front. In this last winter, both men and horses drowned. In the roads. In the transports. Horses and mules and men. It is mud, you see, just there. Those areas are crisscrossed by canals and marshes. And the ground is . . . well, mud. . . ."

He lapsed into silence. Above them, the horse chestnut trees lazily danced in the wind. Bradfield looked away from the horses, and down at his hands. He was quite certain in his own mind that there must be some exaggeration about the mud or the horses coming from China. It was this kind of slack, inaccurate talk of which he deeply disapproved.

Whittaker sat forward on the bench. "But I'm keeping you."

"Not at all."

The younger man held out his hand. Bradfield took it, dismayed at the bony grasp. He saw that Whittaker was not only young and frail, but also fired by a determination that was probably beyond his capabilities. But he also saw that the man's conscience was gnawing away at him. "I can't stay, you see," Whittaker murmured. "I feel I can't."

Bradfield stood up with him. "It is very good of you. Honorable."

"Is it?" Whittaker said. He leaned forward as if he was anxious to hear the answer.

"Of course."

The younger man smiled. "Thank you, Mr. Bradfield," he replied, nodding. "I should like to think there is honor in it. And I shall do my best, you know. That's what we all need to do, don't you think? For king and country? Our very best."

Bradfield watched him go—a scarecrow figure in an ill-fitting set of clothes. Then, sighing deeply, and abandoning his idea of tea on the green, he turned again in the direction of Rutherford.

Octavia Cavendish was in rather less peaceful surroundings.
She was sitting in the glass-walled office of the overseer, looking down on the huge floor of the largest of the Blessington mills. It was one of many rooms, and the glass failed to shut out the noise of the looms. Inside here, it was necessary to raise her voice to make herself heard; but down on the floor, Octavia could see workers using sign language to make themselves understood.

With her was the mill manager, Ferrow, and the overseer himself, Capthwaite. But this visit was quite different from others in one respect: today, Harry was with her.

As they had got out of the car—Harry's sporty little Metz that he had been longing to drive again—Harry had stopped, and stared up at the huge black building.

"When was I last here?" he had asked her.

"Probably eight or nine years ago."

He had companionably taken her arm. "And now you think I should take an interest?"

"It will all be yours," she replied. "Rutherford comes from one grandfather . . . Blessington from another. So . . . yes, dear. You should take an interest."

"Doesn't Father come with you?"

"No," she said. "Not always."

Her son had raised an eyebrow; she could tell that he thought William's absence was unusual.

"And at any rate, he has gone to see someone today. Something urgent, apparently. But we shall all be back for luncheon."

She did not tell Harry that the running of the mills and the well-being of the workers had been an issue with her husband the previous autumn. John Gould had offered her freedom, and, although she had not gone to America with him, he had inspired her to be more than a pretty picture sitting aimlessly at Rutherford. There, William still wanted her as his gilded rose; but she had to have something to do outside the house. And the Blessington mills had been her property entirely before her marriage. She went back to them as much for her own sanity, for a sense of purpose, as for an interest in their industry.

Now Harry sat forward in his chair, listening to the conversation. Octavia saw that he was particularly struck by the overseer, Capthwaite: he was an unpleasant-looking man with a large stomach barely contained in a greasy waistcoat. She knew him of old; he had been her father's man. He had a florid face on which a large, empty-looking grin was permanently plastered. The smile was so false that it made her uneasy just to look at him, and, the more she spoke, the broader his smile became, his frank gaze flitting between herself and her son. She was convinced that she amused Capthwaite. Occasionally he would use the kind of cajoling tone that one would use with a little girl. It made her pulse increase, her hackles rise.

She turned to Ferrow. "Why are children still working here?"

"It's the bylaw," Ferrow replied. "His lordship approved it."

"They look only nine or ten."

"No, ma'am," Capthwaite interjected. "Eleven's the youngest." His bullish tone challenged her to contradict him. She was convinced that he was lying to her, but there was no way to prove it. "I won't have underage children working here," she said now, looking pointedly at Capthwaite and then back at Ferrow. "Is that understood?"

She knew that it was against the law to employ young children, but the mills and factories of Yorkshire and Lancashire routinely gainsaid it. At eleven, both boys and girls worked half-time; at twelve, full-time.

"If you don't mind my saying so, Lady Cavendish," Ferrow added, "it's the families who want it, and the children. They want to work. Now more than ever. The men are going. Someone's got to replace them. And the orders . . ."

She knew about the orders. The mill was working flat out to meet the demand for the army. Last Christmas, they began to work twenty-four hours a day.

She stared down. She could see girls of Charlotte's age, and younger, hurrying to and fro. There was a smell in the air, too: lanolin from the wool, and oil. It permeated the wood, the floors. Wool fibers floated in the air; even in the closed office she could feel it at the back of her throat.

Harry was smiling at Capthwaite. "Do you have children?" he asked.

"Aye, sir. A boy."

"Is he working here?"

Capthwaite flushed. "Nay. He's at school."

"And why is that?"

"He's a gradeley lad, he'll make summat."

"Make something? You mean of himself?"

"Aye, sir."

"And these children won't?"

Capthwaite's empty smile broadened. "Them? Nay." And his hand strayed to the leather strap at his waist. "They're mardy, like. Stubborn." He stuck out his chin as he glanced down at the workers below. "They're good for the looms, and that's all."

"And you know that, do you, of each one of them?"

"Each one, aye," he said, meeting Harry's eye unapologetically, and holding his gaze.

Octavia spoke. "Thank you Mr. Capthwaite," she told him. "Don't let us keep you from your business."

Capthwaite looked at Ferrow, who nodded his approval. They watched the man go, lumbering his way down the metal steps. He strutted up the central aisle glancing from right to left; halfway along, Octavia saw him stare in a leering fashion at a girl.

"Extraordinary," Harry muttered.

"Mr. Ferrow," Octavia said, "will you walk with us awhile outside?"

They left the building by the outside stair; standing on the stone steps, they watched the yard, full of horse-drawn wagons, getting a shipment ready to be sent down to Bradford.

"The flatbed lorries were requisitioned," Ferrow said.

"I read your reports," Octavia answered curtly. "I'm aware of the requisition."

"They were brand new."

"It can't be helped."

"Ma'am," he acknowledged. And there it was again—that small slight smile to himself, as if she were intruding on a man's game. As if to underline the point, Ferrow turned now and addressed Harry. "Perhaps you might ask, sir, if your father will ensure that no more are taken?" he said. "We've one other, but it is needed. It is so much faster than the horses."

"I'm sure that my mother will ensure that herself," Harry replied. This time, Ferrow merely grunted.

"Have any more men enlisted since last month?" she asked.

"Twenty-two, ma'am."

"His lordship has made a case to be presented in Parliament to let no more experienced men go from mills," she told him. "We hope it shall be considered. I don't like taking the women from their children in order to replace them."

"The women work well," Ferrow replied.

Octavia remembered the Sunday that the most recent of the men had left, two months ago in March. She and William had come down from Rutherford to stand on a makeshift stage and wave their own good-bye. They felt it was their duty. There had been flags and a brass marching band, and the men sang "It's a Long Way to Tipperary" as they passed by, each face looking up at her and William broadly smiling. Laughing even, swinging their arms. It had happened all over the country, but especially in the Lancashire and Yorkshire mill towns. Mill towns and factory towns like theirs, emptying of men. Even London offices—government offices. And shops, and railways. And the universities. It made one sick to think of it—those optimistic men in their hundreds of thousands leaving home. Young men and family men who could not be spared by their wives or their employers. And yet they had gone, and continued to go.

The three of them walked on, out of the gates, and turned towards the long street of narrow houses that careered down the incline, so close together that they seemed to be toppling one on the other. In the gutters, grimy children played in the sun. On the doorsteps, old women looked up the street towards her.

Octavia turned to Ferrow. "Mr. Ferrow, I'm aware that you would rather his lordship came to see you rather than myself," she said.

"Not at all, ma'am. . . ."

She waved the lie away. "But you know, I spent my whole childhood listening to my father detailing the workings of the mill." She looked pointedly at him; Ferrow himself—his shortcomings, his abilities—had been discussed on more than one occasion. Ferrow blushed. This, at least, had hit its mark. "So you understand," she continued quietly, "that when his lordship is not available, I shall come in his place, and I shall be fully aware of everything that needs to be attended to."

Ferrow nodded silently.

"It's not only the women here who have to lend a hand," she said. "I must be involved, just as they are."

The manager shuffled along beside her, but did not reply. He half turned to go.

"Do you know a man called Richards?" she asked.

He stopped, perplexed. "Richards? In the mill?"

"No," she said. "He doesn't work in the mill anymore. He used to, before he was injured and his boy killed. He would, I suppose, be in his fifties now."

Light dawned on Ferrow's face. "Francis Richards?"

"Yes. His daughter Mary is one of our maids."

Ferrow nodded. "He sweeps the yards. Does odd jobs for us."

"Is he reliable?"

"About as reliable as any broken-down man can be."

She looked at Ferrow keenly. "I see," she said. "Thank you so much for your time, Mr. Ferrow."

On the way home, she asked Harry to stop his car on the ridge before the moors.

They sat looking back at the belching chimneys of the mills and the towns huddled beyond them. It was hard to believe that only on the other side of the moors, Rutherford lay in such peaceful glory.

"Do you miss it?" she asked Harry now. "England, I mean. Home."

"Every moment."

"Is it . . . very bad?" She paused. "The newspapers talk of victories, but I don't believe it, Harry."

"Yes," he said at last. "It is very bad."

She was very thankful that he could be honest with her; she waited, thinking that perhaps he wanted to tell her just as much as she wanted to hear.

"The strangest things haunt one," he murmured, gazing straight ahead. "Near one of our billets was a little country railway station. It must once have been attractive; there was a signal box." He smiled wanly to himself. "And a train standing just outside the platform. It was a sorry sight; it had been used for target practice." He turned to look at her. "There are pockets of civilians left here and there. Lost souls, you know, who won't leave. And every morning, the signalman used to come to the signal box. He would pick his way among the debris and sit there—quite 'ten-a-penny'—demented, you see?"

"What happened to him?" Octavia asked.

"I don't know," Harry admitted. "We moved along. But very dead by now, I expect. Like the beekeeper."

Octavia was briefly distracted by Harry's hands. He kept the right one quite rigid, but the left was trembling, the fingers describing small circles on the material of his jacket. "There was such a nice old lady in a farm," Harry told her. His voice was muted, almost dreamy. "She actually walked along one of the army supply trenches to get water. She was very sweet; she brought us honey. She was very interested in our aircraft, and kind to us all. It was ridiculous, though. So absurdly dangerous. She was told to leave. She said that the bees didn't mind the shelling; the hives were busier, if anything. And then one day, her cottage took a direct hit."

"Oh, no."

"It had to be. Shells fly everywhere, you know, sometimes a great deal off target. We never saw her again—blown to atoms, I don't doubt. But the hives, at the back of the house, were untouched. And you know . . . those bees flew in and out. They went on without her. And the birds sing among all the hell of it. . . ."

Octavia saw that his eyes were full of tears.

"Harry, darling . . ."

He suddenly wrenched away from her. "This won't do at all," he said loudly, and he restarted to engine; the Metz revved up with its usual coughing roar. "Waste of a good bit of leave to talk about it," he told her. "Waste of a lovely day."

And he put his foot down, and they sped away.

*I*t was the time for morning coffee at Rutherford, but only Louisa and Charlotte were home. The two girls sat together on a bench filled with cushions in the gardens, enjoying the sunshine.

Louisa was watching Charlotte's expression of concentration over the book in her lap; eventually, she snatched it away and looked at the spine. She loved her sister, but Charlotte's incessant preoccupation with current affairs and risqué literature had the capacity to annoy her. "What on earth is this?"

"James Joyce," Charlotte told her. "*The Dubliners.*"

"Sounds awfully grim."

Charlotte took the book back. "You're not much of a politico, are you?"

"I'm liking books more, but not ones like those. Don't tell me that you do."

Charlotte smiled. "Everyone in England ought to be interested in Ireland just now."

"Well, I'm not," Louisa said. "There's too much upset in the world. I'm heartily sick of it. Let's go and sit in the orangerie," she suggested. "Let's see what's in flower."

Charlotte sighed, but obeyed. Arm in arm, they wandered into the sultry heat of the elaborate Victorian glasshouse, and sat down eventually on the bench near the far door. To an outsider looking in, they would have seemed like two elaborately lovely flowers quite at home in their surroundings, and each almost a matching copy of the other in their white pressed linen dresses. Only a very much closer inspection would have seen the worldliness, a trace of sad experience, in the older girl; and the flash of rebellion in the younger. But for now they presented a picture of tranquility, and all that could be heard was birdsong and the subtle rush of water in the heating pipes. Then abruptly Charlotte asked, "Do you ever think of him?"

"Think of whom?"

"You know very well. Charles de Montfort."

"No," Louisa answered.

Charlotte prodded her. "Go on—you do."

"I try not to."

"Did he—you know—"

Louisa raised an eyebrow. "I don't have anything to tell you, little beast."

"I'm old enough to know."

"There's nothing to tell."

Charlotte picked up a leaf and slowly shredded it. "I think it a very poor show when one's own sister won't let on."

Louisa sighed. "There's nothing to let on about," she said. "I wish I could thrill you, but there it is."

"Not a kiss?"

Louisa withdrew her hand from Charlotte's arm abruptly. "Do you think this is a subject I want to talk about?" she demanded.

"You ought to."

"Why? So that you can delight in it?"

Charlotte bridled. "That's unfair. I just want to know."

"Oh, you must know everything, mustn't you?" Louisa complained. "What's going on with Father and the government and the war, and the Irish question—as if it had anything to do with us—and the women's vote. It's very exhausting, Charlotte, it really is. It's none of your business, and neither is Charles de Montfort."

"I should think whatever goes on in the world is my business, and yours," Charlotte retaliated. "Father says we have a responsibility—"

"Excuse me," Louisa interrupted, "but Father says the thinking *man* has a responsibility. He said it at breakfast yesterday. He said nothing at all about women. You know very well he loathes women interfering in politics."

"Well, Mother seems not to want to stick her head in the ground, even if you do," Charlotte told her. "Look at all she's doing in Blessington."

Louisa sighed. "It isn't right."

"The mills are Mother's property!"

"They are *not* Mother's property. Not since she married, you dolt. They are Father's property."

"Well, they're her family's. Why shouldn't she do something about them?"

"Because it isn't attractive. Just like politics for a woman. Not in the least attractive or appropriate." She looked at Charlotte for some moments, frowning. "I hope that you haven't got it into your head to oppose Father, Charlotte."

"You did."

"I did not!" Louisa said.

"Anyway, I don't see that being attractive took you very far," Charlotte retorted. "In fact, it took you to entirely inappropriate places."

Louisa stared at her, hurt.

"I'm sorry," Charlotte relented after a moment or two.

"That was a cruel thing to say."

"I've said I'm sorry."

Louisa sighed. "Look, Charlie, I've made my mistake. You'd better learn from it. Be guided. You're only seventeen. Listen to what people tell you. Listen to Father and Mother."

Charlotte got to her feet. She stared about herself. "It's too hot in here. I'm going out. What are you going to do?"

"Probably lie down awhile."

Charlotte huffed her disapproval. "Listen," she said. "I'm not interested in men telling me what to do," she said flatly. "Or marrying one, or going to Paris with one, or letting someone like Father, who may be a dear but who is actually a *lot* older than me . . ."

"Charlie!"

"Well, he is. Some people have *grandfathers* his age."

"He's a much respected man."

"I know that. But it's 1915, Louisa. Not 1815. Father's ideas are out-of-date, especially when it comes to women."

"He adores you, Charlie. Mother, too. Remember that."

Blushing, Charlotte turned away. "I do remember it," she said. "But I've got a brain in my head, and I intend to use it." She started walking to the door. "I won't let anyone command my life," she muttered. "Not a type like de Montfort, or Father, or anyone else."

Out again in the garden, she hesitated a moment, and then turned towards the house. But, instead of going in, she walked around the terrace and right around to the front. Here, on the broad stone steps, she looked down the drive and out across the lawns; then, she continued on around the exterior, following the same herringbone path.

Halfway along the east wing, she stopped and looked down at the pattern under her feet. The path was very old, made of the same brick of the center of the house; before Rutherford was extended, it would have been out in the gardens. She looked carefully at its surface, smoothed down in places by generations of feet, and pitted in others by the rain of hundreds of winters and the heat of hundreds of summers; each crack, each undulation had a history. Mr. March, the gardener, had told her once that the bricks came from a village on the Ouse to the east of York; he claimed to know their provenance by their color. He said that the villagers there had been digging out clay pits in their fields for so long that the place was now surrounded by water-filled rectangles and ditches. And it had all come to Rutherford, to make the place pretty, to provide a dry place to walk.

She stood and looked east, in the direction that the anonymous village must lie. Out there in the world, whole communities existed to service Rutherford, but she had heard her parents discussing how the country was running dry of men. She had listened to what the war was doing, she had read the newspapers, and she had said nothing, but she felt more and more like a traveler stranded on a desert island—a beautiful island in a green sea.

Out there in the world, lives had a raw edge, not one smoothed by time and routine. The bricks of the world—the people, the cities— did not lie flat and prettily patterned. They broke up; they changed, they re-formed themselves. They were smashed to pieces, and they rebuilt themselves, or they were lost, or decayed, or buried; they sprang up in new shapes, or flung themselves into new ventures. They invented and moved and imagined and achieved. Time did not stand still out there as it seemed to at Rutherford. The world rushed hotly by somewhere beyond the great gates and the parkland. She wanted to be in it; she felt that she must. But she would not go rushing at freedom like Louisa had done. She would think of a way, a plan.

She walked on, past the eastern edge of the house. Here, the formal gardens at the back of the main building were revealed in all their glory. Gravel paths dissected the knot gardens, and, farther on, laurels and bays had been cut into topiary shapes. Around the edge was a thick border of lavender; at the wall to the kitchen gardens were pollarded limes. "I don't see why the trees have to be tortured into shapes," she had once complained to her father. "It makes them look so ugly in winter, and so strange in the spring."

"March knows best," Father had responded. But she looked at it now and thought that March's own brutish character was reflected in the trees. "March is hardly a brute," Louisa had admonished her when she had shared this thought with her sister. "How can he be, when he produces such lovely roses?"

But Charlotte thought she saw something else than delicacy in the chief gardener. She saw him—a bad-tempered old man—laying about the boys sometimes; she saw the way he hacked at the trees and hedges with his pruning shears and axes. Some of the March children were fat little bullies at the Christmas party, stuffing their faces, slapping their friends. "You are very judgmental," Louisa had commented.

Charlotte wondered now if that were true. She thought perhaps that she saw too much, thought too much. She was not sentimental, but still the trees disturbed her. She worried that Rutherford stood for something more than prettiness. Way back in the family history, blood had flowed, and Beckforths had spilled it. It was as if the trees, with their blunt-fisted branches, and their curious topiary rectangles, represented this unnatural, domineering strain. She wondered if it was in her. She wondered if she had any of the determination, the bloodlust and courage, of her distant ancestors. She knew that Louisa didn't feel it, but she wondered if Harry did, up there in the sky dropping grenades on human beings below.

She sighed to herself, irritated somewhat at the frustrating way her thoughts were going. She walked to the far wall, to the shade of a cherry tree. It was planted on the other side, but the blossoms were dropping all over this side and onto the path. She stood there for some time, at last absently picking the petals from her dress and hair.

Out in the stable yard, the clock chimed eleven; soft brass notes falling with the petals.

William was back at Rutherford before his wife and son, but he did not go out to see his daughters. Instead, he went up to his own bedroom and sat in the large chair looking out at the view of the valley.

His conversation with Henry Atticker had been protracted and difficult; although Henry was an old friend, William had still not liked to admit the real reason for his visit.

They talked for some time of their own estates, of whether a shoot could now be organiszd in August, given the lack of manpower, and of Rupert Kent and the worries that now faced that family.

"You know of course what happened at Langemarck?" Atticker asked.

William admitted that he knew no details.

"Gas," Atticker said. "The damned Boche used gas."

"In what way?"

"Five thousand cylinders of chlorine, I'm told." Atticker lit a cigar, blowing out the smoke with a great sigh.

William sat aghast. "Surely that is against the Hague Convention."

Atticker began to laugh in a sour fashion. "The Hague Convention?" he repeated. "What cares the enemy for a convention? They launched their chemicals against the Algerians. The Canadians next to them thought that some sort of new gunpowder was being used: it came over in a yellow green color. Poor bloody French Colonials ran amok, choking."

"My God," William murmured. "And this was what killed Rupert Kent?"

"Most likely. Rupert and his men were brought in as reinforcements to the line. We had three thousand casualties."

William closed his eyes briefly. He was thinking of Hamilton and Elizabeth Kent in their grand Palladian mansion forty miles away. He hoped that Elizabeth especially would not dwell on the new horrors, but he almost worried more for Hamilton, the sort of man who was all charm and all smiles. Hamilton had a desperately soft nature, and was childlike in his enthusiasms. How he might be coping now was hard to imagine. *I must write to him at once*, William thought.

He looked up at his friend. "Harry has come home last night," he said.

"He has? Good show. How is he?"

"Slightly wounded, but . . ." William again hesitated, before drawing out the letter from his breast pocket. "You know Charles Banbury, I believe?"

"Charles? Yes. Distant cousin, in the Flying Corps now."

"He is Harry's commanding officer."

"None finer."

William fingered the letter. "He has written to me about Harry."

"Has he? What for?"

"He says that Harry is behaving strangely."

"Good Lord," Atticker said. "Very odd. And what is your own impression of Harry?"

William considered for a while before replying. "It's hard to say."

"Stiff upper lip and all that?"

"Yes." William handed the letter over for the other man to read.

It was, in its way, a very charming missive. Charles Banbury made very light of the dangers facing the air crews; he talked for a while of their being billeted in a place called Chateau de Rose—*"although any resemblance now either to a chateau or a rose is quite gone, I fear . . ."* He spoke of Harry's courage, but also of his inability to sleep, and of his drinking. *"Naturally we are not averse to alcohol. . . ."*

Atticker must have reached the same line now. He gave a derisory guffaw. "You know of course that the Banburys come from Nonconformist stock in Gloucestershire."

"Do they?" William asked, puzzled.

Atticker tapped the letter. "Teetotal. But they can't stop a fighting man drinking. Quite unnatural."

He went on reading. Banbury had not described specific incidents, for that would have been censored, but he spoke of Harry's reaction to them. *"We have found him sleepwalking; he does not seem to eat very much. . . ."*

Atticker at last put down the letter. "You've spoken to the boy?"

"Not yet."

"Need my advice?"

"If you don't mind."

Atticker considered a moment before replying. "We've sent last-century troops into this war with last-century tactics," he said at last. "Tactics of the sort that we used against the Boers and Zulus."

"It worked for us then."

"Indeed. But it won't work now. This is a war of machines. We are sending cavalry against machine guns. The laws are being rewritten out there; it's a young man's game. And Harry is a young man, making up this war as he goes along. He's got no lines to follow, no rules. We're banging them up there, William, in these cardboard and tin planes, and these boys survive by wits and cunning. They have to be reckless to be alive."

"And so . . ."

Atticker folded the letter, and gave it back to William. "Banbury says that Harry has a week's leave. Take the boy out riding. Fishing. Something peaceful. Or let him rest. It's all you can do."

"Banbury asks me to speak to him."

"I'd advise against it. Don't let on that his CO has written. It's not a reprimand, it's information. Most irregular—one would hardly credit that Banbury has the time. But keep it to yourself. It would just inflame Harry, that's my guess."

The two men walked to the door, and Atticker put his hand briefly on William's shoulder. "And if I were you," he added, smiling, "I wouldn't tell Octavia about this either. We mustn't make the dear ladies overly anxious, must we?"

By noon, Harry and Octavia had returned to Rutherford. As it was still an hour before luncheon, they parted company on the stairs, and Octavia went to her room.

Here, she flung off her coat and sat down with a sigh in the armchair. Amelie was soon at her side. "May I get ma'am anything?"

"No thank you," Octavia replied. "Don't bother with my hat—I shall do it myself. Please come back in a half hour and bring my afternoon dress then."

"As you wish, ma'am." And Amelie was gone, closing the door softly behind her.

Octavia sat stock-still for a few seconds and then, "My *God*," she gasped in exasperation. She tore off the hat, scattering the long peacock-tailed pin that kept it in place. She threw her gloves on the floor.

It was not just Ferrow's attitude at Blessington that infuriated her so; it was not just that awful feeling that crept up on her whenever Harry was home—the feeling that the longed-for event was come and was fleeting away too quickly—no, it was not just that. It was not even that she had to bear William's puzzled, inquiring looks, as if he was trying to see into her soul.

The source of her frustration was much deeper.

Sometimes she would sit in her bedroom and think of John Gould—think of him here, with his hands on her; think of the things that he had told her. Think of the things he had done. At such times she felt cold, and every bone in her body ached as if she were carrying an enormous weight. It wasn't only a physical longing; it was a need for John's cheerful outlook on life—his enthusiasm, his humor. She wanted to hold his hand; she wanted to hear his voice.

And there was a secret about them both: a secret brought into this house, and hidden in this very room.

John Gould had been writing to her for months.

Amelie, her maid, brought her his letters; she had instructions to intercept them before they were ever delivered to the breakfast room.

Octavia did not want to offend William, and yet she had to have these letters for herself. It was all she had left of the wild, brief happiness of last year. The messages were like little patches of water in a desert; they were points of light in the grey dreariness of a dutiful life. She read John's words over and over, and tried not to weep over them, for weeping was too absurdly adolescent. But they broke her heart nonetheless.

His latest letter was even now concealed in her pocket; and, though she had tried—and still tried—to turn her face from him, his words always found a way through to her. *What are you doing there, this spring?* he had asked. *I hope you have rattled the bars of that pretty cage of yours.* He did not say that she should come to him, however. He did not need to; it was written between the lines. He told her about the house he was building on Cape Cod, but he did not call it *our house*. He only described it to her as if she would need to know in future.

It's pretty darn good, Octavia, he wrote. *There's a fine deck all around it looking toward the sea, real deep so that it could take a sofa and chairs. The eaves come low. I've ordered storm lanterns, a very nice kind, and plain. Can you imagine how beautiful they'll be, all lit up at dusk? The grass has been bleached right down by the winter, though. Perhaps it was a mistake. Mother recommends sea grass so that the house would simply be part of the shore. I wonder what you would say I should plant to give color out here or if you would say that she's right. . . .*

Octavia had never replied to him. Not once. She did not trust herself to put pen to paper. She was afraid it would be a letter of despair. But her silence had not dissuaded him; John Gould just kept on writing.

She couldn't blame William for their situation. She couldn't bring herself to blame anyone. It was simply a dire dead end that they all found themselves in. She knew that William felt it, too. Last Christmas he had done his utmost to try to change things.

He had made an enormous effort to make Rutherford charming. He had invited a large number of guests; he had, to her surprise, brought in actors and musicians to entertain them at New Year. He had told her—he had told everyone—that the home fires must literally be kept burning; that the season must be celebrated in the face of all the horrors across the Channel. It was an act of defiance, Octavia surmised; and, in the midst of their own long winter, their own long standoff, she rather admired him for it.

As if to underline his determined optimism, he gave her presents that had made her gasp with their extravagance. A full-length sable coat had come from Debenham & Freebody in Wigmore Street, lavishly boxed, nestling in soft layers of tissue and silk. On Christmas Day, in her own bedroom, she had woken to find that he had himself made a little Christmas stocking and placed it on the foot of her bed. It had contained an exquisite leather-bound volume of Amy Lowell's *A Dome of Many-Coloured Glass*. She was both perplexed and intrigued, for William did not like poetry, and the author was American. After Gould, he had good reason to despise the country. On the flyleaf, he had written, *To Octavia, Christmas 1914.* There had been no other words. Not *to my dearest wife*, or even *to my wife*.

He had come to her room before breakfast, while Amelie was styling Octavia's hair, and looked at her in the dressing mirror like a blushing schoolboy. She had indicated the book. "This is very nice," she said. She felt embarrassed; he was not a man for little trifles like this, or affectionate gestures. He had actually shuffled his feet while Amelie carried on curling and setting with a small smile on her face.

"I hear she is quite the thing," he told her. "I thought you might like it."

Actually, she had not liked Lowell's poetry much. But one poem had haunted her. It was about petals cast on water and being carried away out of sight, and the necessity of remaining while the petals made their own unmarked journey. It echoed her own life. She had stayed, while Gould went away. William had stayed, while his one-time mistress, Helen de Montfort, was stranded, in who knew what circumstances, in Paris. She and William were both the spectators at the drifting sections of their life, or they were the petals themselves, helplessly carried in a greater current. None of them had what they really wanted. What they had had before was gone; what they had now made no real, feeling sense. But they went through the days. That was the most that could be said for it. They went through their days.

Octavia had gone down to breakfast on Christmas morning, and felt moved enough to kiss William on the cheek and take his arm while they stood waiting for Louisa and Charlotte and their guests. "You are very thoughtful," she had murmured. "I hope you continue to think so," he replied, and struck the old formality of pose that she was used to.

And so they lived, and continued to live, in this strange detachment. She had told herself that she must get used to it. She told herself that she was inordinately lucky to be living at Rutherford when so many struggled in worse circumstances, that she was lucky that her husband—a man who, only a few years ago would have considered her own affair grounds for punishment or divorce, whatever his own infidelities—seemed to have forgiven her. That he now allowed her to at least superficially make decisions in the running of

Blessington. But just occasionally—and the issue of new housing for the workers was one of them—her temper got the better of her, and William's reluctance to build infuriated her.

"We are making a fortune from this war," she had blurted out that night after dinner two months ago. "Don't we owe it, morally, to Blessington to at least provide decent houses?"

William's expression had darkened suddenly. "I don't care to be lectured on morals," he had replied.

She had steadfastly ignored the veiled warning that she was trespassing on delicate ground. She tried to keep her voice level. "It is an injustice," she carried on. "Many of the men who have left those hovels will never come back. Their wives are doing their work, and their children. The least we can do is provide them with a good place to lay their heads."

William had glanced at Bradfield, whose impervious face as he stood by the door of the dining room betrayed no clue that he heard Octavia's tone of voice.

"I think, my dear, that it smacks of hysteria to say that many of the men will not come back," William said. She felt the blood rush to her face, a mixture of embarrassment and anger.

"But"—William continued in the placatory way that she knew of old, the tone that she had always found patronizing and which she struggled not to interpret as such—"it is very touching that you think of the families. We shall see what's to be done."

She had taken a deep breath. "Yes," she told him. "We shall indeed."

Octavia found herself staring at the floor. She tore her gaze away from the complicated pattern of the Indian carpet and glanced back at the bed, and the bluebirds, and the old family portraits lining the walls—every eighteenth- and nineteenth-century face seeming to carry an expression of superior criticism as they glared down at her.

"Damn you all," she murmured softly in their direction. "You cannot touch me. I am half a world away."

*M*ary Richards walked out into the sunshine, carrying the curtains in her arms.

In the small yard between the kitchen garden and the house, rails had been set up to take the ironed laundry and the curtains taken from two of the guest suites. Mrs. Jocelyn came out, watched the material spread, and watched the village laundry maids sprinkle the sheets with lavender water. She took several of the pieces between thumb and forefinger while the housemaids stood behind her. "Let them air for an hour, then take them upstairs," she instructed. She looked them over critically, trying to find fault with their appearance.

Then, apparently satisfied, she turned on her heel. "I shall take my tea, and be on the stairs at four," she said. "Don't keep me waiting. In the meantime, unfold all the sheets from the linen closets that I left in the laundry room. Shake them out, air them for half an hour, and refold them."

Mary watched the housekeeper go. At the door to the house, she saw Mrs. Jocelyn take hold of the doorframe for a second or two too long. She wiped the edge of her thumb along it, then reached up and did the same to the top of the door. Finding nothing to reprimand the girls for, she disappeared inside.

Mary looked at Jenny. "She's getting dafter," Mary commented dryly.

Jenny smiled. "Best not say it."

"She is, though. I saw her going along the corridor to the kitchen. It were like a little dance. She'll take a step forward and two back at each light. Don't you see her? Right peculiar."

"Did she always?"

"Not that I remember. Just these last few weeks."

Jenny shrugged. Mrs. Jocelyn inhabited another world, as removed from them as Mars, and just as unfathomable. They went to the laundry room. In the gloom of the house, the small annex behind the kitchens was full of steam and the smell of starch. Yesterday had been wash day, and today the girls brought in from the village labored at pressing every piece of clothing and linen that had dried. The nearest looked up as Mary entered. "It's bad enough doing the regular without the fookin' curtains," she complained. "They was done after Christmas. She's gone off her head."

Mary had to bite back a smile, because the girl was right; however, she was far senior to a village laundry maid, and it wouldn't do to agree, or laugh at her language. "Just get on with it," she retorted, taking from the pile of sheets.

Once the linen was on the rails in the sunlight, Mary and Jenny paused, hands on hips. "I wonder where David is now," she murmured. "I wonder when he'll get here."

"Is he off to Southampton afterwards?"

"No. Shropshire. More training."

"They say when all the Kitchener volunteers get out to France, it'll end the war."

Mary considered awhile before replying. "I don't know," she murmured. "I expect they volunteer in Germany, too."

"You don't think we'll beat them?" Jenny answered, aghast. "That's not a very patriotic thing to say, is it?"

The two of them leaned against the wall of the house, shutting their eyes against the glare of the sun for a moment or two. Mary muttered, "That's what we're supposed to be, is it? Good old decent British, aren't we? They say 'murdering Hun,' don't they—but what do you think *we're* doing out there?"

She opened her eyes to find Jenny staring at her doubtfully. "But we're in the right. We didn't start it."

Mary laughed shortly. "And they think the same, I don't doubt. They'll have been told they *had* to do it. Invade Belgium and France. To right some sort of wrong, I expect."

"Mary," Jenny whispered. "You'll get yourself in trouble talking like that. What would his lordship say?"

"Yes," Mary agreed. "So I keep my mouth shut. But don't expect me out there waving and smiling and saying what jolly good fun it all is, because I won't. Harrison might like it . . ."

"He can't wait to hunt them down," Jenny whispered. "Like the hunt goes after foxes, he says. Ain't that horrible, though?"

"I told you," Mary replied. "When you first came here last year—he's a strange one. You can never tell what's really on his mind."

Jenny raised her eyes. "Do you think he will? Kill someone, I mean?"

"It's a war, isn't it?" Mary replied. "What do you think they do to Germans? Dance with them?"

Jenny sat down abruptly on the low wall just inside the kitchen garden. "Really kill someone," she murmured. "Not to play at it. To kill someone just like them. It don't seem right."

"That's what it is, though. That's what I'm saying to you."

"My brother's gone. My younger one, Georgie. He's sixteen."

"Sixteen? That's not allowed."

Jenny played with the tie of her apron, frowning. "He lied to the recruitment officer, and he lied to Ma that they wouldn't take him—said that he was just going along to the hall as a joke. But he went ahead and signed the paper. My ma went along and complained, but they showed her the form. She's got no birth certificate. She can't proper remember like, what year he was born. But he says eighteen, and he's big, you know? Six foot two. So they took him. Ma says they must be getting desperate."

"He must be keen."

"Yes, but I don't know how he'll get on. Georgie couldn't tie his own shoelaces till he was eight, he's that clumsy." Jenny gave out a great ragged sigh. "Just a big bloomin' ox, he is, and twice as stupid. He says it'll take more than a bullet to stop him, but a bullet would stop anyone, wouldn't it? He doesn't believe it. He thinks he'll just get up and go on." Her voice dropped.

Out beyond her, Mary could see the sun shining on the neat rows of bean sticks, yards and yards of them in military formation. She thought of men lined up in rows like that, but with no sun shining on them, and no heavy peace weighing on them until the lines seemed asleep in the long, drowsy afternoon.

"It's like he don't understand," Jenny was saying. "And there's more than bullets, ain't there? My friend's brother went out on a raid at night, and he never come back. They don't know where he is. He just never come back. They say he's missing. Not alive and not dead, just 'missing.'"

She got up now and stood beside Mary, looking out at the kitchen garden. "His father got up out of his bed—he's been ailing a year—and he got dressed and he went down to Stepney and asked what it meant," she said softly. "He went out every day and he collapsed in the street and they took him to the hospital and he's there yet. And he keeps saying, "My boy's missing." Just keeps saying it. I mean, how could they lose anyone? Why don't they know?" Her voice wavered.

Mary caught hold of Jenny's hand. "Your brother will be all right."

"Oh, Mary," Jenny whispered. "Ain't it all so awful, though?"

"We just won't think about it," Mary told her resolutely. "We won't talk about it and we won't think about it, neither Nash nor Harrison nor Georgie nor any of them."

"No," Jenny echoed unconvincingly.

"And we'll just get on with it."

"Yes, we'll get on with it." And the two girls looked at each other, each with a brightly despairing smile.

Suddenly, from the house, they heard a reedy voice singing. The door to the laundry and kitchen corridor swung open, and Alfred, the hallboy, came striding out into the sunshine, covered from head to foot in coal dust. He was grinning, carrying a slab of bread and butter in his grimy fist.

Mary looked at him severely. "Where'd you get that?"

"Ay-up," he greeted her casually. "Cook give it me."

"And look at the state of you!"

He shrugged. "I don't care."

"I know *you* don't care, you barmpot," Mary retorted. "But you get one dot of soot on those sheets and I'll string you up."

Alfred shoved the last of the bread into his mouth. He shuffled off across the yard, swinging his arms haphazardly. He made a clumsy attempt to march up and down among the waste bins, where he picked up a stick and balanced it on one shoulder. "I'm going to be a soldier," he said.

"God help us," Mary muttered. She looked pityingly at the boy's gangly, dirty shape, the string around his waist holding up his trousers, and a thick misshapen knitted coat on his back. A cap was positioned far back on his too-large head. He turned, and grinned at her and began to sing "*There's a silver lining through the dark clouds shining . . .*"

"They don't want daft folks. Get along with you," she shouted.

He took no notice of her, just kept stamping up and down with his makeshift rifle. Eventually, he went to the archway through to the kitchen garden and there he half kneeled down, pretending to shoot at an enemy among the bean sticks and mounded potato rows.

"Ay-up," he yelled. "I got yer, dirty German, dirty German! I got you proper dead, I did!"

And all the while, watching him, Mary was thinking, *not Alfie, please. Not Alfie.*

Chapter 3

Donald Harrison was as far away from Rutherford as he could possibly be, and he was very glad of it.

Not in miles. No, not that. Not as far from home as some who wore the uniform of the Allies. But as they sat in the open coal carts of the makeshift troop transport—these slow-rumbling tracks had once served the coal mines that were close by in the French countryside—he had heard Canadian voices, and he had seen colonial troops. He hadn't come as far as they had, across vast oceans, to fight here. But he had traveled through solar systems in his head, and he was still flying, still hurtling away from his past.

The Canadians had told him where they'd been born—places with odd-sounding names like Saskatchewan—and he'd been asked his. "Yorkshire?" one had queried. "What are you doing in a London regiment, then?"

"Running away," he'd told them. They had laughed. But it was true.

He'd run away from one world, and fetched up in this one, and he was grateful for it. All around him, men talked about working in docks, on roads, on farms; sweating through their days, going hungry. Sometimes he heard a man say that he had been in a store, or had been a salesman, or in a bank; but for the most part they were just poor. Desperately poor. He never told them what he had done, back there in the faraway other world. "Footman," would be like admitting to being a jumped-up lackey, a groveler, a fairy boy. No, he had kept his mouth shut. No one pressed him on it. No one cared.

On the ship across the Channel, Harrison had been standing behind a rail when he overheard an officer saying that all the London volunteers were "rats that ran out of the slums for something to eat." But Harrison didn't bear a grudge. The man had been right, standing up there with his swagger stick tucked under his arm. Right about them all as they had trudged past at Le Havre, straight off the boat: they were all wily hard-faced men relishing the fine adventure of war, and—rats or no rats—he was proud to be one of them.

Next to him in line had been a Cockney who claimed he was eighteen, although he looked much younger. He swore and shrugged and coughed and giggled; he couldn't finish a sentence without obscenities. Harrison had watched him admiringly. Rats swam in sewers and came up stronger than ever. They bit and fought and fled. This boy alongside him would live if he could, and spit in the Kaiser's eye. He was someone to keep near, to copy, to follow, young as he was, a boy who had been dragged up in a tenement near the East India Docks. He'd asked the boy what he would do if faced with a German. "Piss in his sauerkraut," had been the cheerful answer. "Wear 'is bollocks on a fine Sunday 'at." He'd stuck out his hand. "Ned Billings."

They had been left there in the French port for twelve hours, and they had all put their packs down on the cobbled street, and after a while they had slept, slumped in disorganized piles. Harrison had stretched out among them all and felt relaxed and happy. He had just wanted to be free of it all, free of his old self, and he had left Rutherford as soon as war had been declared; not going to Catterick or Carlisle or York as he had hinted to Bradfield, but straight on to the London train. He knew London from working there whenever Lord William was in London, knew it like the back of his hand.

He had gone to Finsbury Square; there was a recruiting booth there. Volunteers had been arriving in droves, packing the pavements, clogging the streets. He had been given a cursory examination; they made sure that he was over five three—that was all that really mattered. He was asked his age and occupation. "Twenty-seven." That had been the truth. And his job? "Laborer." A mild lie. His smooth hands would have given him away if they'd bothered to look. But what did it matter? The army needed him.

He had gone straight into training in the first week of September and was billeted out to a reluctant woman whose husband had left her and who consequently had three empty bedrooms in the little Edwardian villa on a quiet village street in the middle of nowhere forty miles outside London. She'd had no choice. The men had descended on the Hertfordshire countryside, and they were the rat army. Tommy rats. Jolly Tommy rats. It was grand; he loved it. Leap-frogging through the stubble-rough fields; running, marching. Tearing up the same fields by digging practice trenches. Day after day, charging about with a bayonet and, screaming at the top of his voice, sticking it to a sack.

They were sent next to manoeuvres at Salisbury, and then had gone to a proper camp. The army had got itself more organized by then. They all had full uniforms for one thing. They all got three square meals a day, even a Christmas Day meal, sat down under canvas at long tables with paper tablecloths and steaming plates of a fat-rimmed roast. The catering corps had served them. He had thought it was bloody marvelous. Served at table! Him, who had stood for all of his working life to serve others who never noticed him.

Now and then he wrote to Jenny back at Rutherford. The others wrote to their sweethearts, so he pretended that he had one in Jenny. Skinny Jenny, not a scrap of meat on her. Blushing Jenny. He really had no idea what she thought of him, but she was a nice memory; something to hold on to, the memory of that palely timid girl.

The day after disembarking at Le Havre, the regiment had walked for twelve miles until they had come to a barn where they had camped out. The next day, another twelve miles, and the next. And then finally to the station in the middle of rolling fields where they had waited for the coal trucks to transport them. They were all joking and singing all the time. In good voice, in good humor. Singing rats, grinning from ear to ear, and waving their tin hats in the air when a photograph was taken. "That'll be in the *Illustrated News*," the photographer had told them. "Jolly picture for the ladies and gentlemen at home."

Harrison let himself roll now with the motion of the truck, jammed between other bodies, stepped on by other feet, jostled, smirked at, pushed and pulled. Ladies and gentlemen back home. Yes, he knew all about the ladies and gentlemen. In that world, he had stood for hundreds of hours in a starch-pressed uniform and watched the dinners and parties. He had listened many times to Lord Cavendish expound his theories of the working man; heard him talk about *the lower classes* as if they were, at best, a kind of devoted dog to the land-owner, the man stuffed into a suit, the man who permanently looked down from his lofty heights. The ladies and gentlemen of England.

Donald Harrison laughed to himself. Cavendish wasn't malicious, he wasn't unkind; but he knew nothing. He imagined he was sitting on the top of a tree that would never fall. But you could feel it falling, Harrison thought. Oh, yes. It would fall, all right. He had no doubt about that.

Along the line, he saw half a dozen soldiers leap off the train and run into an unfenced orchard, and come back with apples that they began throwing into the slowly moving trucks. Hands reached up to grab them; a yell of triumph went up, a cheer. Harrison joined in, and caught an apple when it came. He surveyed it lazily, seeing that it was tiny and sour; attached to the same little branch were the faded brown residues of blossom.

He tore the old blossom away, pressed the fruit to his face, and smelled its beautiful scent.

*I*n all his travels, John Gould had perfected one art. He had learned to stand still.

It came in useful, particularly in a place like Pier 54 in New York. The noise here was deafening, but he managed to tune it out. He managed to persuade himself that he was not in the Customs Hall, but on the beach before dawn as he had been four days ago.

He was barefoot, he told himself; and a warm, fresh wind was blowing across Cape Cod Bay. He was standing just below the new house, and, if he had turned back to look, he might have been able to see its white shutters and long veranda and the cedar-clad walls above with their short line of windows.

He liked to stand on the beach and look at the house now that it was almost finished. He liked to see the shingle roof. He was proud of its modesty. He could have afforded something big and broad and four-storied, something more like a hotel than a house, but that was not what he wanted for Octavia. He wanted a plain place with a white sand path to the beach.

The sand and the water were important, because the very first thing that they would do when she came here would be to take off their shoes and run down to the shore through the grassy dunes. She had always said that her husband did not like her to walk barefoot at Rutherford—that it was not dignified. But she would do it here— she would go barefoot all day if she wanted. He could still remember the shock of seeing her naked feet that first day in Rutherford's impressive library; the feet peeping from under the elaborate lace hem of the morning dress. The way her hair was dropping from a loose chignon. He remembered everything. He always would.

He often traveled out from New York onto the Cape to see how the house was progressing, and he would camp out there when the builders had gone home. He brought a little truckle bed and positioned it in the one room that ran along most of the front of the house, where he had designed huge windows and French doors at intervals. He would lie at night looking at the colors over the sea, and the stars, and the racing clouds; he had seen winter and spring here, and now it was coming on to summer when visitors would come to the Cape. He had bought a huge stretch of coast here, but he would still soon start to see sailboats marring his piece of sea.

He wished she would come. It was an idle dream, and barely probable, but he still allowed himself to imagine. He would get a letter someday. Perhaps a telegram. *I'm boarding at Liverpool*, it would say. Or she would surprise him even more. She would arrive with one of his own letters in her hand; he would look up and see her getting out of a car at the front of the house, with that small smile on her face. *I'm here, John*, she would say. *Why did you ever doubt it?*

Lying alone in the empty unfurnished shell of the house, the sound of the wind picking at the wood boards, thinking of her, was the closest he ever came to crying. He tried not to do it, though. It wasn't that he was ashamed of crying—he wasn't one of those men—in fact, he wept easily. His father was the same, "a dynasty of blubberers" his mother fondly called them—they were all the same. Softhearted, impetuous, restless, interested and interesting. Intrigued by the human race. Vociferous and talkative and funny. Oh, Lord, it was months since he'd really found himself able to be genuinely humorous. He'd lost it somewhere in the mid-Atlantic when he was sailing back to the USA after Octavia had decided to stay with William after the debacle with their daughter.

He'd left her at the railway station in York, and he had straightaway got a train across the Pennines and went straight to Liverpool and got on a boat, almost at a run. Almost without stopping, without thinking. Because if he had thought about it, he might have thrown himself in the Mersey, or over the side as the liner churned its way westwards. He'd tried to obliterate her, and he half succeeded until he got home and spoke to his father.

He recalled every word of that conversation.

It was late summer. New York had been hot. He arrived that afternoon weary and travel-creased and with a crooked, beaten smile on his face. As soon as his father had seen that expression, he grabbed his son's arm and pushed him into the study, and shut the door behind them.

"You might as well tell me the whole story," he'd said.

Oscar Gould was a practical man. He was comical, too. All his life, John had heard his father's stories, and understood that the world was a strange and moving and ridiculous place, and that he was fortunate to live in the best city in the world and mix with the best people in the world. Oscar Gould was rich, but he was, unusually for a wealthy man, happy. He had taught his sons and daughters to be charitable towards their fellow man, and told them that everyone had their good qualities.

But his face had darkened when John confessed that he had fallen in love with a married woman. "This is the one you kept mentioning?" he'd asked.

"Yes."

"Married to a title, John?"

"Yes."

"Good God above." His father had turned his back and looked out the window for quite some time. The city beyond the glass rushed and thundered, but there was silence in the room. And then he turned back. "That's no good, Son," he had said. "That can't be."

"I know it's no good. I have to mend it somehow. I want to build a house for her on the Cape. She can't be in one place and me in another."

His father had flailed his arms in a gesture of helpless frustration. "I don't mean that!" he exclaimed. "Man alive, boy, what's got into you? I mean it's no good to be involved with her at all. Not in any shape or fashion."

"I can't help it."

"You can. You will." He sat down at John's side. "You did right to come back."

John gazed at him. "You want to know the truth?" he said slowly. "I can't be anywhere and feel alive. I thought I would. I hoped when I got home I'd feel different. But it's not going to change. It was bad enough on the ship, but as soon as I put my foot in the door, I knew for sure. I'd hoped that I'd see the street and the house and put my key in the door, and see Tilly there in the hallway waiting to take my coat. . . . I thought I'd crash back to earth. I thought that. I hoped for it. But evidently it's not going to happen."

And he put his head in his hands. All the despair he'd been trying to suppress flooded over him. He felt worse in those few moments than he had ever felt. It was like being enveloped in choking soot: like being buried. He balled his fists and pressed them to his eyes, making an effort not to gasp.

After a while, he became aware that his father's hand was on his arm. He had dropped his hands, opened his eyes, and looked miserably at him. His father was frowning. "Now look, John," the older man began quietly. "You've had a hell of an experience here, and I can see what it's done. I don't say you planned it, and so far as that goes, you couldn't help it. I know what these things are. It's like a railroad crash. The damn thing comes roaring out of the dark and its plain pushed you flat. But you've got to get up and walk away. The woman isn't yours, and she's the mother of children. I didn't bring you up to wreck families."

There had been a long silence. In it, John wondered for the first time what was in his father's past. He'd spoken as if he knew the kind of hell that John was living through. *A railroad crash.* Yes, it was exactly like that. All the life had been knocked out of him: he felt thin, transparent.

"I can't forget her."

"You won't," his father replied. "You don't have to. But you can never go back." He sighed; his concern for John was obvious. But his voice was firm. "I'm telling you the decent thing here, John," he said. "Whatever's gone on over there, you have to put it from your mind. You're home now. You'll get over her. You have to look forward. And that's all that matters."

John had never discussed it with his mother. That in itself was unusual, but she had perhaps taken advice from his father and tried to move him on. She arranged several parties that autumn and winter, and invited suitable women. Pretty, available women of good stock, women of his own age and younger. He was as polite to them all as he could be; he dutifully danced with them and he accepted one or two invitations in return. But the moment that he got near a girl, he got a kind of twisted feeling in his chest, a sharp and penetrating ache. He thought that he understood then why people said "a broken heart." Sometimes the pain was so acute that he thought he must be ill, and he tried to ward off his longing with activity. He went sailing, and he started swimming in the sea in the depths of winter. The cold made him gasp so much that he felt sick, but at least his body was numb.

But nothing turned the slow music of Octavia down. She was a constant subtle chemical running in his bloodstream. He only confided in one other person all winter—a man he played racquetball with in New York City. This man had gone into his father's banking business—he had had to shape up and be the pillar of respectability—and he had eyed John sympathetically. "I had a girl in California," he said. He had sighed and shrugged. "Can't have those kind," he had told John. "Got to get a good girl to marry. Think of that. Focus on it. Let the other one fade. And she will."

But Octavia would not leave John's head. In January, he had done as his father suggested and tried to work at the giant department store that had made the family fortune. He had really made an effort, getting up at six and being there even before his father, walking the empty floors, trying to drum up an interest. He had an idea that if he exhausted himself, he would find a cure for Octavia.

He found that he had quite a talent, but it was not for selling curtaining by the yard, or lace for elaborate trousseaux, or the vast mahogany bedroom sets. He rediscovered what he had always had: the ability to tell charming stories and laugh people out of their indecision. He could smooth ruffled feathers, and the sunny glow he imported as he walked his rounds was a quality that he turned on quite deliberately. He was saying to himself, *See? I can do it. I can be happy. I can get along.* Sometimes he amused himself for whole days at a time with this fantasy, until he would get home and go to his own room and sit at his desk, and find himself pouring words onto a page, addressing them to Octavia, sealing them in an envelope, and sending them to her.

He dared not plead—that would be as cruel to her as this whole charade was to himself—but he tried to be subtly persuasive. He tried to say appealing things. And in between the words he hoped she could feel him leaping out towards her, wrapping her in his arms. That's all he wanted to do, in the end. Have her with him, in his bed, in his days. Christ! It was unbearable. It was purgatory. And it went on, and on, and on.

One evening, his parents held a dinner party. It was late March; there was the scent of spring in the air. There was a cherry tree in the garden, and it was all in bloom. One of the guests, a newspaper editor, remarked on it; and, as Harry stood at the man's side, he had turned to him and held out his hand. "Joshua Bellstock," he had said. "I hear you've written a book."

"Yes," John had replied. "On English houses."

"Travel there much?"

"Yes, last year. There, and Europe."

"Know the English?" he had asked. "Know how they think?"

John had had to stop himself laughing out loud. He was afraid it would come out rather bitterly. "Some," he had replied.

"Anyone in government? Anyone who could get you into France?"

John had frowned. "Well, I guess we can all travel there if we want. We're neutrals, after all."

Bellstock had considered him, assessing him. "I want a man to go there and give a view."

"Why is that?"

Bellstock had smiled. "There's a few of us who think opinion needs directing."

"You mean to enter the war?"

"Perhaps."

John had nodded. He knew why he was being asked at this particular time. Just a day or two before, on March 28, the British merchant ship *Falaba* had been sunk by a German submarine. New York was buzzing with the news. Over a hundred people had been killed, including one American, a mining engineer from Massachusetts. As a matter of fact, the incident hadn't surprised John; merchant vessels were regarded as auxiliary navy, and the German Admiralty had already said a month before that they would attack any merchant ship they could find in the water surrounding England and Ireland. And their point had been soundly proved when the *Falaba*'s end was hastened by the thirteen tons of high explosives that she was carrying.

Five days later, the *New York Times* had an editorial. "Shall we go further, and let loose the sympathies we have labored to repress in the struggle against barbarism?" it had asked. John could feel his own countrymen being whipped up and into the Allied cause. At the same time, the agriculture minister was soothingly saying that the war in Europe would be over by October, and the new Cape Cod magazine wrote lyrically about the spirit of the Cape calling, and softly lapping waters and gentle breezes.

Like most of the men of his generation, John felt himself pulled this way and that. He didn't like Germans—at least, he didn't like the couple of Germans he had met recently, the unpleasant preening military attaché Von Papen and his sidekick Karl Boy-Ed. They always managed to ingratiate themselves into society galas, but they made his flesh crawl. It didn't help that one of his father's diplomatic friends had overheard Boy-Ed calling them all "idiotic Yankees." There was a rumor too, that they were whipping up opinion in the Irish dockworkers against American shipping—causing strikes, disputes, and bad feeling.

He didn't know if that were true, but one thing he did know. He didn't want to go to war. He felt that it would stain his country. And then he would think of Octavia, and her son in France. He supposed Harry must be in the thick of battle by now—he couldn't imagine him sitting on his hands while the flower of England, its gilded youth, flocked to the recruiting stations. And yet, Harry . . . He couldn't begin to imagine Octavia and William's anxiety. He had already read heartrending stories of only sons, heirs to businesses or estates, dying in France. And so he had looked at Bellstock with mixed emotions. "You want what, someone banging a drum?"

"No, no," Bellstock had assured him. "But personal views. What England's really thinking? How things really are."

"And out in France?"

Bellstock had shuffled his feet. "The fact is, the Canadians are there. And Indians and Australians. They're coming from all over while we stand back."

"We ship them arms," John observed.

Bellstock laughed rather too heartily. "Well, to quote yourself, we're neutrals," he said. Then the smile left his face. "I don't want to ship arms and do nothing else," he said. "Do you? It's like handing a gun to a guy in a fistfight. You can't do that and then say we're neutral. We're in this already. I say we should stand out front, not in the background."

"Well," said John thoughtfully. "I'm not sure at all I want to stand in front."

Bellstock has raised an eyebrow. "That so?" he asked. "I'd do it in a minute. Got to do it, like it or not."

John had thought about it for a few days. Then, at breakfast in the first week of April, he had broached the subject with his parents.

His mother had blanched and laid down her knife and fork. "You are not going to France," she said.

"As an observer for Bellstock's newspaper."

"No," she said firmly.

He had looked at his father. Oscar Gould had pushed himself away from the table. "I guess that damn traveling bug is rearing its head again," he sighed. "I told you when thirty came, I wanted you here."

"I've been here," John had replied equably. "But I'm not thirty till August."

Gradually, the two smiled at each other.

"Keep yourself way behind the lines," his father warned.

"I've no desire to get a bullet," John replied. "They sure must spoil the cut of a good suit."

At the other end of the table, John's mother had exclaimed in exasperation, thrown her napkin at them, and missed by a mile.

He opened his eyes now, and looked around him.

Outside, he could see the coal elevators on the wharf; theirs was a constant drumming, lifting five thousand tons of coal into the ship. All around him the passengers milled, some carrying today's newspapers. He could see that a few conversations were going on even in the ticket line, and, at that very moment, a lovely woman ahead of him turned around. She was with another man who was talking to a porter. "My goodness," she said anxiously. "Do you think there's anything in it?"

He touched his hat. "In what, precisely?"

"All this talk of the Germans trying to sink us."

He smiled at her; she was very charming in her dove-grey costume. Under the broad brim of her hat, she shyly smiled back. Her husband turned around. "This is Robert," she said.

John shook hands with the man. "Annie here is worrying," her husband said, grinning. "But how can you sink a ship that can outrun any submarine on earth?"

"You can't," John replied. He'd heard the rumors, and he had read the newspaper.

"But the warning they printed today," Annie murmured.

Robert Matthews had a copy of the very page in his hand, John saw. There was a boxed item halfway down the page among the advertisements for Cunard shipping. *Notice!* it was headed in bold type. *Travelers intending to embark on the Atlantic voyage are reminded that a state of war exists between Germany and her allies. . . .* It was signed *Imperial German Embassy* at the bottom.

"Read it all the way down," Robert gently encouraged. "Vessels flying the flag of Great Britain or any of her allies are liable to destruction. . . ."

"You see!" Annie exclaimed.

"But we don't fall into that category. We're not an ally," John told her. "And she's not flying a British flag, is she? I don't see one at any rate."

"Precisely," Robert agreed. He smiled at John. "Just an attempt to get us all rattled," he said. "Their U-boats can't outrun us. And how could you smuggle anything onto the ship with the secret service around?"

He nodded in the direction of two men who were mingling with the Cunard clerks.

"Is that who they are?" Annie whispered.

"Looking for suspicious persons."

Annie, at last, began to smile. "Then you're not safe, darling." And the couple laughed.

He laughed with them. He hoped the woman felt better, for he really believed what he had told her. He wondered if, at any time during this voyage, he would be able to say to her, "Look, this ship won't sink. You know why? Because it's charmed. It's carrying me back to England. And I'll be on the same soil of someone there . . . it's carrying me back to her." He stole a glance at Annie, so sweet, so charming, so evidently in love with the man she was with. She would understand, he knew.

John watched as his luggage was marked with chalk and loaded onto a conveyor belt. It lumbered off with the Matthews' steamer trunks alongside, and soon it was joined by a huge series of matching cases. Annie nudged John's arm. "Rita Jolivet," she said. "The actress, you know."

"Is that so?" John knew nothing about the theater, though he had been tempted to go and see Barnum & Bailey before he left. But in the end he had not found the enthusiasm for skating bears and warrior elephants, nor the miraculous motorcyclists in their suspended golden globe. And he had not relished pushing his way through the ice-cream-eating crowds at Madison Square. He would have done so once, however—he would have enjoyed it. Now, he couldn't decide if it was his lethargy in missing Octavia that stopped him, or the fact that he might be—at last, his mother would say—growing up.

"Anyone else I should look out for?" he asked Annie.

"Alfred Gwynne Vanderbilt," she replied.

"Please ignore her," Robert told John. "Society pages. She drinks them up."

"I certainly do not," Annie said. "But if Mr. Vanderbilt should cast an eye in my direction . . ."

"He'll certainly do that," Robert replied. "You're female, aren't you?"

John suppressed a smile. He knew Vanderbilt. He was a handsome man, and fond of his sports. Some years before, his divorce had been the scandal of the day. But John could not glimpse him among the crowds. Perhaps he had canceled at the last minute, but John hoped not. Three years ago, Vanderbilt had canceled his voyage on the Titanic so late that they assumed he had actually been on board, and listed him as a casualty. Superstitiously, John crossed his fingers behind his back; then, a moment later, he rapidly uncrossed them as he saw Vanderbilt's familiar profile at the Customs Hall door. He allowed himself a small smile of chagrin. *This ship won't sink*, he told himself again. *She's as fast as they come.* In a week, he would be in England.

He looked about himself with sublime satisfaction. It certainly was a glorious day. Sunlight poured into the departure hall: outside, the dockside was drenched in blinding midday light. He loved departures, the start of adventures. This more than any other.

"You look awfully happy," Annie remarked, laughing over her shoulder as she walked away.

"I *am* happy," he murmured.

It was almost half past midday when the great liner finally eased out of the dock and into the Hudson River.

On the boat deck, the ship's band were playing the same song that David Nash would sing later that year as he trudged towards Albert and the front line in pouring rain. But there was no rain today, only bright sunlight as the strains of "Tipperary" mingled with the voices of the Royal Gwent Male Voice Singers, going home to Wales and belting out "The Star-Spangled Banner" for all they were worth.

John stood at the rail and watched New York slip past. Above his head, flags fluttered from the fore and aft masts; black smoke poured from the liner's four stacks, and under his feet, he could feel the vibration of the steam turbines far below deck. He put his head back, relishing the sun on his face and the cold salty air coming from the Atlantic. He was determined not to lose his good feeling about this voyage. For at the end of it, he would make sure that he saw Octavia again.

*I*t was not long before the ship passed Sandy Hook, and the pilot boat left it. The man on it glanced up at the huge vessel once or twice, watching it pull away.

It was strange, the pilot considered, not to see the name or the port of registry on the ship's side, but they had been painted over since war broke out. Nevertheless, he knew the ship very well. He had seen her come into New York on her maiden voyage, and he had accompanied her then. She was a fine vessel, and she would be off Ireland in seven short days, plowing ahead at a hearty pace.

The wake of the great ship gave his boat a jolting. The pilot looked back one last time; high on the decks he noticed that the party of women he had seen that morning—nurses bound for the western front, dressed in pretty finery with the voluminous white veils pulled back on their hats—were still enthusiastically waving their little paper flags.

Although there was not a chance that they could see him, he waved back.

"God bless the *Lusitania*," he murmured.

On the last day of Harry's leave, Octavia arranged a small party for him.

It was not to be a very grand affair; only the family, and one or two from Richmond and York who had always known him. The Kents, as was to be expected, declined with their apologies; "Do tell Harry how much we wish him well," had been Elizabeth Kent's words to Octavia over the telephone. Octavia replaced the receiver slowly: she had made arrangements with Elizabeth to visit her in two days' time, but the anguish in Elizabeth's voice had been plain to hear. Octavia did not doubt that it would be a difficult meeting.

In the afternoon, William asked Harry to accompany him on a ride along the valley. "I would like your opinion on the two tenant farms," he had explained.

Harry agreed, and they set out on a blustery and grey afternoon, seeing the blossoms from the orchards shaken like confetti and the petals strewn across the lane.

It was over an hour later that they stopped on a hill that over-looked the network of fields that spread out towards the stony spine of the Pennines. Getting off their horses, they sat alongside each other. Harry gave his father a sideways look: he had not a doubt that the ride had been engineered for a purpose, and it soon became clear what that purpose was.

"Harry," William began. "After last year, when we went to Paris together . . ."

He stopped. Harry felt a surge of embarrassment on his father's behalf: the old boy had never been very good at expressing himself. Harry remembered when he had ruled with a rod of iron—his father's philosophy once had been *spare the rod and spoil the child*—but he could see that some sort of change had come over William since he was away. His father looked less sure of himself; the rigor had gone out of him.

"Is Louisa all right?" Harry asked now, suddenly worried that the subject of this conversation might be his sister's welfare. "There isn't another romantic entanglement that we have to sort out?"

He had meant it as a joke, but it fell flat. William frowned. "No, indeed," he murmured. "Louisa is much changed."

There was a tense silence. Above them, buzzards wheeled in the currents of air.

"It's you that concerns us," William began again. "Your mother and I. You seem not to be eating, Harry—you are rather thin, my boy."

Harry continued looking up into the sky. "It's not exactly a picnic out there," he said quietly.

"No, of course not . . ."

"I would appreciate it if you could manage not to worry at all."

"That's a difficult task."

"I'm sure. However." Harry began to put on his riding gloves again, as if the topic were over. But William placed a hand on his arm.

"Harry," he said. "Tell me what worries you."

"Nothing at all. Shall we go?"

But William did not get up. He looked up perplexedly at his son. "Are the fellows out there treating you fairly?" he asked.

Harry laughed in surprise. "Treating me fairly?" he repeated. "It's not school, Father. One doesn't get the cane. One doesn't get bullied. We're doing a job of work."

"Of course, of course."

"And as for the fellows . . ."

Harry had looked away again. The distant and preoccupied look that William had noticed on his son's face all week returned. And William noticed now what Octavia had pointed out to him—a reflex tic in Harry's right hand, now pleating and repleating the cuff of his coat sleeve.

"The fellows?" William prompted.

Harry sat down again with a sigh. "It isn't as if one has the chance to form a friendship," he said distractedly, in a kind of monotone. "One would like to of course . . . being treated fairly or unfairly doesn't come into it . . . but one tends to get along with someone— work together, that sort of thing—and then they're gone."

"Gone?"

"Dead," Harry replied bluntly. "Or injured. Or medically bumped off. We've had one or two of those."

"How so?"

"Insanity shouldn't be surprising," Harry muttered, as if to himself. "It's all insanity out there."

William let this go: he had no idea how to delve deeper, and Harry's face was wearing that closed-down look again.

"Tell me about your operations . . . your missions," William ventured.

It was then that he saw a little spark of Harry's old enthusiasm ignite in his son's face. He thought with a pang of how Harry had been last year, so energetic, so happy at the thought of flying. But now that energy was obscured, as a blanket of cloud obscures the sun.

"The thought that I have most of all is . . . well, the disorganization," Harry began slowly. "I suppose you saw the accounts of Neuve Chapelle in the newspapers."

"Yes."

"A jolly fine show, wasn't it?" Harry asked. "Or so they say. I read the accounts when I got to London."

"You flew during it?"

"Oh yes," Harry said. "We flew."

With a sudden gesture, he threw his riding gloves on the ground. "I was in a BE2c," he said slowly. "Just myself, and no observer. The plane stripped down to basics."

"Why so?"

"The target was Courtrai station. Haig sent for Trenchard—our top man, you know—and said that the RFC had to back up the First Army. Up till then, if we bombed something, it was a routinely haphazard affair." A small twisted smile came to his lips. "We carried makeshift bombs and aimed them at our German tormentors, but I suppose we had no effect on the campaign on the ground. Not much, anyway."

"And Haig wanted you to stop that?"

"No. But he wanted it to be specific. German reinforcements were pouring in behind the lines. He wanted us to target their troop trains."

"I see. . . ."

"I had three French bombs on racks under the plane," Harry continued quietly. "There were three aircraft. We flew in midafternoon. There's a lull then with the infantry on both sides below. They get rather tired after killing each other for eight hours or so. The slaughter gets tiresome."

William was shocked at Harry's sarcasm, but said nothing.

"It had been a clear morning, but the cloud started to come down," Harry murmured. "I went north of Courtrai until I saw the town. I followed the railway track at two hundred feet. Then really low—less than a hundred. When I got closer, they started firing on me. Small-arms fire. A sentry with a rifle was taking pot shots, for one. I pulled the bomb release lever. I was right over a train. They were unloading men and horses."

"And were you hit by the firing?"

"Me?" Harry asked. "Not a scratch. Up and away. I looked back, that was the trouble. I looked back."

"I don't understand," William said. "Why was that a trouble, if you weren't struck?"

Harry now turned and looked his father full in the face. "Can you imagine the effect of a large bomb on a full railway station?"

"Oh, I see."

"I doubt it," Harry retorted. "I'm sorry, Father, but I hope you don't see at all." He crossed his arms, staring now back at the sky. "When I landed, there was a piece of railway track embedded in the fuselage. A bloody great piece. I don't know how I got home."

"And the others who flew in with you?"

"Ah, the others."

"Were they hit?"

"I saw them wheel about. One was fine. The other was trailing. He got down at the airfield, but he had taken a bullet. More than one, in fact."

"I'm sorry."

"Yes, so were we all. I went with him to the field station. It was three miles away along a dirt track. We had him in a staff car. What a bloody awful ride that was."

"This was someone you knew well?"

"Pretty well."

"A mature pilot, a skilled man?"

"Mature for us. He was twenty-two."

"It is a great deal to contend with, I'm sure."

Harry abruptly got to his feet, laughing in a kind of astonished gasp. "To contend with?" he repeated savagely. "As one might contend with one's footman being rather slow, or breakfast being rather lukewarm?"

"Harry . . ."

"*I went with him to the field station,*" Harry repeated with aggressively slow emphasis. "He couldn't breathe. He'd been shot through the lungs." Suddenly, the twitching right hand was scratching through Harry's hair repeatedly. "He called out for his mother, you see? I told him to bloody well shut up. They all do that. You can hear them. They don't make a terrific fuss, of course; they try not to groan too much or be too much trouble. But it gets on one's nerves, you see? '*Mother, Mother!*'"

"Sit down a moment. . . ."

"I can't," Harry said. He seemed to recognize the scouring motion of his hand then and shoved it into his coat pocket. His whole body was rigid. "I'm sorry, Father," he managed to say at last. "Ignore me."

William got to his feet. He walked up to his son, but was too afraid to touch him now. He had a feeling that it would be like touching an electric current. "You must try not to dwell on such things," he said. "For your own sake."

"Yes, yes," Harry muttered. "Of course."

"It can do you no good."

"No."

"If you might try to put it aside . . ."

"Yes," Harry snapped. "All right." He hunched his shoulders, sighed, and smiled. It was a dreadfully blank and empty smile.

"Shall we go back?" William asked. "Your mother has her little party arranged. We mustn't disappoint her."

"Of course," Harry replied. He picked up his gloves from the ground. "A party, yes. How nice of her. A party. . . ."

*I*t was indeed a pleasant affair.

Harry appreciated that his mother in particular had tried to make his last evening at home special. He spoke with the parents of his old school friends from Richmond, and one or two of Louisa's acquaintances, all the while making a tremendous effort at inconsequential conversation.

The dinner itself was beautiful, and the dining room looked perfect, lit by candles, the great swags of the curtains drawn back to show the last of the evening light in the grounds and on the terrace. In the reflection of the window glass, he saw their own blurred shapes and faces: muted colors in the ladies' dresses, their bare arms shown as rosy lines among the flowers; the shine of glasses, the sparkle of silver. He felt he must be dreaming from time to time: this was an enchanted world, unreal. Reality lay outside the room, miles away, across the English Channel. He tried to take his father's advice and turn his mind away from that: he tried very hard to focus on the flowers and the glasses and the silver and the pretty colors.

He sat for some time in the drawing room—so gloriously done with its sprays of blossoms arranged in the great blue-and-white Spode urns by the windows—so comfortable in the deep couches, so warm by the fire blazing in the broad limestone hearth. And with

Louisa's two girlfriends on either side of him, placed there, he had no doubt, for his especial entertainment.

He liked to listen to all the voices. The voices of the girls as they leaned towards him, all lightness, all merriment, their fingertips brushing his sleeve; the voices of his family, well-known and loved, weaving in and out of their conversations. It provided a kind of melody. And later in the evening, Charlotte played the piano. It was a piece that she had been practicing for him, apparently: a Chopin Étude, piercingly lovely—so lovely that it made his heart ache.

He had kissed his mother good-night when it was over, and thanked her. He kissed Louisa and Charlotte, and shook his father's hand. "Thank you so much," he told them. "It was very fine. I did enjoy it. I shall remember it."

And he had taken himself up to bed. His train was leaving at six the following morning.

But it was only as he had closed the door on his room that he was able to let the pretense drop. Octavia would have been distressed indeed to see her smiling son walk over to the window, lean heavily upon it, and lean his head on his clenched hands murmuring, "Oh God, oh God. . . ."

Standing there, gasping for air, he wished so much that he had not spoken to his father that afternoon about Neuve Chapelle.

They had taken poor Masterton—the pilot in the other plane—to a field dressing station, and found that it was in a shattered church. Two miles away, they could hear the battle thundering.

In the glimmering light of lanterns, as they got to the door, he saw beyond the medics a white figure moving. Just for a second,

Harry imagined it was some kind of ghost—horrors were plucking at him, it was all too easy to watch phantoms, for he felt at that moment that they were all phantoms—the men, the horses, the mules, the wagons, the screaming pitch of shells, the muffled crump of explosions—it was the seventh circle of hell, he thought. This dark doorway was surely the Styx; devils were coming for them all, dragging them all farther into the underworld. And yet . . . and yet . . . she was there—the ghost in white, a nurse walking between the stretchered lines of the injured.

She looked up briefly, and met his eye.

Behind him, the medics were dealing with several men, Masterton among them. He heard one say, "Seven thousand in twenty-four hours." Seven thousand casualties, he thought, was that possible? Or seven thousand dead? *In one day?*

The nurse that he had thought was a ghost was busy taking off one apron, and tying another around her; but he could still see the rim of chalky mud and dried blood on the hem of her skirt.

He looked along the wall of the church. There seemed to be no space for Masterton; the beds were only inches apart in the flickering gloom. In the corner, behind them, he could see that the wall held pictures of the Stations of the Cross. The church was crumbling—there were holes in the roof as well as the walls—but the wall niches with their little plaster figures were intact. "*Christ, who died on the tree.*"

There had been no trees along the road outside. Broken stumps, shattered poles, stood where there had once been woods. Just half a mile away—at a crossroads, at a point in a rutted swamp—he had seen a man's torso pierced on such a relic, a fragment blown by the murderous tide. "Someone get that man down, why can't you?" he'd shouted to the few troops gathered by the side of the car. "We'll get round to him, sir," had been the reply. "He don't care no more." Stations of the Cross; hung on a tree.

Here in this room, so far from France, he could hear the nurse talking now. She had been intent on giving the poor devil by her feet a scrap of material soaked in eau de cologne. The man, grimacing with pain, had thanked her. "Better than I've smelled for a month," he had muttered. She nodded. She had a soft voice reminiscent of Sussex on the south coast; soft, burring tones. It was a voice full of melody and kindness in that awful place.

There was precious little melody out on the battlefield. A man might start out kind—might even retain some of that kindness despite everything—but in many of the men he knew even the kindness had been overlaid with a blank look. They would have the "thousand-yard stare," something that he had glimpsed in his own face: the weary, stunned look of a man determined not to show how afraid he really was.

The nurse was moving away from him now in this all-too-real memory. He was, as he often felt at night, intimately back in that church while Masterton whimpered behind him. The vibration of the shelling had got down inside him somehow that night and never left him; even when the noise stopped for a second, he could feel the jarring throughout his body. The earth shook too, from time to time.

The driver of the staff car had come alongside him and offered him a cigarette. "Do you suppose they've got any brandy here?" he asked him.

"I shouldn't think so, sir."

"No," Harry replied, drawing the smoke into his lungs. "No, of course not."

"Had we better go?" the man asked him.

"Yes."

They turned around, and Masterton's stretcher was on the floor by the entrance. The faint light of dawn was filtering over him. He looked like a memorial in some English country church; his arms were crossed over his chest, and a note was pinned to him. His eyes were closed; he looked peaceful.

Harry squatted down next to him; he touched his hand. And then he saw that the fingers were blue, and the hand itself was grey.

He breathed hard now, trying to control the feeling of panic that sometimes overwhelmed him. It often caught him unawares, even here at Rutherford.

Breathe once; breathe twice, he told himself. Hold the air a little; let it go.

And again . . . slow now . . . slow now . . . and again.

He started pacing the room, trying to walk it away. Faster and faster, faster and faster . . .

Fear was the raw adrenaline of flight. It was a kind of ecstasy. It was visceral, and it could be fought and conquered. But this panic—these horrible phobias—could not be so easily dispensed with. Panic was a slippery beast; it was vile, getting into his bones, getting into his heart and rummaging about inside him, turning his gut inside out. He tried to stamp it down, and it slid out from under him and snapped at his heels.

He kept seeing Masterton's plane limping home; he kept seeing it slam into the runway like a dead duck. He kept seeing them hauling Masterton out of the cockpit; and he kept hearing himself shouting at Masterton to shut up when he called for his mother, heard the raw fury of his own voice, the cruel bluntness of it.

And he kept seeing the first light outside that ruined church that might have been the first light of the world, except that its growing brightness revealed nothing at all like Eden.

Chapter 4

Two weeks later, Jack Armitage was fulfilling the promise that he had made to Louisa to find a little horse for Sessy to ride. The livery yard was in a village eight miles from Rutherford, on the way to Catterick.

It was late in the afternoon of a beautiful day as he came down the lane towards the farm tucked into the hillside. The weather had been hot this last fortnight, ever since Master Harry had gone back to France. The crops were getting higher in the fields, the new lambs on the farms were getting heavier, and all around him, the land barreled away, lit by sunshine. He was whistling to himself with lazy contentment as he came to the farm gates; and then he noticed that the first one, and all those beyond, were standing open. Jack walked on farther, into an unnaturally empty yard.

He had not been here in more than a year; it had been May then too, and the cow parsley all out in the verges. At this time twelve months ago, Lady Cavendish had been back at the big house for several weeks, and the American had just arrived, and Louisa had still been in London. It had fallen to him then to take the last of the small ponies that the children had ridden to be sold, and Grassington Farm was the nearest; other families came here to find mounts for their children. He had patted Thistle, the little Shetland, as she had been led away. It was four or five years since Charlotte had ridden her, and to keep her at all was sentimental. Charlotte showed no interest at all in riding anymore.

But now, ironically, he was back to find a mount for Cecily. Or, more accurately, for Louisa. He was anticipating how pleased she would be if he could find a little horse for the child that Louisa seemed to care for so much.

As he stood in the yard and looked around him, he saw Mrs. Hallett come out of the barn. She was dressed as always, in corduroy breeches and a waistcoat, like a man. He noticed that her hair had been cropped. "Mrs. Hallett!" he called.

She turned and looked at him, squinting in the sunshine. "Jack, is it?"

"Aye."

He walked over; they shook hands. She was almost as tall as he was, ruddy-faced.

"Horses all out?" he asked.

She put her hands on her hips, but said nothing.

"I come to see for a pony for the little one up at the house," he told her. "Only a bairn, mind. I don't reckon Thistle's still here?"

"You've not had them at Rutherford, then."

"Had what?"

"Yeomanry out requisitioning, buying up."

"What, not yours?" he said, shocked.

"All but four. All gone today."

He stared at her. The Hallett horses were just for hacking out;

they had, for the most part, been taken in when they were unwanted for work. Mrs. Hallett bought old milk-cart horses and even pit ponies, and little runabout geldings like Thistle, and turned them out into her fields and let them lead a better kind of life in their last years. He'd seen many a one get strong, and afterwards go trotting by Rutherford gates pulling a little dogcart, or being led in a group of children. Two years ago, the Hallett horses had been in the Catterick fete all dressed up in ribbons and pulling a wagon decorated with blossom for the May Queen. But for all that they were mild, broken-backed beasts. No good for war.

"Every one but the smallest," Mrs. Hallett told him now. "They left me those that measure under fifteen hands." She took a step close to him, and put her hand on his arm. "They want heavier horses," she told him. "That's what they said. Complained about the slightness of mine, but paid me sixty pounds each. Complained like they weren't right enough. But they had all the forms, and they took them for the Army Remount. You're sure they're not at Rutherford today?"

A cold chill went through Jack. He'd left his father at the stables while he himself went to Richmond to fetch a few errands. He'd taken his time. "What, they said they were coming to us?"

"No, not right off," she replied. A sympathetic smile—half smile and half grimace, in truth—hovered at the corner of her mouth. "Lord Cavendish only let a few go last year, didn't he?" she asked.

"Only the half dozen we had up at the tenant farm. We've got a fair few left."

She nodded. "That'll be his lordship keeping them back, I'd guess. He's a soft spot for his livestock, that I know."

"Well, we bain't have many."

"You've got a couple of Shires, though."

"No," he said, "we only got Wenceslas now." And a picture of the great, soft-natured Shire came into his head. He and the horse had worked alongside each other for several years, winter and summer. The Shire was massive, but as biddable as a baby. Even as a colt, he had been enormous, and they had named him when they had first plodded after him through the snow. "Like the king in the Christmas carol," Jack's father had said, smiling. "Feet the size of four counties."

"They're wanting heavies for artillery guns. Clydesdales, mostly," Mrs. Hallett was saying now.

Jack felt warm, angry. "He'll not go."

"You've never a choice. They got forms and the like. They'll write a check for him."

"Not for Wenceslas."

She looked at him long and hard; her hand was rubbing his arm as if by way of comfort. "There now," she murmured. "The boys go, and the horses must. It's the way of it."

He tried to find something to say to her. He knew that she loved her horses; was a fool for them, in fact. She would feed them and starve herself if it had ever come to it. She had never had children; he had always supposed that the creatures took the place of a family. They *were* her family, in fact.

He scanned her face, and saw unhappiness there, but he didn't know how to comfort her. He couldn't imagine her going back into her cold, flagstone kitchen that night. There had never been a Mr. Hallett, not for years. It was said in the village that he had left her soon after they had been married, long before the turn of the century. She had grown old up here on the sweeping slant of the hill, living more with horses than people. He wondered what she would do tonight. Perhaps she wouldn't go back into the house at all, he thought. Perhaps she would stay out here in the yard, and cry when there was no one to see her.

"I won't let them take him," he told her. "Not him. Not guns."

"Ah, Jack," she muttered. There was a world of grief in those two words.

When he thought about it afterwards, he knew that he had been rude to her. He had turned around and walked straight out of the yard, and he had heard her calling out to him that he must stop for a drink of tea, but he didn't heed her.

He set off to walk the six miles back to Rutherford, and ran some of it as much as he walked. Suddenly the lanes weren't beautiful anymore, not as beautiful as they had been that afternoon when he had set out cadging a lift from the grocer's van, and walked around Richmond whistling, and then on to Mrs. Hallett with a brisk step, thinking of how happy he could make Louisa by finding a pony for Cecilia.

Now it was all gone; he had forgotten what he had gone to Mrs. Hallett for. All he could think of was the woman's stricken face as he had turned on his heel and walked away.

He reached the stable yard at Rutherford at six, and went straight to the Shire's stall, and looked in over the painted green door. The great grey, all eighteen hands of him, turned his head and looked at him with the patient and soulful eyes Jack knew so well. "You're here, then," he said out loud, relieved. *My God*, he thought. What would this animal do, under fire? What happened to beasts like them if they were hurt? Did they leave them at the side of the road, just leave them, what? What happened out there? They couldn't just leave them, surely. His heart started to beat rapidly. He had never had to put a horse down himself.

He'd heard one man say at York races last spring that his own racehorse had known when his time had come. "He looked at me with a mother's eyes," the man had said. There had been a pint of porter in his hands, and he was maudlin, of course, and he was perhaps exaggerating, but Jack had still accepted what he had said. Horses *did* look at you like that: a liquid, understanding gaze.

The beasts had character; that was what people didn't know. They cried sometimes if they were truly hurt, and they could scream. A team of horses had come down in Blessington once, taken a bad turn on the hill and overturned a wagon, and they had screamed like children, caught under the load.

He couldn't imagine a horse in war. What did they do with them, what did they ask them to do? Pull guns, for God's sake? Pull a gun through what, through lanes like these? He doubted it. No parsley growing in the verges now in Flanders. No tunnels of overarching trees. And the ships. They put them on ships. There had been a photograph in the newspaper of a horse being swung over the side of a ship in a kind of harness. And Jack knew that they took them over hundreds, perhaps thousands, at a time, and that some of them died in the holds. Frightened, he guessed.

No, it couldn't happen to Wenceslas. He wouldn't allow it. For Wenceslas, this great soft docile boy? No, it wasn't possible. For a start, Jack reasoned to himself, the Shire was too big by far. He wouldn't fit in a normal wagon to pull a gun, never mind those cramped ship's stalls. And he would be slow, too slow. Jack had never seen Wenceslas rise to more than a lumbering trot, and that only grudgingly. He'd be no good for battle.

Jack ripped open the door and went over to Wenceslas across the fresh straw, and stood trembling—half in fury and half in exertion—by the horse's side. At last, he put a hand out and stroked the warm flank.

"Over my dead body," he promised. "I'll see to it."

He walked back to the house he shared with his father and mother. Josiah Armitage was washing up for supper in the outhouse; Jack went in and stood by the stone sink. "I've been to Hallett's, and her horses are gone," he said. "I went over to find a little pony for the bairn. For Cecily."

"I know," Josiah replied. He was soaping his arms to the elbows, carefully cleaning his nails. Jack's mother hated it when either of them sat down at the table with a speck of dirt on them. He looked weary; older and more dispirited than Jack could ever remember.

"Are they coming here?"

"March and Bradfield both came over an hour ago," his father said. "The Yeomanry rang the house. Lord Cavendish only said a year, they told Bradfield. That we was keeping what we had a year. But no longer."

Jack stared dumbly at his father as the old man meticulously dried himself on a thin towel that hung on a nail above the sink. Josiah replaced it with elaborate care, then turned and faced his son.

"They'll not take Wenceslas," Jack said. He heard a childish twang in his own voice, the pitiful sound of childhood when he had lost something dear. A pleading sound. "I've looked after him for five years, Father."

"They're back in the morning, eight sharp," Josiah replied. "They'll take them to the train. They're going to Romsey eventually." He paused. "Wenceslas, too."

"Where is Romsey?" Jack demanded.

"Down south. Hampshire. Then on to the coast."

"And what then?"

Josiah Armitage shook his head. "Wash up, and set your'sen down for supper," he told him quietly. "Your mother is waiting."

The sun was not shining the next day.

A cool breeze was blowing from the west, off the top of the moors. Bradfield had not been able to sleep; he woke far ahead of the alarm clock by the side of his bed. He thought he could hear sounds in the main house in addition to the faint moaning of the wind. He could always tell when the wind changed direction; somewhere in the turreted chimneys far above him the air sounded a low, stuttering note. He had got up and washed and dressed, sighing. He disliked routines being disrupted. It jarred his soul.

Going down to the kitchen at five, he had been surprised to find Mrs. Jocelyn seated at the servants' table. He stopped on the threshold. She had a Bible open in front of her. "Good morning," he said.

"I've seen to those girls," she replied, not acknowledging his greeting. "They were not up. I have spoken to Miss Dodd. Time was that a head housemaid had control of her staff."

So that was what had awoken him: the tread of the housemaids' feet on the back stair. "Mrs. Jocelyn," he said with quiet puzzlement. "It is ten past five."

She frowned at him as if she had not understood him. "It is light," she said.

"True enough," he agreed. "But it is still ten minutes past five." She looked up at the clock. "They are not due to rise for another fifty minutes," he pointed out.

A ring of heightened color showed above the collar of her dress. She slammed the Bible shut, and got to her feet. "I should think I might say what hour they begin work," she told him. "If I want them up at three in the morning, they are obliged to obey me."

He came fully into the room, and closed the door behind him. At the far end, the range was faintly glowing. The hallboy would be in soon enough to stir it up, and the cook soon after. But there was absolutely no need to have disturbed the housemaids so early.

He drew out a chair some feet away from her. "Do share a cup of tea with me," he said.

The housekeeper hesitated. She was fully dressed, as was he; there was nothing immodest in their being together there, even in the absence of the kitchen staff. He saw that her hands shook a little. Then she relented. Sitting down again, she poured him the tea.

"These days are upsetting for all of us," he observed. "It's not surprising to mistake the time."

"The days of wrath are upon us," she replied darkly.

"Yes, indeed." He drank his tea slowly. "But you, Mrs. Jocelyn . . . are you well enough? You seem . . ." He searched for the word that would not infuriate her. "Preoccupied."

She looked at him as if inspecting his reliability. Then she leaned forward. "There is something wrong here," she whispered.

"Wrong?" he asked. "In what way?"

Her hand fluttered towards the ceiling as if indicating the rooms upstairs. "There will be a visitation." She sat back, nodding. "You've not heard it, in the rooms?"

"Heard what?"

"The . . ." Her fingers walked along the table top in a skittering motion. "The rustling. The movement."

He frowned. "You mean there is some sort of infestation in the main rooms?" he asked, perplexed. "I've seen no evidence of it."

"Infestation," she repeated, and she gave him a brilliantly disconcerting smile. "That is exactly the word, Mr. Bradfield. The exact word."

"Then we must have someone see to it at once." It was not unknown, in country districts, for rats to be on the property; the London houses were regularly infested too, from the Victorian sewers and the sheer volume of people. He had heard rumors that Buckingham Palace itself was positively alive with vermin. "I shall make a call myself," he said.

But Mrs. Jocelyn's gaze had slipped away from him and was

focused on a point somewhere behind his head. The way she stared, as if watching something, made the hairs prickle on the back of his neck. He resisted the temptation to turn around in an effort to see what she was seeing.

"Oh, it's far too late for that," she murmured to herself. "It's the time of harvest."

"Harvest? But it is not harvest yet, not for another two or three months at least."

Her focus strayed back to him. She gave him a smile, patting the closed Bible in front of her. "The Son of man shall send forth his angels, and they shall gather out of his kingdom all things that offend, and them which do iniquity."

He did not know, quite, what to say to her. She seemed happy at least, relaxing back in her chair, smoothing down her dress. The keys rattled on the chain at her waist. "Harvest," she repeated softly. "The purging of the threshing floor, and the gathering of the wheat into the barn. And the burning of the chaff in unquenchable fire."

She was holding his gaze with that same disconcerting smile on her lips. "The New Testament, Mr. Bradfield," she said. "It's all written there, if one cares to read. It's what shall come to us. It's what has already come to us." She nodded to herself in satisfaction. "It's in the bones of this house, in the walls, in the floors. It's with us already. You'll see if I'm not right, Mr. Bradfield. It's the time of harvest in this house."

*B*radfield was to think of this conversation later that morning, and it was then that the memory of Mrs. Jocelyn's words sent a cold chill down his spine.

He was walking in the grounds, out of sight of the main rooms of the house, but with a perfect view of the long driveway, when he saw a motor vehicle come around the corner from the estate steward's house and start the long incline towards Rutherford. It was doing such a speed that it trailed a plume of dust behind it, and Bradfield immediately turned on his heel. He reached the half circle before the Tudor doors and the long line of steps just as the van came to a halt, and a man got out.

Bradfield's intention had been to reprimand whoever it was who had come in such a hurry through the main gate, but then he recognized the driver, who even now was hesitating as he looked up at the house.

"Mr. Rissington," Bradfield said.

The man turned around. In his hand he held an envelope. The postmaster was dressed, Bradfield noticed, in his best uniform and not the common-or-garden suit he wore in the village. He held out the telegram. "I'm afraid it's this," he told Bradfield.

The butler took it from him. "I'll see to it," he said. "If you'd like to go around the back with the van, I'm sure that Mrs. Carlisle might find you a cup of tea."

The agitated postmaster did as he was told, and, after watching the van make its exit, Bradfield climbed the steps of the house and opened the door.

As luck would have it, it was not Lord Cavendish that he saw in the hall, but Charlotte. She was so much quicker than many of them, Bradfield thought; as soon as her eyes strayed to the envelope, her hand went to her mouth in horror.

"Is Lord Cavendish in his study?" Bradfield asked.

Charlotte advanced on him. "Give it to me."

"I think it ought to go to his lordship," Bradfield said quietly. "If you'll beg my pardon."

The girl hesitated a moment, then, "You're right," she said. "I shall go and fetch Mother."

He watched her run up the vast stairway, heard her run along the gallery, heard, distantly, her knock at her mother's door. Then he walked along the length of the hall and turned towards William Cavendish's study.

*L*ouisa and Charlotte were the first downstairs, running to the drawing room, where their father sat with the opened telegram on his knees.

"Mother was just bathing," Charlotte said. "She's coming."

"What did you tell her?" William asked.

"Just that there was something you wanted to talk to her about," Louisa replied. They hesitated, not sure if they ought to sit with him: at such times, William always set himself apart, sought privacy. He was as likely to push any expressions of grief away as welcome them. They stood uncertainly, watching his face. Many another man might have run up to his wife's room directly; he might have wanted to speak to her alone, and, while the two girls recognized his customary rigid calm, his composure baffled them.

Very soon, they heard Octavia's footstep in the hall. She came into the room, and looked at the three of them. Her smile of greeting abruptly vanished. "What is it?" she asked. "What's the matter?"

"Oh, Mother," Louisa exclaimed, and promptly burst into tears.

Charlotte snatched hold of her sister's hand. "That won't do any good," she hissed.

William had got to his feet. "A telegram has come," he said.

"Is it Harry?"

"Yes," he replied.

Both parents stood as if carved in stone; it was Charlotte who moved eventually, going up to William, gently disengaging the piece of paper from his hands, and delivering it to her mother. Octavia read it; the blood drained from her face. Both daughters then took an arm, and guided her to a chair. After a moment or two, Octavia glanced at her daughters and patted their hands. "Don't fuss, girls," she murmured. "Don't fuss."

"May I see it?" Charlotte asked. Octavia handed her the telegram.

"Wounded," she breathed. "*Regret to inform you Flying Officer Harold William Cavendish wounded . . .*"

"Alive at least," William said. He had sat down again on the couch nearest to Octavia. "Ring for that idiot footman Hardy," he told his daughters brusquely. "I want a fire in here. The room is too damned cold. And tell him to get tea."

In short order, two of the housemaids arrived, one carrying a tea tray, shepherded by Mrs. Jocelyn. The faces of all three women were blanched; they looked stricken. Mrs. Jocelyn's gaze hardly left William's face. "We are all very sorry, your lordship," Mrs. Jocelyn said, ignoring Octavia and both Louisa and Charlotte.

William waved his hand. "Thank you," he muttered.

The tea tray was settled with a clatter.

"That's all right," Charlotte said suddenly. "I can light the fire, Mrs. Jocelyn."

The housekeeper hesitated, and then the two maids were ushered out as quickly as they had come in.

Charlotte rounded on her mother. "Did you see that?" she exclaimed. "She kicked poor Jenny's feet as she was kneeling down, to hurry her up! What a dreadful old dragon she is."

"No doubt she's as distressed as we are," Octavia murmured.

"And that gives her the right to kick someone?"

"Let it be, for heaven's sake," William told his daughter. "There's more important things to consider."

Louisa had once more begun to cry, sitting on the arm of Octavia's chair and chafing her mother's hand.

"You won't help Harry by crying, or Mother," Charlotte said.

Louisa glared at her. "I sometimes wonder that you aren't made of stone!"

"I'm not stone at all," Charlotte retorted.

"Girls, please," Octavia begged.

"Pour the tea," William instructed.

Charlotte did as she was bid, distributing the cups. Eventually she sat next to William, frowning at him when he was not looking at her, wondering why it was, at this most awful of moments, that he could not go to her mother and embrace her, or take her hand. And then she saw, with sudden perception, that William was immobilized by shock. Carefully, she gave him his tea and quickly kissed his cheek.

"Thank you, dear," he murmured.

"Can we go to him?" Octavia asked. "Can we go to France to see Harry?"

"I doubt it's allowed," William said. "We may hear more shortly— of where he's been transferred—that sort of thing."

"It says—" Octavia hesitated. "It says he's at a dressing unit at Festubert. Where is that?"

"Near a place called Béthune, east of Lille."

Both parents looked in surprise at Charlotte. "How do you know that?" William asked.

"I read the papers, and I have a map of France," Charlotte replied with hauteur. "I should think anyone does the same when they read the reports, don't they?"

Octavia gave a watery smile. How typical it was of Charlotte to pay such attention. "Lille," she murmured. "We once went there, I think. A charming town."

"I shouldn't think it's charming now," Charlotte said.

Octavia tried to ignore this. "There is not much detail," she said, and, although she had been trying to take a note from William and appear to be calm, her eyes filled now. "It may be serious, may it not?"

No one replied. Louisa held her mother's hand tighter, gazing at her father with a desperate expression, as if he could hold the answer. But of course there was no answer available; no one knew. The telegram gave no further clue.

Suddenly, Octavia wiped her eyes and straightened her shoulders. She got abruptly to her feet, pushing the low table that held the tea tray out of her way. "We must go to London at once," she announced firmly. "We must be nearer him. Either to have him at the Grosvenor Square house when he's back in England, or to be close to France if you are allowed to go over, William."

"Can't we all go over?" Charlotte asked.

"No," Octavia told her. "They won't want whole families turning up. We would only get in the way." She paused. "And perhaps he's already in a Channel port. The telegram will have taken a while to get here . . . perhaps in that time he's been transferred to Boulogne?"

She was looking at William for answers.

"I simply don't know," William told her. "But yes . . . they will have hospital trains going to Boulogne from the front."

"Then we must hurry. We must leave directly."

"We'll come with you," Charlotte said.

"I would rather you stayed here," William told her.

"I shall stay with Sessy," Louisa said. "I don't think I could bear London."

Octavia was walking to the door already.

In her wake, William followed her.

Charlotte looked back at the telegram: such an innocuous piece of paper carrying such a terrible message. In doing so, she caught Louisa's eye. "You're right," she said. "Stay here. Perhaps you should ask Mrs. Jocelyn to make up a room for Harry downstairs. That would be an idea, wouldn't it?"

"Yes," Louisa agreed feebly.

Charlotte regarded her for some seconds. "Dear heart," she murmured, "you could win a prize for sobbing, you really could."

"I should think you ought to hurry up and pack, don't you?" Louisa said, taking out a handkerchief. "You utter little pagan."

When the train from Yorkshire at last arrived in London, it was almost midnight.

Although the station concourse was eerily devoid of crowds, it was instead packed with wagons and delivery trolleys. In the half-lit darkness, the breath of the delivery horses wound slowly upwards in the air, showing hazily against the high glass roof and the night beyond. Octavia took William's arm as they made their way towards the street. After the cushioned luxury of first class and the quiet of Rutherford, the city was a shock to the system.

Two porters went ahead of them with the luggage; behind Octavia and William came Amelie, Octavia's maid; and William's man, Cooper. Charlotte strode now at her parents' side, swinging an overnight case in her hand and resisting her father's frowns. "There is no need to carry that," he had said to her, as they had got on the train at York. "I might need something in it, so might Mother," Charlotte had replied airily. It had proved to contain chocolate and two cheap novels.

William had watched the country go by hour after hour, wondering where Harry was, wondering more so what state of mind his son was in. Watching as the green of England was gradually replaced with the sprawling suburbs of the capital city, William thought of Emily Maitland, and Harry's guilt. Perhaps, he considered, the memory had got into his son's mind somehow, knocked him off course in a more dreadful way than either he or Octavia had appreciated.

He had stolen more than one glance at his wife. Of course, Octavia was more subtle, more understanding than himself. He had never been trained to consider a man's heart. It had not been required of him.

Soon, the three of them arrived at the Grosvenor Square house. Charlotte got out of the cab after them and ran up the steps and rang the bell.

"For heaven's sake, what has got into that girl?" William said to Octavia.

"She is seventeen," Octavia murmured. "Don't you remember being seventeen, William?"

"I would have been castigated, even at seventeen, for ringing my own doorbell," William replied. But his words were lost in a volley of sudden exclamations.

Behind the London housemaid, Florence de Ray had emerged from the hallway, and had at once drawn Charlotte into the house. The de Rays had been known to the Cavendishes for many years, and Hetty de Ray—Florence's mother—had befriended Octavia from the first days of their marriage. Watching the two girls ascending the staircase, William thought with benign partiality that Florence was as plain as Louisa was pretty—the girls were the same age—but, then, Florence had her compensations. She was level-headed and modest; he hoped that her influence on Charlotte would be more effective than it had been on Louisa last year—but then. Who was to tell? Women were an unfathomable species.

Florence's mother, Hetty, now too came into the hall: a broad and smiling vision in some sort of purple lace dressing gown. Hetty held out her arms to Octavia. "My dearest girl!" she boomed. "How was the train? No, don't tell me. Dreadful, I expect," she continued, shooing them all into their own sitting room as if they were a couple of reluctant sheep. The housemaid hopped backwards to avoid her and retreated down the hall. All the while, Hetty de Ray kept up an unstoppable flow of observations.

"You must be thoroughly exhausted," she observed. "I know that I am! We've been in town all Season and beyond. Florence would insist upon it. She's become quite the busybody up at St. Dunstans. They take the blinded there, you know. Did you know? Well, I expect not. Do sit down, my dears. Sit down."

Octavia had gratefully slumped to the nearest sofa already. "You simply wouldn't recognize Regent's Park!" Hetty blithely continued. "Have you seen it? No, of course you haven't. Well, don't." She gave a theatrical sigh. "Where all this shall lead, I truly can't guess. Staff are deserting us even here. My second chambermaid is making bombs. Can you imagine! Bombs! One's blood runs cold. She couldn't thread a needle when she worked for us."

All this was delivered in the hearty, braying tone that they both knew so well. Hetty was a force of nature, one of the old school, a daughter of Britannia who had followed her husband all over the world. Trailing an overpowering scent of jasmine in her considerable wake, she lowered herself back into the sofa in which she had been sitting before they arrived. "I've rung for tea," she said. "Though heaven knows how long it might take your staff to deliver it. You've only one cook here, Octavia! A cook, a housemaid, and a footman. Although where the footman might be this evening I can't guess. Such desperate nonsense, isn't it, this war?"

Octavia glanced up at William.

"Darling man, do sit down," Hetty admonished. "It's your own house after all." He obeyed, stiffly, in his own time.

"You're very kind to come here and get things ready for us," Octavia said, taking off her gloves.

"As I say, it's impossible to get staff," Hetty replied. "And so I don't mind coming here and setting a firecracker under the apologies you've got left. But really! May I send a man or two over from Dalletts? We've got a few left. The halting lame and sick, of course. The one-eyed and pea-brained. But beggars can't be choosers. They're trustworthy at least."

Dalletts was the de Rays country house in Surrey. "We couldn't . . ." William began.

Hetty brushed his objections away with a wave of her hand. "We must help one another out. And talking of which, can you guess? Not in the remotest!" She gazed at them with true affection, and clapped her hands together. "Herbert has found news of Harry."

William saw what looked like a small electrical charge run through Octavia; Hetty's husband, a diplomat, worked in Whitehall. She leaned forward. "He has? But how?"

"A man who knows a man who knows a man and all that. This particular man in question is a chaplain. He's related to the Bickersteths, but then you don't know the Bickersteths. Their son Morris was with Herbert when Balfour gave his speech. He turned to Herbert and said, 'It makes one realize that dying for one's country is a magnificent thing.' What a tremendous family they are. But then you don't know them."

"I think we have established that," William said, with an edge. In the face of Hetty's infernal chatter, his patience was beginning to desert him.

"The Bickersteths," Hetty repeated, giving William a very straight look, and slowing her words as if she were explaining to a small child, "know the RFC chaplain. He saw Harry when he was first brought into the field hospital. Or rather, he saw the nurse who had seen Harry. And he then wrote to his father, who works with Herbert's secretary. That is what I mean when I say a man who knows a man who knows a man. Or, in this case, a man who knows a man who knows a chaplain." And Hetty sat back with cheerful triumph, slapping her hand on her lap as if this were absolute proof of her husband's genius.

The door opened, and the same housemaid who greeted them on arrival came in with the tea. It was set down before them.

"There now," Hetty said, waving her hand at the girl. "You can go, child. Has that cook woken from her torpor to at least give us a tray of sandwiches?"

The girl blushed. "Yes, m'm." The girl retreated. Octavia had been staring at Hetty this whole while. She watched now as Hetty leaned over the tea tray. "Hetty," she prompted. "What else?"

"I shall send Sara, my best girl, to you," Hetty was murmuring, surveying the tray. "She'll make a decent housekeeper for you for three or four days."

"Hetty!"

Mrs. de Ray glanced up at them both. "Legs, darling," she said, smiling. "Both legs broken. And a wound or two from the aeroplane. Metal. But he'll recover. Quite dazed, couldn't quite understand where he was by all accounts, but he's all right. The Northumberland Fusiliers got him out, we're told. Harry's due in Boulogne very soon."

There were a few moments of complete silence, and then to William's dismay, Octavia burst into tears. With a fluttering gesture of annoyance, Hetty indicated to William that he should leave Octavia alone. She herself got up and placed a large linen handkerchief in Octavia's lap.

"Now then, dear, don't you think I'm being extraordinarily useful?" she asked, smiling.

Octavia had taken Hetty's proffered handkerchief. "Yes, yes indeed you are. Thank you, Hetty."

"I'm sure William will like to go and see Herbert, won't you, William?" Hetty asked. "He's expecting you first thing in the morning. He has all the details."

Octavia was gripping Hetty's hand. "But you're quite sure?" she asked. "This chaplain . . ."

"It's quite amazing how the letters get through in such double-quick time," Hetty observed. "That's the transport division for you. They have motorcycle couriers, I'm told. Cameron is with them, did you know?"

Cameron was the de Rays' eldest son. They had three boys; and the last that William had heard was that all were in the diplomatic corps, following in their father's footsteps. He recalled Cameron as a good, dull boy, very tall and rather gaunt, who possessed poor intelligence and not an ounce of humor. "But surely he was in South Africa?" he asked.

"He was," Hetty said. She had settled herself back in the sofa. Her voice was absolutely calm. "And he enlisted and came home, and he is attached to, of all things, the veterinary corps." She gave a small smile. "Anyone less able to empathize with a horse one would be hard pressed to find. He loathes most animals. He was thrown, you remember, by a camel when we were in Kathmandu." She delivered this gem as if it were the most natural event in the world. "He would *not* get back on again. Ridiculous. As a result, I fear he wouldn't know the right way to sit in a saddle. But there. Can't be helped. And it's not all horses, he tells me. They requisition, and they oversee the unloading in the ports and that sort of thing."

"So he's not at the front?"

"Rarely."

"And Gordon, and James?" These were the other sons. "Are they still here in London?"

"Yes, in the Foreign Office. Gordon shan't go. His eyesight is too poor. James is terribly ambitious to be in the War Office. So . . ."

"You've heard of Rupert Kent?" Octavia asked. She was now much more composed.

"I read of it in the *Times*," Hetty answered quietly. "Really awful, darling. Awful."

The three of them remained quite still. William gazed out into the street. He was glad to have to go and see Herbert de Ray. It would give him something definite to do. He would arrange, if he could, to go to Boulogne, if that were possible.

Failing that, he would go to Folkestone and meet the hospital ship.

*I*t was deepest night in Flanders.

Harry was thinking of the Wastleet running in its great curve around Rutherford, soft and low in the summer and brilliantly clear.

It made him think of the place where he had swum as a boy, lying on his back and drifting despite Jack Armitage's warnings about the current. Trees rose above the water there, and he would look up into them and see the sky in a blue fretwork beyond the branches, and he would feel the water turning him round and round.

Blissful times. Summers that had no end. But all that was gone now; it was no more than a fragment of memory. Water . . . irrigation. But the irrigation that he was enduring now was nothing like the river at Rutherford lost in a summer haze.

This particular new irrigation consisted in a nursing Sister pouring saline and iodine into one of his wounds. When he had been carried onto the hospital train that morning, they had made a tremendous fuss about the filth he lay in. He had been stuck to the stretcher with his own blood.

"What time is it?" he asked now. The flushing and the pain continued. No one answered him.

He looked past the Sister to the face of the nurse who was studiously watching the process. "Please—what day is it?"

No reply. He closed his eyes. He had lost the pattern of time; he couldn't think now how days were held together. *My God, that was painful. Why didn't they stop? Wasn't that enough?* He tried to distract himself. Was it Tuesday? Wednesday? He told himself to think back. On Sunday he had flown on reconnaissance again. Sunday, or Monday? And what was the month? Was it May still, or June?

"Please stop," he heard himself whimper.

"We can't stop," the Sister said, "Until it is very much cleaner."

The train was moving now; grinding its way. The man on the bunk above him started to groan hideously.

Could it be that he was still alive? He felt the pain of his legs: he saw and heard the other people. But it was somehow all so surreal. He had been above this world; he had been flying his favorite, the Sopwith Tabloid, the single-seater. Perhaps he was there still, and this was a dream? There was a screech of liquid agony from somewhere else close by. Had that been his voice? He could not tell.

There had been, days ago, whatever it was—weeks, perhaps years, who knew?—a whining and rushing sound. He recalled the piercing volume of it, and the shock with which he had felt the plane tip over. The Sopwith had been descending to earth and the rushing noise was the wind tearing at the Sopwith's superstructure. He must have been hit; he tried to remember.

He had pawed at the controls like a madman; there was a coughing sound from the propellers. "Christ damn you!" he had screamed. The plane had rocked and bumped; some charmless bastard had been firing on him from below.

And then the engine had caught. Was that right? He wondered now. Had it fired again, and saved him? He frowned in desperate concentration. No . . . it had not been enough. He had brought the nose up, and the Sopwith had chattered and hopped in the air. And then, while he had still been wrestling with it, it had plowed into the ground at an oblique angle, skittering along the surface. He had hit something: a mound, a slough of water. A thread of track way had gone past, and with a loud and high-pitched jagged squeal, the left-hand wing tore away in pieces. He glimpsed the large rubbed-edged wheel from the left-hand side go bouncing around in the debris.

And suddenly, all had been still.

He had sat for a second. The force of the impact made him feel as if every tooth in his head was loose. He began frantically trying to extricate himself from the shattered Sopwith.

Then he heard shouts. He looked up to see men running towards him. He swayed uncertainly in the cockpit with what felt like scald-ing fire running through his thighs and knees, and he shouted, "Shoot me then, you bastards, if that's all you can do!"

They kept on running.

He thought that he had perhaps started to laugh when he had realized that they were British.

*I*t was later—perhaps it was hours, perhaps only minutes—that they came to clean the wounds again. It must have been the early hours of the morning—perhaps near dawn. The train was still bumping slowly along.

He tried to be jovial this time. His head felt a little clearer. "I'm sorry for being a bally nuisance," he said.

This time, it was the nurse on her own.

"What do they call you?" he asked.

"Be still," she told him. "Be quiet while I do this, and I shall tell you something strange."

"Will you?" he remarked, trying to smile. "I doubt that you could tell me anything stranger than the things I've known recently."

"We had a very nice billet neat Béthune," she said, ignoring him. Her hands worked deftly in the lantern light of the train. "I had a proper room, up in the roof. You could hear nightingales."

He thought he had misheard her. "Nightingales?"

"Isn't it perverse?" She had given him a bright smile. "We were only a half mile from the line. On our last day there, the garden was shelled. But the nightingales still sang."

"The men told me that you could hear larks," he agreed, almost dreamily. He concentrated on the thought of nightingales and not what was being done to his legs. "They said that the artillery would stop, and the larks would sing."

"It's as if they must," she murmured. "They absolutely must, or die." She glanced at the note pinned to his jacket. "You're an airman, aren't you?"

"Yes."

She leaned a little closer to him. He could feel her breath caress his face. "Do they sing up there?" she asked innocently. "Can you hear the larks up there?"

My God, he thought. *Such a bizarre conversation. But humor her.* "Not with all the *minenwerfers* and what have you."

"Are they the big ones?" she asked. And then, with a harder glint in her eye, "We've seen what they can do."

"Yes," he said. His eyes were pouring water. Jesus Christ, it was awful. "They make a wuffing noise," he said, with effort. "Rather like a very large friendly dog. *Wuff wuff wuff.* And then it stops and goes straight down. Shifts rather a lot of earth. Turns out not to be such a friendly dog after all. We feel the bump up there—the ripples come up to us."

"I imagine it's like being on a fairground ride, of sorts. The kind that bumps up and down."

"Yes, a kind of ride. A strange sensation. But one is used to it."

Now, the nurse was frowning, silent.

He knew that some people disliked the aircrews, thinking that they were glamour boys, and thought highly of themselves. It wasn't true, of course—not that he knew of—but newspapers did talk such unbelievable rot about how marvelous it all was to be in the air. He hated it, personally: hated being thought of as wonderful—more wonderful, the implication was, than the poor bloody infantrymen. "Gladiators of the air," he had read in one such rag. He wished he could write to the journalists and get them to describe the fellows down in the trenches as "gladiators of the ground."

"Get on with it, and be quick," he muttered.

"I'm doing my best," she told him.

"I'm sorry," he replied. "Tell me something else. Anything else at all."

"We had an adjutant in here three days ago," she told him. "He had been buried. And while they were digging him out, another *minenwerfer*—if that's what it was, he said it was a vast beast, anyway—came over and buried the digging party with him."

"Did they get them out eventually?"

"Well, him," she replied.

"Just him?"

"He had lain with a dead man's hand pressing onto his face for hours," she said quietly. "His chest was crushed, his ribs broken. He had had an awful struggle to breathe." She finished the dressing and patted his arm. "Quite raving I'm afraid, poor man."

"Glad to hear an adjutant's had his portion," he observed.

"The Germans had hit our own bomb store," she replied. "He told me the sky was raining things. He kept saying it. All kinds of things . . ." she paused. "Still, I shan't go on." She looked cheerfully at her handiwork. "You'll do."

Her voice was soft, and he noticed now that her eyes were fantastic, an astonishing piercing green. The thread of hair that escaped the cap was red. "Are you Irish?" he asked.

"Yes," she said. "Once upon a time, long ago. In another world to this, in another life." She gave a little dismissive shrug.

"What's your name?"

She smiled. "You won't remember it."

"I'm Harry Cavendish."

"So I see on your label."

"And you are . . ."

"Get a little sleep now, if you can."

"What did you do," he asked her. "Before all this?"

"I lived in London."

"Doing what?"

She smiled. "Enough now." She was glancing up the train at the Sister's back. Then she whispered. "It's Caitlin."

"Caitlin," he repeated quietly. "That's pretty."

She pointed at his leg. "How does it feel now?"

"Oh, jolly good," he told her. Pain was a peculiar thing; it was almost visible in the train—a writhing spirit that pressed itself down on the bodies.

"It's nearly over," Caitlin told him. "It won't be long until we're at Boulogne. Then you'll be transferred to a proper hospital. The Casino, probably, on the seafront."

"Is that true?" he asked. "The distance bit. We're not far from Boulogne? We're nearly there?"

She rewarded him with a dazzling grin: impish, and entirely human. "Sorry," she admitted. "But I really have no idea at all where we are."

The train rocked and rolled. Caitlin got to her feet, still professionally regarding his two splinted legs. Every now and again, at immense cost, he wriggled his toes. Some of them.

All the while that they had been speaking, the man in the bunk above him had been singing a broken tune. Harry couldn't make it out. It was like no other song on earth, anyway: it was the song of a dying man. He didn't need to see the poor devil to know that. The dying had an aura all their own; a man could sense it. Sometimes a strange quiet came over where they were, or the sudden loss of sighing or crying or screaming left a void like no other.

He angled his head towards the upper bunk. Caitlin was adjusting the pillow for the man, and folding back the blanket with a small frown of concentration. He heard her give a short sigh as she did so. Under them, the rails clacked and whistled, and the trembling cadence of the man's song over his head kept a sort of accompanying rhythm.

She started to step away. "What injury has he got?" Harry whispered to her. "A bullet in the brain," she said, as quietly as some other girl, before this war, might have said, "It's raining," or "I shall go for a walk," or "The roses are so nice." She bit her lip before continuing. "I've heard repetitions," she said. "It's as if some parts of the brain hold memories. It's affected, and so . . ."

"They sing a song?"

"Or repeat a word." She gave a small, sad shrug. "Would you like a little cocoa if I can find some?" she asked. He gazed at her.

"How old are you?" he asked.

"Why? Does it matter?"

"Not really." He smiled. He guessed at twenty or twenty-one, and realized that she was his own age. It made him wonder if his twenty-first birthday had been and gone without him knowing. "Yes please," he said. "To the cocoa. If you have time. But only if you do." He reached out for her hand, but she was starting to move away. "What's the other name?" he asked. "Caitlin what? What's your surname?" But she had gone, turned her back to him.

When the train caught speed at last, it had grown dark outside. Mercifully, he had a small window next to him. Although the little glass pane was halfway down his body, he could still glimpse the shadows of the passing French countryside at an oblique angle. The cocoa never came—he forgave her of course, she would have been so devilishly busy—and while he looked out at the darkness, he gradually fell asleep.

Sometime later, the train came to a halt. The lack of movement woke him. The singing in the bunk above him had stopped.

Harry turned his head to the window. Dear God, it was an endless night. He wondered, rather academically, if he had better odds now of coming through it. He could hardly remember the names or faces of the men who had been in that Flying Corps mess with him. More familiar to him were the controls of his aircraft—he could feel his hands on them still, feel the air rushing past him. Feel the descent, the whirling corkscrew that he had somehow survived.

And then he noticed something miraculous.

His eyes had fixed on the little square window, and he suddenly realized that out there in the half darkness there was a field of cherry trees. He tried to raise himself on his elbow, smiling. The trees were half in blossom and half in leaf, and a slight wind was blowing, moving among the trees. There must have been a thousand trees out there in the breezy darkness. Was it a beautiful dream? he wondered vaguely. Did such things still really exist? Every branch lifted and swayed. It was like looking at a softly moving sea.

It was true that there was a world out there, and it was quiet.

He thanked heaven for it.

A quiet spring night in the fields of France.

The next morning in Rutherford, March was waiting with Josiah Armitage.

The yeomanry had not come the day before: Jack had taken it as a sign that they might not come at all. And then Bradfield had walked over last evening, and relayed a telephone message. They were coming the next morning. The horses were to be made ready.

The clock on the yard tower read almost eight when they heard the sound of a lorry coming up the lane that led to the "outsiders'" houses—they could hear the grinding of the gears on the slight hill that led under a lane of lime trees at the very rear of Rutherford, shielding the coming and going of tradesmen and laborers from the main house.

Josiah glanced at March. Both men were in their seventies, March by far the more grizzled and weather-beaten. They held each other's gaze in apprehension.

The lorry rounded the last corner and came in through the gates. Half a dozen men got out of the lorry—three from the cab in the front, three from the rear. They let down a ramp, and pushed straw out onto it with their feet, and then stood leaning on their rifles, looking back at the yard.

"No need for a bloody armory," March muttered.

An officer in the Yeomanry was walking towards them. He was a slight, bowed man in his fifties. He was not the Yorkshireman who had come two days before. Neither March nor Armitage recognized him, and when he opened his mouth, they knew why. He had a West Country accent.

"Good morning, gentlemen."

Armitage touched his cap.

"Well, we've come to do our job," the man said briskly. "Where's your stock?"

Josiah inclined his head. "We've four in the paddock. We mun keep two. Can't mow the fields and bring in t'harvest without."

"Your nearest tenant farmer has two."

"Right enough."

"Well, can't you use his here at the house?"

"'Tis seven miles to Bates's farm, nine to the other."

The man consulted his list. "His lordship declared twenty-two horses. Eleven went last year. We can leave one other. But we must take the Shire."

Neither man spoke. Josiah glanced around the yard. He knew that Wenceslas was not here. Jack had taken him that morning down to the lower meadows, by the river.

"The Shire's being worked," he said.

The man raised an eyebrow. "I sincerely hope there's to be no trouble."

"No trouble, sir."

"Then bring the Shire up, if you will."

"He's not a fast horse," Josiah prevaricated.

The man gave him a sardonic smile. "I've yet to see a Shire that was," he replied. "They're needed for strength, not speed."

Josiah looked at his feet. He was a patriotic man; he wanted to give what he could. And yet he felt that the horses were his, much more so than Lord Cavendish's. He had seen half of them born, nursed others through illness. Every time in the past forty years when a horse had to be sent to the butcher's yard he had been unable to sleep; sat in the stables keeping a vigil with those who had to go. And he had done the same last night with Wenceslas. Which was where his son Jack had found him at first light.

Neither man had spoken a word. They would have been ashamed if anyone else had known their feelings. Only a horse, others might say. Just a horse. But they were not horses to either father or son.

Josiah had eventually got up, laid a hand on his son's shoulder, and gone into the cottage to bring them both a mug of tea. When he had returned, carefully carrying the tray across the yard slippery with morning dew, he saw that the stable door was open, and both Jack and the Shire were gone. He had put down the tray and walked slowly to the far yard gate, and looked down the long slope to the river. He saw Jack leading Wenceslas through the spring meadow; both man and horse had their heads down as they walked, as if in private conversation.

Josiah had considered going after them, but thought better of it. Jack was not running away—there was nowhere to run to, after all, with a gentle giant like Wenceslas—but he needed this time, his father knew. Josiah had turned away, gone back to the stable, and sat down alone.

He looked up at the Yeomanry captain now. "I'll fetch them," he said.

Three floors above, out of the small nursery window, someone else was watching the scene unfold.

Louisa had got up and wandered to the nursery still in her nightclothes and dressing gown; as she had entered, the nursemaid was bathing Cecily.

"Oh, ma'am," she said. "The bairn's not ready." Yesterday evening Louisa had said that she would give Cecily a treat: she would come down and eat breakfast in Louisa's own room, and Louisa was to open her travel trunk—the fine one, from London, with its many compartments—and find some of her own childhood toys.

"It's all right," Louisa had said. "I shall just wait."

She smiled for a moment, seeing Sessy's pleasure in such random things as a trail of soap bubbles, or the edge of the enamel bath, or the ridges in the pink flannel with which she was soon routinely scrubbed; then Louisa walked to the window and looked out.

"There are people down there in the yards, I think," she murmured. There was a very narrow view of the kitchen gardens from here; she could just glimpse the roof of a vehicle.

The nursemaid did not look up: she had Sessy on her knee and was wrapping her in a towel. "They've come for the horses, ma'am. So they were saying last night belowstairs."

Louisa turned around. "Which horses?"

"They say all of them, bar two."

After a moment's consideration, Louisa gave Sessy a brief kiss on the top of the child's head. She left the room, walked down the flight of stairs, and went to her own bedroom. The housemaid who was tending to her in Amelie's absence had laid out a set of clothes— rather beautiful ones today. A lawn dress and very pretty matching shoes, and a linen jacket.

Louisa stared at them, then ran to the French armoire and dug in the bottom drawer. She pulled out riding clothes—much faded. She had not worn them for years, but she was as slim—if not slimmer, since last year—than she had been at sixteen. In a minute or so she was dressed and running down the vast curving stair. She went out through her father's library into the gardens, and through those to the kitchen plot, and through that past the greenhouses to the large wooden door in the wall that led out into the stable yard.

A group of men, some in uniform, turned to look at her. She strode over to March. "What is happening?" she asked.

He touched the brim of his hat. "'Tis the requisition for the horses," he said.

"Where is Jack?" she asked. "Where is Josiah?"

March hooked a thumb over his shoulder. "Bottom meadow."

She knew exactly what Jack thought of his horses. Growing up, he had told her stories about each one. Such silly stories about how they fitted into fairy tales. This chestnut was the prince's horse from Cinderella, and so on. He had been ten years older than she and she had hung on every word with her usual naïve trust. She had sat with him once while Grey Ghost was shoed, and he had reassured her that the horse felt no pain.

But her mother had gently told her, when she was older, that it was not appropriate for her to sit with the staff and chatter. "But Harry sits with Jack all the time!" she had protested. "Harry is a boy," her mother had replied. The frustration and injustice of it had rankled with Louisa for days.

She looked from one face to another. The captain had saluted her, but she had not acknowledged it with any grace. He seemed to her rather pompous, standing there in his ill-fitting uniform with his thin fringe of a moustache and his dry, obsequious manner. He was puffed up with his own importance. *Perhaps you enjoy your moment of power*, she thought sourly. She glanced at the lorry. "You'll take them in that?"

"Yes, madam."

"How far?"

"We'll go to Crewe today."

"Crewe!" Louisa exclaimed. "But that must be over a hundred miles."

"A hundred and fifty," March muttered.

"But why Crewe?"

"For the train," the captain explained. "And then on to the south coast."

She stared at the lorry. "But these horses have never traveled so far," she said. "Some of them were born here on the farms."

No one said anything. A cold sensation of horror began to crawl over Louisa: she felt the hairs rise on her arms. "And then on to France, I suppose," she said. She stepped towards the captain. "What happens to them, out there?" she asked quietly.

"There are more than a million," the captain said. "These chaps here are lucky, you know. Over a hundred and fifty thousand went to France in the first few weeks of the war."

She held his gaze. "And how many have come back?" she asked.

There was no reply. She turned on her heel and walked across the yard. Four ponies that she knew by sight were being led out of the field as she drew level; she stopped to let them by, unable to look at their docile, obedient expressions. They were just sleepy farm ponies, she thought. There was no verve, no spirit in them such as one saw on paintings of army horses. Ponies like these didn't charge, or paw the ground, or have the least capacity to look glamorous. They had never been trained to anything but a plow or a wagon; half of them shied away at the sound of cars.

When the last was through, she started to run. "Ma'am!" March called out. She ignored him. She ran down through the grass. It was just getting to knee height; in a few weeks' time it would soon have its first cut for hay. All kinds of flowers grew in it; the jodhpurs she had dragged on in such haste became covered with the yellow pollen of buttercups. She saw Josiah coming her way; he held up his hand. She stopped next to him, out of breath, trying to see over his shoulder to where the river was fringed with trees.

"Is Jack down there?"

"Aye, miss." Josiah was pulling at the collar of his jacket in an uncharacteristic gesture of unease. "He won't bring the Shire up."

"Oh," she murmured. But it was no surprise to her. "They'll come down and get it if he won't bring it, you know."

"I know," Josiah agreed.

The two looked at each other. "I'll speak to him," she said. "Go up and tell them to wait a little."

Josiah opened his mouth as if to object; then he clamped it shut and walked away. She watched him go: an old man trudging as if he had the weight of the world on his shoulders.

She went on down to the river.

She soon saw Jack there in the shallows, holding Wenceslas on a loose rein while the great Shire drank the cool water of the river. The idyll of it stopped her in her tracks for a moment: it was like something out of a Constable picture, so quiet, and dappled with a slanting light.

Jack glanced at her as she approached them. She stood on the bank and looked down at him.

"It's time, Jack," she said softly. "Will you walk back up with me?"

He said nothing for some moments; then, "He don't like noise."

"Yes," she said. "I know. He hates Harry's sports car, doesn't he? But then, there'll be no sports cars in France, and no idiots like Harry driving them at breakneck speed."

Jack still said nothing.

"They'll treat him awfully well," she told him. "There is a special veterinary corps out there, you know. And they're needed, Jack. Lorries and cars and things can't cope with cratered roads. Horses and mules are the only things that can get to the front. I read that in the newspaper."

Wenceslas shifted his feet, causing spirals of sand to swirl in the water. Both of them watched the patterns unfolding and then disintegrating, and drifting away.

"It's not that I don't want to do our best," Jack said, finally. "To make sacrifices, and so on. I know it's our duty." And he looked up at Louisa with such a complicated expression on his face. "But they never asked for it, the animals. They didn't have anything to do with it. But we bring them in, and we use them and make them do our dirty work. And they obey us, but they don't know what it's for. They go on—they go on into guns and mud and shells and murder, but they don't know why. That's the pity of it." Louisa's heart turned over.

She stepped down the bank and across the gravelly border to the river, and, looking at the man and his helpless grip on the reins—his hand first pulling and then releasing the tension, a perfect picture of agonized indecision—she walked into the water.

The horse turned its head to stare at her, and she could hardly bear to touch the warm flank. She watched a flicker run along under its skin, a momentary trembling in the muscle. "Dear boy," she murmured. "Good boy." She put her hand under Wenceslas's soft mouth. The horse's lips searched in vain for the sugar lump or piece of apple that she would normally have given him. "I've nothing for you at all," she told him. "I'm so sorry."

Jack was staring down still at the water: with his free hand he rubbed his eyes and looked away, then, up the length of the river to the bridge. She put her hand gently on Jack's shoulder and leaned against him. Such a kind heart this man had. Such kindness. She rested her forehead for a moment on Jack's shoulder, then turned up her face and kissed him.

The water rippled, the sun danced, the world passed away. She felt him shaking in her arms. "Ah, but no," he murmured. When they parted, he was looking at her with astonishment.

Then, she put her hand over his on the reins. "Come," she said gently. "It really is time, Jack. We'll take him up there together."

Chapter 5

*H*arrison, in the farthest corner of the barn, was thinking of harvests. It was pitch black in the hour before dawn. He had no real idea where they were, except that it was near the front: they were going up into reserve, they had been told. They had got here close to midnight, and it seemed to him that he had dreamed almost at once, dropping off halfway through eating, with the hard tack biscuit still in his hand. Dreamed of sun, and not the strong wind and rain that they had marched through that day. Dreamed of the Yorkshire lanes in May: sweet smelling, scattered with flowers.

He woke in the death's hour just before dawn. An eerie claustrophobic silence seemed to have its own vibrating echo as he strained for the sound of shelling. They had heard it yesterday. Now there was nothing.

Next to him, Nat was awake.

"Here comes another one," he whispered.

They waited for the noise of the rat snuffling along over the prone bodies of their sleeping mates. It was unaccountable that they couldn't sleep now. Only a few hours' oblivion, and then this damned wakefulness. They'd marched up through Givenchy the day before, and something about the pitiful place had stuck in his throat at the time.

They said that there used to be six thousand people there, but now all that could be seen were shattered ruins and the contents of the houses spilled anywhere, soaked, broken beds and cupboards scattered between tremendous holes in the road. He'd seen a photograph of a family, the glass shattered, and the children's faces peering from the frame spattered with mud. Farther along others like these were churned into a lathered mess of splinters and tattered cloth.

It got worse as they went on, however. They came to the La Bassée canal, bright yellow in color, poisoned by the Hun so that it was unfit for horses to drink, and full of wreckage floating at a snail's pace. They had walked along the old towpath and seen doors and shattered tree branches and bodies in the water. Harrison had looked at it all and felt nothing but mild curiosity and sadness. War was a sodden, strewn, shapeless affair.

He nudged Nat now. "Ever seen a harvest?"

"In Mile End? Naw. Why, have you?"

"Have you never got out to the country?"

"There's no country in London."

"There's squares and parks."

Nat laughed to himself. "Up west maybe." He let out a sigh. "That where you worked, up west, in the city?"

Harrison didn't reply. He was touched, almost in a ghostlike tremor, by the memory of Rutherford on a summer's day, and was surprised at his own sentimentality for it. If only, he thought, he could see Jenny again before he had to go up to the front this morning. Just a moment or two; he would trade his next month's pay to lean back on the kitchen wall and close his eyes against the sunshine and hear the voices of the maids in the kitchen behind him. Instead of which . . . well, there was nothing for it. He was here, and he would face the horror out, if horror was what was in store for him.

But even while thinking this, there was no panic or fear in him. He wondered if he were strange in some way; unable to be moved very deeply. Unable to draw close to anyone. After a moment or two, his line of thought was broken as Nat whistled a few lines of "Daisy" through his teeth. Then the Londoner began to sing in a surprisingly melodious tenor: soft and soulful. "Daisy, Daisy, give me your answer do. I'm half crazy, all for the love of you. . . ."

"Give it a rest," someone said nearby, and he shut up at once, grinning.

After a moment, he commented in a whisper, "You wouldn't ask about bleedin' harvest if you saw where we was," he said. "Me and the wife. Two kids, we got. Babies, like. But I suppose we got a nice view of the river past the railings—on the roof, if you go up there. Over the roofs to the river." He seemed to think about this for a while, his eyes growing vague recalling it. "But these buggers—" he listened again for the skittering of the rats, "—all over. In the beds, even."

Harrison was still lingeringly thinking of Rutherford. "Harvest used to be done by horse and wagon and teams of men," he said. "Teams of scythes. Then the threshing machines came. The mowers would go round a field and leave a patch of grass in the middle, and then the dogs would go in and fetch out the rabbits and the rats. Seen a terrier with a rat?"

"Naw, mate."

"Sight to see. One, two seconds. It's dead. Then the next and the next. Proper-quick dispatch."

Nat snorted. "Quick as us?"

"Naw," Harrison replied, mimicking the man alongside him. They laughed. And then they felt him—scratchy little claws on their sleeves, quick as lightning, trying to get up to their necks, following the scent of warm breath. They had tied wire around their wrists and collars, and bunched their greatcoats around their knees so that it couldn't run up their legs, but it was still going for their faces.

Harrison snapped out his hand and found its tail. The rat bundled itself into a ball, writhing, trying to bite. He threw it into the air, and it landed somewhere out in the rows of recumbent bodies. "Bloody hell!" someone yelled. Harrison and Nat sat with their backs against the barn wall, pleased.

There was a silence of two or three minutes. In that time, the light subtly altered. It was almost four o'clock.

"Coming up dawn," Nat observed quietly. Harrison felt him turn; Nat's breath was suddenly on him, fetid from cigarettes. "You saw that church?" he said. "You saw that crucifix?"

He had. It was just outside Givenchy, in the ruins of a graveyard where memorials were knocked flat and coffins uprooted from their resting places. Someone had tried to cover them again with earth in haphazard mounds. The walls of the cemetery were merely rubble. But, in among them, was a crucifix—ten feet high and carved and colored. In the growing darkness of the march, Christ had looked down at them from His own agony. The cross was unmarked.

"They say it happens a lot," Nat murmured.

"What does?"

"Statues of saints and Mary and all that, staying put, never a mark on them."

"Well, so what?"

Nat shuffled, drawing up his legs and holding his knees. "Seems peculiar. Protected, like."

"They're not protected," Harrison replied. "Nobody is. It's just luck."

"What, God ain't looking down on some? Those that get away with it?"

"No," Harrison said. "God is looking somewhere else, if He's anywhere. Personally, I don't believe it."

"What, not believe in God?"

"No. There's no God."

Nat said nothing for a while. "Bad luck talking like that," he said at last.

Harrison sighed. "It's not luck, and not God. There's no God here, or anywhere. Just what happens, happens. Got to look out for yourself. That's all there is."

He could see a little more of Nat's face now. He was so spare, so thin, and he looked thinner now that he had been shorn of his hair and his weedy, pencil-line moustache. But he was grinning there in the shadows, showing uneven and discolored teeth. "I believe," he whispered. "Yes, I do. In Jesus, in God."

"Good for you," Harrison murmured.

The sergeant came round as soon as dawn broke. When they lined up, he stood there yelling at them, reserving his loudest shouts for the Kitchener volunteers that had been drafted into the regulars. "Pathetic bleeding sight," he'd told them. "Square up, because soon enough you'll be staring at some six-foot Prussian guard. They're facing right at you where you're going." A trembling hiss had gone through some of the men. "That's right, fucking Prussians. Two words of advice. If you stop a bullet, if you get pipped, then stay still. Got it? Wait where you fall, don't make a run for it. Second, do what you're fucking told. No more, no less. All right?" He gazed at them all with distaste. "Get into squads of sixteen. Leave a good space between each squad. Listen to what the lieutenant says; you're going to Aubers Ridge."

They obeyed. Outside, the rain of yesterday was over: it was a bright morning. "Nice day," the lieutenant said, and gave them a sardonic smile.

Each man was loaded with ammunition—two full bandoliers across their bodies; field dressings were stitched into their tunics. Nat fingered the identity disc around his neck. "Let's get at 'em," he muttered. "Going ter bag me one. Going ter run him through."

Harrison looked at him. "Keep it in check," he said. "We're not there yet."

Nat was smiling nonetheless. Harrison wondered if that smile ever really left his wizened little face.

They set off, walking two miles until the swing bridge at Gore. Another two hours, and the firing was much closer. Instead of the distant woolly rumbles they had heard until now, the sounds became distinct punctuations in the brilliantly shining day. Now and again they came upon a group of stones that had once been houses, and negotiated deep shell holes in the road filled with water. Then, barbed wire was alongside the road and, turning a bend, they came upon a wagon. It had been carrying food—it was anyone's guess what the men were eating who had been waiting for it; they were starving today, Harrison supposed, going without—for the peeled-back tins had been shoved into a heap at the side. Some of the tins looked like flowers with open petals, disgorging a kind of fluid waste tinged with phosphorus. The wagon was on its side, and, as they walked forward past it, they saw the bodies of two horses.

"That's put me right off me dinner," Nat observed dryly. Harrison turned around to look at him. The smile was stretched and wavering.

Another mile, and something damned awful wailed to their

right-hand side, a high-pitched ear-shattering whine followed by a thump that they felt in the soles of their boots. A spray of earth went up like a fountain five hundred yards away. Nobody said anything; they averted their eyes.

Five minutes later, the lieutenant caught up with their squad. He seemed deep in thought, frowning; he walked forward to the sergeant and there came orders for them all to halt and take cover. They got down at the side of the road in the verge, or where a verge would have once been. "We're too exposed," Harrison muttered. "The Hun have got our distance."

"It was only one shell," Nat said.

It was not yet seven in the morning, but it was getting warmer. There was another crump. They saw the road ahead explode in a shower of earth. Harrison regarded the way ahead dispassionately. They had been told how random shells sometimes scattered along the lines that the enemy had already measured; the dead horses were proof that they may have done the same earlier that morning, or during the night. Nat shuffled at his side. "You'd think they'd get tired of it," he muttered. "Why don't they go 'ome."

With a blur of black smoke a motorcycle sped up the road and spun to a halt alongside the officer. Nat sighed. "We could brew tea, if they'd let us."

The warmth in the morning air was wafting a strange mix of smells over them: cordite, dust, and something like nasturtium or lilac.

"That's gas," Nat whispered. "Gas shells."

"You don't know that."

"Bloke told me at Boulogne. Oranges, too."

"It can't smell of all of them, can it?"

Nat shrugged. "It's what it is, though. Out there somewhere."

They watched the courier go, hearing the machine whining

through the rutted track long after they lost sight of him. But still there was no movement, no order.

"Where was you working, then, to see harvests?" Nat asked.

"Country house."

"What, a big 'un?"

"Big enough."

"What doing?"

"Fetching and carrying."

Nat was smiling again. "Cushy number."

Harrison thought about it. "Yes, probably."

The conversation was interrupted by the lieutenant walking briskly back to them. They were the last two men in the squad. The lieutenant hooked his thumb over his shoulder, back the way they had come. "Harrison," he said. "Go back and make sure the water cart's with us."

Harrison did as he was told, running back around the bend. Just beyond the line of trees—which were cut off around waist height, split to the ground—the water cart was coming, pulled by a pair of mules. He could see two men on the cart talking to each other, laughing about something. He waved his arm at them as if to say, *come on*. They did not wave back, but kept coming at the same seemingly meandering pace.

"Idiots," he muttered.

He turned back and ran the way he had come, and at that moment he heard another whine—it was so short and seemed high up, the nagging whine of a mosquito—but in the next second there were several deafening crashes. First behind him, and then in front. He stood stock-still in the road.

Then, turning round, he looked at the water cart. No water, no mule—unless that was a mule, thrown over the wire. And no men. He heard his own breath hitching and snagging; knew that he had to go back to the lieutenant. That was his job. That was what he ought to do. Go back and report on the water cart. He felt himself shaking uncontrollably, and cursed himself. *Stop the fuck shaking*, he thought. *Stop the fuck. Stop.* He wondered where the other mule and the other man had gone, then ran towards the bend, heading for his squad.

It was a clay road: that was all he could think for what seemed like hours on end. It was only a few minutes, probably only a few seconds. But it seemed so much longer. He hadn't realized that the battered surface of the road wasn't stone but slicked clay, and now it lay in ridges and clumps. While his back had been turned, some almighty hand had rippled the road and thrown parts of it in every direction. And there was a crater exactly where his squad had been waiting.

Men were running around pulling at other men lying on the ground. He heard the sergeant shouting orders. Harrison's legs carried him forward, but some disassociated part of his brain was running backwards, back the way he had come, back past Gore and Givenchy, back all the way to Boulogne.

He got to the shell crater. The lieutenant was dead, that was obvious: he stared down at a crumpled body, the face turned to the ground. Harrison looked down objectively; his heart had slowed from its first initial shock and was now sluggishly thudding. The noises around him were unnaturally clear: crystal clear in the morning air after the dazzling crash of the shells. He could swear that he could hear blackbirds singing somewhere close, and he started to laugh at the absurdity of it.

He felt a slamming blow on his arm, and turned his head and saw the sergeant, spattered with blood but apparently unhurt, glaring at him. "What you laughing at?" he demanded. "Get these men off the road and move on. Form up with the other squad."

Harrison looked left and right. There seemed to be half a dozen injured: and there on the grassy verge was Nat—sitting propped up, huffing and puffing, his eyes widened, one hand to his chest.

"Nat," he said. "You all right?"

Nat was trying to say something; then he stopped, and infinitesimally shook his head as if the effort were too much.

"We'd best be going," Harrison told him.

The sergeant was still yelling. Harrison looked away, up the road at the milling panic, and at one or two of the men who were being pushed ahead. Half turning back, Harrison held out his hand. "Grab a hold," he told Nat. "On your feet."

There was no reply, and he turned full face to his friend. Nat was absolutely still. His gasping for air had stopped. In fact, for Nat, everything on earth had stopped. Harrison leaned down until he was level with Nat's face. The man's eyes were open, and there was a faint remnant of Nat's perpetual smile. "Nat," he murmured. "Nat, mate . . ."

"Get moving!" the sergeant roared suddenly at his side.

"He was . . ." Harrison began, and stopped. He was suddenly fearful that he would scream, or sob. Something dreadful, something horrible. Curse or cry, like a child.

The sergeant grabbed his arm and hauled him almost off his feet. "Move, now!"

Harrison dragged his gaze away from Nat and ran up to the next squad, and they started marching. He didn't look back.

One two, one two.

Someone shouted back for a cigarette.

"What was it?" he asked the man next to him.

"What're you talking about?"

"The bomb . . . the blast. . . ."

"Whizbang," the other replied. He looked like an old sweat, a regular. "Seventy-seven-millimeter. The crump's bigger. Five-point-nine inch. You wouldn't know about that one. None of us would."

"Seventy-seven-millimeter," Harrison repeated. "Shit."

"About right."

They walked solidly at a hard pace, their feet slipping from time to time on the clay.

As he walked, he thought of songs.

Just songs. Only songs.

He repeated the words to himself and they went around in his head, around and around and around while the sun got hotter and he waited for the next shell to come wailing out of the bright blue sky.

Daisy, Daisy, he thought.

Daisy, Daisy, give me your answer, do.

It would come now, or tomorrow, or sometime soon. Or it may not come at all. He might walk through it all singing songs in his head. He might be here in a week, or gone in an hour.

He set his face and trudged forward.

Give me your answer, do.

In the house in Grosvenor Square, Octavia was awake.

She felt very much at home here in London, far more so than she really felt in Rutherford. Soon after they had been married, William had taken full advantage of the fortune that Octavia brought with her, and rebuilt Rutherford Park. His design had been quite set in his own mind, and he had barely consulted her about the alterations to the fifteenth-century house—he seemed to think that, coming from trade, she would have no inkling what a grand home should look like—but, here in London, he had graciously allowed her a freer rein.

She sat in the deeply upholstered wing chair in her bedroom now, gazing out through the open curtains at the London square in the first light of dawn, and smiled wryly to herself. It had often crossed her mind what her father might have said to the spending of the inheritance on Rutherford; he had certainly been no shrinking violet, and she could easily imagine both William and her father coming to blows—beneath their dignity as it would have been, of course, but nevertheless—in the vast Tudor hall of Rutherford. Her father liked all things new, and abhorred what he called "the rotting mansions of the titled few."

It gave her a nice sense of satisfaction to know that her bullying father's money had been poured into such a rotting mansion as Rutherford was in 1892. He would have loved the intricacies of the new bathrooms and heating systems, of course, for he loved anything mechanical. But the glasshouses and the library. She shook her head now, her smile fading. What a waste of money he would have thought those to be. A place to grow pineapples, and a place to read. "Damn waste!" he would have blustered, his flabby face mottled with fury. God, she had endured so many of his rages after her mother had died. It was the utmost irony that a man like William—titled, calm, straight-backed, superior—had closed his fist on her father's millions. She liked that very much indeed.

Rutherford was entirely William's domain even now. Oh, she had furnished a little and he cared not a jot for the upper floors, where she had secretly given the nursemaid a good bed, and the children, when babies, lavish cots and carpets and playthings; but the public places—the halls, dining room, morning room, music room—all those kind of spaces were determined to William's taste.

But Grosvenor Square more accurately reflected her. She had made it more modern, refusing the heavy damasks and brocades of William's generation. She had employed artists to fashion the Art

Nouveau stairway and beautiful furniture of the black-and-white tiled hall; she had commissioned an Oriental room, superbly done with canary yellow silk wallpaper, and every chair upholstered with a peacock's tail flowing over the seats.

Her taste in art was everywhere; William had tolerated the two small Monets and a rather larger Renoir, but disapproved of the Cubist drawing by some dangerous Spanish upstart called Picasso, and he had finally drawn the line at her prospective purchase of a Gustav Klimt. "The man is a pornographer," he had opined when Octavia had mentioned how much she admired his paintings. "I think he's terribly fine," she had objected. "What about *The Kiss*, don't you like it? Everyone raves about it." William had shaken his head. "Too glittery by far, too fussy." But Octavia had also seen *Judith with the Head of Holofernes,* and it had stuck in her memory. She thought perhaps it was the expression of triumph on Judith's face that so stirred her, the luxuriant smile of power.

How often she herself has wished for a little power, how often in what seemed like a very long marriage. But at least here, in London, something of herself was reflected in the house. And she would see that the housing for the millworkers in Blessington was changed. That would happen. Whatever William said—and he had mentioned the word "socialism" rather darkly when the subject had last come up, hinting that this was a trend equivalent to some mudslide into the end of civilization—she would make it so. She would write a letter today in fact, asking what progress the manager had made since her last visit.

She sighed, and looked at her bedside clock. Five thirty.

Where was Harry now, she wondered? Surely in Boulogne, in the hospital. Perhaps today they would get him onto a ship and bring him home. Unconsciously, she wrung her hands in her lap. It was desperate to be so much in the dark. Every time that she thought of

Harry injured, she felt sick to her stomach. Even when he was a baby, the slightest fall or cut had the capacity to make her feel faint. He had once cut his lip while trying to climb a gate, and she had found—to her surprise, actually—that the world swam in front of her eyes.

How useless she would be in the heat of a true emergency! Perhaps it was easier faced with wounded men en masse, a group of strangers—perhaps one wouldn't feel one's heart turn over, one's pulse stagger. So many very well-brought-up girls were now becoming VADs, but Octavia felt that she would be unequal to the task. If she fainted at the sight of a cut lip, what earthly use would she be in a hospital ward? And yet she must, she absolutely must, brace herself for seeing Harry. For dressing his wounds, too. She was his mother, after all. It was her duty.

She wondered what else she could do. She had thought a lot about it since seeing the Kents on that dreadful day. Rupert was lost, but there were so many others coming back who would never again lead a normal life. For all she knew—and she put her hand to her throat at this choking thought—Harry might be one of them. What if Harry could never again manage to keep steady, let alone marry or keep Rutherford? What treatment could be given, what shelter offered? In addition to writing the letter, she decided, she would talk to Florence de Ray about this hospital in Regent's Park where the girl was working. She could offer money, perhaps, if it would be accepted.

The whole subject was so fraught, so confusing. France was only a few miles across the Channel, and yet it might as well be a whole world away. Despite William's visit to Herbert de Ray yesterday afternoon, there was very little information. It was "war-classified." How men loved to pretend to importance with such phrases, she thought. "War-classified" and "need-to-know basis" and all such other perfect rot. As if she would run into the street and proclaim any news to a random passerby! What arrant, strutting nonsense.

The world was at the mercy of men, and that was the entire problem. Although she had never said a word to William about it, Octavia agreed with the suffragette cause in that if nothing else. Men were far too fond of their little pieces of territory—their fences, their boundaries, their rules. One day, perhaps in the not-so-distant future, such boundaries might be washed away by the common man and woman. Wealth and power might pass to tradespeople completely. The titled classes might become mere footnotes in history. William, of course, would snort at the prospect. But she thought it entirely possible.

How she would have loved to march into Herbert de Ray's office in Whitehall and demand to know what was really happening in France. She had come, lately, not to believe what was being written in the newspapers. She had shown the *Times* to William last evening. "It says here that there was a jolly good showing at Aubers Ridge," she said, incredulous.

"If it says it, it must be so," William had replied.

She had frowned at him. "I cannot believe that you would be so gullible."

"I am not gullible," he replied calmly. "But there must be a picture of success projected."

"Even if it is a lie?"

"The *Times* would not perpetrate a lie," he said.

"But William, it is rumored that we have lost thousands and thousands of men so far, and the French far more. They say we are entrenched. I mean, literally. As in a stalemate." She pointed to the newspaper article. "This is mere drivel, isn't it? This jingoistic talk of bashing the Hun."

He had raised an eyebrow. *"Bashing?"* he repeated with pointed sarcasm. "Not a word I would use."

And that was the end of the subject. She had used an inappropriate phrase, a slang word, and her husband seemingly took this as evidence that a sane conversation could not be conducted with her. He got to his feet, smiled indulgently, and rang for his brandy and cigar.

She had looked at him and wondered if he really believed what he was saying, or if he felt an obligation to be blindly supportive of the French and English leadership in France. "They are old men!" she felt like screaming. But of course it could not be said, especially in front of the servants. Everything was marvelous, everything was a success. The Hun were being given a good hiding. She had screwed the newspaper into a ball with frustration and flung it aside, while William watched her with a deeply perplexed expression of dismay.

She shivered now, not from cold but from helplessness. She got to her feet. When she thought of her conversations with William, she felt increasingly as though she must break away. How she would love a little room of her own, an apartment somewhere, a place of refuge. She fantasized that it might be high up in some anonymous place, just a little room or two up a narrow stair, where she might be nobody, with no name, no position, and no responsibility.

And yet it was a selfish longing. That she was Lady Cavendish she could not avoid; she could not be nameless, nor alone. But God in heaven, how she wished for it: that same breaking free impulse she had felt last year with John, when the idea of fleeing to America had seemed, for a few brief shining days, entirely possible. *You can walk barefoot on the sand all you like,* he had promised her as he talked about the Cape Cod house he had planned. *You can walk all the way around the bay. Alone, if you like, or together. Whatever you want. . . .* John had understood. *You want your freedom, don't you?* he had asked her. *To find out who Octavia might be.* And she had answered, *yes.* But that was before Louisa, before Harry's injury, before the war. Before, before . . .

Across the room was her little bureau: her eyes lighted on it and she went over to it, turning the key on the lid and running her fingers along the drawers inside.

At the farthest end, on the right-hand side, was a tiny lever. She pressed it, and a secret drawer slid out. Inside were the letters of John Gould. She slowly reached out and took the first. She had put it here only yesterday, and the very act had flooded her with guilt. She drew the letter from the envelope, gazing at the postmark. New York City, and the letter was on marked stationery, the name of a shipping company.

All the way down in the train yesterday she had kept the letter in her handbag, and the handbag close to her side. It had arrived just as they were leaving, and Amelie, having intercepted the postman, had pressed it quickly into Octavia's hands once William's back was turned.

It was disgraceful, of course—disgraceful even to have involved a servant in such apparent intrigues. She was sure that Amelie thought that a grand passion was being conducted between herself and Gould across the Atlantic. Weeks ago, seeing the little smile on her maid's face, Octavia had softly reprimanded her. "Mr. Gould is receiving no replies from me," she had commented. Amelie had nodded. "Of course not, ma'am." But it was quite plain that Amelie did not believe a word of it, for the complicit smile was still there every time a letter from America found its way to Octavia's dressing table.

And this letter . . . *this* letter. *My God, my God.*

Her hands trembled as she unfolded it and read it for the twentieth time.

"*I can't stay here any longer,*" he had written two weeks ago. "*I am coming on the* Lusitania. *I hope that you will let me come to see you, darling. I arrive in Liverpool on May 8.*"

She bit her lip, full of anxiety.

John Gould would be here, in England, tomorrow.

*I*t was a dazzling vessel.

All the way across from New York, the weather had been beautifully calm. Every morning, John had taken a turn about the deck before breakfast, and the verandah deck was wide, gleamingly clean. The *Lusitania* was a "wet ship," because her delicately flared bows cut deep into the sea and sent up almost vertical walls of water that were flung onto the decks. And so, despite his determination to keep a straight line, John walked with an inadvertent slight roll: the decks had a distinct camber to let the spray roll off.

There were lifeboats all along the ship, and collapsibles. Standing now at the rail and looking back along the line of the ship, John decided that the *Titanic* had done that for every sea passenger—it was the only decent legacy of that tragedy—there were lifeboats aplenty. Collapsibles, too.

He wondered, without very much concern but rather out of idle curiosity, when the passenger lifeboat drill would be. The crew had come up here at five o'clock in the morning—it was what had woken him today. He had peered out of his door and seen them milling about, looking disorganized. Eventually, an officer had got some of the men into a boat and they sat there holding the oars for a while, and then simply got out and were sent on their way. They had been a motley collection of cooks and stewards and officers of various ranks, and among them a few coal-stained stokers, but nobody looked to have the slightest idea how to lower the boats. John had gone back to bed bemused.

The ship as a whole was much less busy than he expected. When he had asked the steward if there would not be more people seated at dinner on the first night, he was told that first class was only half full. Second class was oversubscribed because a discount had been offered on the tickets, and because the *Lusitania* second was generally thought to be just as good as any other ship's first; but, lower down in the ship, third class—so the steward insisted—was "nearly empty." Three hundred or so, anyways, when it could carry over a thousand down there.

There were a lot of children, however. He liked the little brats, but it wasn't the same for everyone. One of the ladies had asked for her stateroom to be changed because she couldn't stand the hollering of the six children next door, their fractious nursemaid, and the wearied parents.

The weather was fine, however, despite the spraying of the waves. John stood on the deck and felt a balmy, almost tropical breeze come rolling over the Atlantic. There were few whitecaps on the ocean; it was actually calmer than the Hudson on a summer afternoon. Enormous well-being flooded him. He could now count the hours until he was in England. He would go straight to Rutherford, William Cavendish be damned. He *would* see Octavia. Nothing and no one could stop him.

Not everyone seemed to be as happy as he on board, however. There was some spiritualist woman, the archaically named Theodate Pope, and, as he had sat in the Verandah Café after breakfast on the second morning, she had unceremoniously lumped down beside him in a wicker chair. "We're a quiet shipload of passengers," she remarked. "Don't you think so?"

He had agreed with her, but found her a strange sort of bird, walking arm-in-arm everywhere with a man she called Edwin. She was an architect, but she and Edwin were traveling to England to the Society for Psychical Research. "We are fortunate enough to be seeing Sir Oliver Lodge," Edwin had told John. "Have you met him?"

John had to admit that he had not.

"He wrote *Life and Matter*," the man persisted. "An expert in magnetism." Still, John had to admit ignorance. Edwin had given John a rather pitying glance. "A brilliant man, quite brilliant. An advocate for our everlasting souls."

John made sure not to sit next to the couple again. They made him feel odd. The afterlife was all the rage—had been for years now, fanned by the Victorian love of a good séance—but personally he preferred not to think of eternity. Life was what interested him. Ghost-botherers made him queasy.

He took to others more; particularly a man called Charles Lauriat, seated next to him in the dining room on the second evening. Lauriat was a handsome man from Boston. John had held out his, saying, "I hear you're in the book trade."

Lauriat had smiled. "Family business. And you?"

"Newspaper. Though that's *not* the family business."

"That so?" said Lauriat. "And what is?" John named his father's store. They spoke for some minutes about their respective trades, Lauriat pointing out others who were traveling on business. "Gauntlett there, and Knox. Shipbuilders. Armor plate."

"I guess the war draws us together, one way or the other."

"And . . . newspaper, you say. Writing for one?"

"Yes."

Lauriat looked about him. "There's another war correspondent on here," he said. "Did you meet him yet? Forman. Justus Forman."

"No. But then I'm no professional."

"Neither is he. He's a playwright. His last one flopped. Hence the journalism. He's with Frohman—that impresario theater fellow—up in the suites."

John shook his head to signify his ignorance of both man and stateroom.

"Not seen the suites?" Lauriat said. "All kinds of styles. The Regal, there's a piece of grandeur. Marble fireplace and fine curtains and a drawing room modeled on Fontainebleau. Standing in there, it's hard to believe you're afloat."

John laughed. "Too rich for my taste. You?"

"No, no. Plain old cabin. This is a regular trip for me. My twenty-third, in fact. But the first on a greyhound. I like to paddle across usually on a slower boat."

John was impressed. "You like sea travel?"

"Certainly I do. You don't?"

"I'm happier on dry land."

Lauriat smiled. "Ah, hence the *Lusitania*," he said. "To get there quickest."

John admitted it, but Lauriat put his hand on his arm, and dropped his voice. "You'll be disappointed then, this time."

"Why is that?"

"We're going slow. You hadn't noticed?"

"Seems we're going fast to me. Five hundred miles on the first day. That's a fine speed."

"It's slow for the *Lusitania*," Lauriat replied. "You know they have a pool every night, a game, to bet who can guess how many miles she'll cover the next day?"

"Yes, I've seen the tickets being bought."

"Well then, don't waste your money," Lauriat said. "This ship has got a boiler room closed. Number four. She's doing no more than eighteen knots."

John thought about this. "But they said we'd do full speed to outrun any submarines. They said that. I asked about it as we came on board."

"And so did I," Lauriat replied. "I asked in the Boston office when I bought my ticket if the ship would be convoyed and if she'd keep to the fastest speed. With all this talk . . ." He lowered his voice still further so as to not concern the ladies nearby. "All this talk of being a target. And I was told, 'every precaution will be taken.'" He sat back in his seat, regarding John levelly. "What do you make of that?"

"Then every boiler room should be working, shouldn't it?"

"Precisely old boy, precisely."

"Well, why isn't it?"

"Who knows? Saving money, maybe. Or they couldn't get the men, the stokers. Did you know that a hellishly fair number jumped ship in New York? Came over from England, and vamoosed? Not everyone wants to fight for king and country, it seems." *You won't read that in the newspapers*, John thought. *Especially not in England.*

"Then there's the Irish and Germans, stirring up bad feeling. The workers boycott British ships."

"But not in sufficient numbers to close down boilers for want of men, surely?"

Lauriat gave an eloquent tilt of his head. "Eighteen knots," he murmured, tapping his index finger on the tablecloth. "Speaks for itself."

They finished their meal. It was certainly worth their attention— oysters, followed by beef and roast gosling normande; though the steward told them, as he poured the champagne, that German lager and Austrian claret had been embargoed. "Ah well," a woman sighed opposite them. She raised her glass in a toast. "I prefer French any day." She smiled at them. "Here's to all the brave soldiers," she said. "And seamen and flyers." She drained her glass, looking a little tipsy.

John drank a sip, wondering if Harry had ever done as he had promised, and got his license. Had he gone to France, had he joined up? Was he flying there now, in those scratchy little machines? He'd seen the photographs and read the stories. If Harry really was in France, perhaps he would try to find him. Getting an airman's view of the war would be something different.

And then he thought of Octavia sitting in Rutherford, thinking of her son. He couldn't imagine what was worse—fighting out there, or staying at home wondering what the hell was going on. He hoped then, suddenly and fervently, that Harry hadn't got his wings at all, despite the boy's enthusiasm. He hoped he'd even taken some sort of knock, hurt himself training, or just grown disappointed with the experience, and was waiting at home to be called up. They'd make him an officer, train him. That would keep him away from the front for a while. *Don't do anything stupid, Harry*, he thought to himself. *Keep your head down, and don't be a hero, for your mother's sake.*

At John's other side was Lauriat's friend, Withington; an older man, a genealogist by profession, with a twinkling eye and a most manly and luxuriant moustache. They soon fell into conversation. "I've had an interest in English ancestry myself," John told him. They spoke of various families and bloodlines, and the makeup of the English aristocracy.

"I spent part of last year at Rutherford Park," John said. "That would interest you—the correspondence and the history."

"Perhaps I should go there myself. Where'd you say it was?"

"Yorkshire. But they're not always home."

Withington was looking at him intently with a worldly smile. "There is an interest for you there beyond history, if I'm not mistaken."

"What makes you say that?"

"I've rarely seen a grown man blush," Withington replied amicably.

As he went out of the door of the dining room at the end of the evening, Lauriat passed by him, smiling. "Don't take the eighteen knots to heart," he said. "I guess they'll be as good as their word. We'll pick up speed closer to Ireland, I'm sure."

John wondered if he looked terribly young to the older man, that he should try to reassure him. "I'm not worried," he replied.

"That's good," Lauriat said, and went on his way.

The voyage, it seemed to John, went quickly, despite all that Lauriat had told him about their speed. John took to walking for most of the day, pacing backwards and forwards, as if that could get him to Liverpool quicker. But everywhere he went, he heard conversations about submarines, and the preoccupation increased the closer they got to Ireland.

"When we see the Irish coast, we ought to have the Royal Navy alongside us," one elderly gentleman opined. "You'll see them coming. One destroyer, or two. They'll keep us company."

John wondered at it—surely the navy had better things to do than send two ships to a boat-load of civilians—but, on May 6 he did find himself looking ahead, and every now and again starting as he saw something in the water—vertical dark shapes that were soon revealed as pieces of wood, or simply the shape of waves. One of the men that Lauriat had identified as a shipbuilder caught him in this occupation, to his embarrassment.

"By the time you see a periscope, a torpedo would have hit us," he had said, smiling. The man stopped alongside him, and lit a cigarette.

John realized that he had caught the onboard infection: a kind of subdued hysteria, certainly a distinct nervousness. "I guess I'm impatient to be on land," he said.

"Impatient to see somebody?"

"I'd like to see someone before I go to France, yes."

"Pretty lady?"

"Naturally."

"Name of?"

"Ah, that I can't say."

"A pretty lady of some mystery," the man observed. "Quite the best kind."

John had turned to look at him seriously, leaning on the rail, squinting against the strong sunlight. "What are the odds?" he asked. "Frankly. Everyplace I go people talk of it. A submarine, I mean." He inclined his head the way they had come. "Back in New York, on the dockside, there was a couple. She had to be persuaded. We all joked of it. Were we right to joke? Were we right to persuade her?"

The man considered. "Do you know how many U-boats there are?"

"No. Does anyone?"

"No, I guess not. But there's more sinkings than reaches the public ear."

"That so?"

"Merchant vessels. All the time. Little steamers, most of them."

"But not ships like this."

"No," the man conceded. "Nothing like this. Except, I've been thinking of something. Something that's eased my mind. The *Wayfarer*..."

"Another merchant?"

"On war business. They hit it a month ago just off the Scillies. It was taking the Warwickshire Yeomanry to France. Two hundred soldiers and seven hundred horses."

"What happened to it?"

"A friend of mine down at Boston Harbor heard tell it got struck by a torpedo, but didn't sink. Forty-foot hole below water, but it didn't sink."

"Any killed?"

"Five men."

"And all those horses . . ."

"Not one lost."

John was amazed. It hadn't occurred to him that a ship could be hit and not sink.

"So you see, if a ship like the *Wayfarer* doesn't sink, even if struck . . ."

"Then nothing can hurt the *Lusitania*," John said.

"That's right," the man agreed. "Nothing. Nothing in this world."

*O*ctavia was dressing, with the help of Amelie, before breakfast, when Charlotte burst unceremoniously into her room. As the girl rushed across, Amelie made a slight sibilant noise under her breath; she abhorred a lack of decorum far more than her mistress. It made Octavia smile, although as Amelie was dressing her hair she was unable to move, and watched her daughter through the reflection in the looking glass.

Charlotte came close and rested her chin on her mother's shoulder. "Oh, you positively can't guess," she said, grinning.

"Then you had better tell me."

"They just delivered another telegram, addressed to Father. I took it up to him."

"I expect you have made the maid very cross, then. That is her work."

"She's not cross. I just danced in the hallway with her."

Amelie dropped her hands, and Octavia turned in her chair. "You did what?"

"Oh, Mother," Charlotte laughed, and dropped to her knees, and put her arms around Octavia's waist. "Harry's coming on a ship tomorrow. He's coming home."

The relief that poured through Octavia was a positive wave: it actually seemed to wash over her from head to foot. Charlotte was looking at her keenly. "Oh, don't cry," she exclaimed suddenly. "Amelie, give me Mother's handkerchief. . . ."

The two of them fussed around her. Charlotte pressed the still-warm teacup into Octavia's hands. "Drink a little, Mother. Amelie, ring for fresh."

"No, no," Octavia said. "It's quite all right. Just—well, such lovely news."

"Isn't it!" Charlotte said, and jumped to her feet. "I shall go with Father to Folkestone. May I go with him? Are you going? Shall we see him get off the ship? Wouldn't it be wonderful?"

Octavia waved her hand to stop Charlotte's dancing on the spot. "No. We would get in the way, darling."

Her daughter's face fell. "But Mother . . ."

"There will be hundreds of men being brought off the ship, and I expect a lot of ambulances waiting, and medical staff. No, no, dear. We must wait."

"But what was the point of coming down, if we don't go and meet him!"

"Your father will do that. We will get everything ready here." It was almost comical how quickly Charlotte sank to the recesses of the nearby chair. She slumped with disappointment. "He's going to be awfully tired," Octavia pointed out as gently as she could. "And not well. They may not even allow him to be nursed here. It will depend on his injuries."

She regarded her daughter. If it had been Louisa sitting in the same chair, there would now have been a sudden outburst of tears at the thought of Harry's wounds. But Charlotte sat clear-eyed. One could almost see the thought processes racing across her brain, and, sure enough, in the next moment she was sitting forward in the chair. "I can't just wait here all day," she said. "Can you?"

"Probably not."

"Then may we go with Florence to Regent's Park this morning?" Charlotte asked. "To the hospital? She's learning Braille, you know. It's so very clever. She's going to be a helper, to teach the men who've been blinded."

"Darling," Octavia said. "I don't think that's appropriate."

Charlotte reacted as though she'd been stung. "We can't talk of what's appropriate and what isn't now, Mother. People need help."

Octavia opened her mouth to object, but Charlotte was once again on her feet, and in a flash back again in the same position kneeling at Octavia's side. "Can't we go, you and I?" she begged. "They're organizing some sort of fete at the weekend with games and things, to raise money. We could help with the preparations for that, surely?"

Amelie finished Octavia's hair, and caught Octavia's eye in the looking glass. There was, just for a moment, the slightest frown of criticism. *Perhaps*, Octavia thought, *my own maid thinks that mother and daughter are capable of extraordinarily reckless behavior.* And she found herself thinking, quite involuntarily, *How very old-fashioned.*

She turned in her seat, brushed down her dress, and smiled. "I think that's a very productive way to spend our time," she said. "I shall speak to your father about making a contribution to the hospital."

"And go there? After breakfast?"

"If you would like to, yes."

"Be-yong!" Charlotte said, bounced to her feet and did a little twirl as she made for the door. She blew a kiss on the threshold, and disappeared.

Octavia glanced again at Amelie. "What on earth does she mean?"

Amelie's face became even more disapproving. "It is *bien*, ma'am."

"Then why doesn't she say so?"

"It is slang, ma'am. It is what is done to my language, by the soldiers who come back from France." She made a full-throated tut-tutting sound this time as she gathered up the hair things. "And I think . . . I *think* . . . it is said by thieves here, by bad persons."

Octavia stifled a smile as she got to her feet. "Yes," she murmured ironically. "Of all the things that happen in wars, mispronunciation of a native tongue must be quite the worst."

They were able, after some considerable wait, to get a taxicab from the house to Regent's Park.

It had always been a pleasant journey; Octavia had occasionally taken the children to the Zoological Gardens here when they were in London during the winter. She sat in the rattling cab now with

Charlotte at her side, and wondered if it was only fourteen months ago when they and Louisa had taken a horse-drawn hansom from the dressmaker's to Claridge's. Nowadays, one rarely saw the old hansoms. She pined for them a little; they had been more private than the motorized cabs.

Now, as they paused at intersections, those on the crowded pavements looked in on them, and, indeed, down on them from the teetering heights of the omnibuses. Octavia was awfully glad that there would never be a need for her to use an omnibus; they looked so flimsy. It was said that three hundred had gone over to France to transport troops, but she found that hard to believe, for there seemed to be just as many of them as always. Here and there, a woman conductor stood on the outside spiral staircases, balancing in the swinging motion of the vehicle, a ticket machine around her waist, holding back her long skirts with one hand as she stepped up or down. It looked so incongruous, though not nearly so strange as the women porters had been at the railway station, their hair stuffed under large cloth caps and with floor-length canvas aprons over their clothes, hoisting suitcases on their shoulders. Charlotte had thought it thrilling; Octavia rather less so. William, of course, had considered it not worthy of comment. He had looked away, with a small and disapproving shake of his head.

"Look," said Charlotte, tapping her mother's arm. Outside in the sunshine, standing in a group on a street corner, was a section of the Royal Field Artillery Horse; unsaddled, the horses were being led. "Florence says that another lady VAD at the hospital lives in Camberwell, and there's a huge number of horses just stabled in the street," Charlotte said. "I mean, outside ordinary houses. Just tethered in the road. Why do you suppose that is?"

Octavia frowned. "There must be tremendous numbers being

brought into the city for training," she ventured, "Perhaps there was nowhere else to put them." Although she really had no idea.

"Poor horses," Charlotte murmured. Octavia did not dare tell her that William had broken the news that the last horses from Rutherford had gone, including Wenceslas. They sat silently after that, not even remarking on a contingent of Australian troops marching along by the barracks. And, if it had not been for these two sightings—the horses and the troops—it might have been possible to believe that England was not at war at all, for London looked as it always did: busy, ordered, and, when the cab stopped at the park lodge gates, wonderfully green.

"It's up on the Outer Circle," Charlotte said, when they had got out. "Florence said that she would meet us."

And so she did. Unlike her mother, Florence was dressed very somberly in a dark skirt and jacket. "Hello, Lady Cavendish," she said, smiling. "Shall we walk in the grounds? They are putting up a marquee for the fete on Saturday. I think our director might be there. And, of course, you will see some of the men."

She led the way, out from the white portico into the park.

The grounds were very quiet—one could only just hear the hum of the London traffic beyond the gates. Stepping out onto the graveled paths, Octavia felt a moment of apprehension. This was a hospital, and the men were blinded; it was not merely a stroll in the sunshine, no matter how routine Florence seemed to be in her introductions to various helpers along the way. Just up ahead, Octavia could see a group of three or four men and two nurses sitting together on a wooden bench. As they drew level, she saw the familiar white stick of the nearest man, and a youthful hand gripping it. He was talking animatedly, his face averted, but, hearing their footsteps, he turned his head.

There was, she thought at first, nothing much to see. No terrible scar. No distorted face. It seemed that his eyes were half closed, though as small as a child's. It was only as he spoke, holding out his other hand to shake Charlotte's—Florence was introducing them—that Octavia saw the jagged blue line at his left temple. It was more like a pencil scribble than a wound, lines radiating into his hairline.

"Captain Preston," Florence was saying.

Octavia held out her hand. "How do you do."

He was smiling. "We are just discussing a game we might play on Saturday," he said. "Pushball. What do you think it might be?"

"I really can't say."

The other men were laughing. "A gigantic rubber ball," Preston replied. "Six feet high. A very good invention by our founder. Two teams of men try and wrestle it over a line. It's rather fun."

"There are rowing races on the lake on Saturday, too," Florence said. "Captain Preston and Corporal Turner here are in opposing teams."

Corporal Turner was quite another matter. Octavia looked quickly at her daughter, but Charlotte seemed not to be fazed by Turner's injury. The left-hand side of his skull, though perfectly smooth—too smooth, too pale and plastic in appearance—was depressed inwards. It was, to Octavia's dismay, most horribly fascinating. But Charlotte was speaking quite openly to him, while he tilted his gruesome face this way and that.

"Where were you injured?" she was asking.

"A place called Fosse, miss," the man replied, "Second week of October last year."

"And was it . . . was it a bomb?" Charlotte asked.

"Not a bomb," he said. "Rifle fire."

"Oh, in the second week. That would be around the time that the

Germans recaptured Lille?" Charlotte asked. Both Octavia and Florence looked at her in amazement.

"Yes," the man said. "Lot of cavalry round there. Death's Head Hussars. We caught some of them. It was about the last thing I saw—their fuzzy old busbies with the silver skull and crossbones on the front."

Octavia realized that he was turning his head because he had hearing only on the left side. It was so curious to watch him rolling his misshapen head to one side to speak, and back again to listen. "They wanted the five railway lines, and they got them. They've still got them."

"And you were marching along?"

"No. We was dug in, waiting. Stray bullet. I never knew I was properly hit. The others said, 'Take yourself back to the clearing station.' It felt like a punch, see? Never knew what it was. Knew I was bleeding but my cap was—well, it was like, welded in there." Octavia shuddered involuntarily, but Turner merely laughed. "I helped somebody else, and we walks back. I kept walking, like. On a bit and on a bit. And I kept thinking, 'I'll blink a few times, and it'll come back.' But it never did. Walking and walking, and carrying some other bloke's pack, too and with 'alf me head left behind." And he laughed again. Octavia realized immediately that the injury had taken away some faculty, some part of the brain that inhibits speech, or moderates actions.

Captain Preston shifted a little in his seat. "Don't encourage him," he said, in a smooth, well-educated voice. "The fellow can't stop once he starts. Bores us all half to death."

"Begging your pardon," Turner remarked, smiling.

Charlotte was absolutely calm. "Thank you so much for talking to me," she said. "I shall watch out for you in the boats on Saturday."

Florence ushered them onwards. They had only gone a few yards when Octavia stopped. "I must go and apologize to those men," she told the girls. "I didn't say a word to them. I've been very rude." She felt both anguished by their injuries, humbled by their optimism, and hopelessly embarrassed at her own inability to talk as her daughter as done—relaxed, and in a kind way. It was truly amazing, she thought, what one's own children could reveal to you. She began to turn, but Florence stopped her.

"It would be better not to," the girl said quietly. "It sort of emphasizes it, you see. Your hesitation in the first place. They don't mind your being shocked. But we are all absolutely lectured against apologies or sympathy, that sort of thing. It doesn't help."

They walked onwards; Charlotte hooked her mother's arm. Octavia glanced at her as if a stranger had materialized alongside her. They smiled at each other.

"And besides," Florence added after a moment or two, "He's a fine chap, but he really is awfully common."

Despite all Florence's good works, Octavia decided, there was a portion of Hetty de Ray's blithe insouciant snobbery here after all.

Chapter 6

The passengers on the *Lusitania* were not allowed to send messages, but they could receive them.

John knew Alfred Vanderbilt by sight—they had sailed together once or twice at the yacht club—and late in the afternoon he saw Vanderbilt coming towards him, smiling, and pocketing a wireless message. He held out his hand and Gould shook it; Vanderbilt smiled. "Someone is looking forward to seeing me soon. She wishes me a safe crossing."

John made small talk with him, all the while envying his message. He would have given anything to receive such a one from Octavia. It seemed to him that Vanderbilt had everything simply enclosed in those few words, everything a man could really wish for.

"You're going to England on business?" John asked.

"Going to buy hunting dogs," Vanderbilt replied. He was well-known for his driving jaunts across several states, all dressed up in full English hunting gear. As John looked at him, he thought that Vanderbilt gave off a wonderful air; smooth, exquisitely dressed,

handsome. He was resplendent in his riches and gave off the unmis-
takable aura of being in charge. A man's man, a woman's man. John
watched him go, thinking he had all the luck in the world.

Never mind, he told himself. A person's luck could change. His
own was changing now: finding a direction. He realized that he
never visualized himself going back across the Atlantic unless Octavia was with him. He had come to get her. It was as plain as that;
his determination was increasing with every mile. And his father
knew him better than he knew himself.

The night before he left, his father had called him into his study.
"Now then, John," he said, "Do what you have to do, and get out,
and come home."

"I shall be gone quite a few months," he had replied.

"You're thinking of staying until the war is over?"

"It could be over this year, who knows? But maybe not."

"And, if not, you'll stay out there?"

John had hesitated, and his father had come around his desk,
looked him straight in the face, and laid a hand on his shoulder.
"Don't break any hearts, John," he had said. "Your own, or your
mother's, or anyone else's."

The message had been quite clear. "I've never wanted to disgrace
you," he had said. "I hope I never will."

And they had stood in silence, neither speaking. Both knew that
John didn't see Octavia leaving William as a disgrace, but a deliver-
ance. He was driven by wanting her happiness. Nothing else mattered. Not what people might say. Not what William Cavendish
expected his wife to do. Not even—and he knew this himself, though
didn't like facing it—not even Octavia's love for her own children,
and her inability to leave them.

Whenever his thoughts butted up against this intractable problem, he simply rode over it with blinkered and dogged determination. The children could come with her. Or he would wait until they were a year or two older. Louisa might get married, and Harry, too. Charlotte was headstrong enough to leave home of her own accord. And what would Octavia do then, rattling around in Rutherford on her own, while William no doubt went off pursuing his own interests? No; sooner or later she would come with him. And she'd be able to come back to England at any time to see them, or they could come out to her.

Oh, but sometimes the pain of it. God, he had never known anything like it. This preoccupation with her that wrenched his soul; the need, the terrible awkward need that made him stagger. The strength of it was unnerving, and this fixation would have been incomprehensible—laughable even—before he had met her. He couldn't explain it to men like Withington or Lauriat, because he knew that it would make him sound a fool. Perhaps he was a fool, though. She'd never sent him a word; wasn't that evidence enough that she didn't want to see him?

And then he would reassure himself. She was holding back, afraid to contact him, afraid to put what she felt on paper, afraid to look back at the happiness they had known. Still the doubts nagged at him. He would never rest until he could look in her face and see the expression in her eyes. He would know straightaway what it was that she really felt, instead of his being placed in this terrible no-man's-land. "You think that I don't want to live as we lived this summer?" she had asked him last year, with anguish in her voice. "You think that I want to lose that, to never have it again?" He must remember that and not doubt her, he told himself. He must remember it. And he did. By God, he thought, it was *all* he did, the only real way he spent his time. Remembering.

He looked over the rail and he wished himself closer. She ought to have got his letter by now: *Please God, let her send a message*, he thought. Let him have a message folded in his pocket like lucky Alfred Gwynne Vanderbilt.

The water far below rippled in the evening light.

That night, there was a party in aid of Seamen's Charities in the first-class saloon. When John walked in, he thought that there seemed to be a dismal air, even though the Welsh choir was singing. And, after them, a pianist played "I Love a Piano." It was a new song, and John stopped to listen to it. He heard the soft eroticism in the words, about how the songwriter ran to the ivory keys to run his hands over them. "Who wrote this?" he asked Annie Matthews.

She was standing next to him with Robert, laughing, showing John the medal that Robert had won in the egg-and-spoon race on board. "Isn't it silly?" she said. But she kissed it, and held it against her chest as if it were the most precious thing in the world. "Who wrote this?" she asked Robert now, passing on John's question.

"Fellow called Berlin or Beilin. Irving Beilin, a Jew."

"Isn't it sweet?" she said.

"Rich Jew?" he asked Robert.

"Street boy," Robert replied. "Or was, once."

John had seen those boys. God alone knew how they survived. They were survivors of the Russian pogroms that Tsar Nicholas had encouraged; their families had swarmed across Europe to the haven of the good old US of A. The country with the open arms. And out of all that oppression came music like this. A dear little song about a piano.

"Lord," John said, "the human race is resilient."

Annie leaned on Robert's shoulder, misty-eyed. "You can survive anything," she said, and she exchanged a look with her husband. "All kinds of storms."

But just as she spoke, the piano went silent, and the crowd parted.

Captain Turner came into the room, glancing about him at the passengers with barely a trace of a smile. He wasn't known for his bonhomie, but John was glad of that; he'd rather that a captain concentrated on his responsibilities than whoop it up at dinner or on the dance floor. Turner stepped up onto the small podium now, and a hush fell.

"No doubt you have heard," he began, "of the warning of submarines in the area that we're approaching." No one said anything, no one even moved. Distantly, they could feel the thrum of the engines and hear the whispering rush of the waves. "We shall be entering the war zone tomorrow," he continued slowly. "But the Royal Navy will look after us, and there's no need for alarm."

John stole a look at Annie Matthews several times during this speech. She seemed all right until she was told that there was no need for alarm, and then she blanched a little. John stared down then at his shoes. Saying that there was no need for alarm was like telling someone in a doctor's surgery that there was no need for worry; they might not have been worried until that moment, but the very mention of the word put the thought in their heads. *Don't say alarm*, he thought wryly to himself. *And for God's sake don't mention the word "sinking."*

Thankfully, the captain did not. He continued in the same measured, somber tone. "We shall go ahead at full speed tomorrow," he said. "And arrive in Liverpool in good time." A murmur of positivity and a few smiles went through the crowd. But the good feeling was rapidly extinguished by the parting shot as the captain got down from the podium. "May I remind male passengers not to light their cigarettes on deck tonight," the captain said. "No need to advertise our position."

"Lord above," John heard Robert Matthews murmur.

Annie's grip on her husband's arm tightened.

As he turned to go, John heard another woman say, "I'm sleeping in my clothes on the boat deck. Tell the steward to bring me a blanket."

Her companion murmured by way of reply, "Sleeping? You'll manage to do that?"

When John got to his cabin, he looked about him at the seeming solidity of the room: the gilding on the mirror, the thick feather coverlet on the bed, the washbasin and mirror and the white paneled walls. The light holder with its two electric candles. The curtain on the door held back with a tasseled rope. It all looked so perfectly sound: untouchable, indestructible. But it was not solid and it was not sound and it was not indestructible. They were on water, and they were, as the captain had said, in a war zone.

He stood before the mirror and started to take off his clothes, and he saw that his hands were shaking. He stopped, and decided to lie down as he was, and pull the coverlet over him. He had always been afraid of drowning, and the old terror now seemed to rush over him all at once. He tried to steady himself, but as he took a few deep breaths he suddenly noticed that a lifejacket had been laid out on the end of the bed, and an exclamation of black humor, an exasperated laugh, escaped him. "Who the devil put that there?" he muttered. Had it been the steward? And why? Because of the captain's announcement? Was it a general order, or simply the anxiety of his particular crew member for these cabins? He didn't know. He hardly liked to think about a steward who might be more nervous than he was.

John sighed, staring at it. "For Christ's sake," he said. "It doesn't mean anything." But he knew in his gut that it certainly did. He had not touched the damned ugly thing before now out of sheer superstition; but now it seemed to occupy double its rightful space. It looked huge: cumbersome and complicated. He reached out a tentative hand and touched it, thinking that he ought to try it on, to make sure how to tie it. Just in case. Just in case . . .

"Lord," he muttered, grimacing as he picked it up. "Just get us there. Get us there quickly."

*I*t began to rain. Soft, soft beautiful rain that they could hear dripping slowly from the roof.

They were some two or three miles from Rutherford, high up in the moorland. They had come there separately, Louisa from the front of the house, and some time later Jack walking from the farthest point of the meadows, his track describing a wide loop northwards. Only when the roof of Rutherford was out of sight did he at last turn back and climb steadily upwards.

Louisa was already there, sitting quietly, when he arrived. They had said very little to each other, for nothing needed to be said. They sat hand in hand, her head on his shoulder, gazing at the sunken path and the moor beyond, until the misty cloud of rain had come. The windows in the ruined cottage were low to the ground, and the place smelled of the centuries of wood that had once been stored here: oak and cedar. It used to be a stopping place once, on the track over the top of the moors for those coming from the west and over the Pennines.

There was a kind of rough bench in one corner, and a hearth that was now stopped with debris—leaves and nests that had gradually fallen down the narrow chimney. But the cottage had no use now, and Rutherford's land enclosed it and it had decayed, sinking into the rising swathes of gorse, the roof bowed.

There was a drystone wall, put up many years before—probably two or three hundred years ago, its mossy base still intact but the upper stones cracked by frost and tumbled down; but it must have enclosed a garden once, a patch of green. There were speedwell and campion all over it, and up through the mass of heather and knotted turf and pink flowers came two or three incongruous dahlia, rosettes of lurid orange.

They listened to the rain falling on campion, gorse, and broken stone together. Gradually then—after an hour or more—they could see the sky change and become lighter. But the summer rain didn't stop. Light came through the dripping division of the window, and color fell across the floor: blue, indigo, and violet.

"The far end of the rainbow," Louisa murmured. She lifted her head and looked at him. "That is where we are," she said. "Way down in the receding colors, in shadows. Hiding here together."

"Nay," he told her. "Never in shadow. In the light, and all kinds of difference through it."

"That's one way to see it."

"I do see it," he told her. And he always would see those colors softly shedding across the flagstones. There was the color of speed-well in those blues: there was plenty of it outside in the small sweet faces of the flowers pushing through the grass. Mary's flower, his mother called it, for a reason he had never understood.

"Speedwell," Louisa said, as if she had read his thoughts. "The shade there, in the center." She smiled. "It's called 'men's faithfulness,' too."

"Why is that?"

"Because the petals fall off very quickly," she said. "As quickly as a man's faithfulness. There is a book in my father's library. A botanical book."

He stroked the hand that lay in his. "For some men," he said. "Not all."

"Ah, I know that," she said.

They remained there for much longer; he wouldn't be able to remember, looking back, for how long. It was enough to be next to her; he wanted nothing else. He asked nothing of her, thinking that it was shelter that she needed—not just this place and its anonymity—but kindness and time. He had all the time in the world just now. That might change; but he wanted to give her this afternoon, peaceful, gentle, quiet as the rain.

At last, towards the end of the afternoon, the rain stopped and they heard the buzzing of bees in the gorse. Jack wondered idly how far the bees flew, and if it was as far, to them, as men traveled. All the miles to London, where Louisa's parents waited for Harry. All the miles to France. Unraveling miles. So many miles, so many journeys. All the earth was moving, India and Canada and New Zealand, coming from all over. Horses and men across the seas. That made his heart ache, a thing he would not admit, even to her.

"We can't stay anymore," he said grudgingly at last. "Father will wonder where I am."

But they did stay, touching only in the entwined hands.

"I've something to tell thee," he said, finally.

She turned and looked at him. "What is it?"

"I'm thinking of enlisting."

She didn't object, or speak: she stayed looking at him with almost no expression. "You've a reserved occupation here. There's so few left," she said.

"I know," he replied. "And I don't like this war. Not that I don't say to drive the Germans back—they've no need to come through another country, they've no right—but there's nothing but grief. No man wants to be a part of grief." He knew he wasn't explaining himself properly. "Places get stained with it. We do, even here. There's lies in the paper. There's no victory in standing on a million dead men."

Her gaze didn't leave his face. "You think there'll be so many?"

"And more," he said. "And what for? What's it for?"

She had begun to frown a little. "You're a pacifist," she said. "Pacifists are spat upon. They put them in prison, even. It's a dirty phrase, Jack, a conscientious objector. I don't want that for you."

"I don't doubt there's a label for me."

"Then why on earth would you enlist?"

"The things you read in the papers, how they need men."

"And so you would go to support a war you don't believe in?"

"No," he told her. "Go to support the men like me that's out there. Those got roped into this and are trying to find a way out."

"By killing others."

He thought about it for some time. "You'd not think the best of me, then, for signing up?"

She smiled. "I wouldn't think less of you, Jack." She squeezed his hand tighter. "Some might say you are braver than most, for doing what you hate to do."

He looked past her to the still-wet remains of the garden. "I want to get into a veterinary corps. There are veterinary hospitals. I want to do that."

"Ah," she murmured quietly. "Now I understand."

"I would like to speak to his lordship, if he'd hear me. I thought he might know how to go about it. Make sure that it was with horses. I could be some use, then."

She extricated her hand, and touched his arm so that he looked back at her. "It's not like here, on the farms. It's nothing like that."

"I know it."

"You could do a lot. I know you could," she said. "There would be no one better than you to care for animals. But there wouldn't be time to do what you and your father have done here. Sit through the night nursing them. Letting them take things steady if they're ill.

Watching them, taking time. There would be none of that at all, Jack. No time, no peace."

"I know."

"And you could bear it? To see an animal suffer?"

"If they go through it, so could I."

She looked at him for a long time, then said quietly, "I don't want you to go, Jack." She eventually leaned back into his body, reaching for his arm and drawing it about her. He felt her shiver. "It'll break your heart."

"Aye," he replied softly. He pressed his lips to her hair, and closed his eyes. "I've no doubt of that."

William Cavendish sat in his study at Grosvenor Square, holding a thin piece of paper in his hand.

It had been delivered that morning, just after Octavia and Charlotte had gone out. The regular post had come and gone; it was now after midday, and he had been in the hallway trying to obtain a connection to Folkestone from the telephone company. It was a complicated business; he had put in his request, and been asked to wait, and thereafter told that the company would ring him back when they had found the person to whom he wished to speak.

"Good heavens," he had muttered irritatedly. He had only wanted to make contact with the shipping company to make sure of the hospital ship's time of arrival. Then, however, he had realized that this was probably highly classified information. As he had turned away from the telephone, a courier had come to the door.

"What is it?" William had inquired of the servant, thinking that it may well be a telegram from Harry.

It was handed to him: a very thin yellow envelope with a Liverpool postmark and the insignia of the Cunard Line. It was addressed to Octavia, and he had paused, confused; then, frowning, he had torn it open.

He looked at it now for the twentieth time.

"Confirmation of transmission to Mr. J. Gould . . ."

Sent late yesterday, to the *Lusitania*. He labored to understand it. The *Lusitania*? Was it on a voyage to England, to Liverpool? Was it coming here this week? Evidently that was the case. Not only that, but Gould was aboard the ship, and Octavia had sent some kind of message to him, and asked that confirmation be sent to her. She was, it appeared, very anxious to know that her telegram to Gould had reached him. He dropped the paper on his desk, fisting his hands on his knees, and then looked at the clock.

It was now a quarter to one. Luncheon was about to be served. Octavia would be home at any moment. He tried to search for a reasonable explanation of Gould coming back to England, and of Octavia contacting him, and he found none. He could feel the blood beating behind his eyes; his head ached. He sat in his chair, seeing nothing, thinking nothing further, until he heard the doorbell ring and the door to the street being opened. Out in the hall came the familiar lilt of Charlotte's voice. And Florence de Ray's. And Octavia's.

He got up and went to the hall door. Octavia was standing there, calmly removing her hat and looking at her reflection in the hall mirror. She saw him through the glass, and smiled and turned.

"Whatever is it?" she asked at once, seeing his expression. "Is it Harry?"

"No," he said. "Not Harry."

She walked towards him. "Are you leaving for Folkestone after luncheon?"

"Yes," he told her. "I'm catching the train."

Charlotte came between them, talking, laughing. He barely heard her, though he inclined his head as if he were listening. All the while he watched Octavia ascend the stairs, saw the curve of her back, the lightness of her step. He looked at his daughter and touched her arm. "Will you tell me all about it over luncheon?" he asked. "I must speak to your mother before then."

He opened the door to her room without knocking, and saw Amelie, hairbrush in hand, waiting for Octavia to sit down. Both women glanced at him in surprise: he rarely ventured into the room, let alone without announcing it with a knock.

"I must speak to you," he said.

Octavia motioned for Amelie to leave, and stood up slowly. A half smile on her face died as he walked towards her. "Something is wrong," she said.

He handed her the note from the Cunard Line.

She read it, and spent what seemed to him an inordinately long amount of time quite motionless with it in her hands; then she put it on the dressing table and turned to him. "This is the first time that I have contacted him," she said.

There it was again, the beat behind the eyes. It was painful this time; he put his hand momentarily to his temple. "You expect me to believe that."

"Certainly I expect you to believe what I say," she told him, a steely note in her voice. "He has written to me, and I have not replied. Or only this once."

"Written to you? When?"

She had the grace to blush. "Once or twice."

"That is not the truth." He felt confident enough to say it; Octavia could not lie. It was not in her nature. She betrayed it now by dropping her gaze. "You have been in communication with him."

She looked up again. "It would take two to communicate, and that has not been the case," she said. "But I admit there have been more letters."

"To what purpose?" he demanded. "Saying what?"

She paused for some seconds. "That is a private matter, I think."

The faint reddish haze in his vision seemed to bloom like a flower in the corner of his sight: an unfolding peony of red to the left-hand side. He blinked to try and clear his vision, but he failed to control his temper. "A private matter!" he exclaimed. "There are no private matters between husband and wife."

The faintest suggestion of a smile, rapidly replaced with a look of astonishment. "There have certainly been between us," she said calmly.

"That is all over," he retorted. "If you are referring to Helene de Montfort, and I suppose you are. I can't think what else you might mean."

She studied him; he felt like some sort of laboratory specimen under her gaze. He saw that there was no warmth in her. Respect, perhaps. A steadiness certainly, even loyalty. But no warmth. Not the kind that he wanted from her. He advanced on her rapidly and stood just a few inches from her, momentarily overwhelmed by the perfect sweetness of her look. His resolve wavered for a second; surely a woman who looked like that—who had always looked like that, with such openness and charm—could not chase after another man? It would be utterly beneath her.

"Tell me you are not going to meet him," he said.

"I can't tell you that," she replied. "I have not decided what to do."

"You haven't—haven't *decided*?" he thundered. "What is there to decide? What decision has to be made? You won't see John Gould, here or in Rutherford or anywhere else."

She was unmoved by him, it seemed. She sat down slowly in the bedroom chair with the mirror behind her. He was distracted by the sight of her in that glass, the nape of her neck underneath her curled hair; the rope of pearls; the soft lace collar of the day dress. She looked so neat and fragile; she was his to own and protect. And yet she was writing to another man. His blood was boiling.

"Show me the letters," he said.

She gasped in surprise. "I certainly will not, William."

"Show me the letters!"

She sat immobile. He gazed about himself to left and right. "Where are they? Where have you put them?"

"William, please . . . there is nothing in them. . . . That is, there is nothing to which I've replied. . . ."

He stormed over to her bedside table. It was a lightweight little thing in the French style; as he wrenched at it, it began to topple. He steadied it and pulled open the top drawer. There was nothing there but a handkerchief. He wheeled around. "Where are they?"

"William, please. I have kept my promise to you. I have stayed with you, with the children. I am here still. This is so unnecessary."

Some kind of devil took hold of him then. He almost ran over to her, grabbed hold of her arm, and pulled her to her feet. "Unnecessary?" he said. She was pulling against his grip. "I agree with you," he told her. "It is unnecessary for a wife to write to any man and keep it private. It is unnecessary for her to keep herself apart. To treat her husband with disdain."

"I do not disdain you," she protested. She seemed frightened now. With her free hand she tried to prize his fingers away. "William . . ."

"It is unnecessary for a wife to resist her husband," he said. "Wouldn't you agree with that? Wouldn't you? Is that not correct? Am I owed a duty, am I not owed affection?"

They were wedged against the dressing table; as if from a great distance he heard Amelie knocking on the connecting door and her voice. "Ma'am . . . ma'am?"

"Go away, damn you!" he shouted.

He looked back at his wife. "Haven't I treated you with absolute honesty and generosity in these last few months?" he said to her. Fury was blocking his sight with curious circles and squares; they danced across Octavia's face. For a moment or two, she was stained with their peculiar color. He shut his eyes, and took her by both arms now, pulled her to him, inhaling her scent. Her skin was like silk. The dress rustled against him. He opened his eyes. "I have loved you," he whispered. "All our marriage, though you have chosen not to believe me. I have loved you since last year, though many men would have thrown you into the street. I have loved you. . . ."

Tears were beginning to fill her eyes. All he could think of was that she had not said the same words back to him. He let go of her arm and touched her face. "Do you not care for me at all?" he asked.

"William, for the sake of the children . . ."

"Not for the children," he said. "For myself. Between us. Not for loyalty. But as you loved me once."

Quietly, she began to cry.

He stepped back and stared at her. "Is it lost?" he asked. "Lost entirely and forever? Is there nothing I can do to bring it back?"

She had looked away from him. "I am with you," she said. "I shan't leave you."

"But that is not what I want," he told her. "Simply to stay. I want to make it what it once was."

"I can't go back twenty years, William. I was very young. You taught me that the kind of love I offered then was . . ." She seemed to search for the word. "Gauche. Inappropriate."

"That is not true."

Her eyes widened in surprise. "It is certainly true," she said. "But I don't hold it against you, William. I was only a girl, and you had, as you often told me, your place in society to maintain. . . ."

"Damn society!"

She looked at him searchingly, frowning. "Are you well?" she asked. "Do you feel quite well?"

He struggled to take a breath, to control himself. A small voice in the back of his mind told him to try to make himself appealing to her, not to bully her. It was what had made Gould so attractive, wasn't it? A boyish good humor, a lightness in the way he spoke. William glanced away from Octavia for a second, steadying himself. "I realize that I'm not a man like Gould," he began.

"Oh, William. Please don't."

"I realize . . ." he repeated. Pain had invaded his throat. He tried to cough. She grasped his arm in alarm, but he waved her away. "Let us not talk of twenty years ago," he said. "Let us talk of today. Something fresh now. Something else. Octavia . . ."

She put her own hand over his. "I promise you that I will not leave you," she said. "You are the father of my children."

"I don't want that," he replied. A sort of agony was now building in his chest, pouring down his left arm. A kind of white-hot hell. "I want us to love each other."

"Oh, William," she murmured in a broken voice. And he thought he heard her say very softly, *No, no . . .*

The world closed in on him, compressing the picture of her to a tiny disc of light.

He lost his grip on her then, and experienced a kind of slow dull falling. He thought that he saw the material of her dress, patterned cream and grey, pass in front of him as slowly and deliberately as a screen pulled across a theater stage.

But he never felt himself hitting the floor.

It was late afternoon in the servants' kitchen in Rutherford, and Mary sat with Jenny and Miss Dodd at the long, scrubbed table. The head housemaid was pouring the tea, but it was with a wearied air: all day long the staff had been harried by Mrs. Jocelyn. The housekeeper had become obsessed by cleaning every inch while his lordship and Lady Cavendish were away in London; Miss Dodd, exasperated, had protested only that morning that the house was already spotless.

Mrs. Jocelyn's countenance had darkened. "Cleanliness is next to godliness."

"Then we must be at His right hand," Miss Dodd had said.

The two had glared at each other. Mrs. Jocelyn was a thunderous force to be reckoned with, but Miss Dodd had all the froideur of thirty years' service, and a Yorkshire stubbornness to boot. She was as thin as a whippet, and as God-fearing as Mrs. Jocelyn when she wanted to be: a study in determination and self-righteousness. But she had a heart, and some pity. Qualities that the housekeeper seemed to have burned out of her soul since the episode with Emily Maitland.

Mrs. Jocelyn had the authority, however, and eventually Miss Dodd dropped her gaze. She had a newspaper next to her, and opened it.

"There's no time for that," the housekeeper snapped.

The newspaper was slapped back on the table. "Then we shall all read it at afternoon tea, with your permission," Miss Dodd replied. "'Tis our proper duty to see how the boys are all doing in France."

Mrs. Jocelyn couldn't argue with that. She had walked out, clicking her tongue against her teeth. They had listened to her stopping and starting in the corridor, and Mary had simply raised her eyebrows at Jenny. The housekeeper's eccentricities were now so regular that it was almost an entertainment.

They sat now, taking their teacups, exhausted. They had actually been set to scrub the great hall that day; scrub it, if you please, on hands and knees from one end to the other. Listlessness possessed them, but at least Mrs. Jocelyn had spared them her company.

The newspaper was open. Mary and Jenny watched Miss Dodd scour it for news of her brother; he was in the Mediterranean Expeditionary Force, the Royal Naval Division. "Gone to a place called Gallipoli," she had told them a few days previously. She pronounced it "Gallypolly," and no one knew better to correct her. "Where is that?" Mary had asked her.

"Turkey, or somewhere."

She might as well have said, "the moon." They had no idea where Turkey was, except that it was hot, and it was where carpets came from.

There was no news of him evidently; Miss Dodd pushed the paper in their direction. "Where is Nash?" she asked.

"I got a letter from Lancashire this week," Mary replied. "They've moved again."

"And Harrison?"

Jenny blushed under Miss Dodd's scrutiny. "In France."

"Doing what? Is he at the front?"

"I don't know," Jenny replied. "I haven't heard in a long time."

"Well," Miss Dodd replied flatly. "If he were dead, you'd know it soon enough, so I shouldn't worry."

"I don't worry," Jenny lied, bowing her head. "It's just . . . it seems so odd somehow. He was here at Rutherford, one of us." She stopped, realizing that they were all looking at her. "I can't explain myself very well."

"I understand," Mary told her. "You mean it's like *we're* there. Like it's happening to us, people like us?"

"Yes," Jenny murmured. "Like Rutherford got picked up and put out there, and now it's getting ruined. And if he got hurt . . . or Nash got hurt, or anyone, the boys that went from the stables, or even the horses that went yesterday . . . it's *here*, isn't it, then? Right here, not in France."

Miss Dodd was frowning then she shrugged her shoulders. "What a lot of silliness," she said. "Nothing can touch us here."

Jenny looked as if she was about to reply, but thought better of it. "Yes," she said quietly. "I suppose so. Thank you, Miss Dodd."

Mary opened the newspaper.

Her eyes ran down the column of the dead; all officers. The paper didn't bother printing the deaths of other ranks. She was sensible enough to know that there probably wasn't room. "There is someone here from Workington," she said quietly. "And Ripon." She bit her lip; she remembered the notices posted in the same newspaper in October last year, urging men to sign up—"working together, fighting together"—telling them how they would always be kept side by side.

Articles had been written about the same time saying that "clever thinkers say the war was inevitable." The sense being that if "clever thinkers" were saying so, then all the rest of them—dull thinkers, she supposed they were meant to be—should follow suit. "We must face it," had been a common saying then, and "We must all do something." Well, she thought, reading the lists sadly, they are doing something now all right.

Jenny was reading over her shoulder. Turning the pages, they saw an article by a journalist who had accompanied a midnight inspection of Ypres in the last week of April. "A moonlit night and no sign of life," he had written. "And then on to a place called the Plaine d'Amour. Never seen a place so ill-named, a misery of dead things."

Jenny pointed the sentence out to Mary. "What does it mean, 'Plaine d'Amour'?"

"It's love, isn't it?" Mary said. "Amour."

They read on. "The Canadians are there," Mary murmured. "And Indians. And French Algerians."

"I wonder what they think of France."

"Not much. It says here that it's all flat and there are brickyards and canals and coal waste and mud."

Jenny sat with her chin propped in her hand. "I always thought France was pretty. I thought of Paris and everything, all glamorous. They say French girls are . . . well, you know. Very nice."

"I don't expect the Canadians and Indians think it's glamorous. And I don't expect they see any girls."

Jenny sat back. "To think they've come all that way because of the Empire. I wonder what they say back in those countries, of having to come just because England's at war. I wonder what their mothers say about them fighting, about them going in the first place."

"*England* is not at war," Miss Dodd reprimanded her. "*Great Britain* is at war and if we are at war, the Empire is at war. That is what we have an empire for."

"We know that," Mary countered. "But imagine living somewhere out in India. A village there. Maybe in one of those big old cities, or up in the mountains in the middle of nowhere. Places where they don't even know what London is, or rain, or snow. Imagine being told you have to go to France to fight so that Germans don't cross the Channel and live here. They must think, 'well, what is that to do with us?'"

"They don't think that at all," Miss Dodd replied. "They love their mother country and the King."

"But why are we their mother country?" Mary asked. "We aren't Indians."

"That's enough of that," Miss Dodd snapped. "They are all very brave men, and worth ten of you. Drink up the tea, and go see to Miss Louisa's bedroom when you have."

She left the room; they heard her footsteps clumping on the stairs to her room on the third floor. Mary smiled at Jenny. "Gone to write a letter to her lover boy."

"Mary!"

"Well, she has," Mary replied, grinning. "The girl from the village told me she's seen her on a Sunday afternoon with the butcher from Scorton. Holding hands on the bridge like two moonstruck fools—and at their age!" she said. "It ought to be illegal."

They began laughing; but it didn't last long.

The kitchen door was suddenly flung back on its hinges. Mrs. Jocelyn was standing in the doorway, a letter in her hand, and her face flushed bright red. "What is this!" she shouted.

The girls scrambled to their feet. "If you please, m'm, it's our teatime."

"I don't mean that!" Mrs. Jocelyn said, advancing on Mary, and waving the letter under her nose. "This, this!"

"I don't know what it is," Mary said.

The stinging blow came as a complete shock to her. Never in all the time that she had worked at Rutherford had she ever been hit. She'd had many a dressing down, of course; she'd had the privilege of her monthly Sunday off taken away, too. She had been yelled at by everyone above her, even the footman; she had been groped by Harrison. Worst of all, she had once received a disappointed and soft reproof by Lady Cavendish for singing when she was about her early-morning tasks. But she had never, never been struck.

Behind her, she heard Jenny gasp.

Mary stood openmouthed, her hand on her reddened face.

"This is from the manager at Blessington Mills," Mrs. Jocelyn said. "The mistress has set him to find your father and bring him here."

"Here?" Mary echoed, astonished.

"Don't come the innocent with me," the housekeeper said. "What have you said to Lady Cavendish?"

"Nothing, m'm."

"You must have said something, or else how does she know him?"

"Begging your pardon, m'm, but I don't know. We talked of him when my sister died last year, and that was all."

Mrs. Jocelyn put her hands on her hips and looked Mary up and down. "Oh, talked of him?" she repeated scathingly. "And begged her ladyship for work for him. The outrage of it!"

"No, m'm."

"Then why this?" Again the letter was waved.

"I don't know, m'm, truly I don't. Her ladyship said nothing to me."

Mrs. Jocelyn took a step towards her; Mary backed herself against the table. "Have many a conversation with her ladyship, do you?"

"No," Mary whispered. "Only last year. Only once."

"And I'm supposed to believe that she's remembered that?"

"I don't know," Mary said.

Mrs. Jocelyn was eyeing her much as someone would eye a dangerous animal. "Well, he's to come here," she said. "The manager's told him. He's here in the next few days."

Mary did not know what to say. She hadn't heard from her father in months; he couldn't write, and she only occasionally received messages via tradesmen who might have been over to Blessington. They were all the same. "Say hello to my Mary." That was literally all.

Her heart sank heavily now; she didn't know if her ladyship had ever met her father. She knew that Rutherford was very short of men, but she did not doubt that he would never have been offered a job if Lady Cavendish had seen him. Her father was a drunk, and a pathetic, weeping one at that. He swept the mill yards for a few pence, but lived mostly on street corners by the alehouses, hoping that the workingmen would take pity on an old mill hand, a widower whose injuries had stopped his employment prospects forever. *Oh my God*, she thought helplessly now. *Please let someone wash him before he turns up here. Please, please; before Mrs. Jocelyn lays eyes on him.*

"I'm sure it's a very great kindness from her ladyship," she stuttered finally now. "But Father is quite . . . weak, you know. I don't know what good he'll be able to do."

She could feel Mrs. Jocelyn's stare burning into her. She dropped her gaze.

"I know one thing," the housekeeper muttered finally. "You and her ladyship are cut from the same cloth. That's why she likes you, I'll wager." She brought her face to within an inch of Mary's. "Went without my permission last year to see your sister," she said in a low voice. "Don't think I've forgotten it."

Mary couldn't reply. Her sister had died; she had been there when it happened. The injustice of Mrs. Jocelyn's rant cut her to the quick.

"You're a pair," the housekeeper continued savagely. "A pair of mill girls, you and she both."

Out of the corner of her eye, Mary could see Jenny quivering with shock and fright. The older woman suddenly straightened up, took a step back, and swept her gaze around the kitchen; and the abrupt movement made Jenny spring back, a little cry escaping her.

"Filthy," Mrs. Jocelyn muttered to herself. Her fingers plucked at the great swinging set of chatelaine keys at her waist. "You're all as bad as each other, and this is a filthy, filthy, filthy house."

*A*nother kind of night was falling around Harrison, ruinous and noisy, patched with fractured light.

But he hardly heard explosions anymore; his hearing had shut them out. A man could do that. It was a trick that had been taught to him—how many years ago? He couldn't tell. It seemed to him that a dozen years had passed since Nat had been on the side of the road just ahead of the decimated water cart.

Harrison had grown old; he felt it. Much older than the ground he crawled over. Very old: so old that he was not human anymore, but a piece of organic chemistry, living but not living—a compound of elements. "Tell yourself not to listen to it," the old hand had said as the barrage had rained down on them. Face spattered with mud, hands gripping his rifle. Hunkered down together in a featureless wasteland.

"How can't I listen to it, you bastard?" he'd replied. The man just smiled. A wistful drawing back of his lips over his teeth. A kind of subdued smile, at least, or what served for a smile out here.

"Listen to something you remember. In your own head. Inside. Listen to a woman talking. Or a car along a road." Harrison had tried to think of what he remembered while the inhuman roaring went on. He remembered—well, what? Polishing shoes. Very good leather shoes that belonged to Lord Cavendish. He remembered the shine. He remembered—who was this? Jenny on the stone stairs to the kitchen. Starched white collars of serving maids. Starched white collars. . . . "Well, what are you thinking of?" the man had asked.

Crump, crump, crump. Soil flying through the air. Something

screaming: animal, human? Hard to tell. He tried to listen to Jenny, walking down the stairs. "Women's shoes," he said.

"Go on thinking of them," the man told him.

The second-to-last time that he had seen that man, they were still together, this time dug in along something called La Quinque Rue. It meant "five streets," or "fifth street," the major said. Quinque Rue. Canker-roo.

It soon became "Kangaroo" to Harrison. Big, thumping, blinding and deafening Kangaroo. It sat in his soul with its big thundering feet. He let the ridiculous image wander about in his mind while he marched and ran and dug and fixed bayonet and waited, waited, waited in the dark. It joined all the other odd, disjointed thoughts roaming about in his head: a wailing army of ghosts, of gruesome circus acts. Wheeling fireworks, tumbling water. Hoots and klaxons and horns: the clown cars of the big top, circling in sawdust and murderous dreams. A circus called Festubert.

Sometimes he heard himself speaking, and, more often than not, laughing. They said he had a good sense of skewed humor. If he ever had a silent moment—true silence, the guns extinguished, the men praying or asleep or drugged with the aftereffects of ferocity, of barbaric acts, in times like that, Harrison laughed quietly to himself. It may have seemed peculiar, but at least it made him feel better. The men around him never told him to shut up anymore. He'd become a kind of mascot, as if stopping him laughing would end them all, put out their own lives, turn them all into the greenish mud they slimed through.

And the last time he saw that man along the Kangaroo, they had been sitting in a hole they'd scraped out with their entrenching tools and had to crouch in it as if they were stuffed into a hip bath together, their feet outside while shrapnel whirred on either side. They couldn't move; the sniper had their measure. The evening had come in—thank God for the dark—and they tried filling sandbags with more earth from their tiny scoop of soil. They filled two, and shoved them on the side that faced the enemy.

Somewhere out to their right was an adventurous artillerist; one man acting freelance with a mule and an Indian mountain gun. He seemed to have an inexhaustible supply of small arms, and from time to time he would shower the Germans with projectiles, and then scuttle away, vanishing in the murk. Then he began to shower *them*. They cursed him for his momentary inaccuracy and the withering fire in reply from the enemy.

A gun of a much larger caliber four hundred yards away was searching out the artilleryman in the shadows, like a great snuffling dog nosing about. One reply tore out what remained of the old trench just ahead of them: they sat immobile, feeling dead already because the sound of the shell was known all too well to them. Both of them waited for it to land with a few seconds of utmost clarity that their lives were at an end.

And in that moment, Harrison thought of Jenny's starched collar and her soft, self-effacing voice with something amounting to passion, a sudden surge of poignant love. Why had he never said a kind word to her? He had felt cut off from kindness all his life, given or received; he had been isolated in his mind, cold in the way he spoke. He couldn't fathom where that came from, and now it was too late. Now he was here, at the edge of all life, looking back the way he had come, feeling a strange and hollow loss in his soul. Then, in that same terrible instant, the blast came, humping the ground underneath them, sending up a wall of earth. But after it was all over, they found themselves in the same hellish place, in the same hellish hole, untouched.

During that night, there was no sign of anyone ordering them back; no sign at all, in fact, of other men. They were, they decided, well and truly stranded. When the dawn had come up, they had got back to their own lines by scraping along the surface in a flat panic; slumping in the British trench, gasping out that they'd dispatched the Boche but no one had come to back them up—ah, the major's face, red as a beetroot, blaring about orders, losing his nerve—ah, the snide grins of the others and the disguised thumbs-up signals. "What was it like?" a boy said, staring at him, come up from the reserve trenches. Green as you like with fear and shaking like a leaf. "Like a Chinese execution," Harrison replied. "Death by a thousand cuts."

The boy hooked his thumb over his shoulder. "Like him?"

And it was his nighttime companion, the man who'd told him to think of something else when they were first on Kangaroo. He'd caught a shrapnel blast that Harrison had never even heard as he launched himself back into the British trench; his face was sliced quite neatly in a horizontal fashion. There were red tramlines across his forehead, the bridge of his nose, and the tips of his ears. He was being hauled backwards as they tried to get him to a dressing station. He had looked at Harrison nevertheless and smiled as best he could.

That afternoon, Harrison was allowed back, too.

He lay on his back a mile behind the lines, staring at the sky. He had an injury to his hand—never felt it, just like he'd never heard the shrapnel blast—and someone had given him a smoke. He lay on the stretcher and watched far-distant clouds.

A medico came up to him. He had an upper-class accent, the faintest line of a moustache, and a crisply turned-out uniform. "How are you bearing up?" Harrison was asked.

"Just fine and dandy, sir."

"Sit up for me."

He did as he was told. The man had sat down beside him and the tone of his voice was the kind one might use if you spoke to a child. "Can you tell me what day it is?"

"No sir. Why does it matter?"

"Your unit?"

He couldn't think. Watched the clouds still visible over the officer's shoulder. "The British Army," he said, and sniggered at his own joke.

"Bothered by the bombardment?"

This was such a stupid question that he ignored it. The clouds were dancing a little. He wondered how badly he was shaking and if that was the reason for the officer's concern.

The officer hunched forward. "It wouldn't be surprising," he said, in a confidential tone. "In sixty hours, we have expended a hundred thousand rounds of ammunition."

Harrison looked at him. "A hundred thousand," he repeated. "And they say we've got no shells, sir."

"They do say that. It's been raised in Parliament just this week."

Harrison ground out his cigarette in the mud. As far as he was concerned, the conversation was at an end. He hated these boy-officers from the universities who tried to be matey. He wanted to punch the man in the face. He wasn't his mate. He was a trench rat, a thing that crawled through the soaked gullies, and hid behind shattered hedges and makeshift sandbags.

"Well," he said softly. And he got to his feet. He shuffled about a bit to disguise his tremors. "If you'll excuse me, sir, I have to get back. There's a war on."

On board the *Lusitania*, the early dense fog had cleared, and it was a beautiful day.

John Gould leaned on the rail and looked out over the sea. It was a silent sheet of indigo; the sun reflected from it so that he had to shade his eyes. People passed him arm in arm; many of them smiled and nodded at him. He pondered that there was a definite shift of mood aboard the ship; they were nearing Ireland—they would soon be able to see the Old Head of Kinsale on the southernmost coast— and the passengers were visibly relaxing. They would soon be in Liverpool; all the talk of submarines would be over.

Still, he noticed that more than one person, like him, was scanning the water. He wondered what a periscope looked like. Would, in fact, a submarine surface at all, or, if they were fired upon, would one only see the trail of the torpedo? He didn't even know if a torpedo could be seen in the water. Perhaps, if one struck, it would be so far down underneath the ship that it would never be noticed coming at them. He shuddered involuntarily. No need for all this, he told himself. They were almost there. They were not going to be hit.

A couple came alongside him. He recognized Elbert Hubbard, the man who had written an article in *The Philistine* that had gone on to be reprinted forty million times. John had noticed him many times on the voyage, but those figures—forty million, an inconceivable amount—had kept him from introducing himself. He didn't want to say, "I'm a journalist, a writer," to someone whose work had forty million readers. It made him feel shy, like a schoolboy. Added to that, Hubbard was a big figure of a man with a piercing gaze, a kind of force of nature. The forty-million article was all about getting a job done, stiffening the vertebrae and concentrating the energies. John was terribly afraid that Hubbard would take one look at him and decide that his vertebrae were of a decidedly unstiffened kind.

Hubbard caught his look now, though. He stopped in his tracks. "Watching for U-boats?" he asked.

John wheeled around. "I suppose it's tempting fate."

Hubbard smiled. "Believe in such a thing?"

John considered. "Yes, I do."

Hubbard came alongside him, leaning companionably on the rail. His wife put her head on one side, frankly assessing John, and smiling. "Ah, fate," Hubbard said. He held out his hand to introduce himself. "Hubbard."

"I know of you, sir."

"And you?"

He told the great man his name.

"Working in England?"

John was about to say that yes, he was working, and that he would be going to France. But all at once he realized, looking into Hubbard's face, that the whole history of his taking the commission to write about the war from an American perspective was just a smokescreen. He had told his father and mother of what he was doing; he had told other people on this ship. But now he abruptly realized that it was an elaborate and convenient lie. He was going to England for one purpose, and one purpose only. He always had been.

"I'm going to find the woman I fell in love with last year," he said. "I find that I can't live without her."

Hubbard smiled. "You look determined."

"I am sir, yes."

"A message to Garcia, eh?" Hubbard said, and laughed a great booming laugh. He patted John's shoulder, and walked away with his wife at his side.

A Message to Garcia was the forty-million-copy article. John squared his shoulders and laughed to himself. Elbert Hubbard thought he was all right after all: he was a man with a mission, a man to accomplish anything.

And he was heading, straight as an arrow, to his mark.

He went in to luncheon, feeling so much better.

He wouldn't gaze out at the sea anymore, he decided. He would just concentrate on what he was going to do once he got to Liverpool.

As far as he could recall, there was a regular train service across the Pennines, but perhaps it would be better to take an express to Manchester and then to Leeds. The cross-Pennine trains were sluggish at best, pausing at every little town and lamppost. He had no desire to look at the moors, no matter how beautiful they were.

And as he sat staring into space, a small smile on his face, a steward came into the dining room and made straight for him. He was carrying a telegram.

"Mr. Gould?"

"Yes, that's me."

John took the envelope and tore it open. For a moment, the words danced in an incomprehensible jumble in front of his eyes: he was so surprised to receive it. And then he saw her name.

Tell me when you get to Liverpool. Safe passage. Octavia.

Ten words. He counted them. Ten words.

A woman across the table leaned forward. "Not bad news, I hope?" she asked.

"Oh no," he said, and felt the blood rushing to his face. "No. Rather the opposite, in fact."

He folded the piece of paper, hands trembling.

All he could think of was, *After all this time.*

He looked around himself as if he had landed suddenly in heaven. He noticed the elaborate flower arrangements, the silver, the knife-edge creases in the linen of the napkins. Each detail sprang out at him as if seeing everything for the first time. Somewhere in the bowels of this ship were people who had kept and arranged the flowers, who had served the food, who had pressed the cloths, who had shined the silver. He felt as if he wanted to rush below and shake each person's hand. "Thank you," he wanted to say. "Thank you for making it all perfect." He started to laugh, and, seeing the surprised expressions on his fellow diners, stopped himself just in time, he felt, from making a complete ass of himself.

But it *was* fine.

It was all so very fine, and so very perfect.

*A*fter luncheon, he took himself out to the deck.

He had a notion that he would walk for at least an hour; he had suddenly so much energy to burn away. He glanced again at the sea, and then up at the four tall funnels above him. He looked at his watch: it was just after two p.m. Then, looking ahead, he saw that there were lookouts scanning the ocean. Suddenly, he saw one of them raise an arm, and he followed the direction in which the man was pointing, up to the crow's nest.

There, high above them, were two crew.

They too were pointing to something on the starboard side, his side. He heard raised voices, but could not make out what it was that they were calling.

He looked to starboard.

About a thousand yards away, what seemed like a large bubble was breaking and disintegrating, and just before it in the water could be seen two white streaks, as clearly defined as stripes of chalk on a blackboard. For a second, John recalled being on a motoring yacht off Cape Cod at sunset. He couldn't remember the day or even the year, but he was seeing now, in his mind's eye, that same kind of clear twin stripe in the sea caused by the wake of something moving very fast in a quiet ocean. He stared out, mesmerized.

The starboard lookout had grabbed a megaphone. He had turned towards the bridge and was yelling, "Torpedoes coming on the starboard side, sir!" Above him, the crow's nest lookouts had begun to scramble down, shouting as they went.

My God, John thought calmly. *They've done it.*

The twin streaks of foam disappeared and immediately afterwards there was a distant boom like the sound of some vast iron door slamming closed. John turned in its direction in time to see an explosion of smoke and cinders come up through the funnels, rapidly followed by a plume of water at the side of the ship.

"Oh, we're hit," a woman cried.

People rushed to the rail.

They've hit the coal stores, John thought. The explosions were far too loud for just a single missile; in fact, he thought he had heard three. The first was the torpedo—but that had been a different noise. The second two . . . something *within* the ship. Something more central; something that had been ignited.

The ship lifted right up at the prow, and slumped back into the sea; it was still shaking. Out of the corner of his eye, John saw that the hanging baskets in the café had been flung to the floor. Clouds of steam were circling on the deck farther down. He thought very clearly—almost slowly—that the stokers must have been killed. It was hellish down there anyway; they could not have survived. And then he thought of the men down in the hold who would be preparing the luggage for disembarkation. There was only an electric lift out of the hold; Lauriat had told him so. They would be trapped down there if the electricity failed.

"Will we sink?" he heard someone say.

"Not the *Lusitania*," came a man's voice in reply. "And we're close to land even if we do." John looked up and saw the shadowed pencil outline of the Head of Kinsale on the horizon.

Then, he thought he felt the ship tilt.

He grabbed the rail, assuming that it was his imagination. A ship the size of the *Lusitania* would take hours to go down, surely? The *Titanic* had taken two hours and forty minutes to sink.

He found that his hand seemed welded to the rail, his knuckles white. With slow-motion difficulty, he disengaged his grip. A woman rushed past him, holding a small boy in her arms, crying out that her other son was in their cabin, asleep. There were a lot of women and children on this boat, John thought; they were everywhere. Babies and toddlers and nine- and ten-year-olds. Girls in their summer frocks and little boys in sailor suits.

"My God, my God," he whispered.

He looked up at the lifeboats and realized with horror that, indeed, the ship had tilted. It was at something like a fifteen-degree angle. But how could that be, already? It was only three or four minutes since they had been struck. How could it fill with water so much below that it began to list so much?

An officer hurried past. John caught at his sleeve.

"What's happening?" he asked. "What should we do?"

"The captain has ordered the lifeboats to be lowered," he was told. "The ship is not answering the helm. We've lost electricity. The steering has locked."

"Lost electricity," John repeated, as the man rushed away.

He thought of the men in the hold, and those already in the electric lift.

And, while he was still thinking of that horror, the ship began to turn in a prolonged circle, listing ever further in the mirrorlike ocean.

or a moment, Octavia could only stare at William as he lay inert on the floor. Then, she rushed to him, got down on her knees, and put her hands on his shoulders.

"William," she said. "William—what is it?"

There was no reply. Her husband's face was slowly draining of the heightened color that it had worn while he had been arguing with her.

"Amelie!" she cried. "Amelie, come here!"

Her maid must have been listening at the door all the while, for she rushed immediately into the room, and gave a gasp when she saw William on the floor.

"Tell them downstairs to call a doctor immediately," Octavia said. She was trying to loosen William's collar. "And come back here with whoever you can find. We must get him onto the bed."

Amelie said not a word. She ran straight out of the door, and Octavia could hear her footsteps running down the stairs—then raised voices. "William, William," she whispered. She put her fingers on his neck and felt a pulse. It was thready and faint. "Oh my God," she murmured. Seeing him there, all her previous pictures of him flew out of the window—he was no longer the rigid, slightly overbearing figure she had known, but something faded, helpless, grey.

Amelie came rushing back into the bedroom, pursued by a footman. Together they manhandled William's body to the bed. "Get me some water," Octavia instructed. "Let us try to see if he can drink a little."

"Ma'am, there is the smelling salts—" ventured Amelie.

The little bottle that Amelie found in the dressing room was administered to William. His eyes fluttered once or twice, and then his head jerked violently to one side.

"For God's sake take that away," he said.

Each of them let out a sigh. He opened his eyes fully and stared about him. Then, in an instant, he was struggling to get up.

"No, no," Octavia said. She gave him a firm push back against the pillows. "You must stay quiet, you have had a seizure. The doctor is coming."

"I can't stay here," he protested. "I must go to Harry. I must go to Folkestone."

"You are going nowhere at all," she replied, and took his hand.

Boulogne-sur-Mer. Evening.

What a nice-sounding name it was, Harry Cavendish thought. Sur-Mer, Sur-Mer. On the sea. A nice little seaside town, much like those on the other side of the Channel. A straight, sparsely furnished promenade. A great hotel called the Casino, with a vast blue roof near the harbor wall, now converted to a hospital; it reminded him of places like Scarborough. Flat sands, music halls, hotels. The lights reflected on the incoming tide. Mud flats invaded and wrinkled by currents.

He'd played in such places as Scarborough on the Yorkshire coast when he was a boy. Happy times of sand between the toes, his mother somewhere far behind, smothered in a pale summer dress beneath a parasol, in an ornate chair brought by a servant to the sands. He had run about, a little king, while his mother bore the heat for an hour or so before retreating to one of those wedding-cake hotels with their glass roofs and white-painted arches and rose-fringed walks. A fortunate little king, stamping his feet and yelling at his nurse when he had to come inside. A spoiled little king, he now decided; and his sister Louisa trailing after him in her linen bloomers and starched dress and straw hat tied with a ribbon, looking cool and collected and postcard-pretty on the hottest day.

My God, he was glad that Louisa wasn't here to see Boulogne-sur-Mer today. He hoped that she hadn't got it into her head to volunteer as a VAD; the experience would break her, shatter her into pieces. She had a determination to get her way, but that wasn't the same quality that was needed out here. A girl—and there were plenty of upper-class girls helping the troops—had to be staunchly oblivious, enduring, or hearty. Louisa was none of those things.

He lifted himself up on one elbow.

He had been put at the head of a long line of men: stretchers lay on the ground by the dockside. The dock—and the sparsely furnished promenade, and the sands, and the Casino—everything in fact, even the fishing boats, even the steep streets of poor houses, even the pavements—everything was now part of the war. The noise was incessant. Ships were coming in, unloading, disgorging their crowds of uniformed men, or horses, or guns, or stack after stack of pallets;

other ships were going out, heavy with the wounded, with wrecks of machinery and men.

Single-track railway lines came up to the dockside; the air was punctuated with their shunting and hissing. The horses that were led down onto dry land shied about, and were occasionally wrestled into order; their manure stank, mingling with everything else that was acrid. Petrol, sweat, misery.

Some horses sensed it: you could see it in their eyes, widened, and their heads rolling from side to side. Some came off the boats looking sickened from sea travel, just like the men. Although the soldiers hid it with jokes, elbowing each other and stamping on the ground to show that it was solid, making retching faces. The horses had no language other than the foam flecking their coats, the rolling back of their lips, or the shuddering of the muscles along their backs.

Harry counted eighty stretchers to his right-hand side. Ten to his left. He looked again at the man alongside him, who up to now had been apparently sleeping. It was a captain, a man with an aquiline face. He opened his eyes now and looked at Harry.

"Afternoon," came an upper-class voice. "We've both been a-kip. Rather a neat trick in this bedlam, what?" He smiled at Harry. "One ought to object to being lumped on the pavement."

"Not quite Claridge's."

The man laughed. "Claridge's! My God, when I get to London, I shall take a suite and install a nice lady with me." He winked at Harry. "She'll have to be my hands, though."

Harry glanced down. Both of the captain's hands were so swathed in bandages that they resembled two round white lumps of material.

"I'd shake a paw, but as you see . . ."

"Harry Cavendish." Harry tapped his compatriot's shoulder in a friendly gesture.

"John Hooge-Haldane."

"Ah, Hooge. . . ."

"Of course, by way of irony, where we're fighting at the moment."

"Our line is still there?"

"From time to time." Haldane gave out a great sigh. "The twenty-eighth have been smashed up, I'm afraid. Heavy losses. Ten thousand or more."

"Ten thousand!"

"They say it's over forty thousand since the end of April on that salient. The Boche are dug in with barbed wire we can't cut. And then the artillery . . . there's not enough shells."

Harry closed his eyes for a second. "I've been out of it," he murmured. "In a hospital train. Stopping and starting." He opened his eyes and looked back down at Haldane's hands. "Are you thirsty?" he asked.

"Damned thirsty."

Harry had been given a webbing-covered bottle of water: Caitlin had secured it on the train. Water from the train's own boiler. It didn't matter. It was water all the same. With some difficulty, he edged it from under his blanket. Haldane didn't try to move his hands, which reeked of antiseptic, and the bandages were seeping something brownish. It was a hard job to lean over to Haldane's stretcher; Harry's legs and hips felt like lumps of clay. Eventually he managed to get a dribble of liquid through the man's mouth.

"All right?"

"Thanks."

Harry glanced down at the blanketed shape. There was no uniform, just—rather insanely—a pair of sepia-striped pyjamas.

"They got them from my trunk at Bailleul."

For a moment, Harry thought this was sheer dementia speaking.

He thought that the cultured, clipped voice had said "Balliol." Perhaps the man imagined himself back at university. But then he realized that it was the name of a French town in Flanders. There was a clearing hospital there—Caitlin had told him; she'd tried to keep him conscious by getting him to recite the ones she had been posted to. Bailleul, Armentieres, Ypres.

"Ho-ho," Haldane said. "My damned PJs."

"How so?"

"Whole bloody kit burned off me. I had to strip it. Doused in petrol."

"They're throwing petrol now?"

A hoarse, coughing laugh. "I didn't need a Boche to throw anything at me. This was my corporal trying to light a fire."

Harry couldn't think of anything to say. It was a joke surely. Then he whispered, "Oh, bad luck."

"Bloody incompetent bastard," the man muttered. "Making a laughingstock of me, and a corpse of himself. Whole tent went up." He made a snorting noise. "Not a gallant wound, would you say? Hardly something to boast about to the dear little folks at home."

"No, I suppose not."

"The thing is . . ." he began to cough. He struggled for a few moments, then regained his voice. "You've heard of Hill Sixty? We were in the attack of the first of May. They bombarded us and then sent over the gas."

"I saw some men affected by it."

"Brutal stuff," Haldane muttered. "The gas reached the trenches and then they bombed us on both flanks of the battalion. We retaliated of course. . . . And you know, I survived that. The damned fucking irony—excuse my French—is that I survived it and then got struck with this. When there is so much work to do . . . " His voice trailed away, and then regained its frustrated vigor. "We lost ninety men from the battalion from gas poisoning. Fifty-six in the clearing station." The coughing restarted.

"Rest, old man."

But rest did not seem to be on Haldane's agenda. "The colonel there told me it was chlorine and bromine mixed. D'you know what that does? Makes a man cough up thicker and thicker stuff until it suffocates him. They cough to get rid of it, but it only makes it worse. They drown as they breathe."

Harry wondered if Caitlin had seen that.

"Got past that. Got back to Bois Confluent. Near there at least. Make my report. Felt that I had done something worthwhile that day, repulsed them. Gave them no quarter for the use of their filthy tricks. French were just up the line. They've taken a pasting, I can tell you, worse even than us. I was writing . . . then the bloody corporal . . ."

Haldane started to laugh. He held up his bandaged hands. "I got this trying to tear the clothes from him. Lit up like a regular flare, the fool." He suddenly turned his head. "What in damnation is that screeching noise?"

Harry looked. "Getting horses onto a train."

They both looked over. A large grey, a Shire, was refusing to go up the ramp; it hung its head. It must have been seventeen hands high or more. Frustrated, the soldiers gave up on pushing it, and instead passed a large webbing band around it and pulled hard; there were two men on each side, four in all. Still the horse did not move.

"Poor beast," Haldane muttered.

"Yes. They don't like it," Harry agreed. And then tried to sit upright. "By God, I know that horse," he exclaimed. But so many people were passing between the train and themselves that it was hard to see properly.

"You do?"

"I'm sure that . . ." Harry began. But just at that moment, the Shire began to move, and, in a moment, it had vanished inside, hauled by the straps. Its head was still bowed, half turned away; Harry, frowning, could not now be sure. "Perhaps not," he murmured. "Not possible, surely."

Far away, above the noise, there was music coming from the old harbor. Both Harry and Haldane now turned their heads in its direction. "People having fun," Haldane whispered. "Jolly good luck to them."

"Yes, Harry murmured. "Jolly good luck."

Haldane was peering now at the ship on the dockside. "That's our punt, do you think?"

"Yes, that's the one."

"She's just a banged-up little ferry."

"She's our ticket home, though."

Haldane lay back on the stretcher and stared at the sky. "I would get up and walk around but for these bloody PJs."

"I don't know if I can walk," Harry admitted.

"What, they've not had you perambulating?"

"A sort of shuffle off the bunk onto this."

"On your arse, I'll warrant."

Harry laughed. It was probably the first real laugh he'd had since he had left England, coming out of the depths, recalling his shambling and shuffling in front of Caitlin, and the involuntary swearing that went with it. "I impressed one nurse particularly."

"Oh, we've all impressed nurses," Haldane laughed. "Try having a pee with your hands fucked up like this. The poor dears had to fumble about for the old man and hold it. Pissing by proxy." He raised an eyebrow at Harry. "And I would say your luck's right out, old chap. Because unless I'm much mistaken, you'll have to do it for me soon."

Harry lay back on the ground too, and the pair of them laughed together until the tears crept out of Harry's eyes.

"That bloody corporal . . ." Haldane gasped. "I've got no fucking fingers left. . . ."

It all seemed, in its horror, so wildly funny.

After a while they stopped laughing and lay looking at each other: a pair of privileged, shattered boys—no more than boys in reality, but with the experiences of lifetimes laid on them—and they stared at each other's grimed, sweating faces with pained smiles.

"Got a family?" Haldane asked eventually.

"In Yorkshire."

"Joined the flyboys from there?" Haldane had noticed what remained of his uniform.

"Yes. I shall go back."

"To the family?"

"No," Harry replied quickly. "To the corps. They need every flyer they can get."

Haldane opened his mouth as if he was going to reply, then evidently thought better of it, glancing only briefly down at Harry's inert body on the stretcher. "No, I rather meant, will you go back to Yorkshire when we get over there?"

Harry realized that he had not even thought of what he would do once he was back in England. "I suppose they'll put us in a hospital close to the port."

"They'll send you up country. Can't keep us all close to port, can they?"

Immediately, Harry saw the logic in this. He had only imagined himself, he realized, patched up as quickly as possible and kept close to Folkestone so that he could fly back to France. "I suppose then, home . . ." he murmured.

"Wife waiting?"

"No," he said. "You?"

"Delightfully unencumbered, old chap."

They smiled, but then Harry added, "I have a daughter."

Haldane seemed to think it was politic not to pursue this in the absence of any wife of Harry's; he glanced away, back to the ship. This silence, this unwillingness to discuss one's own tragedies or losses, was part of the fabric of a serving man. Harry had seen it before: talk of children or wives politely deflected. It was not done, and he had never wondered why until now.

He lay back down. It was not done because it was fatal to think of what one had left behind. It was done because it would be unbearable to think of the loving arms of a woman, or a parent, or a child. He had heard one officer say of his own newly married wife, "When I think of her and what might happen to her if I'm gone, my bowels turn to water. . . ." The others in the mess room had turned their faces away just as Haldane had done now. It was not out of disinterest, but rather the opposite. It was the voicing of every man's dread.

Of course, there were others who seemed so full of themselves, their personal glories, and their appetite for a glorious fight that they never considered the families that they had left behind, and never thought of what those families might be feeling. It was not their fault, Harry considered; all their training was designed to eradicate such thoughts from their heads. Women, children, joy, romance—it was worlds away. To think of that sort of thing at all was dangerously distracting. Just occasionally, the sensation of little Cecelia's hand in his would rise up out of a dream, and he would experience a passionate need to see her, a kind of extreme hunger of the soul.

But for the most part, they all acted as if war were a giant disorganized party. A famous man had even said so in public, and caused a furor last year. Harry struggled to remember his name. Granville? No, not Granville. It had been in the newspapers. Grenfell. Julian Grenfell.

He reached out and touched Haldane's shoulder. "That chap, Grenfell. Remember what he said? 'Never so well or happy.' Wonder what he'd say if he could see us now."

Haldane looked back at him with a mixed expression. "Heard he's here somewhere," he replied.

"What, just here?"

"In one of the hospitals. Head wound."

"Where'd you hear that?"

"Clearing station. Outside my namesake town."

"Good God. What a bad show." Harry paused. "All that fuss there was about him calling the war a party, or some such."

"Was he right?" Haldane asked, with a wry smile.

The question was an odd one. "Blasted if I know," Harry said.

But it sent him deep into thought. Well . . . *was* Grenfell right, he and his sort of man, blazing with glory? Grenfell had a DSO. None better. In the Royal Dragoons, a hero. Picture in the *Times*, a handsome chap who had won his DSO dispatching German snipers, stalking them as Harry had often stalked deer with his own father. Talents learned in the fields of aristocratic leisure.

He wondered if Grenfell had lain in the soaking wet earth waiting for that brief chance when the prey raises its head. Except that these had not been game birds or beasts, but men. Hitting a man between the eyes was not the same thing as hitting a stag. Or was it? Was it a game, all this? A game for which he and men like Grenfell and Haldane had been bred? He felt suddenly very sick, and now saw Haldane leaning over him, balancing on his elbows.

"All right, old man?"

"Poor Grenfell," he muttered. He didn't like to voice what had been going through his mind: it would be bad form, he knew.

"He was above me at Eton," Haldane said. "Used to like to crack a whip. Jolly good he was with it, too."

"A whip," Harry murmured.

Whips and stalking guns. All games. All games . . .

Beside him, Haldane stirred. "Can't lie about like this," he muttered. "Won't do at all. Behaving like invalids. It will drive me doolally." He had managed to sit up. "Hi there, you!" he yelled.

There was a VAD moving slowly down the line, dispensing cocoa from a huge, steaming enamel jug. "Hi there, sweetness! Please!"

"I shall come to you in a moment," she said, looking up.

"Please, dearest girl, just a moment."

She relented, and walked over. "What is it?"

"Might you do us the most enormous favor? We've been lying here for hours. Could you bring me that wheelchair contraption over there?"

"Oh no," she said, glancing over her shoulder to where he was pointing. "That would be quite against the rules."

Haldane leaned forward. Harry could see that he was a practiced flirt; not handsome, but with something louche about him, in just the right quantity to make a girl blush. "I say," Haldane murmured. "You're awfully pretty."

"Nonsense," she retorted. "Behave yourself."

"We didn't get stuck on this wretched dock by behaving ourselves," Haldane responded sharply. "Oh no, that wouldn't do. Cavendish here is a flyer. Breaks every rule in the book. He's been on a train for days, poor fellow. Needs to sit up properly and take the sea air. I could navigate about a bit if you'd only bring that wheelchair."

"But you're due to go on board shortly."

Haldane gave her a smile of ravishing innocence. "I promise that we won't miss the boat." He lowered his voice. "My gosh, aren't you the bees knees? Look at those wonderful eyes."

Harry laughed to himself. The VAD went hurrying off for the canvas chair. "You'll never get me in that thing," he warned Haldane.

"Won't I, though?" Haldane said. He had got to his knees, and, by balancing on his elbows for a second, managed to push himself upright. He swayed momentarily, looking absurdly rakish in his pajamas with the overcoat thrown over them. The VAD came back, pushing the chair. It creaked ominously. "Now help me with this gallant flyer," Haldane instructed the girl.

They manhandled him, the VAD holding the chair and Haldane looping his arms underneath Harry's hips. It was hard to tell who groaned most. "Fucking paddles," Haldane swore at his own hands. Harry chewed the inside of his lip. His legs, particularly both knees, were hugely swollen. The VAD reached down and let out the leg supports on the chair. "Oh please don't be long," she whispered. "I shall be in such trouble."

"You never gave me this chair," Haldane retorted, grinning. "I shall knock the man down who says you did."

Bumping over the cobbles was an excruciating experience for Harry. But he soon saw the black comedy in it: a man in pajamas and a great-coat pushing a wheelchair with his elbows, occasionally restraining the chair by slamming his foot against a wheel; Harry lopsidedly propped, feeling like an oversized baby. "Heyho and happy days," Haldane said. "Let's go and see who's singing."

They trundled down towards the wharves, Haldane resolutely occupying the center of the road while trucks, cars, and more mobile pedestrians navigated around them. Haldane acknowledged the protesting horns and the curses of the drivers with a nonchalant wave of his bandaged hand. "Get out of the way, you stupid bastard!" one driver shouted.

"And a cheery halloo to you, too," Haldane yelled back.

Somehow, they got onto a pavement of sorts. To Harry's astonishment, fishing vessels were moored up along the harbor wall in one section: Haldane steered towards them. Tables were set up alongside the quay, and fish were being routinely gutted. Women were behind each table, and the singing that they had heard was coming from them. Haldane stopped the wheelchair and the two men listened. The sun began to set slowly over the sea. "It's a late catch," Haldane murmured. "But then perhaps they're lucky to get out at all."

A girl at the nearest table wiped her hands in her canvas apron, and looked across at them. *"Anglaise?"*

"Oui, m'selle."

She smiled in a friendly fashion. She was a plain girl, with a plait of hair over one shoulder, and a broad, frank-looking face, but the smile was angelic.

"Vous êtes . . ." But Haldane's insouciance with the ladies seemed to have deserted him. Harry turned round in his seat as best he could, and saw Haldane's face crumple midway through his attempt at a compliment. Behind the girl's table, a child was sitting on a bale, chewing on its tiny fist as it stared at Haldane.

"M'sieur . . ." the girl began. She indicated the little boy, as if to say that they might be frightening the child.

At once, Haldane began turning the chair away. He coughed, and began in a forcedly cheerful way, "There's an American company comes here. New York to Rotterdam. It stops here. Or it did. And a steamer comes across every day from England. Or . . . it did, yes. It did. A pal and I came out here in 1911, for a jaunt, you know? It was because of the poster."

"The poster?"

"Sort of poster that brings a young fellow to France," Haldane said. "Nice picture of a ma'amselle on the beach in a pink frock and one of those frilled parasols, and another behind her in a bathing costume. . . ."

Harry felt in his pocket for the piece of paper that was folded there. His fingers connected with it, and he smiled at the memory of Caitlin scribbling her name for him, and an address in London. Caitlin Allington de Souza. "That's an extraordinary name," he had commented as she had shyly handed it to him. "Should I know it?" But she had not replied in the crowds of the train.

He turned his face back to the French girl with the child.

She had scooped up the child, and now held it on her hip. The little boy at once buried his face in her shoulder.

"I should think we look a fright," Harry murmured.

"I daresay, yes," Haldane replied.

They turned back for the boats.

As they got to the lines of stretchers, Harry looked up at Haldane. "Those days will come again," he said. "Jaunts with a pal, and pretty girls on the beach. Just see if they don't."

"I hope to God you're right," Haldane murmured.

It was seven o'clock, and the first stars were coming out when they took their turn in the embarkation lines.

In the Grosvenor Square house in London, it seemed to Octavia that the doctor was in with William for a very long time.

Eventually, he came out of her husband's bedroom and placed a consoling hand on her arm. "I understand your boy is being brought back from France today."

"Yes . . . we just had another telegram. The ship is delayed. They don't expect it now until the early hours of this morning, at the earliest. I expect William is fretting about it."

"He is indeed."

She glanced down the wide stairs and into the lavish hallway. "Let's not stand here," she said. "I've asked for tea in the drawing room."

"That sounds very good."

He walked ahead of her down the steps, gallantly offering an arm at the landing halfway down. She felt slightly embarrassed—she hardly knew him. He was Hetty de Ray's physician, a very much older person than their own man in Yorkshire. He was formally dressed in a long black frock coat, too much like an undertaker for her taste, and his face was similarly somber.

When they were arranged more comfortably in the drawing room, Octavia shooed away the maid. "I shall pour myself."

She waited until the girl had gone, and smiled wanly at the doctor. "They stand about like sheep. There isn't a decent trained girl to be had in London. I think this one has come from somewhere in East Anglia. I can hardly understand a word she says, and I don't think she understands *me*."

She realized abruptly that she was babbling. It really didn't matter just now how good or bad the maids were. "I'm sorry," she murmured. "It's of no consequence. Please tell me about my husband."

The doctor was sitting perched on the edge of the Chinese-upholstered chaise longue, looking uncomfortable in such a feminine room. "From what Lord Cavendish tells me," he began. "This has been a problem for some time."

"You mean his heart?"

"Yes indeed, his heart."

"But he has never said a word to me."

"He has been experiencing chest pain for more than a year."

She put her hand to her throat. "A year!"

"In my experience, such conditions are progressive. Lord Cavendish is of an age and disposition . . ."

"What do you mean, 'disposition'?"

"His diplomatic work is stressful, of course."

"Naturally."

"That, and the prolonged traveling. The news of your son. A general tendency to simply endure, as most men do, without recourse to a surgeon, without advice. All these are contributory factors," he explained.

"You mean a disposition to drive himself too hard?"

"Yes indeed."

"And to ignore his own symptoms."

"Quite so," the doctor said. "And I believe his own father . . . there may be a hereditary cause."

"You think that his father had a heart condition?"

"Merely a guess. I understand he collapsed and died when he was fifty-six."

"Yes, I think so. . . . William was only sixteen."

"No post mortem, but in the circumstances one wonders if . . ."

"Of course," she murmured. She was staring down at the untouched tea tray, realizing that she really knew nothing about the father-in-law that she had never met, other than that he had been kindly and rather unworldly, shut up in Rutherford with his botany and archaeology and his quiet, gentlemanly pursuits. William's life, by contrast, had been much more in the public eye: his work in Parliament. His constant shuttling between Paris and London for the Foreign Office.

She looked up at the doctor, affecting composure that she did not feel. Really, in absolute truth, she knew nothing of William's inner life. He kept so much to himself, sealed himself away from her. If he lay awake and worried about Harry, she would not know; they had not slept together for months.

William's naked plea for them to be closer, his impatience and fury suddenly shown behind his customary mask, had shocked her. She had been living, she thought suddenly, in some sort of paralyzed state since John Gould left. The cracks in their marriage had been papered over. She had tried to ignore her own need, tried to think of the children, tried to think of Rutherford—anything, *anything* in fact but Gould and the crisis of last year.

And she had done it by turning off her own feelings as one might close off a faucet, or draw curtains against the dark. She had tried to tell herself that the whole paraphernalia of Rutherford—the family name, the need for discretion, the continuance of its long history without scandal, without so much as a murmur, a ripple on the smooth running of their lives, was all that mattered in the end.

She had learned to smother whatever memories rose to the surface of that life. She thought that she had been doing the right thing, if not for herself, then for her children, and even for John Gould, who deserved a pretty young wife and a whole train of delightful children of his own. And if she cried about it in the privacy of her own room—well, that was a necessary evil. She poured her energies into thinking of the Blessington mills, if she thought coherently or seriously at all. That was something real that she could control and alter and make good, in a way that she could not alter her own life.

And all this time she had thought that William had dealt with it all in the same way, dismissing it from his mind. He had certainly acted the part of the unconcerned husband month after month. But yet, this afternoon . . .

Blood rushed to her face. It was not William's work that had brought about the attack. It was not that, or Harry's wounds, or concern of any kind for Rutherford. It was she—she and Gould. Gould's letters. Her telegram to him aboard the *Lusitania*. They said that people had a broken heart—that popular, outworn phrase, used so often it could seem meaningless—but she had thought to herself many a time over the last autumn and winter and spring that she really knew at last what it meant. She had felt that uncomfortable grinding pain in her chest herself. But, in William's case, perhaps it was actually true. He had actually felt . . .

"Oh madam," the doctor said. "Come, come."

She had not realized that she was weeping. The man came to her side and patted her hand.

"I'm so sorry," she whispered.

"There is no urgent need to worry," he was murmuring. "Lord Cavendish is, it seems by first examination, in otherwise decent health. He is not overweight. He tells me he has had no gout, no arthritis." He smiled reassuringly. "With your permission, I shall ask a colleague to come, a specialist," he continued. "For a second opinion on the cardiac problem. There is every chance that, given absolute rest, your husband will recover."

"He is not a man to rest. He would hate that."

"He has no choice," was the reply. "Bed rest is the treatment for a heart attack. No exercise, no noise, no heavy foods. Absolute rest."

"But Harry . . ."

The doctor smiled, gathering his things together. "Out of the question. Your husband will not be traveling, in any form at all, for at least a month. May I suggest that his valet goes, perhaps, or a trusted member of staff? If you think it imperative that your son is met at Folkestone."

She rose to her feet, accompanying him to the door of the room.

I am not sending Cooper to meet Harry at Folkestone, she thought determinedly to herself, even as she shook the man's hand and thanked him for his suggestion.

I am not sending a member of staff to meet my son.

The *Lusitania* still described its arcing circle.

It seemed to John Gould that the ship was actually gaining speed, although he guessed that that was impossible. Perhaps it was the lurch of the angle, the tilt towards the water, which seemed to make them go faster.

On deck, it was sheer bedlam, a seething chaos. There was no loudspeaker system, and so every now and then one could hear an officer's voice raised in command or information to the crowds, but John only caught a word here and there.

It was to be women and children first in the lifeboats, of course. A whole family went past him; they looked as if they had come from third class. They were staring about themselves, progressing in an extended slow group like a ponderous snail, with all the children holding their mother's skirt, and, in the center of them, an elderly women was being held up and half carried along. In front of them, a man tried to part the way, yelling at the top of his voice, "My children . . . make way . . . my children . . ."

No one took any notice of him.

As John stood staring at the little group, a man careered into him, almost knocking the breath from his body. John recognized him as one of the men who had been playing cards every day in the smoking saloon. He was red in the face, laughing, holding a cigar. "Sorry, old chap!" he boomed. "What happened? What's the matter?"

"We've been torpedoed," John told him.

"Torpedoed?" the man repeated, laughing harder. He reeked of whisky. "You don't say! Torpedo, eh?"

Someone else, another gambler, came up at the man's shoulder. "It's not a torpedo. It's a mine."

"We'll have to limp in," the first one boomed. "Be buggered! I shall be late for the blasted London train."

As if to answer this, the ship tilted again, righted itself, and settled back at the new angle. There came the shattering of glass somewhere below.

"What's that?" the red-faced man yelled, spilling the contents of his whisky glass over John's shoes, swiveling his head to left and right. "What the devil's that?" He turned back to John. "I had a pair of aces," he said. "Damn and blast the bloody Germans. A pair of aces!"

John left them.

He made his way between the crowds. People were in varying stages of dismay, bewilderment, and panic. He passed two middle-aged women sobbing piteously. He laid his hand on the arm of the nearest. "You must put on a lifejacket," he said.

The woman turned a tear-streaked face to his. "I daren't go back into my cabin," she said. "What shall we do?"

"Where's your berth?" John asked.

"In first class . . ." She gave him the cabin number.

"Wait here," he told her.

He fought his way back until he reached the right door. There, he came face-to-face with a first-class steward. Behind him was a mass of passengers who had, it seemed, made their way up the main staircase. The steward barred his way and turned back to the crowd, shouting, "You need to go to the promenade deck for the lifeboats. The promenade deck!" But the crowds pushed forward. John stepped back and they passed him. The instinct was to get higher on the ship. "It's all right," the steward said to him, over the heads of people. "They won't listen to me, but it's all right. She's not going down."

John looked at him and saw in the man's face that he was lying. Even as he had spoken, John had had to brace his feet on the deck as it slipped sideways. He gave the steward a smile and went in through the door.

He remembered then how the men who had survived the *Titanic* had been received on both sides of the Atlantic; how vilified they had been. He decided that he wouldn't get in a boat while there were still women and children about, no matter how urgent that need might become. Running as best he could towards the women's cabin, he passed his own and shoved open the door. His lifebelt had gone.

In their cabin, he found two lifebelts neatly sandwiched in the wardrobe; snatching them up he went out again and was promptly met by a teenage girl who was clutching a younger boy, her face ghost white.

"Are you all right?" he asked. "Where are you going?"

The girl's breath came in stuttering gasps; he could hardly hear her reply. "We have lost Mother," she said. "Do you think she has gone this way?"

Making an instant decision, not knowing if he would ever find the women again, John got to his knees and put the lifebelts on the children. He guessed that the girl was about fourteen, the boy a little younger. Making sure that the belts were tied tightly, he patted the boy on the shoulder. "You must be brave. Can you swim?"

"I can," the boy said. "My sister can't."

The girl began to shake. The neatly curled ringlets on either side of her face trembled, and he felt a rush of sorrow. Inside her babyish clothes she was quite a young woman, though frighteningly skinny. Growing like a beanpole, he thought. Growing up, growing out of her old self. Even now, in her fright, she was self-conscious, embarrassed. Her brother looked hard at her, and responded with a pout of disdain, and gazed up at John as if ready to take orders. John took both their hands. "Come with me."

There were still people trying to get on deck. On the stairway, in the stifling crush of passengers, a man elbowed John in the face. The man's foot was next planted on John's; he was literally trying to climb over the children.

"Have a care," John said. "There are young ones here."

"Young ones be damned," came the reply.

John let go of the girl's hand and caught hold of the back of the man's jacket. "Act like a gentleman," he hissed in the man's ear.

The girl screamed; the man had almost torn the collar from her coat as he tried to haul her off the steps.

"Have it your own way," John said. He released the boy, grabbed the man with both hands by the hair, and pulled him off his feet. He topped backwards, narrowly missing those below them, his hands grazing along the wall until he slumped in a heap at the bottom of the stairs.

"Oh, good show," a woman beside him breathed.

John grabbed the children again, and they got out into daylight. Turning, John saw that the woman who had murmured her congratulations was wearing her lifebelt in a comically haphazard way; he stopped her, and put his hands on it.

"Don't touch me!" she cried.

"You will sink like a stone with it tied like that," John tried to explain. "Madam, it's on upside down. It'll turn you head down in the water."

"You'll not have it!" she hissed, and tore his hands away.

"I don't want it. You've tied it . . ."

But she was haring away, shooting back little baleful looks over her shoulder at him.

Ahead of him, he saw the familiar debonair form of Alfred Vanderbilt. The millionaire was smiling in his usual relaxed fashion at a woman who that moment had rushed on deck, clutching a baby in her arms. As they passed the little group, John heard Vanderbilt say, "Don't cry. It's quite all right." To which the woman gasped, "No, it isn't!" John paused for a moment, watching Vanderbilt in amazement as he calmly gave the woman his own lifebelt and tied it on her.

John looked down at the children with him. "What's your name?" he asked the girl.

"Annalisa," she said. "And this is Joseph. Mother went to see what the noise was, and we were going to wait, but then another lady said we were to leave the cabin."

"And my name is Gould. John Gould. Is your father here?"

"No," she told him. "Father is waiting at Liverpool for us."

"What does your mother look like? What is her name?"

"She's . . . she's a pretty lady. . . ."

"I guess there's a lot of pretty ladies on board just now. What's your surname?"

"Petheridge."

"So we're looking for Mrs. Petheridge," John said. "And so, Petheridge brood, let's shimmy along to the boats." He glanced at Annalisa. "Can you shimmy?"

She blushed and smiled. "No."

"She's not allowed to dance," her brother said.

"We'll tango for once, shall we?" John asked the girl. "Tango like mad for the Promenade Deck?"

"Yes," she whispered.

"You're crazy," Joseph said.

"You're right," John agreed. "I'm one hundred percent crazy just now."

It seemed to him that the water of the ocean was shining brighter than before, shimmering in a haze. He could see no other ships, but surely the *Lusitania* was sending out an SOS. They were just a mile or two from land; there must be a harbor nearby and any number of little fishing boats, at least. And then, they were in a busy shipping lane. There must be larger boats. . . . He scanned the water.

Out there somewhere was the submarine that had fired the torpedo. Was the captain looking at them now? Was he seeing what his work had done? Just for a second, John thought he saw a periscope way out there in the rippling opalescent mirror of the sea. *You bastard*, he thought savagely. *Got a good seat for the show?*

"That lady is not very well," Annalisa whispered at his side.

He looked where she had nodded. A woman was collapsed on a steamer chair, clutching her heavily pregnant stomach and wailing in distress.

"Someone will help her," he said, and pulled Annalisa and Joseph onward.

They struggled towards the boats, caught up in a wave of humanity. Some men were carrying their wives, circling their waists with one arm and almost dragging them off their feet in the tumult. The children pressed closer to him; he heard Annalisa uttering little cries as she was stepped on and pushed. Joseph, on his right-hand side, said nothing, although at one point he tripped and John had to haul him to his feet. All three of them nearly lost their footing then. "Be careful!" John shouted. "Mind out for the children."

They got to a lifeboat. It was being lowered even though it was plain to see that the ship was listing at something like thirty degrees. John looked up at it swinging in the davits and thought quite lucidly, in a moment of strange calm, that it was not possible to lower boats with the ship at that angle.

Just then, he saw Captain Turner appear on the bridge. He was shouting something.

"What did he say?" John asked an officer who was just three or four people ahead of him, and had been staring up at the lifeboats just as he had done. The officer turned around.

"He says not to lower the boats."

"Why, why?" screamed a man at the officer's side. "Get the women in, get the children in, she's going down!"

"She's not going down," the officer retorted. "She's aground." He started pushing and pulling his way to the front of the crowd. "Everybody out of the boats!"

The man who had screamed that they were sinking now turned and looked John straight in the eye. "The bow's submerging," he said, in a low, brutal voice—a murderous voice of fury. "Can't they see it? She's not aground. She's going under."

There was chaos as the officers began pulling passengers who had fought their way to a lifeboat out of them. John saw one regally dressed woman, still in a massive fur coat, and her hat tied on with a blue chiffon scarf, resisting the command. "Take your hands off me! Take your hands off me!" The lifeboat was shaking, swinging. Other passengers clung on to its rails.

John saw the man ahead of him go to the side of the boat and pull a revolver from the inner pocket of his jacket. He pointed it at the officer. "If you don't lower that boat, I'll fire this," he said. "I mean what I say. I'll kill you. My wife is in that boat."

John pulled at Annalisa and Joseph. "Come with me," he said to them. "Let's try the other side."

"What did that man say?" Annalisa said. She had begun to cry.

"Never mind," John told her.

He pushed; he shoved. And was shoved back in return. Passen-

gers were trying to go both ways, to either side of the boat. Someone
hit him hard on the back; it felt like a fist, but he was too tightly
hemmed in to turn around.

In the wailing scrum of the crowd, Joseph's voice came calmly
and clearly at his side. "Do you know how many boats there are?"

"No, I don't," John said. "But there'll be enough." His heart was
hammering at his rib cage in panic. The blank sun-white sea looked
nearer. Under his feet, he thought he felt another, more muted,
explosion.

"There are twenty-two clinker-built and twenty-six collapsibles,"
Joseph said.

In surprise, John looked down at him. It was the sort of fact a
typical boy would seize on: how many lifeboats, how many engines,
how many decks.

"Well, that's plenty," John said, trying to smile.

"We shall be quite safe," Joseph informed him.

It was barely ten minutes since the ship had been struck. When
they got to the starboard side, John saw that some people were leaping across the gap to get into wildly swinging boats. Others hung
back, looking at the eight or nine feet between them and the boats,
and then staring down below at the sea some eighty or ninety feet
below. John glanced over the side and thought it was a hell of a way
to fall, and, in that instant, he realized that he had no life preserver.
I'm going to die, he thought. It was simply true. He stood watching
the boats and saw people rushing back to the port side, now so much
higher than the starboard. But simple reason showed that a boat
would be much harder to launch from the port than the starboard.

To his left-hand side, some twenty yards away, he suddenly
glimpsed Robert Matthews standing with Annie at the rail. They
were clasping each other, but nothing about their body language

suggested that Annie was preparing to get in a lifeboat. They were looking down at the sea, her head on Robert's shoulder. As he was swept on with the crowd, John glanced back. Robert was saying something to Annie; he raised her hand to his and kissed it. John couldn't help but think of Annie's anxiety while they had waited in the Customs Hall in New York. Both he and Robert had reassured her; perhaps they had even made a little fun of her worries. He regretted that now; he wished that he could apologize to her. In the next second, in the crush, he lost sight of them completely.

He pushed his way towards a boat that was already loaded with women and children, some screaming, some crying, others white and mute with shock as the boat hung precipitously over the ship's side. "Let these children on!" he shouted.

Annalisa stopped moving. "I can't get on without Mother," she protested.

He shoved her unceremoniously towards the side. "I promise I'll find your mother," he said. "Just get in the boat."

She looked at him. "Mother is not there," she said. "She's not in that boat. You're lying to me; you won't look for her at all." She had become rigid, elbows tucked into her sides, hands clenched. He pushed her, but she would not budge an inch.

John turned to her brother. "Joseph," he said, "you must get your sister into the boat, and follow her. Do you understand?"

Joseph said nothing. But he nodded.

The ship was groaning. The Marconi wires and the lines from the funnels were making an infernal straining sound; from below came something monstrous, a combined rushing and crashing noise as furniture was churned to the starboard side in all the public rooms. They were descending faster now; the lower decks must be all but submerged, he thought. And it had only been minutes since they were struck. How many, twelve, thirteen? Surely not more than that. . . .

Men were trying to heave the two-ton lifeboat outwards, but they were just ordinary passengers. *Where are the crew?* John wondered. And realized that they must be belowdecks, trapped. There was no one who knew what they were doing. No one.

He shoved Annalisa and Joseph to the rail and held Annalisa up. She kicked against the deck, against his legs, crying, *No, no,* and, just as he had decided to lower her back down, a man grabbed her and flung her outwards. She landed in the boat and a handful of women caught her. "Now you," John said to Joseph. "Be quick, be quick."

But Joseph had caught hold of the rail. "I can't do that," he said.

"It's only a few feet."

"I don't mean that. I mean ladies first, and little kids. But I'm not little. I'm twelve."

John looked into his pitifully earnest face. The boy was not budging. He put an arm round his shoulder. "All right," he conceded. "If it comes to it, we grown-up fellows will jump together."

Joseph simply nodded. "She's in boat twelve," he said quietly. "We shall have to remember. Annalisa is in boat twelve."

Keeping an arm around him, John watched two men and a woman climb the rope falls to get into the boat. They scuttled like crabs, clinging to each other, none of them wearing lifebelts. A man was standing on the *Lusitania*'s rail, trying to place his foot on the rail of the lifeboat; it began to dip at the bows from the weight of the passengers crawling on the rope falls. An officer shouted, "Let her go faster by the stern."

John switched his gaze from the boat to Annalisa's face. "Joseph," she was calling. "Joseph."

All at once, the lifeboat dipped at the stern. *They've corrected it too fast*, John thought. And, in the next instant, the lifeboat tipped and went straight down, eighty feet stern-first, throwing passengers out as it fell.

It was a matter of a split second; John leaned out in horror; the boat was upside down, with a few bodies in the water, and the scattered faces of a few others rising to the surface of the sea. Annalisa had vanished, together with the women who had been holding her.

He struggled to keep upright; all around them came the screams and shouts of those simultaneously trying to launch boat fourteen. He stared at it now as it was lowered about halfway down, the passengers on it realizing that they were swinging now over the upturned hull of boat twelve, which had been dragged back in the current by the *Lusitania*'s dogged listing speed. To one side of him he glimpsed, rather than saw, a flailing of arms, a tangled shouting scrum, agonized yells as the ropes broke free of boat fourteen. It fell straight down, landing on top of those desperately floundering in the water out of boat twelve.

He turned Joseph away, pressed him to his own body, trying to obliterate the scene.

Farther down the deck, boat eighteen suddenly swung inwards, smashing against the superstructure of the *Lusitania*, crushing a crowd of people who were standing there. He got down on his knees and made the boy face him. "Listen to me, Joseph," he said. "Look me in the face. Don't look anywhere else. Don't listen to anything else. Listen to me, just to me, okay?"

"Yes," Joseph answered.

"Pretty soon the ship's going to go over," John told him. "When she's going, we'll jump up on that rail and we'll wait for the water to come over our feet, and then we'll swim. We'll swim like madmen, okay? There'll be things in the water—people, things from the ship, but don't you look at them, okay? You're going to swim quicker than you've ever done. Make for a lifeboat or a floating chair or a collapsible. Something like that. Do you hear me?"

Joseph was solemnly staring straight at him, ignoring the hell around them. "Yes," he said. "I hear."

"All right, then," John muttered, getting up and taking hold of his hand. "All right, then, all right. . . ."

Fear smothered him, making him gasp.

Somewhere even now he could hear an officer shouting that the ship wouldn't sink.

Way down the starboard deck, he suddenly saw Charles Lauriat jump into a lifeboat and set to like a wild man trying to free its after falls; at the other end, a steward was hacking away at the thick ropes with nothing better than a pocket knife. He saw Lauriat begin to shout at the occupants, but there was no time left. John could see plainly what he was trying to tell them—that the boat was still attached to the ship and would go down with her. They had only seconds to get out. But nobody seemed to be moving at all. They were clinging to the stuff in the boat—the oars, the kegs of water, the boat hooks, the sails, as if the clutter could help them. Above them all, the four massive funnels of the *Lusitania* loomed ever further over, scattering a huge volume of dust and soot. He saw Lauriat climb onto the lifeboat rail and jump.

He looked away. He thought of Octavia. It was the last coherent thought before the end. He saw her face languidly smiling underneath him, he saw the long green lawns of Rutherford; he was at her side again that very first morning in the library.

Images of her enveloped him in a wholesale rush. He thought of her lying with him in the woodland far above Rutherford's parkland. He thought of her hands on him. All the secrets she had told him: her abusive, insulting father; her grief at the realization that it had been money, and not love, that had made William marry her; her joy at the children—running down to the river and helping Harry to fish when he was just a little boy—summer sun on water . . . on water . . .

And then it happened.

The stuff of his nightmares, the scene he had dreaded for years, the imagined terror when he had read about the *Titanic* and the *Empress*. It came rolling wildly towards him now; not the soft whispering water of Rutherford, but the shocking cold of the Atlantic. The sea was suddenly up to the rail.

"Now!" he shouted to Joseph, and hauled on the boy's hand. But at his side he could feel that Joseph was already climbing, almost casually, and he saw the boy's face level with his own for a split second. The water boiled over them; and he felt Joseph's hand dragged through his, his fingernails scoring along John's palm.

And then he was gone. Then everything was gone. John was underwater, and felt his foot caught in the rail as he went down, down, down. He kicked furiously; it came free, and in the next instant a rope wound itself around his body. Maniacally he pulled at it. It was like being in the coils of a snake. He felt extraordinary pressure on his eardrums and opened his eyes.

The sea was a green whirlpool. Past him went torn shapes of chairs, oars, bodies, clothes. In the surreal and ever-growing darkness, a dead man floated past him, and his bloodied hand slapped John's face and snatched through his hair. In the next moment, he was hit by the body's leather-booted foot. It caught him under the chin, and he bit through his own tongue with the force of it.

The suction was appalling; the *Lusitania* was going straight to the bottom like an arrow. He felt the ship move past him, a monster groaning through the deeps, and he put out his hand and he felt her painted side, her enormous bulk, with his fingertips, a sensation of such strange intimacy that he believed he was already dead.

He was alongside the dropping, dropping ship; ever further, floating weightless in the dark, caught in her intimate embrace.

Chapter 8

*D*avid Nash walked from the tiny railway station at Was-
thwaite all the way to Rutherford. It had taken some time
to extricate himself from the congratulations of the station master,
Baddeley, who had insisted on shaking his hand and introducing him
to every bemused passenger waiting for the three o'clock train to York.

It was ironic, because Baddeley had never used to like him much;
once, standing by when David had dropped a piece of luggage, he
had even called him a "nancy boy." Apparently, though, David wasn't
such an embarrassment now. Or perhaps it was just the uniform.
Even snotty-nosed little boys had saluted the uniform as he had
made his way here today from Lancashire.

He reached Rutherford's gates just as the afternoon began to
cloud over. He stood at the entrance to the long, beech-lined drive,
and he felt suddenly overcome by sentiment. He didn't know when
he would be coming here again—and he felt that this was much
more his home than the house in the village a couple of miles back.

He had worked here for twelve years, coming here as a hallboy. Lord Cavendish had approved of him, and Bradfield had taken a sort of shine to him—and—well, all the rest was history. Through all those years, Rutherford had fed and clothed and educated him: it was in Lord Cavendish's library that he had first picked up a volume of poetry, and Shakespeare's plays, and Plato's *Republic*. He had read Dante's *Inferno* here through the course of one winter, page by stolen page in candlelight when everyone else had gone to bed. He had read all the Romantic poets through the length of one glorious spring; and struggled through *Paradise Lost* that same autumn. It had been much more of an education to him than the hapless efforts of the village school. The words had played like a beautiful and secret orchestra in his mind, and, as a consequence, he had Rutherford to thank for his own poems, poor as they were. He would never forget that.

Halfway up the drive, he cut quickly across the lawns of the lower terrace and circled around to the back of the house through the kitchen gardens. As he got to the back door, it began to rain, and he walked quickly into the corridor by the laundry, brushing the droplets from the shoulders of his greatcoat.

He looked up, and was surprised to see Mary Richards standing there watching him. She was out of breath.

"I saw you come up the drive," she said. "I ran down from the drawing room. I'm meant to be cleaning." She laughed, and added in a whisper, "For the fortieth time. She's possessed, that woman." Then she glanced over her shoulder, back along the kitchen corridor. "If she catches me, I shall be for it," she said, and looked back at him.

He'd never so much as held her hand. Not for more than a moment, anyway. But the fact that she was out of breath, the fact that she had run down to meet him, and now stood, plainly embarrassed at herself—Mary Richards, of all people, lost for words, playing helplessly with the tie on her pinafore apron, and such a glad expression on her face—God, it gave him courage.

He walked straight over to her, and put his arms around her, and kissed her. He fully expected her to resist him, to push him away. But she returned his kiss, and, when they parted, she held on to him.

"I thought you might not like it," he said.

She smiled at him. "Not like it?" she said. "Tha's bakk'ud in coming for'add, lad." *You're backward in coming forward.* He laughed out loud. It was a sign that the feisty little termagant he'd known so long, who could slay you with a look if you so much as stepped out of line, was moved so much that she had clean forgotten that she was a parlor maid, and slipped straight back into her broadest Yorkshire accent.

"Like the uniform, then?" he asked.

"It's not the uniform I like, it's the man in it," she told him.

"Maybe I should always have been forward, then," he said. "Like Harrison."

"If you'd been forward like Harrison, I wouldn't give you the time of day," she told him decisively. She turned and walked briskly along the corridor, then looked back at him. "Well, don't stand there with your mouth open," she said. "You'll catch flies."

Grinning, he followed her to the kitchen. "Look who's here, Mrs. Carlisle," Mary called out. The cook looked up from her work, and a beaming smile came to her face. "Well, lad! Look at you! You look proper fine," she said, hands on hips and assessing him.

Shyly, he took off his cap.

"That's right, sit yer'sen down," Mrs. Carlisle said. "You too, Mary."

"Oh, I daren't."

"It's half past five, and past teatime," Mrs. Carlisle said. "Where's the others?"

"She's got them doing all sorts. Donkey-stoning the flight of steps at the main door, and scrubbing the hall; doing the paintings with a fine brush. All sorts."

Mrs. Carlisle looked levelly at David. "Mrs. Jocelyn has taken a bit of turn," she told him. "We do what she says. But I shan't be bullied."

"I ought to go back up," Mary murmured. She still had not sat down.

"You'll do no such thing," Mrs. Carlisle replied. "You'll sit down for a pot of tea and the seed cake I've made this morning. Take down that tin on the shelf there, and bring the plates."

"But . . ."

"If she comes in here, I'll speak to her," the cook replied. "It's not every day one of our chaps comes back to see us. Lord Cavendish would have him up to talk to him, if he were here."

"He's not at home?"

"No, lad. They've gone to London, him and her ladyship, and Miss Charlotte. Amelie and Cooper too, of course. Miss Louisa is still here. She's taken a shine to the bairn." She took the kettle from the range and made the tea.

"That's not all she's taken a shine to," Mary said, and nudged David with her arm. He raised an eyebrow inquiringly.

"Tush, tush. No more," Mrs. Carlisle reprimanded.

Mary, after hesitating another moment, sat down next to David. "We've had such a to-do," she told him. "Master Harry is coming back from France, and they've gone down to the London house to meet him."

"Do you know any more on his injury?" Mary had written to David that Harry had been shot down; he had received the letter only a day or two ago, just before he had been given leave.

"No, not really. They don't tell us much, of course. Amelie said just before she went that her ladyship was very happy about him coming back, though. She cried and everything."

"Well, she's got feelings like the rest of us, I suppose," Mrs. Carlisle said.

David took the offered cup of tea gratefully. He couldn't remember when he had last eaten or had a hot drink. He had been traveling for nine hours. They had only told him at eight o'clock this morning that he had forty-eight hours' leave before the regiment moved on to another training ground. "And what's this about Miss Louisa?"

Mary, glancing at Mrs. Carlisle, said nothing. The cook was holding her gaze with a warning look. But then when Mrs. Carlisle looked away, busying herself by cutting the cake for them, Mary mouthed, "Jack," in David's direction. He widened his eyes to show his surprise. Under the lip of the table, Mary wound her fingers together in a sort of knot by way of illustration, and smothered a smile.

"By heck," David murmured. "A man can't go away for two minutes in this place."

Mrs. Carlisle looked up. "What's that?"

"Nothing," he said, shaking his head in bemusement as he took his plate.

They all sat companionably together for a few moments, and then Mrs. Carlisle abruptly pushed back her chair and got to her feet. "I shall go and find those girls. This won't do."

It was unheard-of for a cook to leave her own domain and go up to the main house, unless summoned. It was trespass, for a start, on the housekeeper's territory.

"Oh, do you think you ought?" Mary asked.

"I've had about enough of this," Mrs. Carlisle replied. "I shall be back as soon as I find her. Those girls and Hardy are entitled to a sit-down at five. Donkey-stoning the steps, indeed! I never heard of such a thing. They're Portland stone, they don't need whitening. Anyone would think we're a mill terrace—that's what they do in those back-to-back streets. Donkey-stoning! It's nonsense."

They watched her leave, still muttering to herself. They heard her go along the stone corridor and tap on Mrs. Jocelyn's door, and then, farther on, at Mr. Bradfield's. They heard his door open, a few exchanged words, and then the door closed again.

"He's let her in," Mary said, surprised. Mr. Bradfield's room was the inner sanctum. She gave David a smile. "It's been very strange," she admitted. "Mrs. Jocelyn . . . well, she isn't right. She's up and down stairs all day, over and over. She goes in all the rooms and walks around them."

"Mrs. Carlisle's right about those steps, though. It'll ruin the look of them."

"We know it. But what can you do? She goes on and on about things being clean. And she prays all the time."

"She always did."

"I know. But it's loudly now. We can hear her from here. "Lord, strike down Thy enemies," and all that. It's right frightening, David." She paused. "And she goes on about his lordship in a funny way."

"What do you mean?"

Mary bit her lip. "How good he is, and how she's always served him since before he married Lady Octavia."

"Well, I suppose that's all true."

"It's just the *way* she says it. And the way she talks about her ladyship. She's called her a sinner, here in this very room, in front of all of us."

"Why? What's her ladyship sinned over?"

"Mr. Gould last year . . ."

"Ah, that," David murmured. "She ought to know her Bible if anyone does," he mused. "Let him that is without sin cast the first stone, and all that."

Mary smiled broadly. "What sins do you think Mrs. Jocelyn has, then?"

"Coveting another woman's husband, by the sound of it."

"David!"

"You don't think so?"

She considered. "I don't suppose it's our place to think about it at all."

They sat in silence awhile, then he slowly took her hand. "And what about your father?"

"He's coming tomorrow. We got word. That's another thing she doesn't like. It's because her ladyship asked for him." She paused, eyeing him. "She hit me over it."

"Hit you!"

"She slapped my face. Said I had gone behind her back, or some such thing."

Blood rushed to David's face. His first instinct was to go and find Mrs. Jocelyn for himself; he half rose, but Mary pulled him back down. "It doesn't matter. She's a bit off her head, like Mrs. Carlisle says."

"All the same," he told her. "It's not right. Things are changing all over, Mary. People like us needn't stand for it anymore. You'll see what I mean when the war's over. You can't have men fighting and seeing their mates dying and then come back and it's all the same. They'll take orders from officers, but to take orders afterwards . . . well, I reckon it'll stick in the throats of most folk."

"We need to work."

"Aye, but not to be treated badly. You know what I mean. You saw the mills. They've not much changed."

"Her ladyship ordered all the children out. It caused a fuss over there," Mary said. "But soon after, the women went to the gates and said they couldn't survive without the wages. Two days later, the overseers brought all the children back. I don't even know if her ladyship knows about that."

"She'll know when she comes back."

"I've heard say that they won't take orders from her."

David smiled slowly. "Well, after all, she's only a woman."

Mary gave him a playful slap. "Some women aren't to be trifled with, my lad."

"Lord, I know that."

Then, "But I'm more bothered about Father," Mary continued, frowning. "I sent word to the mill and I asked the men to make sure he was tidy, and keep drink from him. But I don't know if they will have done. They've probably sent him off with a few jars at the pub. I'm that worried about it."

"I can stay till tomorrow. Do you want me to talk to him?"

"Oh," she said, and she blushed. "Till tomorrow. That's good."

They sat in silence for a while, smiling at each other. Eventually, she said, "You write such a nice letter, David."

"You like them?"

"I'm sure it's not all what you make it out to be, though."

"How do you mean?"

"Well, as if it's fun."

"It isn't. But you've got to see the bright side. And we have some games, and concerts sometimes. They've got me playing football. I can't say I'm much good at it."

"Oh, David," she murmured, looking down at their joined hands. "We've been reading the paper . . . you know about the Kents?"

"Yes. But don't think that's going to happen to me."

She looked up at him with a critical, determined look on her face. "We have to get a few things straight, you and me."

"Such as?"

"Such as not telling me a lot of rubbish. You don't know if it'll happen to you or not. I'm not stupid, David. So don't tell me any kind of silly story that's it's all going to be all right, when it might not be."

"Well, thanks for the vote of confidence."

She gripped his hand tightly. "If it were just you, I know you'd hold on till hell froze over," she said. "I know you'd face down anything. But it isn't a choice like that, is it? It's bloody murder out there, David, and you know it."

He nodded slowly. He turned her hand over in his and smoothed a finger over her palm. "Yes," he said. "We all know. But you can't think that way, otherwise you'd never go. You'd just turn tail and run for the hills. So we'll stick together and mind each other's backs. And keep our spirits up. That's all we can do."

"And not be a hero."

He laughed. "And not be a hero."

"Promise me."

"I promise," he said.

"Neither you nor Arthur. You tell him that."

"I will."

He looked at her with deep affection. She could be such a fierce girl; he liked that in her. "I hope I don't bring sorrow to your door, Mary," he murmured.

Her mouth dropped open slightly; her eyes rapidly filled with tears. "Oh hush," she said. And she put her arms around his neck. "You're right," she whispered into his ear. "You'll come back, and we'll get married, and we'll have a little family, and we'll work here if we're able to, and it will all be just as it was. But better."

And then she sprang back from him, apparently only just then realizing what she had said. He started to laugh, because the look of embarrassment on her face was so comical. "Jumping the gun a bit, aren't you?" he teased.

"Well, I . . ." She blushed harder. David watched her with fascination; he'd never seen her react to anything like that. He hadn't even known until this last hour that she could color up at all. "Well, you've got ahead of me," he said. "You've been thinking a lot while I've been away, by the looks of it."

She dropped his hand as if it were a hot brick and started fussing with the teacups. He snatched back her hand and forcibly turned her to face him.

"Don't make fun of me." She dipped her head.

"Do you suppose Mrs. Jocelyn would give you a week off later this year?" he asked. "Do you think you might be able to come down to Wiltshire?"

"Wiltshire? Why?"

"We're going to Shropshire in two days. Then they reckon Wiltshire a week or two later. To Fovant, the big camp there. But the lads say they'll give us a bit of leave before we go to France."

"And when will that be?"

"Ah, there's the question. Who knows? Sometime in the autumn. People want to get in the thick of it."

She made a small groaning noise.

"I know. But Mary . . . before that. In the leave they give us before going to France . . ."

She looked up at him expectantly. Then, in the silence, they heard footsteps on the stairs from the main house. Several sets of footsteps, and raised voices, Mr. Bradfield's among them.

"Mary," he said, "be quick now, and give me an answer before they all come in. Before I leave Wiltshire, before I go to France . . ."

She shook her head, puzzled. "Well, what?"

"It seems like you've got it all worked out already," he said. "And it looks to me like the best plan, since you mention it."

"You're talking in riddles," she complained.

"So I am," he admitted. "So here it is, plain enough. I'd have liked to do a bit of courting. I'd have liked to take it a bit steadier for you. But since you've brought the subject up, and time's against us . . . will you please marry me?"

*I*t was strange, but, in the darkness, he thought he could hear a bell ringing.

Harrison stood, and listened. It was two in the morning, and he was on sentry duty in the forward trench.

He was tired, although the word didn't even begin to describe it. He thought that, long ago—it seemed like centuries now—that he had used to be tired at the end of a working day at Rutherford. He had thought then that there was nothing more fatiguing than standing in the dining room, especially at a celebratory dinner when the room was full, waiting on his lordship and the family and their friends. In those days, the staff could be standing there for four or five hours sometimes. But, in reality, he had never known what tiredness was until now. This was beyond weariness and beyond boredom. His muscles had strained and ached for so long that it had become normal, and the ache went deep down into his bones, a kind of tortuous rheumatic fever that never let up, never released its grinding grip.

A cool air blew over the land that had once been fields.

It brought with it a sensation of the openness of the ground. The trees were long gone. And Aubers Ridge . . . well, that was a joke if ever there was one, he thought. The Ridge was just a minor ripple, a few yards higher than the churned soil that stretched around it for mile after mile.

The breeze brought more unpleasant things with it than just the sensation of space, however. It brought a kind of dirty miasma, a mixture of wet and cordite and a deeper and more insistent fetid rot. Clay and blood and bones.

He peered into the night.

He thought, just then, that he had seen a shape out there. Someone moving. Something hovering just above the ground. He narrowed his eyes and tried to focus: there couldn't be anything there, surely? It was just not possible. All it could possibly be was ground mist, not a person. He looked up at the sky, where a few clouds scudded. He decided that it was just the shadow of clouds, one degree paler than the inkiness of the night, casting their fleeting impression on the earth below.

One of the lads had said that at Neuve Chapelle, just as the light had been coming at dawn, the battalion had plainly seen a priest walking about the battlefield, leaning down to the dead, and kneeling beside the wounded, giving absolution. A priest wearing a long black cloak.

"That wasn't a priest," one man had said, laughing derisively. "That was the Grim Reaper. Come to get souls."

Perhaps he was out there now, Harrison thought. His face set in a grimace. If it was him, the collector of souls, then he had a bloody busy job lately. A bloody and a busy job, all right. Harrison's hands shook. He looked momentarily away from the ground and down at his feet. Blinked once or twice. Looked up again.

He had spent the last few days trying to hide the intractable jittering of his body. It was as if his own fingers wouldn't obey him anymore. He lived in fear that an officer would see him lose his grip on his rifle, or fumble cleaning it. He thought that it might look as if he was nervous; and he wasn't nervous, and he wasn't lazy, and he wasn't clumsy. He had lost the ability to feel anything striking; he was numb. He really believed that he wouldn't be able to be afraid anymore; it would take an energy that he no longer possessed. Courage or cowardice didn't come into it. It all seemed so irrelevant to him, to be afraid or to be strong. After all, strength or weakness weren't required of him. He was required to be an automaton, a body moving about or standing still or lying down. Just a body that did as it was told, that obeyed orders.

But his damned hands wouldn't do what he wanted them to do. He had to concentrate hard, chewing on his lip, making his mouth hurt so that the distraction jolted his fingers into action.

He clutched his rifle now, staring out to the German lines four hundred yards away.

He could feel something other than the smell of the ground. He could feel other men looking back at him, at the British lines. Other men waiting and, beyond them, thousands of others. He didn't doubt that there were reserve lines and communication trenches and arms depots and railway lines and troop trains behind that four-hundred-yard-away parapet. Lines that stretched all the way back to Germany. Here he stood, facing another man just like himself, staring at the dark, clutching a rifle. And both of them, perched at the edge of an abyss, standing at the edge of a bottomless cliff, teetering on the rim of it while, behind them on both sides, others pressed forward, full of anxious misery and bravado. But he didn't feel any of that. He was scoured out, empty.

He kept thinking of Nat, and others. Only a few hours ago, he had run back to a reserve trench, carrying a message, and there on the edge of the trench was a hand, cut off at the wrist. A wedding ring, greasy with mud, was on the third finger, but otherwise it looked like marble, the hand of a statue. No one knew nor cared to whom this oddly displaced hand belonged. No one would ever know.

There was a cursed and continuous ringing in his ears. It was just like the bells in Rutherford before the new electrical system was put in, he thought. All the little bells on the yards-long rail belowstairs, each bell with a painted notice saying who was calling upstairs. *Her ladyship's room . . . drawing room . . . upper bedroom five . . .*

Such a long time ago and so far away.

He put one hand to his head. Perhaps it was all the noise over here that had done it. Caused the ringing. After a bombardment, sometimes you couldn't hear at all for a while. It was like a hundred thunderstorms raging around you. And in the silence, if there was silence, a man's ears would hiss and rumble, replaying the noise. He swayed slightly, trying to focus his eyes. *Clang, clang, clang* went the bell in his head. *Clang*, like the village school bell. *Clang*, like all the bells in Rutherford going off at once. *Clang*, like the bells on churches. *Clang* . . . ruined churches.

He pulled his mind away from the associations. *Don't think about bells, even if you can hear them*, he told himself. Think about the bloody Boche. Think about fixing a bayonet. The battle was coming; they'd got word only an hour ago.

What time was it now? He looked along the trench and saw the officer making his way towards him. They checked every hour, checked each man on sentry duty. It was a court-martial offense to be asleep. They shot you for it. You could be a serving soldier, an old hand, a regular, and you'd still get treated the same, no matter how many years' service you had. They took you away and shot you along with the deserters and the madmen and the crying boys.

But he wouldn't fall asleep. He didn't know if he really slept at all now. He had no sensation and no recollection of it. Dreams were nightmares, and the days were nightmares. It was all the same, waking or sleeping. All the same.

The officer had reached him. "All right, Harrison?"

"All right, sir."

"Bombardment at five a.m. Leading battalions over the top at five thirty. That's us."

"Right, sir. What time is it now?"

"Almost three."

"Thank you, sir."

"Flying Corps will be up there. Should see them after dawn."

He watched the officer go. A few days ago they'd been taken into the reserve trenches and had Sunday service. There had been hundreds of them in a semi-circle, and he couldn't hear the priest. There were two of them—the first sermonizing, the second giving the Sacrament. And blow him down if the second one hadn't been old Whittaker from the village. Looking frail and trembling, but Whittaker all the same.

He'd wanted to rush over and say something, but what was there to say? And maybe . . . maybe he'd just imagined it was Whittaker. Like a lot of imaginings he'd had lately. Imagined he'd seen something moving in no-man's-land, and imagined he'd seen the aircraft above them guarded by real wings, like birds' wings, massive, hidden in the streams of clouds. Imagined he was tasting tea with his elbows on the scrubbed table in the servants' kitchen. Ah, that would be lovely. That would be good. But it was all useless, for the imaginings had no power.

At four a.m., the sun rose, and all was still.

They let him stand down, and he had a breakfast of sorts there in the trench alongside the others who had been brought up. There was nothing hot to drink; there was only hard tack. He tried to chew it, but his mouth was dry. He swallowed a few bites. They all gave up and threw the rest away, and they started to clean their rifles. They did it thoroughly, and whenever he felt his hands shaking, he would tell a joke.

"You're a riot," someone said. "Regular comedian."

It was all in whispers, hunkered down below the parapet.

Five o'clock came, and the sky was streaked with a fine pattern of cobalt blue and pink. And the bombardment began. Field guns were firing shrapnel at the German wire, and howitzers were sending high explosive shells onto their front line. Earth shifted, a stench came out of the broken ground; mud was flung in all directions. The shells wailed as they sailed overhead, high pitched and mournful, like numberless girls crying and keening, and then crashed with blinding force.

Oh. Make it stop, he thought.

He crouched in his line, inhaling the cold sweat of the man directly ahead of him.

"Get up," came the order. "Stand by."

Five twenty. They hung together, looking up at the edge of the trench where they would soon fling themselves. They hung word-lessly, panting, drifting, shoulder against shoulder, arm against arm, feet knocking against other feet as they shuffled. Hung like a row of dirty washing, pinned in the breeze, elbow nudging elbow, face alongside face, hearts thudding.

The bombardment got suddenly heavier. Field guns firing at the German breastworks in an effort to wipe them out. In the cacophony, somewhere out to their left, they heard whistles blowing. Brigades of First Division were moving. The Northants and the Royal Sussex were out there, and the Royal Munster Fusiliers and Royal Welsh Fusiliers. Men from the farmland of middle England, and men from the Welsh mountains and mining valleys. Somewhere too, the Indian Corps, the Dehra Dun Brigade and the Ghurkhas and the Seaforth Highlanders.

Ready now, ready.

Wildness surged into the blood. A thickness of spirit, as if his soul had got heavy inside him and needed to be shrugged off, as if it would weigh him down. Let go his soul and his sanity. Ready now. Foot on the ladder. Raining soil and stink. Ready now.

They started up. In an orderly line, with the officers behind them making sure that no one waited too long. But there was no need. The infantry pressed forward, struggling to get purchase on the steps, heavy with their packs and ammunition and guns, forcing themselves out of the shadow of the trench and into the smeared dawn light. Then they were properly up, and half walking, half shambling along in a jogging line, trying to balance on the uneven ground, deafened by the blasts of the guns.

He kept his head down for the first few yards. Vaguely, absurdly, he wondered what had been planted here before the war. He won-dered what would be planted here when it was all over, if it would ever be over. They would be good crops, he thought. They'd come up strongly. There would be wheat here, or barley, or potatoes. Or maize. Or meadow grass.

He lifted his head and, for a strange moment, he thought that all the way ahead of him was a meadow full of wild dark flowers. Dark blue streamers, like irises, or reeds at the edge of a river. And then he realized that it was not flowers at all, but other men—mere sketches of men now in the ground mist—as they swayed and staggered. Wild dark flowers bending to the ground.

He looked down again, tripping a little, trying to gain a foothold. And it was then that he saw, to his amazement, a line open up in the earth ahead of him. Little sprouts of soil as if something were trying quickly to grow. Time had shot forwards into the future; something had been planted and was coming up frantically, just like the beanstalk in the fairy tale.

For a split second he stared at the sprouting line in fascination to left and right. He couldn't see where the German front line was. He was surrounded by the sprouting seeds. And then they hit him.

It was then that he knew that they were not seeds at all, but machine gun bullets raking the line of men.

*I*t was midday, and he was lying in a shell hole eighteen inches deep with the pack on his back as a pillow, and after a while he stopped wiping away the rain. At first he'd put himself facedown where he fell, and put his hands over his head, but after a while the filth from the ground was suffocating him, and so he turned and lay to face upwards.

Two men were lying beside him. At first he had thought that they were all lucky; being hit by the machine guns had been like going over a tripwire. It must have been almost funny to look at, all falling down in a row as if they were falling over their own feet.

Then, looking more closely, he decided that they hadn't been lucky after all.

It reminded him of music-hall dancers he had seen a while back doing a show; he tried to think what it was called. French dancers, just outside Paris where the very first train had stopped. It was meant to be a dirty dance, but he couldn't see anything erotic in it. They hadn't been very good dancers; it wasn't the Moulin Rouge, just a village concoction, and some of the girls well past their prime. They flashed their skirts, but a man had no desire to see what they were flashing, poor ducks. They were only trying to get some money. When they had stopped, their faces fell into lines scored by hunger. Poor old fairground ducks in a row.

The three of them that were now in the shell hole had been like that: dancing, but not very good at it. It was hardly surprising. Nothing in their training had shown them how to dance fast enough to dodge a stream of bullets aimed at their knees.

Raining and dancing, raining and dancing.

He'd got a bullet in his hip. Another, bouncing off someone else's body, had scored his neck. The man alongside him had been the best dancer in that tripping line, hopping about like a clown before he fell. Strange, how men reacted in different ways. Some simply threw up their arms; they made a sound as if the air had been punched out of them. Some danced, like his mate here. Some just plain fell flat on their faces, like him. And all three of them had all ended up in the same place: this ten-by-six rectangular hole, showered with debris of all kinds.

Just after they fell, he'd realized that the British bombardment had shifted a bit. The sound was different. *They're moving up*, he thought, and was glad for a few minutes, because he thought that it meant that the advance was working, and that the guns were moving forwards to back them up.

But after a while he realized that the orders were to try to crush the German front lines again. Probably the first bombardment had made no impact. He could hear the machine guns still stuttering routinely. God, did the Germans ever run short of fucking ammunition? It seemed not. Nor did the gunners ever pause for breath. On and on it went, and as it pattered on he could hear more whistles, more shouts. More men advancing. More falling. More screaming.

Somewhere nearby, a voice was calling "Maud, Maud . . ." There would be a pause for a few seconds and then it would come again. "Maud, oh Maud . . ." After a half hour the voice stopped.

"Thank Christ for that," he muttered.

The sun climbed in the sky. He began to feel a raging, piercing thirst. He turned his head, looking down to see his trousers dark red on the left-hand side. He couldn't feel a thing. The foot there was crumpled underneath him, but he couldn't feel that either.

He looked to his right.

The man whom he had first thought had survived with him—when they had first fallen, and he'd thought that they were lucky—was looking back at him. His mouth hung open as if he were in the act of saying something. He had a slightly surprised look, and one hand was at his own throat, clamped tight around what was left of the area between chin and shoulder. The whole of the front of his chest was drenched. He had died quickly, probably in less than a minute; the artery had gone, neatly sliced away.

The third man lay beyond him. For a very long time, he had been slumped in the corner, and Harrison had been fairly sure that he was dead, too; but in this very moment, he opened his eyes. He looked about himself, dazed. "What happened?" he asked.

"The charabanc's got a puncture and we thought we'd have a lie on the grass," Harrison replied.

"Ah," the man said. "The comedian."

"You're the bloke from Smithfield."

He recognized him now; a couple of days ago they had been talking, and the man had told him that he worked in the meat market in London. He'd boasted of carrying a beef carcass on one shoulder.

"Go on, or go back?" he asked now.

"What've you got?"

The man looked himself over. He held up his hand. "This." He had lost three fingers. Harrison could see that the knee of one leg was a bloodied mess. "And . . ." He felt about, scratching the edge of his scalp. "Something caught me under here."

"We'd better wait for orders," Harrison said.

"Orders?" the man repeated. "You're bleeding barmy, mate. Can't you hear what's out there? Hundreds of us stuck in no-man's-land." Harrison looked closely at him. The man was crying quietly as he spoke: an unstoppable reflex reaction to his pain. He seemed unable to prevent his tears, and didn't bother to wipe his face.

"Then we go by the last order. Press on. Or you can," Harrison told him. "I've got no propulsion." He pointed at his hip. "But if you think you can walk with that fucked-up knee, you're the one who's barmy."

"I'm not waiting here," the man said. His voice hitched and broke, but his face was set in an expression of bewildered fury.

Neither of them moved.

"Wait for the guns to stop," the man said, eventually.

"Yeah, mate," Harrison replied. "Like that's going to happen anytime soon, right?" He searched about himself, around the back where his pack should be. "Cigarette somewhere."

"Against orders to light up here."

Harrison smiled grimly at him. "Think anyone would notice a trickle from a smoke?"

The other man sighed. "Nah. Throw it over."

By extraordinary effort, he had managed to get a light; it took him a full minute to strike it, light it, and drag on it. Then, he threw it across the shell hole, and it fortuitously landed on the other man's chest. He grabbed at it and put it gratefully to his mouth. "Thanks," he said. But after a while, he added, "Bit wet, though. Had better."

Harrison grinned at him. "Don't mention it," he murmured.

*S*oon, any attempt to talk was obliterated. A shell came down within ten feet, lifting them up from the ground, dumping them back, rolling the dead man onto Harrison's shoulder, his hand finally loosened and flopping over his waist like a lover's embrace. Harrison's mouth was full of soil. The lip of the hole they were lying in had been smoothed out, and a new ridge of clay had been pushed above them.

The man he'd been talking to now lay buried almost up to his neck in the earth, with just one shoulder and his head showing. There was nothing that Harrison could do but look at him, while the other man stared around himself. At last, seeing Harrison's gaze, he gave a thin smile and, with excruciating slowness, winked at him.

"All right?" Harrison asked.

"Fine and dandy," came the reply. "Just fine and dandy."

*I*t was early afternoon before he realized that the sound of the guns had stopped.

There was nothing anymore: no machine guns, no shelling from either side. From what seemed a long way off, he could hear a lot of voices. It sounded like more men were being brought up to the front.

You might as well run a flag up and tell them you're there, he thought bitterly. He wondered what the new men thought, looking out onto the ground between them and the Germans. All they would be able to see would be a mess of bodies and shifted earth, and, beyond that, thick and uncut yards of wire. They would send them over soon, he supposed. Another attack. Another wave of walking dead. *Christ have mercy.*

The sun was getting hotter, it seemed to him; the sky above was a brilliant blue. Ironic. It almost made him smile. Somewhere back at Rutherford that same sky would be blazing down on beautiful fields, on manicured gardens. The same sky . . . the same sky. It couldn't be, could it? That Rutherford still existed, peaceful and untouched, while the ground here had been churned into a raging and howling mess? He looked back at the pile of shifted clay, and saw that the Smithfield man was staring fixedly at a point on the lip of the shell hole. Harrison wondered what image was in front of him that so took his attention. Was it an image of something like his own, something wonderful, something calm? After a while, he couldn't stand it any longer. "What are you looking at?" he demanded.

The Smithfield man didn't move.

He was so thirsty. So thirsty . . . he could drink whatever it was in the bottom of this shallow hole, like he had done once before. But . . . not that . . . that disgusting mess . . . and then he tried to see whatever it was lying there by his feet. A boot. His own boot. But, no . . . not separated from his body. Not lying there like that. He would have felt it. . . .

He thought of putting both his feet in water. That would be good. Sweet, clean water. He'd only been to the sea once, gone with her ladyship when the children were much smaller. He'd liked the vastness of the ocean, its anonymity. You were nobody out there—the sea didn't recognize names. He would have liked to learn to swim and be carried along by it. That would have been fine.

It occurred to him that perhaps all his life he had just wanted to be washed away. He wondered why that was. Just to be carried off and washed out of his own existence. He had actually disliked everything he was; a servant, a man. He thought of Emily, and Mary, and frightened Jenny, who had quivered under his touch. Perhaps he'd always been empty. It seemed a shame.

He heard someone crying quite nearby, and he thought for a second that it was Jenny come to look at him. "Don't come down here," he whispered. "It's not safe, Jenny."

He saw her face above him, and a pair of white hands reaching down. "Don't bother with me," he told her. "Get under cover. Look after yourself, Jenny. Look after yourself. . . ."

The hands grabbed him. Two pairs of hands. He was being prized from the ground, slippery, unwieldy, covered in filth. "Get hold of his legs," a voice said.

He tried to focus, and saw that the face belonged to the officer who had ordered them over the top. "I'm all right, sir," he said. "The bloke from Smithfield, he's buried . . ."

"He's dead," the officer said. And, with a grunting groan, he hoisted Harrison onto his own back.

They progressed, the RMC corporal alongside his officer dragging another man by the arm, stumbling. With vague irritability, Harrison realized it was a man who had been screaming all day somewhere quite close to them. He was screaming still, yelling curses, fighting the very men who were trying to save him in the heat of the afternoon.

As they approached it, there was no noise from the British trench, and Harrison thought that perhaps he had been wrong. There was no one there at all. *They've all gone home*, he thought to himself, and the very idea of it made him want to laugh.

"Going home," he murmured.

"That's right," the major said, through gritted teeth. "Wherever that is."

"Yorkshire," Harrison muttered. "Rutherford."

And he thought of turning up at Rutherford again, and his heart gave a great lurch of gratitude. He lay on the major's back, felt himself being jogged along. There was no pain at all. It was as if he had never been in a war; it was like lying in the back of one of the wagons that brought you from the railway station to Rutherford in those first years of service. He remembered sitting in one, cardboard suitcase between his knees, looking up at the great house as the wagon rolled towards it.

He could see the trees now, and the long green lawns, and the roses on the terrace, and the lake and the river. The great house rose, shimmering in the sunlight, in the middle distance.

It had never looked so good, so beautiful.

"Home," he whispered, smiling. "Home."

The major and the RMC corporal at last staggered onto the British lines, the corporal throwing the screaming man bodily ahead of him so that he slipped and slid on his knees, landing almost on top of the line of waiting men in the trench.

The crazed man began fighting with them, lashing out with his fists, foaming saliva running out of his mouth. After a furious few seconds, he was pinned by the arms, and then the major was tumbling down, bringing sandbags with him and a stream of brackish and bloody water, falling thudding to the ground. A forest of bodies tripping over each other.

"Suicide, sir, to do that!"

"Take hold—take hold—"

"All right now, sir . . . "

The major straightened up, gasping for air.

"Nobody fired," he said, grinning in wonderment.

"Victoria Cross that is, sir."

"I hardly think so," the major said. He was wiping sweat out of his eyes. "Get that lunatic away from here. Get him down the line to the clearing station."

The men were doing their best. They were frog-marching the man as much as they could in the narrow line that was already choked with troops.

The major knew what was planned for the rest of the day. He had received his orders before he had decided to go out there and get whoever he could out of that vision of hell.

Haig had decided midmorning to renew the attack. Noon had been the zero hour, but there was not time to bring enough supporting units forward. Another attack would begin at two forty. The major looked at his watch.

It was two fifteen: there was a lot to do before the next men went forward. He looked down at his feet, to where the man that he had carried was lying. He saw that the man had taken a bullet in the hip, perhaps the back. His left foot was missing. But he had been conscious; he had survived nearly five hours of continual German shelling.

The RMC corporal, who had been bending over the man, now straightened up.

"We'll get a stretcher down here," the major said. "He's on his way home to Yorkshire. He's been telling me about it."

The corporal gave a shrug that was hard to interpret. Then, "No need for a stretcher," he said, finally.

They both looked down at the man that neither of them knew, the man for whom the major had risked his own life.

For a moment, the major said nothing.

Then, he turned away, shaking his head.

They would say later to him, after the war, many years later when the whole unraveling horror of the time was fully realized, fully understood, that there had been more than eleven thousand casualties that day.

But he only ever remembered one of them.

He would always remember the man from a place called Rutherford in Yorkshire who had been going home.

It was light by five o'clock, and William lay awake.

His sleep had been fitful; the air in the room of the Grosvenor Square house seemed to have choked him. Not wanting to ring for Cooper in the darkness of the early hours, he had managed to get out of bed and go to the window, and with something of a struggle, he had raised the frame.

Coolness had slowly poured into the room. He had stood and listened to the sounds of London—the few mournful and distant hoots of railway engines, the intermittent and now increasingly rare sound of horse's hooves on the roads.

What day was it? He tried to remember.

The ninth of May. His favorite month; he liked Rutherford in the spring. He always began his longer walks in May, and his favorite rides across the moors. But not this year. This year, all that treasured tradition had been pulled out of shape, first with the news of Rupert Kent's death, and then Harry's injury. And their own arrival in London at the very time that they had always left it in the past, after the Season.

They had not been to the Season this year; they had decided not to subject Louisa or themselves to London again so soon after the debacle with Charles de Montfort. And so the year was already peculiarly distorted before it had begun.

He had begun to think of them all—all of England, in fact—as being in the grip of some strange twisted fairground mirror. Nothing was the same. One took hold of a fact, and it disintegrated in one's hands. He was certain now that Octavia had been right, and that the newspapers did not report how the war was really going; the jingoism of hearty victories covered up something much worse: something, again, pulled out of shape, crushed and twisted.

He watched the far side of the square, and saw a horse-drawn cab pull away from the curb outside a house directly opposite. He watched it with mixed feelings and memories.

The cabs were merely relics of a time whose standards and routines were being swiftly erased. He had once been a young man in this city; he had raised a small amount of rakish hell, and much later still, as a married man, returned here as a Member of Parliament, the very epitome of respectability. His younger self had gone, vanished as if his dalliances and indiscretions had never been.

Except for Helene de Montfort. She rarely came to his mind these days; it was odd that he should dwell on her now. Since that business last year—since he had seen Helene in Paris brought low by some affair that had evidently gone sour, abandoned by some anonymous lover—he had managed to put her away, out of his conscious thoughts. He had supposed that she would survive without him; she barely cared for him, and had lied to him for years, suggesting that her son Charles had actually been his. And so, in his mind, after bringing Louisa back to Rutherford from Paris, he had closed the door to Helene in his mind.

He leaned his head down on the cold window glass, and looked down into the empty green square behind its railings. His marriage. Octavia. He had thought that he had saved it, mended his fences, brought his wife and children together again under Rutherford's roof.

But what had he achieved, in reality? he wondered. Octavia had gone last night to Folkestone entirely on her own. Without Cooper, without Amelie—and, of course, without him. She was so brisk, so expressionless, a different woman entirely to the one that he had married. Businesslike almost, with something like only pity in her eyes. "Do as the doctor tells you," she had said to him. He had felt like a great burdensome child; it was all wrong. She was meant to depend upon him, to listen to him and concur with him—not make her own decisions.

He had watched her go, watched the taxicab from this same window. And then Cooper had come in and fussed around him and shooed him into bed. Child again. "Get out of here," he had finally hissed to his valet. "Bring me brandy."

"That I cannot do, my lord," had been the reply.

He stared at Cooper in astonishment, and the man spread his hands helplessly. "Her ladyship's strict orders."

"God damn it!" William roared. And felt his heart flutter like a sparrow against his rib cage. Cooper had seen the change in his complexion, and bundled him into the bed. To William's mortification, he had been powerless to stop it, and lay there gasping like a landed fish.

"Octavia," he whispered when he was alone. He thought of her beautiful face staring at him as she had pulled on her gloves and wrapped the shawl over her traveling coat. "I shall be back with Harry as soon as I am able," she had said.

"Hire a private ambulance," he told her. "Don't let him be shoved onto some train or other. Get a motorized ambulance, and come back with him that way."

"I will," she replied. "It's all in hand, William. I have arranged for two nurses to come here tomorrow. Amelie has her instructions."

And then she was gone.

Unthinkable once that a woman of her class could travel alone on public transport. Utterly unthinkable. Only a certain type of woman did such a thing when he was young. He remembered them now, those women: he thought of himself and other young men going down to Piccadilly; he thought of the painted girls of sixteen and seventeen.

What an enormous joke it had all seemed; he never once gave a thought to them. Why they were there. Only that they *were* there. Girls to amuse him; girls that you paid after twenty minutes in some sweaty room or other; glasses of cheap champagne, false sighs, and then hands snatching his money. *Oh my God*, he thought, the desperate callousness of youth. The mistakes, the greed.

He pushed himself back from the window and looked at the clock on his bedside table.

Ten minutes past five.

He realized that his thoughts were racing. He must try to think clearly. He walked slowly over to his bureau, and from it he took out a sheaf of paper and his fountain pen; going back to the bed, he climbed laboriously into it, resting the paper on the coverlet and an open book that was still lying there from the night before.

And after a while, he began to write.

*M*uch later, a tap came on his door.

"Who is it?" he called. He was lying back, the writing done, the envelope tucked under the coverlet, out of sight.

The door opened, and Charlotte's smiling face appeared. She came into the room carrying a breakfast tray.

"What are you doing?" he demanded. "Surely you've not made that yourself."

"Don't be silly, Father," she retorted, laughing. "I took it from the cook downstairs." She put the tray down on the bedside table and made a place for herself on the edge of his vast bed, drawing her heavily embroidered Chinese dressing gown about her. "Now I'm going to spoil you, and feed you things."

He tried to be angry, but could not. He gazed at her as she poured his tea, ladling far too much sugar into the cup and stirring it briskly. She was a kind girl. Not pretty, like Louisa—or, rather, not pretty in Louisa's fashion. She was not finely drawn, but had a strong, handsome face.

He remembered that he had once murmured to Octavia, watching Louisa and Charlotte play on the lawns when they were little more than babies, that he had wondered where such a lumpish child had come from. Octavia had smiled and objected, of course, and he had only meant it as a joke. But Charlotte as a small child always seemed bold and large next to her sister. The teenage years brought glowering sulks and storms; now, though, she had matured into something entirely different. Dark haired, and bright-eyed under that newly shingled fringe of hair. How he wished that women did not cut their beautiful tresses. It somewhat frightened him, although he could not have said why.

"Here you are," she said now, handing him the cup.

He eased himself up in bed. "Thank you."

"We have had a call from Mother. I thought that you would like to know."

"Thank you, dear. Yes. Did you speak to her?"

"No. They told me downstairs. She was on the train until nearly midnight, and then she got off at somewhere called Plummington. She decided to go the rest of the way by car. She's found someone to drive her this morning."

"My God. What happened to the train?"

"Oh, overcrowded, or signal failure or something." Charlotte smiled, and patted his knee. "She's quite all right," she said. "She left a message that she would ring again when Harry's ship arrived. She's quite happy, just rather annoyed she couldn't reach Folkestone; so you can remove that outraged expression, Father."

"I shall write to the railway company to complain, nevertheless. A woman alone . . ."

"We're not all winsome little flowers, darling. Mother certainly isn't."

He sipped his tea. "No," he murmured. "I realize that."

He sat back, and she looked at him. "You seem a bit better," she observed. "Better color."

"I shall be better when I get out of bed."

"Oh no, it's not allowed."

He snorted. "I'm very tired of being swaddled up here," he said. "I'm going downstairs at least and read my newspaper."

Charlotte's face fell. "Well, I don't think you ought to," she said.

"Not ought to!" he had taken the *Times* every day for the last fifty years, and read it religiously over his morning coffee.

"Well, it's rather horrible news. Mr. Asquith's been talking again about munitions. You know how that gets you annoyed."

"A lack of ammunition is tantamount to murder of our troops."

"There—you see? Stop it, Father. You shan't see the paper at all. You shall stay up here and be spoon-fed milk sops."

He had to laugh. "Bring me the *Times*," he told her quietly. "It'll make me feel human at least, part of the world. I promise I shall not shout."

"Well, you see, that's another thing. There is no *Times* to be had today. The delivery boy was very apologetic, but people apparently came into the shop off the street and just bought up every copy."

"What are you talking about?" he said. "We have a daily order. That is preposterous."

"I know," she conceded. "But it's this thing about the *Lusitania*. They've got the *Daily Sketch* downstairs. Yesterday's. Until we can run a copy of the *Times* to ground, that is. Would you like to see that instead?"

"The *Lusitania* . . . ?"

"I saw a little bit about it yesterday evening. Florence had been past the Cunard offices, and she said there were people all over the place. And there's been some sort of riot in the West End. German businesses, you know, being looted."

William stared at her. "The *Lusitania* . . . ?" he repeated, more loudly.

She gave a little shrug. "Well, I suppose you'll find out about it anyway. I don't suppose seeing the newspaper will make much difference." She hopped from the side of the bed. "I shall fetch it."

"Charlotte," he said softly. "What happened to it?"

She paused in the doorway. "Oh, I'm afraid that it sank," she said. "On the seventh, in the afternoon. It's beastly, isn't it? A submarine torpedoed it, and you know—it was all civilians on board. I know they sink merchant ships all the time, but a passenger liner!"

And she closed the door behind her. He heard her feet going downstairs, and a muffled and hurried conversation. Then the sound of her returning.

All the while he lay immobile, feeling as if the air had been drawn out of him. Of course, Charlotte did not know that John Gould had been on board. And, whatever happened, he must not reveal that it was of any tragic importance to them if she *did* discover that the American had been a passenger. None of their children knew of Octavia's involvement with Gould—only that he had been a visitor to Rutherford. And none of them ever *would* know. He would make sure of that. If Charlotte made the connection—he twisted himself further up in the bed, wincing at a scratching wire of pain that seemed to be lodged in the base of his throat—if Charlotte made the connection . . . he must try to be a good actor. He must try to say, "Oh, the man who was in Yorkshire last summer?" carelessly, as if that same man had not held the power to shatter his life.

His daughter came back in, carrying the newspaper, and laid it on the bed. He glimpsed the headline—"The Huns Sink the *Lusitania*" above a half-page photograph of the great liner at full steam. Beneath were photographs of passengers. He reached for the page, and stared at the faces portrayed there. Charles Frohman . . . Alfred G. Vanderbilt . . . Sir Hugh Lane.

Charlotte was looking with him, her hand on his arm. He kept the paper flat so that she would not see his hand shaking. "I met Vanderbilt once, long ago," he murmured. "Decent fellow. Hunting man."

"And Frohman?"

"I don't know him."

"And Lane . . . ?"

He sank back into the pillows, resting his head, looking up at the canopy above his head. "Did your mother hear about this before she left?" he asked.

"I don't think so. She was in such a rush. Florence only arrived to tell me after she had left. But she said that the editions yesterday got it wrong anyway. A lot of them reported that everyone was saved. It wasn't until late at night that the rescue boats started coming back into Queenstown. There was no news to speak of before that."

He turned his head to look at her. "And that was not correct?" he asked.

"Was what not correct?"

"About all the passengers being saved."

"No," she told him. "Apparently not. Florence says there's a notice in the Cunard windows. A thousand or more have gone. It sank in fourteen minutes. And lots of women and children, you know, on board."

"Fourteen minutes," he repeated. He closed his eyes.

Fourteen minutes, fourteen minutes. And who survived, and who did not? he thought. The pain at the base of his throat worsened slightly, pinching off his breath; it was a most uncomfortable, curious sensation, as if small sharp fingers were pinching his airway closed. He found himself coughing, while the thought still hammered insistently in his head, *Who did not? Who did not?*

Charlotte stood watching him, frowning with concern. After a moment or two, she gently eased the newspaper from under his hands, and folded it, putting it on the bedside table.

"If you particularly want to know, shall I go via the Cunard offices on my way to St. Dunstan's?" she asked.

He opened his eyes. "No, darling," he said. "And please don't go out this morning."

"But . . ."

"There will be more riots over this. Don't go."

She hesitated, obviously struggling with her determination to help at the hospital as she had been doing so often lately, and her unwillingness to oppose him.

He felt for her hand, and gripped it tightly. "Just this once," he said. "Stay with me for a few hours."

"All right," she murmured, biting her lip.

"And get me Cooper," William murmured. "Tell him to come here at once."

It was one of the prettiest little villages that Octavia had ever seen.

She stood outside the public house at seven a.m., pulling on her gloves and appreciating the cool sweetness of the air. Last night, the name *Plummington* had appeared in the darkness, a black-on-white sign on a single railway platform. After five hours of traveling in the train at a snail's pace, she had been beginning to lose her temper. She dozed for a while, much the same as her silent companions in the hushed carriage; but as midnight approached she had felt increasingly irritated.

She had got out of her seat and walked down the corridor. Every seat was full, and, to her surprise, there were passengers even crowding the spaces between carriages. A young woman was actually on the floor, hunched up, her arms wrapped around her knees. She glanced up at Octavia, her eyes briefly ranging over Octavia's clothes, before she looked resignedly away. She had a small child, a little boy, nestled into her side; he was partly covered over with his mother's skirt, and fast asleep.

At the conjoining of the first-class and second-class carriages, a harassed steward almost collided with Octavia. "Are we stopping here for any appreciable amount of time?" she'd asked him.

"I'm very sorry, but I don't know," he replied. "There's a delay on the line."

She gave him a small smile. "I'm going to get off the train. Please hand me down my overnight bag."

"Oh, but I can't do that," he said, flustered. "This isn't a regular stop on the service."

"That's quite immaterial to me," she told him, not unkindly. "I don't intend to spend the night in this carriage."

"But we're not in Folkestone," he said.

"No," she agreed. "My bag, if you don't mind. I shall make it quite all right with the station master." She turned back, and then paused. "Do you see the woman sitting on the floor ahead of us?"

"Yes, ma'am. I'm sorry about that. People is tired, and they . . ."

"Give her my seat," Octavia told him. "She has a child to think of."

It seemed that the station master had not anticipated anyone alighting at Plummington either. He came rushing out of his house, and stood on the platform hastily buttoning his collar when he saw Octavia. "This isn't a regular stop on this service, madam," he told her, his ruffled hair showing up under the single oil lamp as an unlikely halo.

"So I've been told," Octavia said. The station master's gaze ranged from her to the lavish Italian leather bag, back to her face, and then back again to the bag.

She held out her hand. "I'm Lady Cavendish," she said. "I need to go on to Folkestone in the morning. Perhaps you might tell me where I can stay tonight? And I shall need a car tomorrow."

He gazed at her hand, and then gave a jump as if he had been given a mild electric shock. "Oh yes," he said, fumbling with her hand and after a few agonized moments unceremoniously dropping it. "It's all very messed up, you see? The timetable. The trains. We run to the minute usually. But there's troop transports, and they've taken to running them at night. We never had trains at night. We never know what's stopping." He gave her a helpless grin. "I've taken to sleeping in my clothes, as you see . . . just in case. It isn't right, you know. I like to be spick-and-span. But just lately . . ."

She despaired of him. "Shall I wait outside?" she asked. "Or here?"

"Oh no," he said. "No, no. Come into the house, your ladyship. It's much more . . . more commodious while I find someone to . . . while I telephone someone. . . ."

Standing in the morning light now, Octavia suppressed a small smile of amusement. She had quite inadvertently thrown lovely little Plummington into disarray. A battered motor taxi had come along the road some twenty minutes later; she had been deposited at the public house just five minutes after that. In half an hour, she was in bed in the smallest room she had ever seen.

It was all rather thrilling, in its way. She had found a place to sleep, and she got herself within twenty miles of Folkestone, all without a maid, or staff, or a driver. It was a triumph, although she knew of rather a limited kind; she felt as if she had broken free. It was, she thought, very silly—perhaps even ridiculous in a grown woman—to be pleased by such trifles. She realized that she had never been on her own—truly on her own—anywhere.

Behind her, she heard the door open.

The landlady was standing uncertainly on the doorstep. "The car is coming, ma'am," she told Octavia. "He won't be a moment."

"Thank you," Octavia said. "And thank you for the tea this morning."

"Oh, we would much rather have made you a good breakfast."

"I don't really have time, I'm afraid."

"You're going to Folkestone?"

"Yes."

The woman stepped forward, out of the shadow of the thatched porch and into the sunshine. "You've got a very fine day for it," she observed. "But it's horrible busy now, you know, down there. Camps all over the place. Huts and what have you. There are Canadians everywhere, even just down the road here, billeted. And Belgian refugees."

"Refugees?" Octavia echoed, surprised.

"Oh yes. They started coming here last August. Sixty-five thousand, now."

"Sixty-five *thousand*?" Octavia said. "Oh, my goodness. But Folkestone must be overrun?" All she knew about the place was that it used to be a quiet seaside town that ran occasional ferries to the continent. "I had no idea."

"We're still quiet here, but only a few miles away . . . You just wouldn't recognize it." The woman suddenly stopped speaking. She inclined her head. "Can you hear that?" she asked.

Octavia listened. "Thunder," she replied. "A long way off, though."

"Not thunder. Guns. There must be a big push on."

"Guns?" Octavia repeated. "You don't mean artillery, surely? Not the guns in France?"

"Yes, ma'am. Quite regular. And . . . begging pardon for asking," the woman continued, "but the driver last night said you were going to meet a hospital ship?"

"Yes. My son."

"Oh, I'm sorry. We've had local boys back, and . . ." She stopped abruptly, evidently thinking it was best not to describe those who had returned. "You'll have a terrible job finding him, I'm afraid, my lady," she said, with soft sympathy. "It's very difficult, with all the traffic and the troops. They stop people going to the harbor."

"Do they?" Octavia murmured. "We shall see about that."

They were distracted by the sound of a car coming along the road, the only vehicle in the early-morning light. She watched its approach under the line of horse chestnut trees. It drew up by her side, and a dapper-looking middle-aged man got out. "Good morning," he said, "Anthony Smythe. Your arrival has caused quite a stir."

"I'm terribly sorry for it."

"Oh, no bother, no bother," he said. He held out his hand. "Very honored." She dipped her head by way of acknowledgement. "I warn you, it's a brutal task trying to get into Folkestone."

"So I hear."

"But we shall do it," he continued, with a broad grin. "Yes, we jolly well shall." He picked up her overnight bag. "My pater knows his lordship in a roundabout way. Bit of a coincidence. Drafted into the admiralty last year at Whitehall, you know."

"I see."

"And so we . . . well, the pub here telephoned us last night . . . general opinion was you'll need a comfortable car to take you."

"I'm sorry they disturbed you. The regular cab would have been quite sufficient."

"No, no . . . no trouble." He smiled at her. "And I understand it's to the *Princess Victoria.*"

"I'm sorry?"

"Well, either her or the *Marguerite*. Or with a bit of luck they'll have had the *St. Cecelia*. She's newer." He saw her frown of confusion. "Ships, you know. In and out of Folkestone. Anyhow . . . we must make full steam ahead ourselves. Do make yourself comfortable."

Octavia stopped just before she got inside. "This is rather glamorous. It isn't a British car, is it?"

Smythe at once puffed up with pride. She could see his weakness now, his boyish adoration of anything mechanical; it reminded her painfully of Harry. He self-consciously gave the bodywork a pat. "She's a 1913 Peerless," he said. "I had her shipped over last year. Damnably good cars. I've been to America, and I saw these. . . ."

"America?" she said. "Have you?"

"I rather like Americans. Don't you?"

She didn't reply; she looked along the cream-and-black lines, the soft top, and the white-walled tires.

"Very much the movie star," he admitted. "I had her shipped in the *Lusitania*, if you can believe it."

She glanced up at him, at something peculiar in the emphasis that he had given the ship's name.

"Wonderful boat," he continued. "I sailed in it myself, to bring the car home. It's because she's the fastest, I should think. The Germans just hate that. Can't bear it. Just simply can't, you see?"

He had put her bag alongside him in the front. She climbed in, puzzled. The landlady gave a little wave as they pulled away. Smythe put his foot down, and glanced back at her over his shoulder. "We'll have you there in a jiffy," he shouted.

She tried to lean forward against the momentum. "What is it about her being the fastest, the *Lusitania*?" she asked.

But Smythe, one arm resting on the open window, had begun to whistle as the car hurtled, engine roaring, down the country lane.

Folkestone was indeed overrun.

They came down out of the soft Kentish countryside and through what had once been quiet leafy roads, with large Victorian villas set back in enormous gardens, no doubt each with a view of the sea from their upper windows. They would have once been rather elite, Octavia supposed, although they were certainly under siege now.

The pavements and roads were crammed with every kind of transport, even horse-drawn carts piled high with deliveries. As they had traveled, the green of the Kentish fields was increasingly obscured by tarpaulin tents, and, closer to the town, row upon row of what seemed to her like hastily erected huts with the bare minimum of paths between them.

In the melee, Octavia at last saw the sea. Not the calm blue expanse that she had always associated with past travel, but a patchwork of boats, with warships farther out, and dirigibles dotting the sky. "Always on the lookout for those damned U-boats," Smythe said. "The troopships and hospital ships have to be accompanied, you know. Rotten Hun. Imagine targeting something with wounded aboard, and nursing staff. Let alone women and children. If one could just get that U-boat captain in one's sights; I should like to be the one to pull the trigger, by George, I would. Strikes me as piracy, plain and simple."

Octavia said nothing. In truth, she was only taking in half of what the man said; she was so preoccupied about transporting Harry back to London. After a moment, Smythe slowed the car and looked back at her. "I do apologize," he murmured. "Something of a family trait, opening the mouth and rapidly inserting the hoof. I'm sure your boy's boat is already here, safe and sound."

"It's all right," she told him.

The car had now been stopped at a road junction. "Look," he said, "I shall go for the harbor, but I don't know that we'll get through. But let's give it a try."

But the warnings of the landlady and of Smythe had been accurate. After only another half mile, the car was snarled in a morass of both foot and road traffic; a column of Canadian troops was marching for the harbor, and the street was rapidly lined with people waving them off.

Octavia watched the Canadians responding, waving cheerfully, laughing among themselves; she looked into their painfully young faces and thought of the *Sunday Post* writing last week that there had been a great rush to colors when Canada heard about the use of gas in France. And of twenty-five thousand New Zealanders on active service; their Prime Minister had said that no sacrifice was too great "to keep the old flag flying." She had to turn her face away from the Canadians marching so briskly into the baying artillery on the other side of the Channel.

She reached into her handbag. "I have a letter from Mr. Churchill's office," she told Smythe. "It might help us reach the ship."

Smythe's eyes opened wide in astonishment. "Have you indeed!"

"I sent to the admiralty yesterday morning. He is in France at the moment, but his staff were kind enough to reply. They have sent a letter with his facsimile signature."

"Good heavens," Smythe said, almost to himself. "What a very resourceful lady." He steered the car into a parking position, and got out, helping Octavia onto the pavement. "We ought to walk from here," he said. "I know this path. It's away from the crowds. One can reach the harbor this way."

She went with him, but after only a few steps, Smythe stopped. "I wonder if it's wise to show Churchill's name," he murmured.

"Why ever not!"

"You know what they call him now?" he said. "*The butcher of Gallipoli*. The Dardanelles campaign is a disaster, my father said. And as for the event two days ago . . ." He stopped. "That's hush-hush, I suppose. Some say that our own Admiralty . . ." Smythe bit his lip, and changed tack. "However. I just wonder if the crews down here really might be all that impressed."

"He's still the Minister," Octavia retorted. Her impatience was getting the better of her. Smythe was no doubt being kind, but all she truly cared about was seeing Harry as quickly as possible. "I shall show the letter nevertheless."

"As you wish, of course," he replied.

They walked quickly. It was now almost nine o'clock and the sunlight was incredibly bright as they neared the docks. They came to a sad-looking bench seat at the bottom of a set of allotment gardens. "Would you sit here, just for a moment?" Smythe asked. "I shall go and ask around. No use you trailing through the crowds."

"I certainly shall not."

Smythe's face took on a pleading expression. "If you could just take a breath for a few moments," he said. "I can dodge about down there so much quicker. His lordship I'm sure would be horrified— quite rightly—if I had subjected you to trailing over the whole harborside."

And he was gone in the next second. Octavia seethed quietly for a while. She felt impotent, hampered by her own femininity. Even men whom she did not know assumed that she was not up to the fray of normal life. One might think she were made of paper, able to be torn by the anxious elbowing of a crowd.

She fought down a very severe desire to wrench off her ridiculously expensive velvet hat and her prettily silk-stenciled coat. She ought to roll up her sleeves, metaphorically at least; it was almost embarrassing to arrive in a less-than-workmanlike costume. If Smythe thought her fragile, then it was hardly his fault. She looked down at herself. Velvet . . . silk . . . how could she have been so frivolous, so thoughtless? Rapidly she took off the gloves and pushed them into her handbag. Smythe was only reacting to the picture she projected of herself.

She could almost feel William's admonishments ringing in her ears: traveling alone, getting into strange cars with men of a lower class; sitting alone, in some narrow uneven walkway, on a bench with a broken seat. "Great heaven's sake, Octavia!" It was almost as if he were there at her side.

Well, she thought. *What of it?* Much worse was happening all around. She thought of the sixty-five thousand refugees that the woman had talked of that morning. Good people among them, doubtless people of a certain distinction, people who had owned property and land. They had not been allowed to stand on their dignity; they had fled for their very lives.

War was a great leveler, the destroyer of societies. She wondered how she would ever manage, ever again, to sit at the head of their own dinner table and discuss inconsequential subjects. How would she ever be able to look into the faces of men like Harrison or Nash again, and tell them to wait upon her? And what on earth was she meant to do with her life, to be of use, instead of a mere embellishment?

"I am an anachronism," she murmured, out loud. And, with the sun blazing down on her in the ragged little alley, she realized with a crushing certainty that it was true. They were outdated, she and William. They were out of place and time, and merely bystanders at this great world-breaking war. They sat in their houses and let their sons talk of glory and fun, and watched them being brought home as casualties. Across in France, the British and Austro-Hungarian relics crashed together. They called themselves empires, but they were mammoths of another age.

She thought of William lying in his room in the Grosvenor Square house, pale against the pillows, the very picture of a fading class. She stared sightlessly over the tidily kept gardens beyond the fence at her side. Working people. The woman on the train last night, sitting on the floor, had been possessed of a dogged courage, enduring her discomfort. The look she had given Octavia was one of indifference, almost defiance. *We are dinosaurs*, Octavia thought, *we can't rely on the way things used to be.* And her heart flew out in absolute pity for her husband.

At the same time, at the back of her misgivings and her worry over Harry, John Gould was at the very edge of her mind: standing there in the wings of the theater of her life. He would have arrived in Liverpool two days ago at least; she had not had a moment to contact him. If he had arrived at Rutherford, or telephoned there, he would have found no one home.

She passed a hand over her forehead distractedly. She knew John's impetuosity: he would have gone straight to Yorkshire, and if he had then been told that she and William were in London, she knew he would come there. He would at least be in a hotel in the city, if not actually at the Grosvenor Square house. Had he spoken to William already? Her heart turned over; William's health would not bear Gould's appearance.

She realized that she had no idea at all what she would do when she saw John again. "Perhaps I should avoid it altogether," she murmured to herself. John and William and Harry . . . she felt that she was at the center of an unraveling drama. It was she who must get Harry back to London. It was she who must ensure William's wellbeing. It was she who . . . she paused, and gazed around herself.

The threads of her life were all in her hands. If she dropped a single one . . . she must be blameless. She *ought* to be blameless. She had a duty to her husband and son. She had a duty of care to her daughters. And yet . . . and yet . . . the house on Cape Cod, on the bleached and grassy-duned bay, with its lanterns around the deep verandah. She could see it all as John had described it. "Oh my God," she whispered. "I must tell him to leave." If she saw him, all the delicately held threads would disintegrate. And yet, at the periphery of her mind, the lanterns on the deep porch flickered.

Interminable minutes slipped away. Eventually, she got to her feet. She straightened her back and took a deep breath. She tried to see what ships were coming into harbor, but it was futile; they were too far away. "Oh, this is ridiculous," she muttered. "It won't do. It simply won't."

She scooped up her bag and started down the path.

She had not gone twenty yards before Smythe appeared again, quite out of breath. "It's in," he told her. "Docked forty minutes ago. Bedlam down there. I'm not sure you'll want to see . . . some of the cases . . ."

"Nonsense. Please let's hurry."

"They know who you are. The harbormaster had a call from his lordship." He smiled broadly. "They can't quite believe you've come alone." He offered her his arm. "And there's a motor ambulance. Yours, apparently. But you'll have to talk to the doctor about that one, I'm afraid. It appears they've got your boy booked to go to Liverpool on the next train."

Octavia's expression made it quite obvious what she thought of this news. "I shall be more than glad to speak to the doctor," she said firmly.

*I*n the house in Grosvenor Square, William and Charlotte sat in the drawing room with the newspapers, at last delivered by an apologetic vendor, spread out on the table in front of them.

Charlotte was gazing at the front page of the *Daily Chronicle*. There was a banner headline across the very top—"*Lusitania* Survivors' Terrible Stories"—and, beneath that, column after column of print: "Last Scenes of *Lusitania*," "Full Story of Great Murder," "1,400 innocent Lives Sacrificed," "Tragic Scenes at Queenstown." Overshadowing them all was a large drawing of what looked like an ancient prince all in armor, waving a sword marked "Vengeance."

She laid her finger on this and looked up at her father. "More blood, more dying," she said. "They'll use this to recruit more men, and bring America into the war."

William looked at this very perceptive daughter of his, and could do no more than nod. He had been reading as much as he could since he had heard the news, and he had kept his thoughts private. U-boats had been the subject of many a conversation just before war had broken out: he had heard both Churchill and Grey talk of them.

He knew very little of Admiralty policy now, and certainly not the inner workings of that department, but something was making him uneasy. He knew that a U-boat captain, to score a successful hit, needed to be square on to a vessel. He knew that the vessel had to be sailing at a speed considerably less than the *Lusitania* was capable of in order to be able to make a strike at all. And he knew that to score three direct hits in rapid order was very near impossible.

He glanced at Charlotte's newspaper. "*Lusitania* Struck by Three Torpedoes," and his heart made that peculiar little tripping dance that he had experienced so often over the last few days. He waited for it to assert its normal rhythm, and then turned back to his own broadsheet.

"How can a ship that size sink in just a few minutes?" Charlotte was asking him. "The *Titanic* took a couple of hours, surely?"

"The *Titanic* was not hit by explosives," William replied.

"It says here that she rolled over to one side, and lifeboats just fell into the water, or crashed along the deck." She paused. "Someone called Charles Lauriat was on a rescue ship, and when it got to Queenstown, the captain wouldn't let the survivors off. Lauriat put the gangplank over the side himself. . . . Oh dear," she suddenly murmured. "There were babies just floating in the water; there's a bosun here of an Irish lifeboat saying that the corpses were 'as thick as grass'. . . ."

"Don't read any more," William said. "It will only upset you."

Charlotte gave her father a withering look. "Darling papa," she murmured, and read on, occasionally exclaiming with another fact. "The quartermaster of the *Lusitania* was in the water for hours, and saw half a dozen steamers go past him. . . ."

William read that Charles Lauriat and others had struggled to get a collapsible lifeboat to float properly, telling the screaming people in the water to let go the sides just for a few seconds so that the rails to which the canvas was attached could be raised. The tackle for opening up the seats inside had been rusted and broken, and the oars had gone. In astonishment for the man's courage, William read that Lauriat had dived into the sea to find oars. The collapsible had eventually picked up so many survivors that it lay almost flush with the water, with still more people begging to be let aboard.

"Good God," William murmured.

The stories of the women desperately trying to save or find their children were by far the worst. His eyes ran over the accounts: of someone called Charlotte Pye who had fallen from a lifeboat, clutching her daughter, and lost hold of her child as she was dragged under twice; of another who had lost three children, all killed by the cold of the water as she had struggled to keep them afloat. A father who had held his son until the boy died, and then sank under the water himself.

William read that the water temperature had been only eleven degrees; there were endless stories of passengers losing their grip on the pathetic pieces of wreckage that they had found. Such extraordinary things washed up from the ship—dog kennels and hen coops, part of a piano, chairs and tin cans and oars. Grimly, he read of those who had survived by holding on to corpses, and, almost more horrifying still, of those who had drowned because their lifebelts had been put on wrongly—bodies floating upside down because the belt was the wrong way up, or floating facedown because the belt was on back to front.

A woman called Alice Middleton told how the American millionaire Vanderbilt had helped her and many others, telling his servant to find children, and put lifebelts on them, and get them to lifeboats. But no one knew where Vanderbilt was now; he had not been in a rescue boat, and his body had not been found. It was said that the flags of the Vanderbilt Hotel in New York were flying at half-mast and that Vanderbilt's solicitor had offered a thousand pounds for the recovery of Vanderbilt's body. They evidently did not expect him to have survived.

The grim task of recovering the dead had gone on through every hour of the day and night. Hundreds of corpses were being fished out of the sea, and taken from lonely beaches and the mudflats of Courtmacsherry Bay. The desperate survivors were brought in alongside the dead, and they had come ashore at Queenstown wrapped in clothes that the crew of fishing boats had given them; dripping, pale, injured in every way. They had been sent to hospitals, and hotels and boarding houses; those who could walk had been told to go to the Cunard offices and register their names on a list of survivors.

Americans had complained that the banks would not give them money; many were wandering the streets, dazed, hardly knowing their own names, white with shock. The Queenstown post office on the waterfront had been open all day and all night so that telegrams could be sent; a post office official reported that he had found one woman shaking too violently to make out a message, and that she kept murmuring that "my brother . . . my mother . . ." as the pencil slipped from her hand.

There were bizarre moments recorded, too: of a man called Roberts, for instance, now lying in a mortuary with his cap still on his head, looking quite composed in death. The man's wife had not been found, though the newspaper seemed to suggest that the woman and Roberts had not actually been married, but were fleeing lovers. And some writer or other of whom William had never heard—but who was reputed to have sold forty million copies of an article—whom one American survivor was reported to have seen trying to climb a cylindrical drum that kept turning over and over in the water. He was now missing. Here, too—a woman called Theodate Pope, thrown with a pile of the dead on a rescue boat, had suddenly revived, asking for her companion, of whom there was no trace.

And then. The captain of the ship, Turner, trying—incredulous,

William read on—to buy a hat in a Queenstown outfitters, look-ing "broken down," if the reporter was to be believed. "Broken down and his uniform shrunk too small." Further down, the article noted: *In the same shop window, a notice had been posted as follows: "Missing: a baby girl, 15 months old, very fair curly hair and rosy complexion. . . ."*

William put the newspaper aside.

Where was John Gould? he wondered. And where was Octavia, at this very moment? He imagined her in Folkestone. She must have seen a newspaper by now. She must know; she must be absolutely consumed by the horror of it all. And yet she had not telephoned him. What was going through her mind, at this very second? What was she feeling in the heart she so successfully disguised from him these days? He almost dared not think about it.

And he certainly did not want to acknowledge the very first thought that had come to his mind; he was too ashamed of it. For his first thought had been, *Please God, let him be dead.*

William suddenly realized that Charlotte was looking at him steadily. "It's just too much," she said sadly.

"Yes, it is," he agreed.

She came to him, and put her arms around him.

After a moment, he kissed her cheek. "Would you please make a telephone call for me?"

"Of course," she said. "Who would you like to speak to?"

"My solicitor, Bretherton," he told her. "Tell him to come here this morning, as soon as he can."

*H*arry Cavendish had begun to feel quite desperately bored. Hooge-Haldane had gone long ago, almost rushed out of the sheds on the wharf, holding up one bandaged hand by way of good-bye. He'd be going to Exeter, of all places; the train had been already rumbling in the sidings nearby. "Don't forget Claridge's!" Harry had joked after him, and felt at once ridiculous, propped up on his elbows, and surrounded by empty stretchers.

"I say," he called out. There were a knot of medical staff and army officers by the doors of the shed, silhouetted in the bright sunshine. "Not going to leave me here?"

He slumped back. Christ, it felt as if his body were tethered to two great planks of wood. He could feel his toes, but very distantly; everything else was either numb—in patches—or itching unbearably, or—more of this—thudding with pain, quite distinctly, in seemingly electric lines. One or two of those lines seemed to stretch into his body, his stomach and groin.

The night on the boat had been quite the most disgusting of his life. He had not felt alone, as he had done on the train with the corpse in the bunk above him, nor was he afraid. He had simply been most awfully sick. And he was not the only one. The man next to him had thrown up all over him as the boat pitched and rolled; and, as if that weren't enough, the poor devil stank—a dreadful reeling stench.

As soon as they had got out of harbor, they had felt the ship veer to port, and it had continued that way all night, zigzagging, he supposed, to avoid torpedoes.

"Wretched fellow, the Hun," Haldane had complained. "Chasing ships. Coward's war."

They'd heard about the *Lusitania*; someone who had got off the ship and was bound for the front had told them. It set off a feverish reaction among the troops; there in the hold that night somebody started shouting in an accent they didn't recognize, and men had swarmed over the poor fellow, who, it turned out, was from Scotland,

and had reverted to Gaelic in his fever. It was taken to be German. Four nurses had been obliged to pull three full-grown men off the raving infantryman.

What a comedy we're in, Harry had thought. And then he hadn't been able to hold it in anymore, but he had tried to vomit carefully. "I say, Haldane, I'm about to puke and shall do so in a gentlemanlike fashion," he had joked apologetically. And failed. Haldane was as splashed as the rest of them.

"If I had a fist, I'd connect it with your eye," he'd told Harry sourly.

Seasickness was a wonderful thing. It had the capacity to overrule any other pain a man might be feeling. At least, that was Harry's own experience. He couldn't vouch for the horrible cases on deck, fighting for every breath, green in the face from gas, not mal de mer. "Oh mine papa," he'd whistled brokenly. There it was again, the papa song. He'd sung that a few centuries back when they first picked him out of the aeroplane. Between retches, he tried the word again. "Papa, papa." Would his father come and get him from Folkestone? He hoped so. He would rather like to see his father again. Solidity in the shifting sands of madness: calm in the face of riot and mayhem.

Dawn had come as a welcome shaft of light through the salt-caked portholes. A nurse had come round and given them tea and said that she could see the shore. "England," he had breathed to himself. And, "I should like to see little Sessy." And then to his shame, he had begun to cry. Haldane had slumped down at his side. There had been no jolly words about bucking up or seeing the bright side; Haldane wept too, there in the half-light. They had looked at each other, and knew that it was a moment shared that they would never breathe to another living soul.

The crunching of the ship against the dock, the sensation as she was nudged and tied and the engines died, was glorious. He'd looked down at himself and saw the man alongside spirited away, and all the others.

"I say!" he called again now. "Have pity, fellows!"

One of the RMC officers came striding purposefully towards him. "Cavendish?"

"That's the ticket."

"We have you down for Liverpool."

"Ah no. . . . That won't do at all."

"Awkward lot, aren't you?" the officer replied, unmoved. "You've got a very visible mother on the dock standing by with an ambulance."

"God bless her."

"I shall want to speak to both you and her when we get you on dry land."

"Speak away," Harry said, smiling broadly now. "But for God's sake, let me out of here."

It was Friday, the fourteenth of May.

London was not the city that Octavia had known all her life; it was not even the city that she had known last year when Louisa had been presented at Court.

She sat in the morning sunshine of the Grosvenor Square house, looking out at the street. Thinking of last year was like looking back on some sort of fairy tale. She remembered Louisa in that beautiful pink silk dress at the Chasteris Ball: ethereal almost, lit by candlelight as she had come down the stairs. She remembered her in the dressmaker's, and Charlotte's head on her own shoulder, complaining at the hours that it had taken to fit Louisa's clothes. She remembered going to tea with Hetty de Ray; God, so long ago; twelve months that might as well be fifty.

She looked up at William.

Sitting opposite her, he was regarding her with a mixed expression: concern, sadness, and his old and habitual immovability.

"Tell me what is in your mind," he said.

She gave a small shrug. "I really don't know," she told him. "It's too much, almost. Everything."

He made no comment. His eyes strayed to the newspaper. "Intolerable behavior," he observed.

The *Times* was full of the riots in London and Liverpool. German businesses had been attacked, mobs of hundreds—some said thousands—strong rampaging through streets, breaking windows, tearing shops to pieces. Over one desolate ruin had been painted the words "Go to hell, Hun."

William gave a wan smile. "It was the Kaiser himself that spawned that word," he mused. "He gave a speech when I was in Parliament, a speech to his troops going to China in 1900. He told them to give no quarter. He said that the Huns had gained a name for themselves 'as still resounds in terror a thousand years later.' He said that the name of Germany should sound the same. Hence . . ." He waved his hand expressively at the photograph.

"Then he has his wish," Octavia murmured. "He has his dirty name now." She felt numb. How like William it was to know the political context; how like him to retain his level appreciation of history. She wished she could manage a tenth of that objectivity.

"I've been up to see Harry," William continued quietly. "He's got over it, I think. Not so much angry now, as resigned."

She closed her eyes briefly, not wanting to think of that Monday morning on the harborside. Of the stale-smelling harbormaster's room where the RMC doctor had told her of her son's true condition, while Harry himself fretted outside in the ambulance. "It isn't a case of merely recuperating at home," she had been told severely. "He must be operated on again. The compound fracture of the right leg must be reset. As for the left leg, it's not so bad, but again must be broken back."

"Broken again?" she repeated, aghast.

"We do our best at the front," he replied. "But it's largely a case of clearing out debris, and preventing further infection."

She had gone to Harry, her darling boy, her son, looking so much older, with a curious dead light in his eyes. She hadn't been able to bring herself to tell him then. He, in turn, took her distress for concern at the rickety, shambling state of the ambulance. "I say, this is luxury," he had told her. "You should have seen the places I've been carted through, and other men's problems. Don't cry, Mother, for God's sake."

She obeyed him. She brought him home, and the staff had all turned out on the steps of the house that afternoon, and he was carried into his own bedroom upstairs. They got him settled, and he had slept the sleep of the dead. William had said as much, and she had caught his arm. "No, not that," she told him. "Don't say that." Her throat had felt burned out; she had been on the brink of a fever.

William had taken her arm and drawn her into the dining room. There, among the polished mahogany and the deep fringed curtains and the silver—such immaterial details, but they snagged at her vision luridly, all the patterns and reflections—he had said to her, "You've heard of the *Lusitania* business by now, of course."

She had sat down at the empty table in whose deeply polished shine she could dimly see her own blurred reflection. Only a few hours before, she had asked someone to fetch them something to eat as the ambulance dragged itself out of Folkestone, and a boy had come back with bread and cheese, grinning from ear to ear. He had also got them a newspaper. She had taken it from him, seen the first page, asked the driver to stop, and walked away from the van, the newspaper in hand. Since then, even with Harry, she had felt remote, anaesthetized. The effort to seem calm, and to attend to Harry, had made her feel as if she was slowly dying of some raging heat.

"Yes, I've heard," she told William on Monday.

"I've asked Bretherton to contact the US Consul in Queenstown," he had said. "To find news of him."

She had no words to give William. She looked up at him gratefully. Passing out of the room to see his son, he had placed a hand briefly on her shoulder.

She thought now that it was the most affectionate thing that her husband had ever done; not only instructing Bretherton, but in the wordless and delicate sympathy of that fleeting touch.

She gazed at him now. "I'm not being secretive," she said quietly. "But I simply don't know what I feel."

Already, the newspapers were moving on. Octavia's eye ran over the page, and saw an article about the "scandalous shortage of shells on the western front." She tried to make sense of it. Harrison had been out there; they had heard of his death only yesterday. Tall, blithe-looking Harrison, who had always worn such an air of calm. He was already buried before they had known of the price he had paid; the major involved was mentioned in dispatches.

A telegram had arrived at Rutherford. "The dreaded yellow note has come for Harrison," Bradfield had told William, over the telephone. "And the Reverend Whittaker too, we're told, from the village." Octavia had sat for some time in her room, wondering if Harrison had a family she ought to tell, and realizing that she did not know. It had plunged her further into despair.

The *Times* was full of photographs of those who had survived the *Lusitania*, and those who had been lost. 128 Americans had died, and 94 of the 129 children. In all, over twelve hundred were gone. On the same day that Octavia had brought Harry back from Folkestone, 140 bodies were buried in Ireland with no identification at all; it was estimated that nine hundred more would never be found, for they had gone down in the ship, or been washed farther out to sea.

The US Consul complained that of those Americans who were left, many could not be persuaded to identify the corpses that filled the morgues. It was all too much for the disoriented survivors; those that had no relatives on the ship were already out of Ireland, catching ferries to Liverpool, sitting up all night in the public areas of the ships with their lifebelts on, too afraid to sleep. The US Consul despaired of keeping track of them: the missing, the fleeing, and the dead.

The first train of survivors that had reached London had arrived in London on Sunday—the very day that Octavia had been packing to go to Folkestone. She had not spoken a word to the staff; no one had told her. She had gone for the evening train at Charing Cross, and never seen the newspaper hoardings: shielded from private car to first-class carriage, she had not heard a single voice saying the *Lusitania*'s name. By Monday morning, Smythe had assumed she knew the story.

John Gould had probably been dead for almost three days before she was handed the newspaper in the ambulance.

William began to speak again now. "Bretherton has sent me this letter," he said. He got up slowly, and handed it to her; walking away, he turned his back, and stood by the fireplace, staring down at his feet. The letter was dated Wednesday, May 12.

Your lordship,

Octavia read,

There is a sad state of affairs in Queenstown. I instructed my agent to inspect all mortuaries, and to inquire at the Cunard office and with the US Consul. It has taken some time; as you may imagine, every possible point of information is full of the bereaved.

I'm afraid I have little absolute news of Mr. Gould. My agent was told in the Cunard offices that just before the ship went down, Gould was seen with two small children by the rail close to the lifeboats, and upon further inquiry we have learned that a male child named Joseph Petheridge was brought in alive on the auxiliary patrol trawler the Indian Empire, *and has said that he jumped into the ocean by the side of a man who told him that his name was John Gould. This boy was placed in the Queens Hotel, where my agent has spoken to him. He has given us a description that tallies with your own, but the child did not see Mr. Gould after the ship went down. Sadly, the bodies of the boy's mother and sister have been found; both were buried on Monday.*

The US Consul has compiled a list of identified American bodies, but Mr. Gould is not among them. As it would be impossible to survive in the water for more than a few hours, and as Mr. Gould has not registered his own presence to either Cunard or the Consul, it would seem to be a logical conclusion that Mr. Gould will not be found, although searches are, of course, ongoing. It is possible that Mr. Gould is in a state of shock, or injured and unidentified as yet; I have to say that is possible, but unlikely.

I have left instruction that if his body is recovered, I am to be informed. I understand that a wire has been sent to his parents to the effect that it is likely he is among the dead.

With respect, Bretherton.

Octavia read the letter twice.

"This was very kind of you to inquire, William," she managed, at last. "Thank you."

Her husband said nothing for some time; he seemed to be struggling to frame his words. Then, he walked back to his seat. "Octavia," he said, "don't think for a moment that I don't appreciate the tragedy of this. Simply in itself, of course . . . but for you personally."

"I didn't write to him," she replied resignedly. "Only that one telegram. I want you to believe . . ." Her voice trailed away; with a great effort she began again. "I want you to believe that I tried to forget last year." She paused, and then looked directly at William. "But it's no use us living a life of complete pretense," she said. "Here is the truth. I wanted to see him again."

William's expression did not alter much; if he was hurt, or surprised, he did not show it.

There was a prolonged silence. In Octavia's mind, Bretherton's words kept repeating themselves. Even now the letter felt livid in her hands. She knew how much John had feared drowning, feared a sinking ship; she kept returning to his terror. *Dear God*, she thought, *I hope it did not last long*. It tortured her to think that he might have held on for hours in the freezing water, losing his strength inch by inch.

She glanced up, and saw that William was looking steadily at her. He continued to hold her gaze. "Harry's operation is tomorrow," he said slowly. "A fine way to celebrate one's twenty-first birthday."

"Yes, indeed it is," she murmured.

"I take it that we'll return to Rutherford together with him afterwards?"

"Of course," she replied. Very slowly, she folded Bretherton's letter, and laid it aside. "But you realize that Charlotte will not be coming with us."

"Yes, she has told me," William said. "She has presented that to me as a fait accompli."

"She is seventeen, William. She and Florence wish to train as VADs; they want to stay at St. Dunstan's. What can we do? It's important work."

William looked at the ground, his hands clasped in his lap. Eventually, a small smile came to his face. "I began to tell her that it was impossible . . . but then, of what use are my wishes? She is a most determined young woman. I cannot deny her useful occupation, much as I cannot deny you, Octavia. You must live as you wish."

Octavia stared at him, astounded. She could hardly believe that this was the same man who had been so severe, so reprimanding all her married life until last year. In fact, he bore little resemblance to the man who had railed at her less than a week ago. It seemed that his heart attack had shrunk his spirit. She saw, for the first time, a man frightened by his own mortality.

"When I was in Folkestone," she said quietly, "I realized that my life had been very narrow. I think that will change. I think it must."

"Only in Folkestone?" William asked. "You were not thinking of leaving me before that?"

A denial sprang automatically to her lips, but she stopped herself. Eventually, she said, "What John Gould was offering me . . . what I wanted from him . . . it was not only himself, William. It was the kind of life where I might be free to do as I wish, without constraint. When I got myself to Folkestone, do you realize that it was the very first time that I have traveled anywhere entirely alone? My life is too sheltered, William. I need to do more in the world."

"To go to America . . ."

"Yes, if you like. John Gould traveled. He was a free spirit. I have led a fortunate life, but it's not the life I would have chosen. I had such dreams, romantic dreams, of us both once. I abandoned them, I made myself into the person you required. But now . . ."

She let out a great gasp of exasperation at her failure to tell him exactly what she meant. "William," she said, "it's not that I don't feel a great affection, a great comradeship if you like, with you. We have raised three beautiful children. I daresay that they will concern us all our lives, whatever they choose to do with themselves. But, as much as I love them, I have a life. I have things that I want to achieve in Blessington. . . ."

"The work is going ahead."

"I know that," she agreed calmly. "But it's not enough. The mills are making a vast amount of money. I would prefer to be a better employer. I look at Blessington and feel nothing but guilt. Elsewhere in England there are model villages, and hospitals, and schools, built by more enlightened employers than ourselves. I should like us to do something like that. There are men coming back from this war who need new employment. The blinded, the disabled . . . our own workingmen among them. We must attend to them."

A silence grew between them. She could see that William was trying to understand her, and fighting with his own confines. At last, he sighed. "You must do what you want. Whatever it is that makes you happy." He spread his hands. "I've rewritten my will in the last few days," he told her. "I have left much more to you than previously. You are an entirely free agent."

His pallid resignation, where once he would have automatically opposed her, broke her heart. She got up, and went to his side, and kneeled in front of him, taking his hand. "It's nothing that we have done or not done," she said. "The world has changed, that's all. We can't look back. We must look forward."

His eyes ranged over her face. Finally, he raised her hand to his lips. "If only I could have made you happy," he murmured. "As happy as he did."

She gazed at him over their clasped hands. "You have made me happy," she said. It was not exactly a lie; they had been happy once, and he had tried so hard to make it right. It was not his fault that her heart was elsewhere. She suspected that it would always be so.

William lifted his head and made a touchingly obvious attempt to lighten the mood. "There is a letter there in the bureau from David Nash, our footman."

"Is he not in France?"

"Not quite. But before he goes he asks if he and Mary Richards might be married."

"Good heavens!"

William smiled at her. "I don't know why he has written to me. Observing the old order, I suppose."

"But that is rather wonderful. Mary is a very good girl. I like her. When is the wedding?"

"Very soon, I should think."

A sudden thought came to her. "William, let us give them a wedding in the Rutherford chapel on the estate."

She could see that, instinctively, a denial sprang into his mind; only family were ever married in the chapel. Then, he relaxed. "If you think it wise."

"I think it very wise," she told him. "Let them have some joy. Let us all have some joy in this awful world."

He sat regarding her seriously. "And ourselves?" he asked her. "We shall go on, then?"

"Of course," she told him. "We shall go on together."

She did not know if it were true.

But she would make it true.

There was simply no alternative.

After a few more minutes, Octavia left William to go up to her room, but when Amelie came after her, she shooed the girl away. She closed the door behind her and leaned on it.

"John," she whispered. "My poor love." And she began to cry, sinking to her knees.

Only his name was left, haunting her in the silence.

Chapter 10

August was a month of rain and sun, light chasing dark across the great parkland. At the beginning of the month, a deluge soaked the grass, scattering the petals of the roses in drifts over the terrace, darkening the walls of the house from ash rose to terracotta; the river broke its banks, and the leaves of the beech trees came wandering down in the mist. The moors were obscured.

But the morning of David and Mary's wedding was, thankfully, bright. Octavia rose early, and discussed the day with Amelie as she dressed.

"Do you remember the party we had for Louisa on her sixteenth birthday?" she asked her maid.

"I do, ma'am."

"We had linen flowers pinned to the table covers in the dining room—you and I made them as they would have been for hats in my mother's day. Large flowers in shades of cream and pink, with lace. It took us some time. . . ."

"Like peonies, ma'am."

"Exactly." Octavia smiled. "I've been thinking how pretty they would be on the tables in the tithe barn, for the wedding supper. We could let the ladies from the village take them as mementos, too."

"That is very kind, ma'am."

"Well, they're hardly of much use locked away," Octavia observed. Finished, she regarded herself briefly in the mirror. "Would you go downstairs and ask Mrs. Jocelyn for me? I'm sure they were put away in the linen cupboards, in my old hat boxes."

Amelie nodded briefly and left the room. Wrapping a paisley shawl around her, Octavia went downstairs and out into the garden. From here, she looked out across the terrace and lawns; she walked quickly along the herringbone path and down the steps past the orangerie. Here, she saw the person that she had been looking for, busy on a task that he had taken upon himself like a religious duty every morning. Mary's father was sweeping every inch of the paths of the knot garden with elaborate, dutiful care.

"Good morning, Mr. Richards."

He seemed to jump several inches, and then swept off his cloth cap. "Ma'am."

"A wonderful day for you."

"Yes, ma'am, indeed 'tis." He had blushed a deep beetroot red; he was often tongue-tied in her presence.

"I have the key to the chapel," she told him. "Shall we inspect it? The maids were all busy there yesterday."

He followed her over the garden and down the long path to the fifteenth-century chapel hidden in the trees. When Octavia had moved here, family services were still taken every Sunday morning in what had looked to her like an ivy-covered mound, where the floor inside was spongy and the walls green with damp. During the renovation, it was found that the chapel was standing only because the ivy had been holding it together, and it was taken down, stone by stone, and the floor cleared of several centuries of dirt. When it had been completed, it revealed itself as an enchanting little building. Octavia now unlocked it; the heavy oak door swung back.

The verges along the lanes to the village had been raided whole-sale, and the tiny space decorated in true country fashion: a mass of ox-eye daisies had been arranged in wall niches and on windowsills.

"How pretty," Octavia murmured. Something in the scene struck at her heart; she couldn't help it—flowers in chapels made her think of John Gould's end, and the sadness that, without a body, there could never be a place to mourn him. She had no idea if his family had held a memorial service in New York—she supposed they may have done so. The sensation of being cut off from them, as well as him, was unbearable. Unconsciously, she put her hand to her mouth. Scalding emptiness inside that could never be shared. On some days, she felt that it must drive her mad, but there was nothing for it now but to conceal it as best she could, and smile at Mary's father.

He had evidently seen that she was moved, without guessing the real reason. "'Tis a beauty," he murmured.

"It is," she agreed. "You will have such a lovely ceremony here."

He was clutching his cap in his hands, twisting it around and around. "Will your ladyship come?" he asked.

"No," she told him. "We shan't intrude. There's hardly room in here, and in any case, this is Mary's day. But we shall come to the supper certainly."

"You're very kind, ma'am," he murmured. "I been meaning to say such a long time, if you'll pardon me. But 'tis such a great thing you've done for me."

She patted him briskly on the arm. "Nonsense," she told him.

"It's you who have helped us. Mr. March is very grateful you've been here, and so is Mr. Bradfield. We're awfully short of help."

Smiling, she entrusted the key of the chapel to him. "As father of the bride, you are in charge today," she said.

She left him in the doorway, a thin man with the troubled life he'd led still etched on his face, and still clutching his cap to his chest, incongruously framed by the flowers in the porch and the overhanging horse chestnut trees.

As she came back towards the house across the grass, she suddenly saw Harry come out onto the terrace. She stopped, watching him as he made his way laboriously along the broad flagstone path fringed with roses; saw him sit down and take out his cigarettes.

He didn't hear her coming.

She put her hand on his shoulder.

"Good God, Mother, you made me jump."

She sat down opposite him. "How is it today?"

"Like toothache of the worst kind in both bloody legs."

She would have corrected his language once; now, it seemed to her to be of no importance whatsoever. "Shall I call Dr. Evans?"

"Absolutely not." Harry stared at the crutches. "Lord above, I hate these blasted things."

"They won't be forever. Perhaps just a walking stick in time."

"I'm not going through the rest of my life with a stick," Harry retorted. "Exercise is the thing. I shall take Sessy down to the river this morning. I've been thinking how much I used to like to fish. You used to take me down there, too. I'm sure Sessy would like it just as much."

"Her nurse must come with her. And you must have the wheel-chair. The slope is too much; the grass is still slippery."

He regarded her with a twisted smile. "You do like to fuss awfully, don't you?"

"I consider it my duty."

They remained silent for a while, appreciating the brightness of the day after the torrents of the evening before. Then, Harry leaned forward. "Well, let me out of my misery. Tell me what you make of her." He held up a warning finger. "And no flannel, please."

Octavia considered.

"Very pretty."

"Isn't she, though?" he responded, beaming. "But that isn't what's best about her, of course."

"No, darling. She is a very brave girl; that is evident." She paused. "Tell me about her family."

Harry began to laugh. "I shall not indeed. She can tell you herself if she wishes." He blew out a long stream of smoke. "Really, Mother. That's the sort of question I would have expected of Father. What else?"

"Irish, by her voice. But by her name . . . Spanish? Dutch?"

"I've no idea," Harry replied. "And I can't say that I care at all."

Caitlin Allington de Souza had arrived at Rutherford late the previous afternoon.

At first, when Octavia saw Harry's friend descend from the motor taxi, she had felt slightly disappointed; for Caitlin seemed to be a very slight girl—tall, but very thin, and dressed in a severe gabardine coat of indeterminate color. Her features were hidden by a shapeless hat, a kind of large beret pulled over her hair. She carried a cloth bag, and wore flat laced-up shoes.

And then at the top of the steps, Caitlin had looked up at William and Octavia and smiled. They were confronted with eyes of the most startling shade of green and a face of arresting charm: not exactly beautiful, but unusual, memorable. But—there again—was the look that Octavia had seen in her son's face: blank resolution. A face that had grown used to horrors. It had made Octavia keep hold of her hand and guide Caitlin indoors.

She had watched as Caitlin removed her hat before the hall mirror, and revealed a neatly cut bob of thick red hair. And, past Caitlin's shoulder, she caught Harry's look of pure admiration.

As if summoned by Octavia's thoughts now, the girl herself materialized on the terrace. "How beautiful it is!" she exclaimed as she walked towards them.

Harry tried to get up; she shushed him down, laughing.

Caitlin turned to Octavia, "I've slept like a baby," she said. "This is a wonderful place."

Is it you who shall take it away from me, in time? Octavia caught herself thinking. *Will it be your children who sit here in years to come?*

And, astonished at this idea—sprung out of nowhere, she had not really considered such a future before—in a few minutes she excused herself, and left the two of them sitting in the morning sunshine.

She doubted very much that either of them had really noticed her leaving.

As Octavia came back into the house, she saw Mrs. Jocelyn standing at the foot of the stairs.

"Mrs. Jocelyn," she said. "I'm glad to have caught you."

It was odd; the woman was absolutely still. She seemed not to be going anywhere, but was staring up at Octavia's portrait.

"Mrs. Jocelyn," Octavia prompted, as she walked along the Tudor hall towards her.

At last, the housekeeper turned.

"Did Amelie speak to you?" Octavia asked. "About the linen flowers? Do you have them in storage?"

Mrs. Jocelyn blinked. She had a very high color, and looked almost feverish. "It's not at all appropriate," she said.

"I beg your pardon? What is not appropriate?"

Mrs. Jocelyn vaguely waved a hand. "This mixing of things," she said. "Weddings for the staff in the family chapel, and a footman marrying a maid. And yourself." She nodded as if these last words confirmed the worst. "Yes, yourself, madam."

Octavia was so shocked at the impertinence, that she caught her breath for a moment. "What on earth can you mean?"

"It's not right for them to be married at all, let alone in the chapel."

"Mary and David?"

Mrs. Jocelyn let out a disapproving hiss. "I mean them, yes. Nash and Richards."

Octavia held down her irritation. "It is most extraordinary for you to comment, Mrs. Jocelyn."

"Extraordinary!" the housekeeper retorted. "But it is all extraordinary. It is all quite wrong, you see? It can do no good."

"I don't know what you mean at all. And I cannot see that it's your place to make an objection."

Mrs. Jocelyn let go of the carved bannister, which she had been gripping tightly, and took a step in Octavia's direction, staring at her as if really seeing her in detail for the first time. "It started with you," she said, in a low voice. "Yes indeed, madam. Tearing apart the place, and the waywardness of it all, the upset. It was peace before. Now there is never peace. And it came. Judgment came."

Octavia frowned. She looked about her, hoping that someone else would appear. She had never much taken to William's housekeeper, but Mrs. Jocelyn at least had been rigorously good at her job. She had always been somewhat frightening, though; self-effacing as a shadow—ghostlike in the house, ever watchful, ever sharply to the point. She knew too, how much Mrs. Jocelyn admired William and pointedly deferred to him above herself. But the housekeeper had always—until now—been excruciatingly stiff and polite.

"I don't know what you mean by judgment, Mrs. Jocelyn," Octavia replied now.

The housekeeper smiled. "Oh, they that sin," she interrupted. "That's what I mean. They reap the whirlwind," she said. She stepped even closer now—much too close—her voice low and threatening. "It shan't go on, it must be clean. It's the way of it, the right way. He has gone, hasn't he? Dragged down to the depths for his transgressions."

"In heaven's name, who do you mean?"

"Why—him. The American. And the Lord shall come for others. For you."

"Good God," Octavia breathed. She glanced behind her, looking for the hallway bell to press to summon Bradfield. "Yes, in heaven's name certainly," she heard Mrs. Jocelyn saying. "To be struck down in heaven's name, that is quite correct. Quite correct."

Appalled, Octavia looked back. She saw that Mrs. Jocelyn was calmly, steadily, walking away. She got to the green baize door, and opened it.

"I've put the linen flowers in the tithe barn, on the supper tables," she said. "I take it that was where you wanted them?"

Octavia could not speak.

"And you see, madam . . ." Mrs. Jocelyn paused. Then glanced away, smoothing down her black dress. "To be done in heaven's name, quite so," she murmured. "Master Harry now . . . but he is brought back."

At Harry's name, anger at last ignited in Octavia. "You shall not speak of Harry," she said. "What are you thinking of!"

"Of the lesson of retribution for error," Mrs. Jocelyn said. It was with utmost disdain, as if explaining herself to a stupid child.

She regarded Octavia sourly for a moment—such a strange expression, bitterness mixed with triumph—and then the heavy baize door shut behind her, and Octavia could faintly hear her steps descending to the basement below.

*I*t took some minutes for Octavia to find William.

     He was not, as she had expected, in his study, but seated in the orangerie, reading.

She hurried in, not knowing quite how to phrase her complaint; he looked up, and saw the concern in her face. He put down the book.

"William, something is the matter," she said. She found a chair opposite him. She felt faint, out of breath. Something nearby had a smothering scent; she looked at the rows of lilies, and realized that it was them. Between them, the orchids presented their curious little faces. "Something is very wrong with Mrs. Jocelyn."

"Wrong?" he repeated.

"She has just threatened me, William."

He started to smile. "Ridiculous! Over what?"

"You don't believe me," she murmured.

"What is it exactly she's threatened?" he asked. "I suppose it's something to do with the wedding supper? She seemed very frosty about it, Bradfield told me."

"I don't mean the wedding!" Octavia exclaimed. "William, just this second she has . . . it is really quite bizarre . . . she has suggested that my behavior . . ."

"Surely you've misunderstood her?"

"I have not misunderstood," Octavia snapped, trying to keep her temper. "She is under some sort of strain; that is obvious. Bradfield told you about this fanatical cleaning. . . ."

"I've seen nothing untoward."

She sighed in exasperation. "Of course you would not. . . ."

"And she has said nothing to me."

Octavia stared at her husband. She didn't want to cause him any disturbance; he was supposed to be resting still. "William," she began again. "I think at the very least we must insist that she takes a holiday, a rest cure."

"Mrs. Jocelyn has never taken a holiday in all the time I've known her," William pointed out. "A day or two here and there, but nothing more."

"I want her to go away somewhere," she said. "I want her to have a week away, or a fortnight. She's most agitated."

"Well, I leave that up to you."

Octavia bit her lip. "I would prefer it if you told her, William. She has spoken of . . ."

But no. She couldn't mention John's name. Nor the oblique reference to Harry, and what she supposed was an inference that his injuries had been brought about by his behavior over Emily Maitland, or in London last year—his reckless carousing and spending. "Oh, it's too utterly ridiculous," she murmured. "Please speak to her, William."

He was looking at her with a bemused frown. Then, he sighed and picked up his book once again. "If you insist, " he told her. "If you insist."

*J*ust before lunch, Charlotte came into the drawing room. She stopped on the threshold, looking absently about her, and then, spying Caitlin sitting in one of the far chairs, she shut the door hastily and walked briskly towards her.

"I've been hoping to speak to you," she said. She flopped down in a chair alongside and without any further introduction, reached for Caitlin's hand. The girl looked surprised, but didn't retract it.

"I've come to ask for a favor," Charlotte said. "Where is Harry?"

"Upstairs, I think. Would you like me to call him?"

"No, no. It's just you I need to speak to." Charlotte dropped Caitlin's hand after squeezing it, and sat back a little. "I know we only met yesterday, but you can advise me like no one else. And I've a favor to ask." This last, she let out under her breath, frowning. But she let that go for the moment. "You've seen a great deal of the world, I expect."

Caitlin smiled. "Only a very misbegotten world on the other side of the Channel."

"But you've traveled. Not just to France. You're Irish, aren't you?"

Caitlin paused for a second, as if weighing up her reply. "Not exactly."

"You have an Irish accent. You *look* Irish."

"I had an Irish nurse. She brought me up entirely."

"But your parents?"

"Not around very much." She smiled in a guarded fashion. "This is quite an inquisition!"

"I'm sorry for it, but I hate pleasantries. We can talk about the weather if you'd rather, though."

At this, Caitlin laughed a little. "I see. Ask on, then."

"You met Harry out there, in France."

"Yes. I nursed him briefly."

"It's quite a . . ." Charlotte searched for the word. "An intense thing, isn't it?"

"It is. Your mother tells me that you've been at St. Dunstan's. Is nursing something that you would like to do?"

"Yes," Charlotte said. "I want to volunteer as a VAD. Do you think I'd have the character for it?"

Caitlin's smile, which Charlotte noticed was rather practiced—she wondered briefly how much it hid—became broader. "You can only know if you try it," she replied. "It's interesting how little some apparently strong people can take, and vice versa."

"Yes," Charlotte mused. She had looked away, out of the window, her eyes fixed on the horizon for a second. Then she looked back at the older girl. "Would you tell me about it?"

"Oh, I'm not sure your parents would thank me."

"It's nothing to do with my parents," Charlotte retorted firmly. "I need to know. I've been at St. Dunstan's and I've listened to the accounts that the men give, but they shield me. I'm tired of being shielded altogether. Were you at Aubers Ridge? We've had news that one of our staff was killed there."

Caitlin seemed to assess Charlotte for some time. "It's best to disassociate yourself, if you can," she said quietly. "I mean one's heart. It doesn't do to weep over what you see. It's a job of work. Sometimes the hardest thing of all is to maintain efficiency. But I was in Boulogne recently, not at Aubers. Although we saw the results come through."

"I think I could cope."

"Could you?" Caitlin asked. "It's impossible to know before you are faced with it."

"I can train."

"Yes, you can train. But the pity of it . . . that's hard to bear."

"Did you pity Harry?"

"No."

"Why not?"

"I pity only those who don't come home. And besides, it's not good to form a friendship out of pity, is it?"

The two girls looked at each other. "It's much worse than they say in France, isn't it?" Charlotte asked eventually.

"Yes, it is much worse than any of us can imagine, I think. Think of a horror, and double it. Treble it. I doubt that even comes close, however."

Charlotte was by now looking down into her lap. As she spoke again, she didn't raise her eyes. "I saw you getting on the train," she murmured.

"In London?"

"Yes." Charlotte paused, then went on, "I thought you might be the girl that Harry's spoken of, and I wondered if you had seen me. Father had sent me a first-class ticket and . . . well, I didn't see you afterwards in first class."

"No, you wouldn't."

"I've been staying with our friends in London for a few weeks now. And yesterday, on the platform, as you passed us . . ." Charlotte paused. "Well, I was saying good-bye to a friend. A captain from St. Dunstan's."

"Ah," murmured Caitlin.

At last, Charlotte raised her eyes. "You won't say anything, will you?" she asked. "Not even to Harry. It's not . . . well, it isn't *spec-tacularly* a romance. And it certainly *isn't* based on pity."

"I hope you don't mind me saying so, but you are rather young for a romance anyway."

"Yes . . . yes, I know," Charlotte replied.

At that moment, the door opened, and Octavia entered.

Putting a finger to her lips, and raising her eyebrows eloquently at Caitlin, Charlotte rose to meet her mother. "Is it all ready, the wedding supper?" she asked in a loud voice.

"I expect so, darling."

"Shall we all go and see?" Charlotte asked. "Shall we take Sessy and Louisa and all go and inspect the tables and everything? It's such fun, and that's been in short supply, hasn't it? We've got time before lunch."

"If you want to. . . ."

"Good," Charlotte said, kissing her mother's cheek. "I shall go and root Louisa out."

They watched her leave, and Octavia turned to Caitlin. "She always was a restless spirit," she said, smiling. "One never knows really what is next."

"Is that so, indeed," Caitlin murmured, rising to her feet.

*J*ust after lunch, as the guests began arriving for the wedding, there was one last flurry of rain. The wind scored across the open parkland. Those that were coming up from the village—David Nash's mother among them, and his brother—were hurried into the warmth of the servants' kitchen, where Mrs. Carlisle held court, regaling all and sundry with the merits of the happy couple.

Earlier, Jack Armitage had taken Mary to his parents' cottage across the stable yard, where she was preparing herself, fussed over by his own mother and by Jenny. Poor Jenny, Jack thought to himself. She looked so hollow eyed since the news about Harrison. She kept denying that they had been sweethearts—"He never wrote me anything lovey at all," she had confessed to Mary—or so he had heard. Jack felt for her. To have someone near, to adore them, to fear losing them, all without being able to speak of any future; this, he understood too well.

It was three o'clock, just an hour before the ceremony, and he was sitting in the tack room, when David Nash came in the door. The prospective groom looked flushed and happy.

"There you are," David said. "I'm doing the rounds, making sure everyone knows they're invited. You'll come and see us tie the knot?"

"That I will."

With a sigh, David sat down opposite him; he was laughing to himself. "We've been down at the inn in the village," he said. "You know that Kessington is back?"

Kessington was one of the stable hands; he had gone to France only two weeks ago, and been invalided back only the day before.

"I seen him," Jack replied. "What used to be him, any road."

"Yes," David agreed, suddenly serious. "It's a shame."

"He come up here yesterday," Jack continued. "Looking for the horses. Set him off again when he found them gone."

Kessington—a broad, squat, cheerful lad when he had left Rutherford—had come back literally staggering. His walk was oddly angular; it seemed that he could not control his face and jaw. Jack had felt sorry for him, had tried not to look at him, had apologized that the horses were gone, and felt mortified when the lad had slumped at the empty stable doors, trembling from head to foot.

Taking hold of his arm to guide him to his own mother's, Jack had felt vibration running through the man, both horrible and fascinating.

"He can't help it," he murmured now to David. "But it's a thing to behold, that face. I can't see him anymore in it. He seems like Kessington, but some other man got in there. It's not him looking out at me." He frowned.

"My mother told me they were in a reserve trench and it got struck," David said. "He was the only one that came out of it, and he couldn't stand. Not a scratch, but when they tried to move him on, he kept falling."

The two of them sat and looked past the open door at the rain dancing on the stones of the yard.

"He tried to tell me about the horses there," Jack muttered. "He said there's all kinds of animals. Not just horses, and not just belonging to the Army—but the animals left behind on the farms and the villages. And they heard dogs barking in the German trenches. One of the couriers had a little terrier that used to ride on his shoulders. He said it were like Miss Louisa's dog that she had, little Max." He stopped for a while. "I can't credit it, how animals stick with us after what's done to them."

"Mary told me that you've talked of going out there," David said.

The wind plucked at the tack room door, swinging it on its hinges. Jack watched it for a while. "I've spoken to his lordship," he said in a quiet voice. "He says he can arrange it. In the veterinary corps. Probably sooner than later."

David got to his feet. "I'd best get myself ready."

Jack stood up, too; he held out his hand. "I might see you out there, in France," he said. "'Tis possible."

"Yes," David agreed.

They held the grip of each other's hand, looking at each other.

To Jack's recollection, it was the first time that David had been in the stable yard, let alone sitting down in here. But across the clasped hands, divisions were falling—the past was dust blown away, as the leaves blew across the yard. They felt their sameness and their strangeness all at once, saw themselves in the same khaki walking the same shattered roads.

"You get off and take the girl to wife," Jack said, and smiled. "She's a bonny one."

"She is," David agreed, suddenly beaming. "Come and share the meal with us."

"I will."

Jack watched him go across the yard—so tall, so spare, pulling his uniform cap back on his head, running against the rain.

When the rain stopped, the sky cleared dramatically, and the day turned into one of those old-gold afternoons on the cusp of summer and autumn. Hearing that Harry was at the river, William walked down there. He took his time; it had taken him weeks to learn this lesson—to go slowly, to watch, to listen.

It had not been easy, for all his life William had been the one who spoke while others listened, or acted while others procrastinated. But he was following his doctor's advice for one single and most pressing reason: that obeying it might keep him here longer. And, if his world had now shrunk to Rutherford—no more Paris, no more Whitehall—then he was beginning to be thankful for it. Every day he gathered the house and the rolling acres into his mind, mulling over them, turning them this way and that with greater delicacy and intensity than he had ever before achieved. And there was one crucial, overwhelming point to his thoughts—that he might pass on all he knew to Harry; Harry, who was at last home, and remaining here for good.

He stopped within sight of the bridge where the river curved, and where Harry and his daughter were now sitting. The nursemaid, he noticed, was a little way off, sewing, and occasionally glancing up at her charge.

Harry and Sessy sat side by side on the bank where the grass ran down to a sand-and-gravel shallows. Harry was holding out a box of bait, his fishing rod alongside him, and his child looked down into the box with fascinated delight, reaching out and wriggling her finger in the box. *This one is like Charlotte*, thought William. *Fearless.* He leaned on the bridge and called to them; they waved to him.

As William got closer, Sessy wobbled to her feet. "She's more interested in the bait than the fish," Harry said, laughing.

"Any luck?"

"Not a one."

"There'll not be much for a while yet."

"No," Harry agreed. "But we've seen tiddlers, haven't we?" he asked Sessy.

Sessy nodded mutely, fingers twined in her curly hair.

The nursemaid came up and nodded, smiling at William, to whom she bobbed a brief curtsey. "Your lordship."

"You'd best take her, Agnes," Harry said. "It'll be a while before I get up from here; it was a study getting down in the first place."

Sessy was lifted up and placed in the elaborate perambulator—a rather monumental study in black and silver, heavily upholstered. From here, she waved at them regally for a moment. And, as they moved away, William and Harry could hear the nursemaid singing *"Beautiful dale . . . ."*

Harry listened, glancing at his father. *"As boys we have wandered along beside the river so clear . . ."* he murmured. *"Beautiful dale. . . .* I wonder how old that song is. It could have been written for here."

William, after some hesitation, sat down alongside him. It had struck him with emotive force that this was where he had come while they had waited for Harry to visit so many weeks ago, before he was injured. "This was my own father's favorite place," he said.

Harry said nothing. He was watching the water, thinking that it was also the spot where Sessy's mother almost drowned after he had rejected her. But he kept his mouth shut. Bringing Sessy here had been, in effect, the act of bringing the child to her mother, but he didn't expect William to understand that. His own mother might, of course. In fact, Octavia would have seen it from the first.

"I have been thinking of the estate," William began now, in a slow and measured tone. "I have been giving it considerable thought, in fact."

"Yes?" Harry answered, with most of his attention on the circling currents of the water ahead of them.

"I have been wondering how much you would want to take on, and how soon."

Harry turned his head. "Take on?"

"We might have a meeting next week with the land steward. It will be your concern, after all. You may as well see the accounts, and so on."

"The accounts?" Harry repeated, puzzled. "Well, if I might help, I should be glad to while I'm here."

William smiled at him. "Not quite a case of helping as such," he said. "Rather accustoming yourself to the workings of the estate in detail. To enable you to make your own decisions."

Harry was still looking at his father bemusedly. "I'm afraid I don't follow, sir."

William waved one hand vaguely behind him, encompassing the

vast grounds and the valley beyond. "I imagine you will want to have it under your belt, to understand it, by the time you are recovered." And, seeing that Harry's face still bore an expression of complete mystification, he smiled. "I shall turn the estate over to you, Harry, as soon as you're fit. I had not planned it so early, of course. I imagined that when you were thirty . . ." He paused. "But you have greater experience now than either of us ever anticipated. And there is my health. It's appropriate now, Harry. It is yours, after all. You may as well begin."

"Begin? I . . ." Harry stopped. "I'm terribly sorry, Father," he at last continued. "But there's been some misunderstanding. I must go back."

It was William's turn to be confused. "Go back where?"

"Why, to France, of course. To the corps. They need every man they can get."

William was horrified. "But you cannot fly again."

"I can certainly fly," Harry retorted.

"No, no," William said. "Impossible."

"I beg your pardon, sir, but I don't see where the impediment would be."

"But your legs . . ."

"I don't need my legs as much as I need my hands and eyes. There's nothing wrong with *them*. And I shall be mobile; it's not as if I can't walk."

"You can't possibly serve—you can't be thinking of it. Your injury was too severe. You will break your mother's heart; she thinks you're safe here at last." He paused, most reluctant to reveal his own feelings in the matter. But at last he murmured, "And myself, Harry. I need you here. Rutherford needs you."

"Well. We shall see what the medicos say," Harry conceded,

plainly irritated. "But if they insist I can't fly—which would be the highest idiocy—then I shall still be needed. I'm damned sorry for Mother's disappointment, of course. Truly I am. And yourself, sir. But I must go. I thought that was understood. It's my duty."

"But how can you help in France if you can't fly?"

"In training . . . in command . . ."

"That would take a promotion."

"They may well consider the contribution's enough to merit one, who knows?"

Harry was looking hard into William's face. And, in it, William saw the stubborn, wayward Harry, the Harry of his teenage years, the Harry who could not be controlled, reasoned with. But there was something else there now, too: a hardened, mature determination.

"Harry, you cannot win this war on your own," he murmured. "No one expects you to do more now. You have made a tremendous sacrifice already."

"Sacrifice?" Harry repeated. "Sacrifice? I've done nothing." And he gave a short, exasperated laugh. "One of my squadron tells me that the First Canadian Division had twenty-four hundred casualties at Festubert trying to take six hundred yards of line. They had already lost half their fighting strength at Ypres. Half! That is what I'd call a sacrifice. And Harrison. *That's* a sacrifice. Do you know what kind of place Harrison died in? A rat-infested swamp called Quinque Rue. . . ."

There was a silence, in which Harry took breath. All around them the trees and river whispered; the sun shone through the leaves. William gazed on it, this picture of heaven that he wanted to give to his son so that he would stay grounded here, literally wedded to the ground. Perhaps shackled too, so that he could never escape again; yes, perhaps that. He never wanted to let Harry out of his sight again, let alone to the kind of hell that his son was describing.

"I can't sleep for the thought of sacrifices," Harry said softly. "St. Julien, for instance. They dug a trench near there during a midnight attack. Eight hundred and sixteen started; six hours later, six hundred of those were dead. We hear such things all the time. That is the real state of the war. They come back to the corps by message *'which are the proper trenches? Where is the front line?'* because it's all mixed up, you see. These things are fought over and taken, and lost, and the whole lot blasted to hell by artillery, and new lines dug, and those obliterated in hours. . . ." He looked directly at his father now. "I see those lines, I see them in my dreams. And that's why I must go back."

They sat together for a few moments more, and then William helped Harry to his feet.

They walked together across the lawns, each looking up at the house and then across towards the tithe barn and the path leading to it, which they could see now was banked with potted flowers from the greenhouses.

"Good Lord," Harry murmured. "March has actually allowed his precious babies outside. Romance is not dead."

William smiled. They reached the house, and stood by the open doors to the drawing room. For a moment, William struggled with the desire to say something more to Harry; he felt a helpless, racking disappointment. He respected what Harry had told him . . . but . . . well, perhaps it was an old man's frailty. He *felt* like an old man, for God's sake. Unconsciously, he straightened his shoulders and decided not to burden his son any further. "Go on inside," he said to Harry, patting his arm. "I'm sure that lovely young lady of yours will be waiting for you. It showed delicacy that she let you have time with Sessy alone."

"She is a wonderful girl," Harry said.

"Indeed she is. Off you go . . . I need to talk to your mother."

As he knew she would, Octavia was taking a rest in her room. He stood outside the door a moment, biting his lip, then knocked.

"Come in," he heard her call.

He saw that she was lying on the bed.

"Were you sleeping?" he asked.

"No." She propped herself up on one arm. "What is it?"

"I've been speaking to Harry."

"About the estate?"

"Yes." He sat down heavily in the armchair closest to her. "I'm sorry, Octavia. But Harry intends to go back to France as soon as he can."

"What!" she exclaimed. "Oh no, surely not." She swung her legs off the bed; she was wearing an exquisite silk wrap, one that he dimly recalled them buying together on a trip to Paris. It must have been twenty years old, of a lovely pattern in pink and gold, and Octavia looked almost girlish in it. It made him think of the days of their honeymoon and early life together.

"He has been telling me about the battles," William said quietly. "Some, at any rate. He feels a responsibility to go back there—all hands to the pump, as it were. Every man needed. A responsibility to those fighting on the ground, as well as his own squadron." He paused; then continued, "We traveled through those places ourselves one year, you know. By train and that little barouche that we rented to take us through the countryside. Ypres and Lille."

"It was the year of the Paris Exhibition," Octavia murmured. "Do you remember the medieval Cloth Hall at Ypres?"

"I do. Very beautiful."

"It is gone now, in ruins."

"I remember eating in a little place; we had stopped for lunch. . . ." Octavia was smiling fondly. "Do you recall? It was out in the Somme valley somewhere. There was just a single café, an estaminet. My goodness! Sitting in the shade outside . . . and a very old spaniel came to lie on the pavement. I can still see him sleeping there, on stones so old that they looked like polished glass. We sat there all afternoon."

"St. Julien."

"Good heavens!" she said. "I haven't thought of it in years. Just a little place among fields. It was so warm that day. . . . I believe you're right! Whatever made you think of it?"

"It doesn't matter," he murmured. He leaned forward and put his head in his hands. "I admire Harry of course, for returning. His loyalty and courage. But it's a kind of madness."

Octavia had got slowly to her feet and now paced the room, stopping to lean briefly on the stone sill of the window. "This is dreadful," she said, at last. "I can't bear it. Can't we stop him somehow?"

"I doubt it."

"His commanding officer?"

"The rest here seems to have done the boy good, Octavia. I've seen no nerves of the kind we noticed even a few months ago. He says he sleeps badly, but that's hardly a reason not to fly. Probably in a month or two, if seen by a medical board, he would be passed fit. The whole experience of the crash may well have made him less inclined to take risks. All in all . . ." William paused. "He may even be a better flyer, a better officer."

"But his injuries . . ."

"He says it makes no difference."

He saw the pain on his wife's face, and understood what she felt. She would do anything to keep Harry here. She walked slowly back to the bed, and stood in front of him.

"I wonder," she murmured, "if children ever appreciate what they do to their parents." It was said with a wry, infinitely sad smile. "To let them go, to see them out in the world, to want them to have their own life, of course . . . but to watch them leave. It's hardly bearable. And yet one mustn't say so, of course. I should loathe to be the kind of mother clinging on to him, or any of them . . . and yet . . ."

He had not heard her speak so frankly in some time. "We must be proud of him, at any rate," he said.

"Of course I am proud of him," she answered. "And of course one feels such admiration . . . but to fling one's child into this abyss. That is what it feels like. I think of the Kents; I think of how Elizabeth was when I met her. So faded, so fragile. To lose them, but, worse still, to know *how* they were lost, in such horror . . . my God, William . . . if that were Harry . . ."

She sat down slowly, gazing at him.

He was about to offer some sympathetic platitude; his duty, his role after all, was to be the stalwart center in this house. And yet, he suddenly felt his eyes fill with tears. She was right. It was the thought that Harry might be lost as Rupert Kent was lost. He had seen the notices in the newspapers every day: those touching paragraphs with the grainy black-and-white photographs, accompanied by the inevitable text of grief.

"We must let him go," he tried to say, but the words became blurred; to his embarrassment, a sob escaped him. He was thinking, *those we have lost; those we wish to keep.* And as for Octavia, who even now was kindly placing her hand on his hair and gently stroking it—well, my God, she had lost John Gould, and, before that, as she had painstakingly told him, his own love. Or so she perceived it.

He had trampled over her feelings as a young bride, and destroyed her trust over Helene de Montfort, and he had no idea how to rebuild this empty, decaying place that used to be his marriage. Nothing that he did or felt for her seemed to work; it was as if she were simply drifting away. He felt that he was not competent to reach her, understand her; to be with her was to feel nothing less than something infinitely precious draining through his grasp.

It was no exaggeration, he thought with despair, that one day it might be entirely possible that he would be here alone—without Octavia, or his daughters, or Harry. They might all leave for one reason or another, and then he would be back as he had been before he married: alone in Rutherford.

"Oh God," he said, under his breath.

He was then dimly aware of Octavia kneeling down by his side; he opened his eyes and saw her kindness, her grief, her fears mixed in a single expression.

"Oh, William," she whispered. "What are we to do?"

He put his arms around her. "Lie down with me and love me a little, my darling," he pleaded. "I beg of you. Just today. Just a little."

When Nash had first come home the day before, and gone to see his mother with Arthur on that afternoon, he had at first been grey faced; training that month had been a miserable affair for both the brothers. They had heard of the massacres at Gallipoli, Churchill had gone from office, and on the western front the Germans were employing a new terror—the *flammenwerfer*, liquid fire.

Both David and Arthur had been told that their regiment would be sent to Hooge, the bloodiest battleground of those clammy, wretched months. Hooge was a place passed back and forth between the opposing armies, littered with dead, a place of built and blasted and rebuilt trenches. Someone had told him that you walked on bodies, and all the way to Rutherford he had tried to get this picture out of his mind.

Coming to the parkland gates, however, yesterday evening, he did finally manage to let the ghastly imagining go. He had parceled it up in his head, and determinedly left it at the lodge gates, where the land steward and his wife both came out and shook his hand and wished him well. He would not burden Mary with his anxieties; he had hurried on to see her, to feel her arms around him, through the fading light.

The chapel today was a fine sight.

It choked him to think that it had all been done for him and Mary: all the flowers, and the opening of the private chapel under the trees beyond the kitchen garden. He almost had to pinch himself as he stood waiting in front of the little stone altar, with Arthur as his best man by his side.

There was stillness as Mary entered, and then a sort of sigh went round the staff gathered in the rear pews near the door. The girls, of course, were all in tears; he wondered how they cried so easily before ever a word was said; he supposed they must like it. He had told himself not to cry, and he did not. It was not becoming in a soldier all dressed in best kit, with his mirror-shined boots and his hair slicked back and his cap under his arm.

Mary was clear faced, upright. She came in on her father's arm; the old man had been all gussied up and brushed down, wearing a suit of clothes that Bradfield had given him, with his tie knotted too tight under his collar. He only shambled a little once as he handed Mary over, making an apologetic face to her as he regained his footing. He had turned away, affected, wringing his hands before he found his seat.

She'll see me through, David thought, looking at Mary. *Through this and whatever else comes.*

"You'll do for me," she had told him with a smile, the evening before as they said their good-night in the stone corridor downstairs. "You'll suit me fine."

here was no rain at all that evening.

The sky cleared and, if the sun wasn't strong, at least the sky was beautiful, empty of clouds: a limpid pale blue, the color of the satin sash on Mary's dress. David would not forget that blue. He would see it in moments in the months to come, and in the year after that. He would see it in winter mornings when the frost was thick on mud; he would see it, remember it, right through the spring of 1916. He would see it again in his mind's eye on the morning of the first day of July, as he stood next to Arthur waiting in the reserve line at dawn, near the place that they called Mouquet Farm, on the Somme.

After the ceremony, David thought that the tithe barn looked very fine, all tricked out in bunting and the long trestle tables covered with white cloths and with the best servants' china brought in from the house. Although by then he had felt a sort of lovely stupor come over him, unused to the heavy ale and then the champagne of the toasts; he felt himself a very fine man, a rich man, the luckiest man alive.

Lord Cavendish stood at the head of the table and gave a little speech. David couldn't remember for the life of him what it had been about afterwards: something about holding together, and how that was important. And his lordship had taken Lady Octavia's arm, and they had walked around and shaken his and Mary's hands, and wished them well. And David had sat there feeling rather like a sort of stuffed doll, full of pleasure and self-satisfaction and a numbed delight, while Mary's hand squeezed his arm.

"Mrs. Nash," he murmured to her.

"Mr. Nash," she replied, laughing.

On the other side of the room, the Cavendish family occupied a top table all to themselves.

As darkness fell and the noise levels rose, Octavia noticed that Mrs. Jocelyn was standing stiffly by the door. The housekeeper was glaring at the band of country musicians as if she had never seen such a sight. And she made a little gesture—almost as if she would like to block her ears, hands raised—when they started on "My Bonny Yorkshire Lass," violins keening through the melody, and dancers rose to take the floor.

"William," Octavia said quietly, nudging his arm. "There is Mrs. Jocelyn. Why don't you ask her to take a turn about the floor? It will be an ideal opportunity to speak to her."

William gave her a small smile. "If I must," he said.

He walked over to her; the housekeeper fluttered a kind of half curtsey. He noticed that she had made no effort to wear anything remotely celebratory—she was still dressed in the severe black she wore every day.

"Would you do me the honor of a dance?" he asked her.

To his inner amusement, Mrs. Jocelyn blushed a startling shade of bright red. "It's you who do *me* the honor," she whispered. She took his arm; they walked to the rough board floor that had been put in the center of the room.

"I'm not terribly good at jigs of any kind," he warned her. "Shall we potter about near the edge?"

"As you wish," she replied.

He held her lightly in his arms, quite away from himself. Her hands in his felt unpleasantly wet with perspiration. "Thank you for all you have done for the happy couple today," he said.

She pursed her mouth before replying. "I'm sure it's been a pleasure."

"But not what we would have expected in the old days," he commented, seeing the mixed feelings in her face.

"Not at all."

"The world has changed."

"If you will excuse me saying so . . ." she began, then stopped. She was staring pointedly at Louisa, who was dancing some feet away with Jack Armitage. Realizing her father's eyes on her, Louisa smiled hesitantly. It seemed to William that she moved several inches out of the tenderly close grasp in which Jack had held her. The pair of them looked as guilty as if they had been caught lovemaking in public. Jack raised his chin, but his grip on Louisa's hands did not alter.

"Saying . . . ?" William repeated, confused.

"If I must speak the truth—and I have never done other than that, you may be assured, sir," Mrs. Jocelyn went on, "I found it much easier years ago. When it was ourselves alone here."

He thought he had misheard in some way. The song stopped; the dancers applauded. He maneuvered her slightly away from the floor, next to an empty table. She seemed very agitated suddenly. "Ourselves alone?" he said.

"They were happy days. There was more respect. One knew one's place. I was honored to have run Rutherford with your lordship then."

He frowned. "And not now?"

"Oh well . . . now . . ." She was looking towards the table where Octavia was sitting. "It's all upset. I feel that. Turned upside down. There is no godliness. Such things are happening here . . ."

"I don't understand you, Mrs. Jocelyn."

"Don't you?" she asked. She stepped very close to him. "I am of your age, you know. I am not of this younger generation. I mourn this destruction."

"Do you mean the war?"

"I do not," she told him.

"Well, what do you mean exactly?"

She put her hand on his arm, and gripped it tightly. They were half hidden by the flower displays and the bunting, cornered, William felt, by the edge of the table and the wall of the barn. "I have been your devoted partner at Rutherford," she whispered. "I have honored your lordship. I will to my dying breath."

"Well, that is . . ." William floundered. "Mrs. Jocelyn," he managed finally, in a firm voice. "Perhaps the task has been too onerous, too tiring for you of late. Her ladyship feels that you have exerted yourself too far. That you are in need of a holiday."

She stared at him, aghast.

"Perhaps a week or two by the coast," he continued. "Miss Dodd can manage very well while you're away. A month, perhaps. You have earned it."

"You want me to go away?" she said. "And Dodd is to be in charge? For a *month*?" The grip on his arm had not lessened in the least; in fact, it had increased.

"Yes. We shall pay you, of course."

"And this is her idea."

He tried to remove her hand. "If you mean her ladyship . . ."

"I don't call her that," the housekeeper hissed at him. "In my own mind, never that."

"Mrs. Jocelyn—"

"She doesn't deserve you," she said. To his absolute astonishment, she began stroking the lapel of his dress coat, like a mother preening a child. "Yes, you are perfection," she was murmuring. "Too fine for her."

"That's quite enough," he said firmly. He caught hold of her wrist. "Take control of yourself."

"Control?" she echoed, staring at him. "But I have control."

"No," he told her. "What you have said to me is not acceptable in any way."

"It is her," she repeated; she looked confused, affronted. "I have done nothing. I am God's servant; I am yours. I obey my betters. But she is not my better. I resent that. Not her. As for the American . . ."

"Enough!"

"You have been all to me," she told him. "Don't you understand?"

"I understand you only too well," he said, truly annoyed now. "And if you continue in this way, and with regard to her ladyship in particular, your services will no longer be required."

The effects of his words were quite remarkable to behold. Mrs. Jocelyn at first smiled, shaking her head as if he had said something comical. Then, holding his gaze, she saw that he was quite serious. And at that point, every ounce of color drained from her face.

She stepped back from him. She looked from him to the table where Octavia was sitting. "I see," she whispered.

"I will not have my wife either disturbed or reprimanded by you, or anyone," he told her. "However many years of service they might have. You understand that, surely."

"Oh yes," she breathed. "I understand."

He turned away. In the same instant, he felt rather than saw Mrs. Jocelyn move past him; in a flash she was striding across the floor, across the boards of the dancing area, over the rushes and sand between the nearest tables. She walked with her head high, her shoulders squared, her back straight, almost in military fashion. The thought flashed into William's mind that she was more warrior, more avenging angel than woman. Those closest shrank back from her, and then a murmur went around the tables as Mrs. Jocelyn passed.

One man—William recognized him vaguely as one of the tenant farmers—stumbled to his feet. He stepped out in front of Mrs. Jocelyn, smiling. She put a hand to his chest, and pushed him savagely; the man lost his footing, collapsing backwards in a splintering crash of wooden chairs. A small child squealed; her mother snatched her up in her arms.

At Octavia's table, the reaction was slow. Harry was deep in conversation with Charlotte and Caitlin; the two girls, heads bent, were watching as he arranged pepper and salt pots and cutlery in an evident explanation of formation. It was Caitlin who looked up at the commotion; she looked once, then twice, and then immediately jumped to her feet.

Octavia was sitting sideways to the table, her back to the dance floor. She had just given the woman behind her something; William dimly grasped that it was David Nash's mother, now clutching several of the large linen flowers from the table. She too glanced in the direction of the crash, and the smile vanished from her face.

It was ten, perhaps twelve seconds. Over so quickly.

Mrs. Jocelyn reached the table. Octavia turned her head in

response to a low cry from the housekeeper. William saw the blade only then—a knife taken from the table, probably, where he and the housekeeper had been standing. She stepped forward almost casually, and thrust it in Octavia's direction.

Caitlin had grabbed Harry's arm, and, turning his head, he saw what was happening. He tried in vain to get to his feet. Charlotte stood up.

Octavia was half on her feet—she stepped backwards and stumbled to avoid the knife. Charlotte pushed past Harry's chair and ran to her mother. With the table between them, Mrs. Jocelyn was temporarily halted. Alongside him, Louisa rushed to her father; he heard her abrupt cry, though his whole attention was fixed on Octavia. Mrs. Jocelyn was shouting something—men nearby tried to catch hold of her.

But it was Caitlin, coming around the opposite end of the table, and walking briskly towards the older woman, who reached her; she put both arms around Mrs. Jocelyn's body from behind. She held the older woman there in what looked absurdly like a lover's grip, her head bent to Mrs. Jocelyn's ear.

She talked to her, at the same time gently pulling her away from the table. Mrs. Jocelyn's arm was still held out at right angles, but, in another moment or two, she suddenly relaxed her grip, and the knife tumbled to the floor. Pinioned by Caitlin, Mrs. Jocelyn stared hard once more at Octavia.

And then, she turned her head away.

She looked at William, her mouth moving, but no word escaping her.

David Nash had booked a room in the village for their wedding night.

He wanted Mary to himself, away from Rutherford, away from

the well-wishers, the crowding faces, the nudging elbows, the beery glances, the noise.

They were seen off from the steps of the tithe barn at ten o'clock, to cheers and a rousing chorus of "For they are jolly good fellows . . ." and laughter that decreased to ever-fainter echoes as they made their way, arm in arm, through the dark gardens.

By the front of the house, Mary paused.

"What do you think they would say?" she asked.

"Of what?" he asked. "And who?"

"Jack," she whispered. "He'll go just as you have to. What will Miss Louisa do then, I wonder? What will her parents make of it when they find out?"

David couldn't guess. "Perhaps they'll never find out," he said. All he wanted to do was get Mary to their room and their bed. He kissed her, and afterwards she held his arm tightly as they walked down the drive under the trees.

"It's been coming for a long time," Mary murmured.

"What has?"

"All that with the daft old biddy."

"Mrs. Jocelyn?"

"Oh," Mary said, "she thinks of herself as righteous, that's what it is."

"She's not righteous," he told her. "She's barmy."

Mary laughed softly. "The mistress is all right, at least." And then she stopped walking and gazed at him. He saw, with affection, the sweetness of her round little face in the half darkness; saw, too, the glitter in her eye. "Perhaps she'll go to prison. She should."

"I don't think his lordship would do that."

"What'll it be, then? She deserves it."

"The asylum."

"You think so?"

"I do."

They began to walk again, and began to hurry.

The trees were gently moving ghosts far above them. When they were almost at the gate, David looked up into the vast network of branches, wondering how long they would stand, seeing the moon between the shapes, a drifting coin of light.

"My Lord," Mary murmured suddenly. "Oh my Lord God."

He looked down, and in the direction that she was pointing.

A man was coming through the gate. He wore an overcoat of light-colored camel; he had a soft checked cloth cap on his head. He was something like a ghost too, there in the shadow.

He walked forward, and was about to pass them, when he stopped. "It's Nash, isn't it?" he asked.

"Yes sir," David said, slow with wonder. Beside him, Mary was panting slightly, like some frightened animal.

"And Mary."

"Yes sir," she replied.

"'Tis our wedding day," David told him.

A hand reached out to grasp his own. "Congratulations," he said to them both. "That's very fine news." David thought for one irrational moment that he would be touching something cold—he hesitated a second—but the returning pressure was absolutely warm and real.

"Good night, then," the man said.

"Good night, sir," Mary whispered.

The man paused, looking up the drive at Rutherford, gazing for some time at the house. "Is her ladyship at home?" he asked finally.

"Yes, Mr. Gould," David told him. "Her ladyship is home."

Read on for a special preview of
the next Rutherford Park novel
from Elizabeth Cooke

Available soon from Berkley Books

The rain fell softly on the day that she was to be married.

All night long Charlotte had been dreaming of her old home at Rutherford Park—she thought that the sound of the downpour outside was the water rushing through the red stones of the riverbed by the bridge. It was only when she awoke that she realized she was in London, in the Chelsea house owned by the American, John Gould.

It was half past five in the morning when Charlotte let herself out of the house and into the street. Cheyne Walk was barely stirring, and the road held only a clattering echo of her own running feet. She was at the embankment wall in just a few moments, leaning on the edge, staring at the lively grey ribbon of the Thames. *I shall be married*, she thought, *in a few hours*. She turned her face up to the rain.

It was April 1917, she was nineteen years old, and everywhere there was change. On the fields of Flanders, history was being written in the harrowing of humanity; in the pretty eighteenth-century house behind her, her own mother lived in what some called sin, but what Charlotte could see was a kind of correctness, a way of holding on to life. In Yorkshire, her once happy father habitually mourned in bitterness. The world rolled and altered.

She held on to the embankment wall, feeling its granite strength. Someone had told her that the stones of the wall here had come from Cornwall, from Lamorna Cove. It was supposed to be wildly lovely there, but she had never seen it. She had, despite her nursing service at St. Dunstan's, never seen France. Her brother Harry was back there now, advising the Flying Corps. She had never seen America, as Mr. Gould had done; she had never been to Italy. She had wanted to take the Grand Tour as her male ancestors had once done. But she doubted that she would now. She was to be a married woman.

She turned away from the river, trying to hold down the nonsensical impulse to throw herself into the water. She had nothing at all to be worried about, she told herself. This was just a morbid anxiety, a last-minute rush of pre-wedding nerves. She must grow up, and stop wanting some romantic notion of independence. After all, what did she have to be worried about? Michael Preston was a wonderful man, a brave man. His blindness was no barrier; they were, as he always joked, a good team. Her parents were pleased that she was about to marry into one of Kent's oldest and most respected—not to say very wealthy—families; that she would be secure and cared for. That she would live a stone's throw from her family's London house in Grosvenor Square, in a lovely little mews cottage that Michael's parents had bestowed upon them. Her father had even hinted obliquely at the grandchildren that she and Michael would provide, and she so longed to see him happy again. She was desperate not to bring further disappointment into his life.

Yet the old sense of suffocation threatened to overwhelm her.

She looked back through the trees at the houses on Cheyne Walk. John Gould now owned one of the prettiest, his gift to her mother, Octavia. They lived like two honeymooners here, and for the last six months Charlotte had come here often, absorbing both their scandal and their happiness in equal measure. She was to be married from here, and not the Grosvenor Square house where her father was now staying in solitary and temporary splendor among the dusty relics of his marriage. Now and then, in talking to him, it had become obvious that he expected his wife to eventually return to him. People called him an old fool for it, she knew. It was her older sister Louisa who tended to look after Father, and Charlotte was drawn to her mother. But sometimes the longing for the old untouched days at Rutherford would return in her; the innocence of it all, the feeling that England would never change. The ancient conviction that the Cavendish estate of Rutherford and that charmed and luxurious way of life were eternal.

Charlotte smiled to herself. Well, they had all had that permeability knocked out of them now.

She wondered, as she looked at Cheyne Walk, at the other dramas that had played out in this London street over the centuries. In Number 16, Dante Gabriel Rosetti had lived out his final years with Fanny Cornforth; Number 4 was George Eliot's last home. Just along the way was the Chelsea Hospital and the Physic Garden. And it had been here, last October, that Charlotte had sat with her mother and told her that Michael had proposed to her. In the seventeenth-century green oasis by the Thames, Charlotte had expected Octavia to tell her that she was far too young. In retrospect, she had hoped that this was indeed what her mother was going to say. She would have returned to Michael and told him that, without her mother's approval, she could not possibly marry him, flattered as she was to have been asked. But, to her astonishment, Octavia had not objected at all. In her own half-dazed and happy state, she had simply clasped Charlotte's hands and smiled at her, and given her blessing. But it was not her mother's blessing that Charlotte had wanted. She had wanted her mother's disapproval, and an excuse not to marry at all.

It was very strange, she considered, that in all these months, it had only been John Gould, her mother's lover, who had carefully and subtly questioned her decision. "Shall you be very happy as a little wife?" he had said to her in a joking fashion last Christmas. She had looked at him gravely, the champagne glass in her hand as the dinner guests settled around the dining table on the day before Christmas Eve. "Don't you think that I could be?" she'd replied. John, in his handsome and easy way, had considered her. "You always struck me as a wild bird waiting to fly," he had commented. "Well, one can fly when one is married," she'd told him. And then had blushed scarlet. "I mean, as a couple. We could fly anywhere, anywhere at all."

If he had noticed her embarrassment, he hadn't dwelled upon it. "Come to America when this lousy war is over," he had said. "And see the house I've built for your mother on Cape Cod. I'm sure you'll like it. America too."

Her heart had welled up inside her. Oh, she was sure that she would love the beach, the house, the country. The very words spelled out freedom and space. And of course she could go there with Michael—of course they would love to, she'd told John. She had then deliberately turned away from him and his piercing, appraising gaze. She had spoken gaily to the woman on the other side of her; but about what, she had no idea at all.

Since then, she seemed to have been swept forward by events. Michael's parents were charming; their grand home in its beautiful gardens outside Sevenoaks was charming; Michael himself was, of course, charming. But how "charming" grated on her to the roots of her soul! How maddening she found it. How ridiculously she had painted herself into this lover's corner. Into maturity and security and all those other things that her father so approved of. She thought she should die of it.

"Stop it," she said out loud, to no one at all but herself. "What a silly, selfish fool you are."

She walked back to the house and let herself in the gate. In six hours, at midday, her father would come here in the Rolls-Royce he had lately acquired. They would be chauffeured to the parish church of St. Margaret's, Westminster Abbey, within sight of the Abbey itself and the famous clock tower of the Palace of Westminster that was familiarly called Big Ben.

There would be crowds at the church door because society weddings were food and drink to a war-weary London, and because it was seen to be a great romance, this union of the blinded war hero and the youngest child of a loyal servant of the Crown. Police on horseback would hold back the throng; there would be cheers as she emerged from the car dressed in what she—oh so privately, oh so secretly—thought was a completely idiotic costume of a white silk dress and a vast tulle veil. Her sister Louisa would be there at the church door, laughing prettily and scattering rose petals. And, after the ceremony, the thunder of the *Meistersingers* march on the church organ would compete with the pealing of bells of St. Margaret's. And she and Michael would stand together at the porch, smiling, arm in arm.

And all the time, she would be wanting to run.

The door of the house opened as she approached it, and there was the housemaid, looking frightened that someone was already outside as she reached to polish the doorframe and the brass handle of the bell. "Oh, miss," she said, beaming when she saw that it was Charlotte. "The happiest day of your life. We are all that excited, miss, if you'll pardon me saying."

Charlotte stepped over the threshold, and shook off the coat that had become saturated with rain.

"Yes," she murmured. "You're quite right, Milly. It's the happiest day of my life."

READERS GUIDE

FOR

The Wild Dark Flowers

BY

ELIZABETH COOKE

DISCUSSION QUESTIONS

1. The story opens with William Cavendish overlooking Rutherford. What does Rutherford symbolize for the Cavendish family, and how does its significance change, especially for Octavia?

2. When the Cavendishes visit the de Rays, they have a conversation about their sons who are not in active posts: "[James is] in the Foreign Office. Gordon shan't go . . ." Octavia brings up Rupert Kent's death, the group falls silent, and there is the presence of implicit guilt. How does guilt function as an influence in the story, both in this scene and elsewhere?

3. Harry's plane crash and subsequent injury are narrated in chaotic terms: a "high-pitched jagged squeal . . . A scalding fire running through his thighs." How do the raw physical experiences of Harry mimic the emotional experiences of his family?

4. When Harry is being transferred, the author writes: "Pain was a peculiar thing; it was almost visible in the train—a writhing spirit that pressed itself down on the bodies." Where do we see pain most acutely in the book—and where is it physical versus emotional or mental?

5. Harry considers the phrase uttered by the "drunk" officer, and he thinks: "The snuffing out of candles; and they were all candles. Particularly the young ones. Brief candles flickering in the dark." Whose lives fulfill this description of flickering candles during wartime?

6. Octavia thinks, "The world was at the mercy of men, and that was the entire problem." Discuss how men and women cope with their problems differently in the story. How might the world be different if it were "at the mercy" of women?

7. Harrison tells Nat he thinks that "God is looking somewhere else," if there even is a god. Nat disagrees, and just after, is blown to bits. Sometimes it is said that the best men don't survive wars—why is that? How are we made vulnerable by faith and goodness?

8. When Louisa has to urge Jack to give up the Shire, they have a conversation about sacrifice. What do both ultimately lose, and how is this moment—giving up an innocent and unknowing creature—a symbolic reflection of that?

9. After William's heart attack, Octavia laments the way in which both she and her husband have dealt with their emotions: turning off feelings "as one might close off a faucet, or draw curtains against the dark." What happens in the long and short term when the characters, and we, cut off or ignore our true feelings?

10. When Harrison's line is fired upon, he first sees the machine gun bullets as "sprouting seeds." How does the author juxtapose these

images—of bucolic Rutherford, the flora and fauna, new growth—
with those of death? What comment does the book make on the
circle of life and how it is impacted by war?

11. While William is recovering, he thinks back on the young pros-
titutes of his youth, "painted girls of sixteen and seventeen," and
he realizes he never considered their plight. He considers the "desperate callousness of youth. The mistakes, the greed." Where do
we see those mistakes and greed manifest in youth, like Harry?
How do the older characters' actions—like those of William, John,
and Octavia—differ?

12. Octavia finds herself very frustrated by the limitations of being a
woman when she goes to meet Harry. In what ways does Octavia
subvert the expectations of her sex and position, and in what ways
does she bend to them?

13. How does William change from the cold, pragmatic young man
that he was, to the remove of his middle age, to his empathy later
in the book? Most dramatically, he is sympathetic to Octavia
regarding the fate of Gould—he seeks out information and, if
subtly, comforts her. What prompted this evolution?

14. The story begins with William at Rutherford and ends with the
marriage of Mary and David Nash at Rutherford. How do the
masters and servants affect each others' lives in an imperative way,
for better or worse? How might Mrs. Jocelyn serve as a microcosm
for society, in the manner that she obstructs the comingling of
classes?

15. Octavia says to William, "I wonder . . . if children ever appreciate what they do to their parents." What does she mean? How do not only children, but lovers, spouses, friends, and comrades, not "appreciate" what they do to each other?